Raves for Elizabeth Hand's
WINTERLONG

"Elizabeth Hand's epic WINTERLONG reminds us why we started reading SF to start with: it does things 'mainstream' fiction doesn't dare try . . . [a] remarkable first novel."
—Terry Bisson

"With elegant and evocative prose, Liz Hand has woven a richly embroidered tapestry of dreams and madness. WINTERLONG is a compelling drama, a beautiful and terrifying vision of a world where science borders on magic."
—Pat Murphy

"A wonderful new talent that's ready to knock the socks off the SF field."
—George Alec Effinger

"Franz Kafka said a book should be an ax for the frozen sea within us. WINTERLONG is such an ax, sharp and quick, shattering our complacency about what it means to be human. Not since *A Canticle for Leibowitz* have I encountered landscapes quite this rich in psychological, cultural, and mythic resonance. Elizabeth Hand has rendered her epic in a style so precise and poetic you want to give her a standing ovation."
—James Morrow

"Elizabeth Hand is already an important writer, and may be destined for greatness. WINTERLONG is an ambitious debut."
—Lewis Shiner

SPECTRA SPECIAL EDITIONS is a program dedicated to masterful works of the fantastic by today's most visionary writers. Look for these remarkable works in Spectra Special Editions.

WINTERLONG

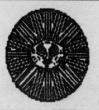

A novel by

ELIZABETH HAND

BANTAM BOOKS
NEW YORK · TORONTO · LONDON · SYDNEY · AUCKLAND

WINTERLONG
A Bantam Spectra Book / October 1990

Grateful acknowledgment is made for permission to reprint material from previously published material: Excerpt from "The Hollow Men" in *Collected Poems 1909–1962* by T.S. Eliot, copyright 1936 by Harcourt Brace Jovanovich, Inc., copyright © 1964, 1963 by T.S. Eliot, reprinted by permission of the publisher and Faber and Faber Limited; excerpt from "Memorial to the City" from *W.H. Auden: Collected Poems* edited by Edward Mendelson, copyright © 1976 by Edward Mendelson, William Meredith and Monroe K. Spears, reprinted by permission of Random House, Inc.

ISBN 0-553-28772-9

Published simultaneously in the United States and Canada

Bantam Books are published by Bantam Books, a division of Bantam Doubleday Dell Publishing Group, Inc. Its trademark, consisting of the words "Bantam Books" and the portrayal of a rooster, is Registered in U.S. Patent and Trademark Office and in other countries. Marca Registrada. Bantam Books, 666 Fifth Avenue, New York, New York 10103.

PRINTED IN THE UNITED STATES OF AMERICA

OPM   0 9 8 7 6 5 4 3 2

*We know without knowing there is reason for
    what we bear . . .
Whoever the searchlights catch, whatever the
    loudspeakers blare,
We are not to despair.*

When he'd begun to rattle deep down in his throat, I asked him: "What are you thinking about?" I always like to know what a dying man is thinking about. And he said: "I'm still listening to the rain." It gave me gooseflesh. "I'm still listening to the rain." That's what he said.

—Bertolt Brecht, "Baal."

Contents

Part One

The Boy in the Tree

Our heart stops.

I am within her, a cerebral shadow. Distant canyons where spectral lightning flashes: neurons firing as I tap in to the heart of the poet, the dark core where desire and horror fuse and Morgan turns ever and again to stare out a bus window. The darkness clears. I taste for an instant the metal bile that signals the beginning of therapy. Then I'm gone.

I'm sitting on the autobus, the last seat where you can catch the bumps on the crumbling highway if you're going fast enough. Through the open windows a rush of spring air tangles my hair. Later I will smell apple blossoms in my auburn braids. Now I smell sour milk where Ronnie Abrams spilled his ration yesterday.

"Move over, Yates!" Ronnie caroms off the seat opposite, rams his leg into mine, and flies back to pound his brother. From the front the driver yells, "Shut up!" vainly trying to silence forty-odd singing children.

> *On top of Old Smoky*
> *All covered with blood*
> *I shot my poor teacher*
> *With a forty-four slug . . .*

*Ronnie grins at me, eyes glinting, then pops me right on
the chin with a spitball. I stick my fingers in my ears and
huddle closer to the window.*

**Met her at the door
With my trusty forty-four
Now she don't teach no more.**

*The autobus pulls into town and slows, stops behind a
truck carrying soldiers, janissaries of the last Ascension. I
press my face against the cracked window, shoving my
glasses until lens kisses glass and I can see clearly to the
street below. A young woman in rags is standing on the
curb holding a baby wrapped in a dirty pink blanket. At
her ankles wriggles a dog, an emaciated puppy with
whiptail and ears flopping as he nips at her bare feet. I tap
at the window, trying to get the dog to look at me. In front
of the bus two men in faded yellow uniforms clamber
from the truck and start arguing. The woman screws up
her face and says something to the men, moving her lips so
I know she's mad. The dog lunges at her ankles again and
she kicks it gently, so that it dances along the curb. The
soldiers glance at her, see the autobus waiting, and climb
back into the truck. I hear the whoosh of releasing brakes.
The autobus lurches forward and my glasses bang into the
window. The rear wheels grind up onto the curb.*

*The dog barks and leaps onto the woman. Apple blos-
soms drift from a tree behind her as she draws up her arms
in alarm, and, as I settle my glasses onto my nose and stare,
she drops the baby beneath the wheels of the bus.*

*Retching, I strive to pull Morgan away, turn her head
from the window. A fine spray etches bright petals on the
glass and her plastic lenses. My neck aches as I try to turn
toward the inside of the autobus and efface forever that
silent rain. But I cannot move. She is too strong. She will
not look away.*

*I am clawing at the restraining ropes. The Aide pulls the
wires from my head while inches away Morgan Yates
screams. I hear the hiss and soft pump of velvet thoughts
into her periaqueductal gray area. The link is severed.*

* * *

I sat up as they wheeled her into the next room. Morgan's screams abruptly stilled as the endorphins kicked in and her head flopped to one side of the gurney. For an instant the Aide Justice turned and stared at me as he slid Morgan through the door. He would not catch my eyes.

None of them will.

Through the glass panel I watched Emma Harrow hurry from another lab. She bent over Morgan and pulled the wires from between white braids still rusted with coppery streaks. Beside her the Aide Justice looked worried. Other doctors, all with strained faces, slipped from adjoining rooms and blocked my view.

When I was sure they'd forgotten me I dug out a cigarette—traded from Anna that morning for my dosage of phenothiazine—and lit up. I tapped the ashes into my shoe and blew smoke into a ventilation shaft. I knew Morgan wouldn't make it. I could usually tell, but even Dr. Harrow didn't listen to me this time. Morgan Yates was too important: one of the few living writers whose works were still sanctioned by the Ascendants.

"She will crack," I told Dr. Harrow after reading Morgan's profile. Seven poetry collections and two authorized Manifestos published during the last insurrection; an historical novel detailing the horrors of the First Ascension's century-long Night; a dramatic recreation of the biblioclasm, performed before the new Ascendant Governors passed the Dialectic Malediction. Since then, recurrent nightmares revolving around a childhood trauma in the janissary crèche, sadistic sexual behavior, and a pathological fear of dogs. Nothing extraordinary; but I knew she wouldn't make it.

"How do you know?"

I shrugged. "She's too strong."

Dr. Harrow stared at me, pinching her lower lip. She wasn't afraid of my eyes. "What if it works," she mused, and tugged thoughtfully at her cropped gray bangs. "She says she hasn't written in three years, because of this. She's afraid they'll revoke her publishing sanction."

I yawned. "Maybe it will work. But she won't let me take it away. She won't let anyone take it."

I was right. If Dr. Harrow hadn't been so eager for the chance to reclaim one of the damned and her own reputation, she'd have known too. Psychotics, autists, Ascendant artists of the lesser rank: these could be altered by empatherapy. I'd siphoned off their sicknesses and night terrors, inhaled phobias like giddy ethers that set me giggling for days afterward. But the big ones—those whose madnesses were as carefully cultivated as the brain chemicals that allowed me and others like me to tap in to them—they were immune. They clung to their madnesses with the fever of true addiction. Even the dangers inherent to empatherapy weren't enough: they *couldn't* let go.

Dr. Harrow glanced up from the next room and frowned when she saw my cigarette. I stubbed it out in my shoe and slid my foot back in, wincing at the prick of heat beneath my sole.

She slipped out of the emergency lab. Sighing, she leaned against the glass and looked at me.

"Was it bad, Wendy?"

I picked a fleck of tobacco from my lip. "Pretty bad." I had a rush recalling Morgan wailing as she stood at the window. For a moment I had to shut my eyes, riding that wave until my heart slowed and I looked up grinning into Dr. Harrow's compressed smile.

"Pretty good, you mean." Her tight mouth never showed the disdain or revulsion of the others. Only a little dismay, some sick pride perhaps in the beautiful thing she'd soldered together from an autistic girl and several ounces of precious glittering chemicals.

"Well . . ." She sighed and walked to her desk. "You can start on this." She tossed me a blank report and returned to the emergency lab. I settled back on my cot and stared at the sheet.

NAME & NUMBER: Wendy Wanders, Subject 117

Neurologically augmented empath approved for emotive engram therapy.

The pages blurred. I gripped the edge of my cot. Nausea exploded inside me, a fiery pressure building inside my head until I bowed to crack my forehead against the table edge, again and again, stammering for help until with a shout Dr. Harrow's Aide ran to me and slapped an ampule to my neck. He stood above me until the drug took effect, his hands poised to catch me if I began head-banging again. After several minutes I breathed deeply and stared at the wall, then reported on my unsuccessful session with the poet.

That evening I walked to the riverside. A trio of retrofitted security sculls puttered down the river, colored yolk-yellow like dirty foam upon the water. I had always assumed the sculls kept watch over those of us at HEL; but the Aide Justice had told me that their true business lay across the river, within the overgrown alleys and pleasure gardens of the dying City of Trees.

"Smugglers," he had said, tugging at the bronze earcuffs that marked his rank and credit level. "The Ascendants trade with the City Botanists for opium and rare herbs. In return they give them precious metals and resins. And sometimes their generosity is overwhelming, and they leave us dying from some new plague."

A tiny figure on one of the sculls raised an arm to wave at me. I waved back as the boat skidded across the water. Then I turned and wandered along the riverwalk, past rotting oak benches and the ruins of glass buildings, watching the sun sink through argent thunderheads.

A single remaining service ziggurat towered above the walk. It shadowed the charred ruins of a refugee complex built during the brief years of the Second Ascension. That was when there were still refugees and survivors, before

the Governors began to fight the starveling rebels with the
first generation of mutagens.

Or so the Aide Justice had said. He was from the City,
and knew many strange things, although he spoke little of
his people there.

"Do you miss them?" I asked him once. We were awaiting the results of a scan to determine if a woman I had
been treating showed evidence of schizothymia.

He shook his head, then smiled ruefully and nodded.
"Yes, of course I do," he said. "But they are simple people,
it's not like here. . . ."

I could tell from his expression that he was a little
ashamed of them. The idea excited me: *shame* was not an
emotion I tapped often at the Human Engineering Laboratory.

"Are they smugglers?" I asked.

Justice laughed. "I guess some of them are."

He told me about the City then, a history different from
the one given us by Dr. Harrow and the sanctioned educa-
tional programs of the Fourth Ascension. Because at HEL
we learned that after the Long Night of the First Ascension the abandoned capital had been resettled, set up as an
outpost where a handful of researchers and soldiers stood
guard over the Museums and Archives and Libraries of the
fallen nation. But with the Second Ascension the City was
forgotten. Those who had commanded the City's few resi-
dents were killed or exiled to the Balkhash Commonwealth (even then its vast steppes and mountains saw the
deaths of more prisoners than there were now people in
the world). And those who lived in the City were forgotten, abandoned as the City itself had been after the First
Ascension exterminated its inhabitants. They were not
worth capturing or remanding, the few hundred researchers and soldiers and the prostitutes who had followed them
to the City by the river. Their descendants were squatters
now, living in the ruins of the capital, kept alive by cannibal rites and what they could wrest from the contaminated
earth.

But the Aide Justice spoke with respect of the Curators.
His own people he called the Children of the Magdalene.

Only the lazars were to be feared, those who fell victim to the viral strikes of the rebels and the guerrillas of the Balkhash Commonwealth. Lazars and the geneslaves who haunted the forests and wastelands.

"It is beautiful, Wendy: even the ruins are beautiful, and the poisoned forest . . ."

But we had been interrupted then by Dr. Harrow, calling Justice to help her initialize the link between myself and another patient.

The riverwalk's crumbling benches gave way to airy filigrees of rusted iron. At one of these tables I saw someone from the Human Engineering Laboratory.

"Anna or Andrew?" I called. By the time I was close enough for her to hear, I knew it was Anna this time, peacock feathers and long blue macaw quills studding the soft raised nodes on her shaven temples.

"Wendy." She gestured dreamily at a concrete bench. "Sit."

I settled beside her, tweaking a cobalt plume, and wished I'd worn the fiery cock-of-the-rock quills she'd given me last spring. Anna was stunning, always: brown eyes brilliant with octine, small breasts tight against her tuxedo shirt. She was the only one of the other empties I spoke much with, although she beat me at faro and Andrew had once broken my tooth in an amphetamine rage. A saucer scattered with broken candicaine straws sat before her. Beside it a fluted parfait glass held several unbroken pipettes. I did one and settled back, grinning.

"You had that woman today," Anna hissed into my ear. Her rasping voice made me shiver with delight. "The poet. I think I'm furious."

I shrugged. "Luck of the draw."

"How was she?" She blinked and I watched golden dust powder the air between us. "Was she good, Wendy?" She stroked my thigh and I giggled.

"Great. She was great." I lowered my eyes and squinted until the table disappeared into the steel rim of an autobus seat.

"Let me see." Her whisper the sigh of air brakes. "Wendy—"

The rush was too good to stop. I let her pull me forward until my cheek grazed hers and I felt her mouth against mine. I tasted her saliva, the chemical bite of candicaine: then bile and summer air and exhaust. . . .

Too fast. I jerked my head up, choking as I pulled away from Anna. She stared at me with huge blank eyes.

"Ch-c-c-," she gasped, spittle flying into the parfait glass. I swore and grabbed her chin, held her face close to mine.

"Anna," I said loudly. "Anna, it's Wendy—"

"Ahhh." Her eyes focused and she drew back. "Wendy. Good stuff." She licked her lips, tongue a little loose from the hit so that she drooled. I grimaced.

"More, Wendy . . ."

"Not now." I grabbed two more straws and cracked one. "I have a follow-up with her tomorrow morning. I have to go."

She nodded. I flicked a napkin at her. "Wipe your mouth, Anna. I'll tell Harrow I saw you so she won't worry."

"Goodbye, Wendy." A server arrived as I left, its crooked wheels grating against the broken concrete as it listed toward the table. I glimpsed myself reflected in its blank black face, and hurried from the patio as behind me Anna ordered more straws.

I recall nothing before Dr. Harrow. The drugs they gave me—massive overdoses for a three-year-old—burned those memories as well as scorched every neural branch that might have helped me climb to feel the sun as other people do. But the drugs stopped the thrashing, the head-banging, the screaming. And slowly, other drugs rived through my tangled axons and forged new pathways. A few months and I could see again. A few more and my fingers moved. The wires that had stilled my screams made me scream once more, and, finally, exploded a neural dam so that a year later I began to speak. By then the Ascendant funding poured through other conduits, scarcely less complex than my own, and led as well to the knot of electrodes in my brain.

In the early stages of her work, shortly after I arrived at HEL, Dr. Harrow attempted a series of neuroelectrical implants between the two of us. It was an unsuccessful effort to reverse the damage done by the biochemicals. Seven children died before the minimum dosage was determined: enough to change the neural pattern behind autistic behavior; not enough to allow the patient to develop her own emotional responses to subsequent internal or external stimuli. I still have scars from the implants: fleshy nodes like tiny ears trying to sprout from my temples.

At first we lived well. Then the Governors decided this research might lead to other things, the promise of a new technology as radical and lethal as that which had first loosed the mutagens upon the countryside nearly two centuries before. As more empaths were developed and more Ascendant funds channeled from the provisional capital, we lived extravagantly. Dr. Harrow believed that exposure to sensation might eventually pattern true emotions in her affectively neutered charges. So the Human Engineering Laboratory moved from its quarters in a dark and freezing fouga hangar to the vast abandoned Linden Glory estate outside the ruins of the ancient City.

Ascendant neurologists moved into the paneled bedrooms. Psychobotanists imported from the momentarily United Provinces tilled the ragged formal gardens and developed new strains of oleander within bell-shaped greenhouses. Empties moved into bungalows where valets and chefs once slept.

In an earlier century Lawrence Linden had been a patron of the arts. Autographed copies of Joyce and Stein and the lost Crowley manuscripts graced the Linden Glory libraries. We had a minor Botticelli, two frayed Rothkos, and many Raphaels; the famed pre-Columbian collection for which a little war was fought; antiquarian coins and shelves of fine and rare Egyptian glass. From the Victorian music room with its decaying Whistler panels echoed the peacock screams of empties and patients engaged in therapy.

Always I remained Dr. Harrow's pet: an exquisite monster capable of miming every human emotion and even feeling many of them via the therapy I made possible. Every evening doctors administered syringes and capsules and tiny tabs that adhered to my temples like burdock pods, releasing chemicals directly into my corpus striatum. And every morning I woke from someone else's dreams.

Morgan sat in the gazebo when I arrived for our meeting, her hair pulled beneath a biretta of indigo velvet worn to a nap like a dog's skull. She had already eaten, but HEL's overworked servers had yet to clear her plate. I picked up the remains of a brioche and nibbled its sugary crust.

"None of you have any manners, do you?" She smiled, but her eyes were red and cloudy with hatred. "They told me that during orientation."

I ran my tongue over a sweet nugget in a molar and nodded. "That's right."

"You can't feel anything or learn anything unless it's slipped into your breakfast coffee."

"I drink tea." I glanced around the Orphic Garden for a server. "You're early."

"I had trouble sleeping."

I nodded and finished the brioche.

"I had trouble sleeping because I had no dreams." She leaned across the table and repeated in a hiss, "I had no dreams. I carried that memory around with me for sixty years and last night I had no dreams."

Yawning, I rubbed the back of my head, adjusting a quill. "You still have all your memories. Dr. Harrow said you wanted to end the nightmares. I'm surprised we were successful."

"You were not successful." She towered above me when she stood, the table tilting toward her as she clutched its edge. "Monster."

"*Sacred* monster. I thought you liked sacred monsters." I

grinned, pleased that I'd bothered to read the sample poem included with her chart.

"Bitch. How dare you laugh at me. Whore—you're all whores and thieves." She stepped toward me, her heel catching between the mosaic stones. "No more of me— you'll steal no more of me. . . ."

I drew back a little, blinking in the emerald light as I felt the first adrenaline pulse. "You shouldn't be alone," I said. "Does Dr. Harrow know?"

She blocked the sun so that it exploded around the biretta's peaks in resplendent ribbons. "Doctor Harrow will know," she whispered, and drawing a pistol from her pocket she shot herself through the eye.

I knocked my chair over as I stumbled to her, knelt, and caught the running blood and her last memory as I bowed to touch my tongue to her severed thoughts.

A window smeared with garnet light that ruddles across my hands. Burning wax in a small blue glass. A laughing dog; then darkness.

They hid me under the guise of protecting me from the shock. I gave a sworn statement for the Governors and acknowledged in the HEL mortuary that the long body with blackened face had indeed shared her breakfast brioche with me that morning. I glimpsed Dr. Harrow, white and taut as a thread as Odolf Leslie and the other Ascendant brass cornered her outside the emergency room. Then the Aide Justice hurried me into the west wing, past the pre-Columbian collection and the ivory stair to an ancient Victorian elevator, clanking and lugubrious as a stage dragon.

"Dr. Harrow thought that you might like the Horne Room," Justice remarked with a cough, sidling two steps away to the corner of the elevator. The brass door folded into a lattice of leaves and pigeons that expanded into peacocks. "She's having your things sent up now. Anything else you need, please let her know." He cleared his throat, staring straight ahead as we climbed through orchid-

haunted clerestories and chambers where the oneironauts
snored and tossed through their days. At the fourth floor
the elevator ground to a stop. He tugged at the door until it
opened and waited for me to pass into the hallway.

"I have never been in the Horne Room," I remarked,
following him.

"I think that's why she thought you'd like it." He
glanced into an ornate mirror as we walked. I saw in his
eyes a quiver of pity before he looked away. "Down here."

A wide hallway ended in an arch crowded with gilt
satyrs.

"This is it," said Justice. To the right a heavy oaken door
hung open. Inside, yellow-robed Aides strung cable. I
made a face and tapped the door. It swung inward and
struck a bundle of cable leading to the bank of monitors
being installed next to the huge bed. I paced to the window and gazed outside. Around me the Aides scurried to
finish, glancing at me sideways with anxious eyes. I ignored
them and sat on the windowsill. There was no screen. A
hawkmoth buzzed past my chin and I thought that I could
hang hummingbird feeders from here and so, perhaps,
lure them within reach of capture. Anna had a bandeau
she had woven of hummingbird feathers that I much ad-
mired. The hawkmoth settled on the BEAM monitor beside the bed. The Aides packed to leave.

"Could you lie here for a moment, Wendy, while I test
this?" Justice dropped a handful of cables behind the headboard. I nodded and stretched upon the bed, pummeling a
pillow as he placed the wires upon my brow and temples. I
turned sideways to watch the old BEAM monitor, the
hawkmoth's wings forming a mask across the flickering
map of my thoughts.

"Aggression, bliss, charity," droned Justice, flicking the
moth from the cracked screen. "Desire, envy, fear." I
sighed and turned from the monitor while he adjusted
dials. Finally he slipped the wires from me. The others left.
Justice lingered a moment longer.

"You can go now," I said, and tossed the pillow against
the headboard.

He stood by the door, uncomfortable, and finally said,

"Dr. Harrow wants me to be certain you check your medications. She has increased your dosage of acetelthylene."

I slid across the bed to where a tiny refrigerator had been hung for my medications. I pulled it open and saw the familiar battery of vials and bottles. As a child first under Dr. Harrow's care I had imagined them a City like that I glimpsed from the highest windows at HEL, saw the long cylinders and amber vials as abandoned battlements and turrets to be explored and climbed. Now I lived among those chilly buttresses, my only worship within bright cathedrals.

"Two hundred milligrams," I said obediently, and replaced the bottle. "Thank you very very much." As I giggled he left the room.

I took the slender filaments that had tapped in to my store of memories and braided them together, then slid the plait beneath a pillow and leaned back. A bed like a pirate ship, carved posts like riven masts spiring to the high ceiling. I had never seen a pirate ship, but once I tapped a Governor's son who jerked off to images of yellow flags and heaving seas and wailing women. I recalled that now and untangled a single wire, placed it on my temple and masturbated until I saw the warning flare on the screen, the sanguine flash and flame across my pixilated brain. Then I went to sleep.

Faint tapping at the door woke me a short while later.

"Andrew." I pointed to where my toe poked from a rip in a much-patched blanket. "Come in. Sit."

He shut the door softly and slid beneath the sheets. "You're not supposed to have visitors, you know."

"I'm not?" I stretched and curled my other foot around his finger.

"No. Dr. Leslie was here all day. The Governors are angry. Anna said they're taking us away."

"Me too?"

He nodded, hugging a bolster. "All of us. Forever." He

smiled, and the twilight made his face as beautiful as Anna's. "I saw Dr. Harrow cry after he left."

"How did you get here?" I sat up and played with his
hair: long and silky blond except where the nodes bulged
and the hair had never grown back. He wore Anna's bandeau, and I tugged it gently from his head.

"The back stairs: no one ever uses them. That way."
With his foot he pointed lazily toward a darkening corner.
His voice rose plaintively. "You shared that poet with
Anna. You should've saved her."

I shrugged. "You weren't there." The bandeau fit loosely
over my forehead. When I tightened it, tiny emerald
feathers frosted my hands like the scales of moths. "Would
Anna give me this, do you think?"

Andrew pulled himself onto his elbows and stroked my
breast with one hand. "I'll give it to you, if you share."

"There's not enough left to share," I said, and pulled
away. In the tiny mirror hung upon the refrigerator I
caught myself in the bandeau. The stippled green feathers
made my tawny hair look a deeper auburn, like the poet's.
I pulled a few dark curls through the feathers and pursed
my lips. "If you give this to me . . ."

Already he was reaching for my hand. "Locked?" I
glanced at the door.

"Shh . . ."

Afterward I gave him one of my new pills. There hadn't
been much of Morgan left and I feared his disappointment
would evoke Anna, who'd demand her bandeau back.

"Why can't I have visitors?"

I had switched off the gaslight. Andrew sat on the windowsill, luring lacewings with a silver lighter tube. Bats
chased the insects to within inches of his face, veering
away as he laughed and pretended to snatch at them. "Dr.
Harrow said there may be a psychic inquest. To see if
you're accountable."

"So?" I'd done one before, when a schizoid six-year-old
hanged herself on a grosgrain ribbon after therapy with
me. " 'I can't be responsible. I'm not responsible.' " We
laughed: it was the classic empath defense.

"Dr. Leslie wants to see you himself."

I kicked the sheets to the floor and turned down the empty BEAM, to see the lacewings better. "How do you know all this?"

A quick *fizz* as a moth singed itself. Andrew frowned and turned down the lighter flame. "Anna told me," he replied, and suddenly was gone.

I swore and tried to rearrange my curls so the bandeau wouldn't show. From the windowsill Anna stared blankly at the lighter tube, then groped in her pockets until she found a hand-rolled cigarette. She glanced coolly past me to the mirror, pulling a strand of hair forward until it fell framing her cheekbone. "Who gave you that?" she asked as she blew smoke out the window.

I turned away. "You know who," I replied petulantly. "I'm not supposed to have visitors."

"Oh, you can keep it," she said.

"Really?" I clapped in delight.

"I'll just make another." She finished her cigarette and tossed it in an amber arc out the window. "I better go down now. Which way's out?"

I pointed where Andrew had indicated, drawing her close to me to kiss her tongue as she left.

"Thank you, Anna," I whispered to her at the door. "I think I love this bandeau."

"I think I loved it too," Anna nodded, and slipped away.

Dr. Harrow invited me to lunch with her in the Peach Tree Court the next afternoon. Justice appeared at my door and waited while I put on jeweled dark spectacles and a velvet biretta like Morgan Yates's.

"Very nice, Wendy," he said, amused. I smiled. When I wore the black glasses he was not afraid to look me in the face.

"I don't want the others to see my bandeau. Anna will steal it back," I explained, lifting the hat so he could see the feathered riband beneath.

He laughed, tossing his head so that his long blond braid

swung between his shoulders. I thanked him as he held the door and followed him outside.

On the steps leading to the Orphic Garden I saw HEL's chief neurologist, Dr. Silverthorn, with Gligor, his favorite of the empaths as I was Dr. Harrow's. Through the heavy jet laminate of his eyeshield Gligor regarded me impassively. Beside him Dr. Silverthorn watched my approach with distaste.

"Dr. Harrow is waiting for you," he called out. He took Gligor's arm and steered him away from us, to the walk's border edged with tiny yellow strawberries. As he stumbled after him Gligor crushed these carelessly, releasing their sweet perfume into the autumn air. He waved blindly in our direction, his head swinging distractedly back and forth as he tried to fix me with his shield, like a cobra seeking a rat by its body's heat.

"Wendy!" he said. "Wendy, I heard, it's—"

"Hush," said Dr. Silverthorn. As Justice and I passed he leaned back into the tall hedge of box trees until their branches snapped beneath his weight. But Gligor waited on the walk for me. He plucked at my arm and drew me to him. I smelled the adrenaline reek of his sweat as he brushed his lips against my cheek, his tongue flicking across my skin.

"Anna told me," he whispered. "I'll come later—"

I returned his kiss, my tongue lingering over the bitter tang of envy that clung to his skin. I ignored Justice waiting, and lifted my sunglasses to grin at Gligor's keeper.

"I will, Gligor," I said, staring into the dark furies of Dr. Silverthorn's eyes rather than into the ebony grid that concealed Gligor's own. "Goodbye, Dr. Silverthorn."

I dropped my sunglasses back onto my nose and skipped after Justice into the Orphic Garden. Servers had snaked hoses through the circle of lindens and were cleaning the mosaic stones. I peered through the hedge as we walked down the pathway, but Morgan's blood seemed to be all gone.

Once we were in the shade of the Peach Tree Walk I removed my glasses and put them into my pocket. Justice quickly averted his eyes. The little path dipped and rounded a corner humped with dark green forsythia. Three steps farther and the path branched: right to the Glass Fountain, left to the Peach Tree Court, where Dr. Harrow waited in the Little Pagoda.

"Thank you, Justice." Dr. Harrow rose, tilting her head toward a low table upon which lunch had been laid for two. Despite their care in placing a single hyacinth blossom in a cracked porcelain vase, the luncheon servers had not bothered to clean the Pagoda. The floor's golden sheath of pollen was chased with tiny footprints of squirrels and rats and their droppings. Justice grimaced as he stepped to a lacquered tray to sort out my medication bottles. Then he stood, bowed to Dr. Harrow, and left.

Sunlight streamed through the bamboo frets above us as Dr. Harrow took my hand and drew me toward her.

"The new dosage. You remembered to take it?"

"Yes." I removed my hat and dropped it, shaking my curls free. "Anna gave me this bandeau."

"It's lovely." She knelt before the table and motioned for me to do the same. Her face was puffy, her eyes slitted. I wondered if she would cry for me as she had for Andrew yesterday. "Have you had breakfast?"

We ate quenelles of hake with fennel and an aspic of lamb's blood. Dr. Harrow drank Georgian champagne and permitted me a sip—horrible, like brackish water. Afterward a remodeled greenhouse server (still encumbered with its coil of garden hose) removed our plates and brought me a chocolate wafer, which I slipped into my pocket to trade with Anna later, for news.

"You slept well," Dr. Harrow stated. "What did you dream?"

"I dreamed about Melisande's dog."

Dr. Harrow stroked her chin, then adjusted her pince-nez to see me better. "Not Morgan's dog?"

"No." Melisande had been a girl my own age with a history of tormenting and sexually molesting animals. "A small white dog. Like this." I pushed my nose until it squashed against my face.

Dr. Harrow smiled ruefully. "Well, good, because *I* dreamed about Morgan's dog." She shook her head when I

started to question her. "Not really; a manner of speaking.
I mean I didn't get much sleep." She sighed and tilted her
flute so that it refracted golden diamonds. "I made a very
terrible error of judgment with Morgan Yates. I shouldn't
have let you do it—"

"I knew what would happen."

Dr. Harrow looked at her glass, then at me. "Yes. Well, a
number of people are wondering about that, Wendy."

"She would not look away from the window."

"No. They're wondering how you know when the therapy will succeed and when it won't. They're wondering
whether you are effecting your failures as well as your
cures."

"I'm not responsible. I can't be—"

She placed the champagne flute on the lacquer table
and took my hand. She squeezed it so tightly that I knew
she wanted it to hurt. "That is what's the matter, Wendy. If
you are responsible—if empaths *can* be responsible—you
can be executed for murder. We can all be held accountable for your failures. And if not . . ." She leaned back
without releasing my hand, so that I had to edge nearer to
her across the table. "If not, the Governors want you for
themselves."

I flounced back against the floor. "Andrew told me."

She rolled her eyes. "Not you personally. Not neces-
sarily. Anna, yes: they created Anna, they'll claim her first.
But the others—"

She traced a wave in the air, ended it with finger pointing at me. "Things are changing again in the world outside,
Wendy. You are too sheltered here, all of you children;
which is my fault, but I thought . . ."

Her voice drifted into a sigh, and I noticed that her
fingers were trembling as she let go of my hand. "It doesn't
matter anymore what I thought," she said. She stared up at
me, her eyes glittering with such desperation that I
yearned to taste it, know what it was that could terrify a
woman like Dr. Harrow.

She took a deep breath and said, "There is a rumor that
NASNA plans to strike against the Balkhash Commonwealth. They will never succeed. NASNA and the present

Governors will be overthrown, and the Commonwealth will do to us what they did to Brazil and the Asian diarchy: more mutagens and viral strikes and burnings, until only the land remains for them to claim."

I yawned. It had been decades since the last Ascension. The Commonwealth was on the other side of the world. To myself and the other empties at HEL it was nothing more than pink and crimson blotches on a map, separated from us by a blue sea that would take weeks and weeks to navigate. I reached for my glass and sipped, grimacing again at the taste. When I raised my eyes Dr. Harrow was staring at me, unbelieving.

"Does this mean nothing to you, Wendy?"

I shrugged. "What? NASNA? The Commonwealth? What *should* it mean to me?"

"It means that NASNA needs new weapons. It means further intervention in our research, and misapplication of the results of the Harrow Effect. They'll treat you like laboratory animals, like geneslaves. . . .

"Don't you understand, Wendy? If they can trace what *you* do, find the bioprint and synthesize it . . ." Her finger touched the end of my nose, pressed it until I giggled. "There'll be nothing left of you except what will fit in a vial."

She tapped her finger on the table edge. The westering light fell golden upon my head, and I shook my hair back, smiling at its warmth. From a peach tree outside the Little Pagoda came a mockingbird's sweet treble. Dr. Harrow remained silent, listening.

After a few minutes she said, "Odolf Leslie was here yesterday. They are sending a new Governor—"

I looked up at that. "Here? To HEL?"

"No." She smiled wryly at my disappointment. "To the City. The Governors wish to monitor it more closely: the black market has grown too successful, and the Governors have professed a sudden interest in the Archives.

"Or so NASNA says; my sources say otherwise. There were stockpiles of weapons there once, within the City; weapons and secret things, things lost in the Long Night."

I must have appeared dubious. Dr. Harrow gave a small

laugh, a bitter rasping sound. "Did you think you knew everything about this place, Wendy? I assure you: you children know nothing, *nothing* of the world, even of the world across the river. That was a great city once, greater than any city standing now; and there are still things hidden there, things of great knowledge and power that the poor fools who live there now cannot begin to comprehend.

"But the Governors have decided it is time to look again at the City of Trees. I think they are searching for the engines that brought the Long Night; else why would they be sending an Aviator to govern the City?"

"An Aviator?" I repeated; but Dr. Harrow seemed not to have heard me.

"A hero of the Archipelago Conflict. Margalis Tast'annin: a brilliant man from the NASNA Academy. We knew him there, Aidan and I. He is to assume control of the City, set up a janissary outpost."

I thought of what Justice had told me, of the people who lived in the Museums and the ruins of the ancient Embassies. "What about the people there now?"

Dr. Harrow tilted her head back and shut her eyes as the afternoon sun touched her face. "I suppose they will be killed if they resist, or enslaved. Although Margalis Tast'annin doesn't seem the type to take prisoners.

"He arrived yesterday with Dr. Leslie, Wendy. Dr. Leslie told him about you, about Melisande and Morgan Yates and the others. He wants you for—*observation.* He wants this—"

She pressed both hands to her forehead and then waved them toward the sky, the unpruned fruit-laden trees, and the rank sloping lawns of Linden Glory. "All this, Wendy. They will have me declared incompetent and our research a disaster, and then they'll move in. They've been looking for an excuse; the Wendy suicides will do nicely."

The garden server returned to pour me more mineral water. I drank it and asked, "Is Dr. Leslie a nice doctor?"

For a moment I thought she'd upset the table, as Morgan had done in the Orphic Garden. Then, "I don't know,

Wendy. Perhaps he is." She sighed and motioned the server to bring another cold split.

"They'll take Anna first," she said a few minutes later, almost to herself. Then she added, "For espionage. They'll induce multiple personalities and train them when they're very young. Ideal terrorists."

I drank my water and stared at the gaps in the Pagoda's latticed roof, imagining Andrew and Anna without me. I took the chocolate wafer from my pocket and began to nibble it.

The server rolled back with a sweating silver bucket and opened another split for Dr. Harrow. She sipped it, watching me through narrowed gray eyes. "Wendy," she said at last. "There's going to be an inquest. At Tast'annin's request. It will probably be the last time I will supervise anything here. But before that, one more patient."

She reached beneath the table to her portfolio and removed a slender packet. "This is the profile. I'd like you to read it."

I took the file. Dr. Harrow poured the rest of her champagne and finished it, tilting her head to the server as she stood.

"I have a two o'clock meeting with Dr. Leslie. Why don't you meet me again for dinner tonight and we'll discuss this."

"Where?"

She tapped her lower lip. "The Peacock Room. At seven." She bowed slightly and passed out of sight among the trees.

I waited until she disappeared, then gestured for the server. "More chocolate, please," I ordered, and waited until it creaked back across the dusty floor, holding a chilled marble plate and three wafers. I nibbled one, staring idly at the faux vellum cover of the profile with its engraved motto:

HUMAN ENGINEERING LABORATORY
OF THE
NORTHEASTERN FEDERATED REPUBLIC OF AMERICA
PAULO MAIORA CANAMUS!

deus ex machina — god fr. machine
— ascention / (remember)

" 'Let us raise a somewhat loftier strain,' " Gligor had translated it for me once. "Virgil. But it should be *deus ex machina,*" he added slyly.

God from the machine.

I licked melting chocolate from my fingers and began to read, skimming through the charts and anamnesis that followed. On the last sheet I read: "Client requests therapy in order to determine nature and cause of these obsessive nightmares."

Beneath this was Dr. Harrow's scrawled signature and the blotchy yellow star and triangle that was the Republic's emblem. I ate the last wafer, then mimed to the server that I was finished.

We dined alone in the Peacock Room. After setting two places at the vast mahogany table the servers disappeared, dismissed by Dr. Harrow's brusque gesture. We ate in silence for several minutes beneath the hissing gaslights.

"Did you read the profile I gave you?' she asked at last, with studied casualness.

"Mmmm-mmm," I grunted.

"And . . . ?"

"She will not make it."

Dr. Harrow dipped her chin ever so slightly before asking, "Why, Wendy?"

"I don't know." I sucked my fork.

"Can't you give me any idea of what makes you feel that?"

"Nothing. I never feel anything."

"Well then, what makes you think she wouldn't be a good analysand?"

"I don't know. I just—" I clicked the tines of my fork against my teeth. "It's like when I start head-banging—the way everything starts to shiver and I get sick. But I don't throw up."

Dr. Harrow tilted her head. "Like a seizure. Well." She smiled, staring at me.

I dropped my fork and glanced around in impatience. "When will I meet her?"

"You already have."

I kicked my chair. "When?"

"Fourteen years ago, when you first came to HEL."

"Why don't I remember her?"

"You do, Wendy." She leaned across the table and tapped my hand gently with her knife. "It's me."

"Surprised?" Dr. Harrow grinned and raised the sleeves of her embroidered haik so that the early morning sunlight gleamed through the translucent threads.

"It's beautiful," I said, enviously fingering the flowing cuffs.

She smiled and turned to the NET beside my bed. "I'm the patient this morning. Are you ready?"

I nodded. There had been no Aides in to see me that morning; no report of my stolen dreams; no blood samples given to Justice. Dr. Harrow had wheeled in a rickety old wood-framed cot and now sat on it, readying her monitors. I settled on my bed and waited for her to finish. She finally turned to me and applied electrolytic fluid to the nodes on my temples, placed other wires upon my head and cheekbones before doing the same to herself.

"Justice isn't assisting you?" I asked.

She shook her head but made no reply as she adjusted her screens and, finally, settled onto her cot. I lay back against the pillow and shut my eyes.

The last thing I heard was the click of the adaptor freeing the current, and a gentle exhalation that might have been a sigh.

> *"Here we stand . . ."*
> *"Here we stand . . ."*
> *"Here we lie . . ."*
> *"Here we lie . . ."*

> "Eye to hand and heart to head,
> Deep in the dark with the dead."

It is spring, and not dark at all, but I repeat the incantation as my brother Aidan Harrow gravely sprinkles apple blossoms upon my head. In the branches beneath us a bluejay shrieks at our bulldog, Molly, as she whines and scratches hopefully at her basket.

"Can't we bring her up?" I peer over the edge of the rickety platform and Molly sneezes in excitement.

"Shhh!" Aidan commands, squeezing his eyes shut as he concentrates. After a moment he squints and reaches for his crumpled sweater. Several curry leaves filched from the kitchen crumble over me and I blink so that the debris doesn't get in my eyes.

"I hate this junk in my hair," I grumble. "Next time I make the spells."

"You can't." Aidan stands on tiptoe and strips another branch of blossoms, sniffing them dramatically before tossing them in a flurry of pink and white. "We need a virgin."

"So?" I jerk on the rope leading to Molly's basket. "You're a virgin. Next time we use you."

Aidan stares at me, brows furrowed. "That won't count," he says at last. "Say it again, Emma."

"Here we stand . . ."

Every day we come here: an overgrown apple orchard within the woods, uncultivated for a hundred years. Stone walls tumbled by time mark the gray boundaries of a farm and blackberry vines choke the rocks with breeze-blown petals. Our father showed us this place. Long ago he built the treehouse, its wood lichen-green now and wormed with holes. Rusted nails snag my knees when we climb: all that remains of other platforms and the crow's nest at treetop.

I finish the incantation and kneel, calling to Molly to climb into her basket. When my twin yells, I announce imperiously, "The virgin needs her faithful consort. Get in, Molly."

He helps to pull her up. Molly is trembling when we

*heave her onto the platform. As always, she remains hud-
dled in her basket.*

"She's sitting on the sandwiches," I remark. Aidan hastily shoves Molly aside and retrieves two squashed bags. "I
call we break for lunch."

We eat in thoughtful silence. We never discuss the failure of the spells, although each afternoon Aidan hides in
his secret place behind the wing chair in the den and pores
through more brittle volumes. Sometimes I can feel them
working—the air is so calm, the wind dies unexpectedly,
and for a moment the woods glow so bright, so deep, their
shadows still and green; and it is there: the secret to be
revealed, the magic to unfold, the story to begin. Above me
Aidan flushes and his eyes shine, he raises his arms and—

And nothing. It is gone. A moment too long or too soon, I
never know; but we have lost it again. For an instant
Aidan's eyes gray with tears. Then the breeze rises, Molly
yawns and snuffles, and once more we put aside the spells
for lunch and other games.

That night I toss in my bed, finally throwing my pillow
against the bookcase. From the open window stream the
chimes of peepers in the swamp, their song broidered with
the trills of toads and leopard frogs. As I churn feverishly
through the sheets it comes again, and I lie still: like a
star's sigh, the shiver and promise of a door opening somewhere just out of reach. I hold my breath, waiting: Will it
close again?

But no. The curtains billow and I slip from my bed, bare
feet curling upon the cold planked floor as I race to the
window.

He is in the meadow at wood's edge, alone, dark hair
misty with starlight, his pajamas spectral blue in the dark.
As I watch he raises his arms to the sky, and though I am
too far to hear, I whisper the words with him, my heart
thumping counterpoint to our invocation. Then he is quiet,
and stands alert, waiting.

I can no longer hear the peepers. The wind has risen, and
the thrash of the beech trees at the edge of the forest
drowns all other sounds. I can feel his heart now, beating
within my own, and see the shadows with his eyes.

In the lower branches of the willow tree, the lone willow that feeds upon a hidden spring beside the sloping meadow, there is a boy. His eyes are green and lucent as tourmaline, and silvery moths are drawn to them. His hands clutch the slender willow wands: strong hands, so pale that I trace the blood beneath, and see the muscles strung like strong young vines. As I watch he bends so that his head dips beneath a branch, new leaves tangling fair hair, and then slowly he uncurls one hand and, smiling, beckons my brother toward him.

The wind rises. Beneath his bare feet the dewy grass darkens as Aidan runs faster and faster, until he seems almost to be skimming across the lawn. And there, where the willow starts to shadow the starlit slope and the boy in the tree leans to take his hand, I tackle my brother and bring him crashing and swearing to earth.

For a moment he stares at me uncomprehending. Then he yells and slaps me, hits me harder until, remembering, he shoves me away and stumbles to his feet.

There is nothing there. The willow trembles, but only the wind shakes the new leaves. From the marsh the ringing chorus rises, swells, bursts as the peepers stir in the sawgrass. In the old house yellow light stains an upstairs window and our father's voice calls out sleepily, then with concern, and finally bellows as he leans from the casement to spot us below. Aidan glances at the house and back again at the willow, and then he turns to me despairingly. Before I can say anything he punches me and runs, weeping, into the woods.

A gentler withdrawal than I'm accustomed to. For several minutes I lay with closed eyes as I tried to hold on to the scents of apple blossom and dew-washed grass. But they faded, along with the dreamy net of tree and stars. I sat up groggily, wires still taped to my head, and faced Dr. Harrow, who was already recording her limbic system's response from the NET.

"Thank you, Wendy," she said without looking up. I

[handwritten marginalia: "constrmtimay the desire, based on desired other" / "nausea - sign of self-ness" / "Me." vs. "He."]

glanced at the BEAM monitor, where the shaded image of my brain lingered, the last flash of activity staining the temporal lobe bright turquoise.

"I never saw that color there before." As I leaned to examine it an unfocused wave of nausea choked me. I staggered against the bed, tearing at the wires.

Eyes: brilliant green lanced with cyanogen, unblinking as twin chrysolites. A wash of light: leaves stirring the surface of a still pool. They continued to stare through the shadows, heedless of the play of sun and moon, days and years and decades. The electrodes dangled from my fist as I stared at the blank screen, the single dancing line bisecting the NET monitor. The eyes in my mind did not move, did not blink, did not disappear. They stared relentlessly from the shadows until the darkness itself swelled and was absorbed by their feral gaze. They saw me.

Not Dr. Harrow; not Aidan; not Morgan or Melisande or the others I'd absorbed in therapy.

Me.

I stumbled from the monitor to the window, dragging the wires behind me, heedless of Dr. Harrow's stunned expression. Grunting, I shook my head, finally gripped the windowsill and slammed my head against the oaken frame, over and over and over, until Dr. Harrow tore me away. Still I saw them: unblinking glaucous eyes, tumbling into darkness as Dr. Harrow pumped the sedatives into my brain.

Much later I woke to see Dr. Harrow staring at me from the far end of the room. She watched me for a moment, then walked slowly to the bed.

"What was it, Wendy?" she asked, smoothing her haik as she sat beside me. "Can you tell me?"

I shook my head. "I don't know," I said, biting the tip of my thumb. Then I twisted to stare at her and asked, "Who was the boy?"

Her voice caught for an instant before she answered. "My brother Aidan. My twin."

"No—the other—the boy in the tree."

This time she held her breath a long moment, then let it out in a sigh. "I don't know," she said. "But you remember him? You saw him too?"

I nodded. "Now. I can see him now. If I—" And I shut my eyes and drifted before snapping back. "Like that. He comes to me on his own. Without me recalling him. Like—" I flexed my fingers helplessly. "Like a dream, only I'm awake now."

Slowly Dr. Harrow shook her head and reached to take my hand. "That's how he found Aidan, too, the last time," she said. "And me. And now you." For an instant something like hope flared in her eyes, but faded as she bowed her head. "I think, Wendy," she said with measured calm; "I think we should keep this to ourselves right now. And tomorrow, maybe, we'll try again."

He sees me.

I woke, my heart pounding so that for a dizzying moment I thought I was having a seizure and reflexively braced my hands behind my head. But no: it was the dream, it was *him*—

I breathed deeply, trying to keep the dream from fleeing, then slowly opened my eyes to my room bathed in the glow of monitors and a hint of dawn. In the air before me I could still see his eyes, green and laughing, the beautiful boy's face adrift in a sea of young leaves more real than the damp sheets twisted around my legs. He reached a hand toward me, beckoning, and intense joy filled me as I smelled new earth, apple blossoms, the breeze carrying the promise of sun and sky and burgeoning fruit. I leaned forward in my bed, clutching the sheets as I began to reach for him, to take that white hand in my own—

When like the rind of some bright fruit peeled back to reveal squirming larvae, the boy's skin shriveled and fell from him. A skeletal hand clawed desperately for mine. Beneath its shell of flesh the skull shone stark white. I screamed and snatched back my hand, then staggered from my bed to the window. He was gone.

I don't know how long I knelt there, resting my forehead against the sill, blinking against tears: real tears, my own tears. Because it was not that awful cadaver that burned within my mind's eye but the boy with green eyes and fair hair, heartbreakingly lovely, new leaves brushing his brow, and the cry of tiny frogs piercing the shadowy air about him. A sense of terrible desolation filled me at waking alone in this dark place. I thought of Aidan Harrow weeping: to have had the radiant promise of those eyes before him and then forever gone . . .

From outside came a sound. I lifted my head to see a phalanx of wild geese, black against the pale September dawn. Their cry held nothing but regret and sorrow for the summer gone, and a shrill hope for distant warmth. I watched until they disappeared, their grief fading into the rising wind, and fell asleep there with my head pillowed upon my arms. Hours later I woke to Dr. Harrow's knock upon my door, and her announcement that we would not repeat the experiment that day.

Several days had passed since Morgan Yates's suicide. As standard procedure Justice ran a standard post-trauma scan on me early one evening. I sat patiently before my window, staring out at the sun setting over the tops of the yellowing lindens while Justice ran the wires and stimulated the rush of recent memory.

Blood racing across dirty glass. The imagined thud of janissaries' feet upon cracked macadam. A feathery explosion of bone and tissue from Morgan's skull. I made my breathing quicken as I lingered over the memory of Morgan's fury and held for a moment her words in my mind—

Bitch! Whore! How dare you laugh at me?

—recalled the poem in her datafile—*Sacred Monsters*—and her face as she screamed at me. Justice stared at the screen, finally nodded. Then he pressed a sedative to my neck, as I knew he would, and left me with an extra hand-

ful to be taken as needed. I nodded goodbye as he left the
Horne Room, and waited for the others to arrive.

"Hello, Wednesday," croaked a voice. A triangular face
hung upside down in the window, dusky black and
pinched as a bat's.

"Hullo, Gligor," I said, and moved over on the bed to
make room for him.

His hands scrabbled at the sill and I thought he might
fall; but he caught his balance, sighting me or the lingering
warmth of the monitors that showed up as bright blue
pulses in his mind. He swung clumsily into the room, one
hand grasping the edge of the sill while he paused to catch
his breath. He twisted until he found me, waited a moment
for his shield to set me on the grid. Then, suddenly grace-
ful, he sidled onto the bed beside me.

"What did they give you?"

I handed him a sedative. He pressed it to his temple,
waited a few moments before making a face and discard-
ing it.

"Nothing else?" he whined. "Merle said she saw Dr.
Harrow here yesterday with the NET."

I started to nod, then stopped. Suddenly I didn't want to
share Emma's memories with Gligor or Anna or anyone
else. Reaching beneath the bed, I withdrew a hand-rolled
cigarette and lit it. I went to sit on the windowsill and
stared moodily down at the lawns where servers were
clipping the grass.

"So?" Gligor prodded. He sniffed hungrily.

"Leave me alone." I blew smoke out the window, refusing to look at him or offer him a cigarette.

From the other end of the room echoed a faint creak, a
muted giggle. Gritting my teeth, I glanced back. The door
swung open. Andrew slipped into the room.

"Hah! Merle was following me but I took the back stairs,
the secret way, and now she thinks I'm in the north turret.
What's the matter, Gligor?"

He flopped onto the bed next to him, breathing on the
smooth surface of Gligor's eyeshield and then drawing a
squiggle in the condensation.

Gligor took his hand and nipped at his bare shoulder.

"Mmmm," he murmured. He leaned back, drawing up the shield so that I could see the empty white balls of his eyes, and licked his lips. I knew he was trying to annoy me. I snorted and stared at Andrew.

"What's the matter?" he repeated. He leaned over the little refrigerator at my bedside and rifled its contents.

Gligor snapped the shield back down. "Wednesday won't share," he said petulantly. "Harrow did something with her yesterday and now she won't share—"

I took a last long drag on my cigarette and flicked it out the window. "Nothing happened," I said, glaring at the back of Andrew's head.

Abruptly he turned around to stare at me. His eyes widened. He blinked once, very deliberately, and lowered his head. The face that lifted itself to me a moment later was dark with cunning, and Anna's huskier voice rang out.

"*I* know," she said triumphantly. "Something about the poet, something about the suicides!"

Gligor hissed admiringly. I stiffened, tightening my grip on the windowsill where I sat. Anna grinned. Then, before I could dart away, she lunged at me and pulled me to the floor.

"Come on, Gligor!" she barked, pinning down my arms and kneeing me viciously when I tried to push her back. "She shared with me the other day and it was *wonderful*—"

"No!" I protested, kicking at Gligor as he slid behind Anna and slapped ineffectually at my feet. "It wasn't the poet, I swear—"

"That's it, get her feet," she ordered Gligor. She straddled my chest and looked at me, grinning, her face flushed with delight just as mine had so many times before in the same circumstances. "Now, Wendy, hold still—"

Anna's strong hands gripped my head and held me steady. She lowered her face to mine and kissed me, her tongue probing my mouth before she nipped my lower lip gently and then bit it, hard enough to draw blood. She shut her eyes and threw back her head, letting out her breath in a long sigh. I waited several seconds to be sure her rush had begun. Then I shoved her from me and kicked at

Gligor, taking him by surprise so that he sprawled onto the floor with a groan. I turned back to Anna, furious.

There was nothing I could do. It was too late to revoke whatever response the neurotransmitters in my blood now carried to her brain. I could only hope that there had not been enough blood, or enough of the resonant chemicals within it, to satisfy her hunger for sensation.

I glared, waiting to see how she reacted. Beside me, Gligor rubbed his leg and watched too. Occasionally he darted furtive glances at me, so that I saw my sullen face reflected in the matte surface of his shield.

"Look, Wednesday," he whispered.

Anna had sunk back on her heels, eyes closed. A rapturous expression crept over her, making her face seem remote and otherworldly. I watched, fascinated, wondering if she saw the same unearthly figure I had, or if she was still tapping in to Morgan Yates's death. Gligor moved his head back and forth, back and forth, his eyeshield tracing some invisible pattern in the heat emitted by Anna.

Suddenly her eyes opened. She stared at a point some distance above her head and smiled in delight, as though she greeted some beloved friend in the empty air. I caught myself leaning forward to grasp her hands as she reached for whatever it was she saw. But before I could touch her, her expression changed. She snarled and wrenched back her hands as though someone had tried to grab them, then turned to me blindly.

"Oh, Wendy," she breathed, awe tingeing her disbelief. "What have you done?"

Then she began to scream.

I tried to muffle her cries and yelled for Gligor to help. But he had immediately jumped onto the bed and now sat there whimpering while I restrained her. She swung at me wildly, clipping the side of my head so that I reeled back but did not let go.

"Him!" she shrieked over and over, her jaws snapping each time so that she bit her tongue and blood covered my hands. *"Him!"*

I shouted at Gligor to get one of the sedatives from my bedside, but still he refused to move. And then I heard voices and running feet in the hall. Several Aides and Dr. Silverthorn rushed into the room.

They restrained her, though not without a fight. The Aide Justice swore fiercely when Anna bit him. Dr. Silverthorn pushed him away before administering a sedative to her. It wasn't until after they carried her out that he noticed Gligor cowering on the bed.

"Gligor!" Dr. Silverthorn shook him gently until the boy stopped whimpering. "What happened?"

"Something was there—" He gasped, clutching at his head. Dr. Silverthorn put his arm about him and drew him close. To me he turned eyes so cold that for a moment I forgot my own anger and disappointment.

"What the hell were you doing, Wendy?"

I shrugged. "Anna tapped me. I warned her—"

"Don't you know what this means?" he shouted. Gligor winced and tried to pull away from him. "They'll take him away, they'll take all of you—"

"But it's true," said Gligor. "It wasn't Wendy's fault—but I'm so tired, Dr. Silverthorn. Can I go to my room?"

Dr. Silverthorn nodded and helped Gligor to the door, all the time regarding me with icy revulsion.

"I'm going to recommend that you all be forbidden to see each other. But I'll let Dr. Harrow handle you, Wendy," was all he said as they left.

"Didn't you hear anything I told you the other day, Wendy?"

Dr. Harrow paused in front of my window, eyeing with disapproval the cigarette ashes blown into the corner in a small gray heap. She fixed me with a probing stare. "Don't you understand what's going on, why we need to be careful while *they're* here?" She motioned toward the outdoors, where Dr. Leslie led a group of Governors and their accompanying janissaries on a tour of the grounds.

I sat on the bed, playing with the wires she had carefully arranged on the frayed counterpane in preparation for our session. "Yes," I replied.

She continued to watch me closely. "I don't think you do, really," she said at last, then sighed. She glanced at the door. It had been fixed with a new lock. "Anna's resilient, though. She'll be fine."

I shook my head indifferently. I hadn't asked after Anna because I knew she would be fine. Empaths were always fine.

Dr. Harrow's gray eyes narrowed. "You don't really care, do you? None of you really care at all about each other."

I yawned. Fruitless to point out that our lack of emotive response was due to the expertise of the staff of the Human Engineering Laboratory. My main concern had been that Dr. Harrow would learn that Anna had somehow tapped in to the same memory that had haunted Dr. Harrow's dreams for most of her life, and that as punishment she would not permit me to continue with the empatherapy— or, worse, that Dr. Harrow would perversely choose to continue it with Anna. But Dr. Harrow had shown up once again with the NET, and wheeled the splintering cot from its closet, and otherwise behaved as though we were going to proceed as planned.

"Are we ready to start?" I asked.

She sighed again, pushed her hair behind her ears, and removed her pince-nez. "Yes, I suppose so."

And though her hands were steady as she initialized the BEAM, I could smell the dreamy odor of absinthium on her breath, and fear like a potent longing in her sweat.

"Emma," he whispers at the transom window. "Let me in."

The quilts piled on me muffle his voice. He calls again, louder, until I groan and sit up in bed, rubbing my eyes and glaring at the top of his head as he peeks through the narrow glass.

From the bottom of the door echoes faint scratching, Molly's whine. A thump. More scratching: Aidan crouched outside the room, growling through choked laughter. I

drape a quilt around me and lean forward to unlatch the
door.

Molly flops onto the floor, snorting when she bumps her
nose and then drooling apologetically. Behind her stumbles Aidan, shivering in his worn kimono with its tattered
sleeves and belt stolen from one of my old dresses. I giggle,
gesturing for him to shut the door before Father hears us in
his room below.

"It's fucking freezing in this place," Aidan exclaims,
pinning me to the bed and pulling the quilts over our
heads. "Oh, come on, dog." Grunting, he hauls her up
beside us. "My room is like Antarctica. Tierra del Fuego.
The Balkhash steppes." He punctuates his words with
kisses, elbowing Molly as she tries to slobber our faces. I
squirm away and straighten my nightshirt.

"Hush. You'll wake Father."

Aidan rolls his eyes and stretches against the wall.
"Spare me." Through the rents in his kimono I can see his
skin, dusky in the moonlight. No one has skin like Aidan's,
except for me: not white but the palest gray, almost blue,
and fine and smooth as an eggshell. People stare at us in
the street, especially at Aidan. At the Academy girls stop
talking when he passes, and fix me with narrowed eyes
and lips pursed to mouth a question never asked.

Aidan yawns remorselessly as a cat. Aidan is the beauty:
Aidan whose gray eyes flicker green whereas mine muddy
to blue in sunlight; Aidan whose long legs wrap around
me and shame my own; Aidan whose hair is the purest
gold, where mine is dull bronze.

"Molly. Here." He grabs her into his lap, groaning at her
weight, and pulls me to him as well, until we huddle in the
middle of the bed. Our heads knock and he points with his
chin to the mirror.

"'Did you never see the picture of **We Three?**'" he war-
bles. Then, shoving Molly to the floor, he takes my shoulders and pulls the quilt from me.

> "'My father had a daughter loved a man
>   As it might be perhaps, were I a woman,
>   I should your lordship.'"

twins — narcicism — incest is
self w. the
self—no
knowledge of other

He recites softly, in his own voice: not the deeper drone he affected when we had been paired in the play at the Academy that winter. I start to slide from bed but he holds me tighter, twisting me to face him until our foreheads touch and I know that the mirror behind us reflects a moon-lapped Rorschach and, at our feet, our snuffling mournful fool.

" 'But died thy sister of her love, my boy?' " I whisper later, my lips brushing his neck where the hair, unfashionably long, waves to form a perfect S.

> *" 'I am all the daughters of my father's house,*
> *And all the brothers too; and yet I know not.' "*

He silences me with a kiss. Later he whispers nonsense, my name, rhyming words from our made-up language; then a long and heated silence.

Afterward he sleeps, but I lie long awake, stroking his hair and watching the rise and fall of his slender chest. In the coldest hour he awakens and stares at me, eyes wide and black, and turning on his side he moans, then begins to cry as though his heart will break. I clench my teeth and stare at the ceiling, trying not to blink, trying not to hear or feel him next to me, his pale gray skin, his eyes: my beautiful brother in the dark.

After this session Dr. Harrow's red eyes met mine when I first came to, but she left quickly, advising me not to leave my chamber until she summoned me later. I fell soundly asleep until late afternoon, when the rush of autumn rain against the high casements finally woke me. For a long time I lay in bed staring up at a long fine crack that traversed the ceiling. To me it appeared like the arm of some ghastly tree overtaking the room. It finally drove me downstairs, despite Dr. Harrow's warning to stay in the Horne Room.

I paced the long glass-roofed corridor that led to the pre-Columbian annex, brooding. I almost wished that Justice would see me and stop me, send me to my room, and arrange for my medication to be changed or schedule me for tests that might reduce this strange unease. But today the Aides would be meeting with Margalis Tast'annin and his staff. HEL's senior personnel would be in their private quarters upstairs having tea, and the other empaths would be playing at furtive pastimes where they could not be easily monitored. I paused to pluck a hibiscus blossom from a terra-cotta vase and arranged it behind one ear. Then I went on, until I reached the ancient elevator with its folding arabesques.

The second floor was off limits to empaths, but Anna had memorized a dead patient's release code and she and I occasionally crept up here to tap sleeping research subjects. No Aides patrolled these rooms. Servers checked the monitors and recorded all responses. Their creaking wheels and the monotonous click of their datachambers were the only sounds that stirred the drowsy air. At the end of each twelve-hour shift, doctors would flit in and out of the bedrooms, unhooking oneironauts and helping them stumble to other rooms where they could fall into yet another, though dreamless, sleep. I tapped the pirated code into the first security server I saw, then waited for it to read my retina imprint and finally grant the access code that slid open the false paneled wall.

Here stretched the sleeplabs: chambers swathed in yellowed challis and moth-eaten linens, huge canopied beds where masked oneironauts (most of them unfortunate survivors of the previous Ascendant autocracy, or captives taken during the Archipelago Conflict) turned and sighed as their monitors clicked in draped alcoves. The oneironauts' skin shone glassy white. Beneath the masks their eyes were bruised a tender green from enforced somnolence. I held my breath as long as I could: the air seethed with dreams. I hurried down the hall to a room with door ajar and an arched window columned with white drapes. A woman I did not recognize sprawled across a cherry four-poster. Her demure homespun shift, yolk-yellow and embroidered with a five-digit number, was curiously at odds with the mask that rakishly covered her eyes. I slipped inside, locking the door behind me. Then I turned to the bed.

The research subject's hair formed a dark filigree against the disheveled linen sheets. I bowed to kiss her on the mouth, waiting to be certain she would not wake. Then I dipped my tongue between her lips and drew back, closing my eyes to unravel strands of desire and clouded abandon, pixie fancies. All faded in a moment: dreams, after all, are dreams. I reached to remove the wires connecting her to the monitors, adjusted the settings, and hooked her into the NET. I did the same for myself with extra wires, relaying through the BEAM to the transmitter. I smoothed the sheets, lay beside her, and closed my eyes.

A silvery dome shot with sunlight. Clouds mist the dome with a scent of filters and stale air. In the distance I hear the click of solex panels rotating as the NASNA station moves silently through the atmosphere. Turning, I can see a line of stunted gray-green trees planted in a straight line. We walk there, the oneironaut's will bending so easily to mine that I scarcely sense her: she is another engineered breeze.

The trees draw nearer. I stare at them until they shift, stark lichened branches blurring into limbs bowed with green and gentle leaves. Now they are great and verdant trees that would never grow within a station. I sense the oneironaut's faint puzzlement at this change, but in another moment we are beneath their heavy welcoming boughs.

I place my hand against the rough bark and stare into the heart of the greenery. Within the emerald shadows something stirs. Sunlit shards of leaf and twig align themselves into hands. Shadows shift to form a pair of slanted beryl eyes. There: crouched among the boughs like a dappled cat, his curls crowned with a ring of leaves, his lips parted to show small white teeth. He smiles at me.

Before he draws me any closer I withdraw, snapping the wires from my face. The tree shivers into white sheets and the shrouded body of the woman beside me.

My pounding heart slowed as I drew myself up on my elbows to watch her, carefully peeling the mask from her face. Beneath lids mapped with fine blue veins her eyes rolled, tracking something unseen. Suddenly they steadied. Her mouth relaxed into a smile, then into an expression of such bliss that without thinking I kissed her and tasted a burst of ecstatic, halcyon joy.

And reeled back as she suddenly clawed at my chest, her mouth twisted to shout; but no sound came. Bliss exploded into terror. Her eyes opened and she stared, not at me but at something that loomed before her. Her eyes grew wide and horrified, the pupils dilating as she grabbed at my face, tore the hibiscus blossom from my hair, and choked a scream, a shout I muffled with a pillow.

I whirled and reset the monitors, switched the NET's settings, and fled. In the hallway I hesitated and looked back. The woman pummeled the air before her blindly; she had not seen me. I turned and ran until I reached the stairway leading to the floors below, and slipped away unseen.

Downstairs all was silent. Servers creaked past, bringing tea trays to doctors in their quarters. I hurried to the conservatory, where I inquired after the Aide Justice. The server directed me to a chamber where Justice stood recording the results of an evoked potential scan.

"Wendy!" Surprise melted into dismay. "What are you doing here?"

I shut the door and stepped to the window, tugging the heavy velvet drapes until they fell and the chamber darkened. "I want you to scan me," I said.

He shook his head, nervously fingered his long blond braid. "What? Why—" I grabbed his hand as he tried to turn up the lights, and he nodded slowly, then dimmed the screen he had been working on. "Where is Dr. Harrow?"

"I want you to do it." I tightened my grip. "I think I have entered a fugue state."

He smiled, shaking his head. "That's impossible, Wendy. You'd have no way of knowing it—you'd be catatonic, or—" He shrugged, then glanced uneasily at the door. "What's going on? You know I can't do that alone, especially now."

"But you know how," I said, stroking his hand. "You are a

student of their arts, you can do it as easily as Dr. Harrow."
I leaned forward until my forehead rested against his, and
kissed him on the mouth. His expression changed to fear as
he trembled and tried to move away. Sexual contact between staff and experimental personnel was forbidden and
punishable by execution of the Aides in question, since
empaths were believed incapable of initiating such contact. I pinned both of his hands to the table, until he nodded and motioned with his head toward the PET unit.

"Sit down," he said. I latched the door, then sat in the
wing chair beside the bank of monitors.

In a few minutes I heard the dull hum of the scanners as
he improvised the link for my reading. I waited until my
brain's familiar patterns emerged on the screen.

"See?" Relief brightened his voice, and he tilted the
monitor so that I could see it more clearly. "All normal.
Maybe she got your dosage wrong. Perhaps Dr. Silverthorn can suggest a . . ."

His words trickled into silence. I shut my eyes and drew
up the image of the tree, beryl eyes and outstretched
hand, then opened my eyes to see the PET scan showing
intrusive activity in my temporal lobe: brain waves evident of an emergent secondary personality.

"That's impossible," said Justice. "You have no MPs, no
independent emotions. . . . What the hell *is* that?" He
traced the patterns with an unsteady hand, then turned to
stare at me. "What did you do, Wendy?"

I shook my head, crouching into the chair's corner, and
removed the wires. The last image shimmered on the
screen like a cerebral ghost. "Take them," I said, holding
out the wires. "Don't tell anyone."

He let me pass without a word. Only when my hand
grasped the doorknob did he touch me on the shoulder.

"Where did it come from?" He faltered. "What is it,
Wendy?"

I stared past him at the monitor with its pulsing shadows.
"Not me," I said at last. "The Boy in the Tree."

* * *

They found the sleep researcher at shift-change that evening, hanging by the swag that had decorated her canopied bed. Anna told me about it at dinner.

"Her monitors registered an emergent MP." She licked her lips like a kitten. "Do you think we could get into the morgue?"

I yawned and shook my head. "Are you crazy?"

Anna giggled and rubbed my neck. "Isn't everybody?"

Several Aides entered the dining room, scanning warily before they started tapping empties on the shoulder and gesturing to the door. I looked up to see Justice, his face white and pinched as he stood behind me.

"Margalis Tast'annin has ordered evacuation of all senior staff to the provisional capital. They're bringing in new personnel for reevaluation of the Harrow Project. You're to go to your chambers," he announced. "Dr. Harrow says you are not to talk to anyone until Tast'annin has seen you individually." He swallowed and avoided my eyes, then stared directly at me for the first time. "I told her that I hadn't seen you, Wendy, but would make certain you knew—"

I nodded and looked away. In a moment he was gone, and I started upstairs.

"I saw Dr. Leslie before," Anna commented before she walked outside toward her cottage. "He smiled at me and waved." She hesitated, biting her lip thoughtfully. "Maybe he will play with me this time," she announced before turning down the rain-spattered path.

Dr. Harrow was standing at the high window in the Horne Room when I arrived. In her hand she held a drooping hibiscus flower.

"Shut the door," she ordered. I did so. "Now lock it and sit down."

She had broken the hibiscus. Her fingers looked bruised from its stain: jaundiced yellow, ulcerous purple. As I stared she flung the flower into my lap.

"They know it was you in the sleeplabs," she said. "Dr. Silverthorn matched your retina print with the masterfile. How could you have thought you'd get away with it?" She sank onto the bed, her eyes dull with fatigue.

The rain had hung back for several hours. Now it hammered the windows again, its steady tattoo punctuated by the rattle of hailstones.

"I did not mean to kill her." I smoothed my robe, flicking the broken blossom onto the floor.

She ground the hibiscus beneath her heel, then picked it up and threw it out the window. "Her face," she said, as if replying to a question. "Like my brother Aidan's."

I stared at her blankly.

"When I found him," she went on, turning to me with glittering eyes. "On the tree."

I shook my head. "I don't know what you're talking about, Dr. Harrow."

Her lips tightened against her teeth when she faced me. A drop of blood welled against her lower lip. I longed to lean forward to taste it, but did not dare. "She was right, you know. You steal our dreams. . . ."

"That's impossible." I crossed my arms, shivering a little from the damp breeze. I hesitated. "You told me that is impossible. Unscientific. Unprofessional thinking."

She smiled, and ran her tongue over her lip to lick away the blood. "Unprofessional? This has all been very unprofessional, Wendy. Didn't you know that?"

"The tenets of the revised Nuremberg Act state that an Ascendant should not perform upon a subject any research which she would not undergo herself."

Dr. Harrow shook her head, ran a hand through damp hair. "Is that what you thought it was? Research?"

I shrugged. "I—I don't know. The boy—your twin?"

"Aidan . . ." She spread her fingers against the bed's coverlet, flexed a finger that bore a heavy ring set with cabochons spelling NASNA. "They found out. Instructors. Our father. About us. We were betrayed by another— *promising student.* Do you understand?"

A flicker of the feeling she had evoked in bed with her brother returned, and I slitted my eyes, tracing it. "Yes," I whispered. "I think so."

"It is—" She fumbled for an explanation. "A crime. They separated us. Aidan . . . They sent him away, to another kind of—place. Tested him."

She stood and paced to the window, leaned with a hand upon each side so that the rain lashed about her, then turned back to me. "He went mad.

"You see, something happened that night in the woods." Shaking her head, she pounded the wall with flattened palms. "He was never the same. He had terrible dreams, he couldn't bear to sleep alone—that was how it started—

"And then they let him come home for a visit, in the spring. He wouldn't leave his room. We went out one morning, Father and I. And when we returned, I looked for him, he wasn't there, not in his room, not anywhere. . . .

"I was the one who found him. He had—" Her voice broke and she stared past me to the wall. "Apple blossom in his hair. And his face—"

I thought she would weep; but her expression twisted so that almost I could imagine she laughed to recall it.

"Like hers . . ."

She drew nearer, until her eyes were very close to mine. I sniffed and moved to the edge of the bed warily: she had dosed herself with hyoscine derived from the herbarium. Her words slurred as she spoke.

"Do you know what happens now, Wendy? More janis-saries arrived tonight. They have canceled our term of research. We're all terminated. A purge. Tomorrow they take over. New personnel. Representatives of the Governors. Specially trained *NASNA* medics, hand-picked by Margalis Tast'annin."

She spat the name, then made a clicking noise with her tongue. "And you, Wendy. And Anna, and all the others. Like the geneslaves: toys. *Weapons.*" She swayed as she leaned toward me. "You especially. They'll find him, you know—dig him up and use him—"

"Who, Dr. Harrow?" I asked. Sweat pearled on her forehead. She stretched a hand to graze my temples, and I shivered.

"My brother," she murmured.

"No, Dr. Harrow. The others—who betrayed you, who—"

"I told you, we were friends," she cut me off. "Aidan trusted him—"

"*Who?*"

"Margalis." Her hand rested on mine now, and I felt her fingers tightening about my wrist.

"And the other—who was the other, the Boy in the Tree?"

Smiling, she drew me toward her. She reached for the NET's rig, flicking rain from the colored wires.

"Let's find out. . . ."

I cried out at her clumsy hookup. A spot of blood welled from her temple and I touched my face, drew away a finger gelled with the fluid she had smeared carelessly from ear to jaw. Then, before I could lie down, she made the switch and I cried out at the dizzy vistas erupting behind my eyes.

Aniline lightning. Faculae stream from synapse to synapse as ptyalin floods my mouth and my head rears instinctively to smash against the headboard. She has not tied me down. The hyoscine lashes into me like a fiery bile and I open my mouth to scream. In the instant before it begins I taste something faint and caustic in the back of her throat and struggle to free myself from her arms. Then I'm gone.

Before me looms a willow tree shivering in a breeze frigid with the shadow of the northern mountains. Sap oozes from a raw flat yellow scar on the trunk above my head, where, two days before, our father had sawed off the damaged limb. It had broken from the weight. When I found him he lay pillowed on a crush of twigs and young leaves and scattered bark, the blossoms in his hair alone unmarked by the fall. One hand lay upon his breast, the Academy ring glittering in the sunlight. Now I stand on tiptoe and stroke the broken willow, bring my finger to my lips and kiss it. I shut my eyes, because they burn so. No tears left to shed: only this terrible dry throbbing, as though my eyes have been etched with sand. The sobs begin again. The wrenching weight in my chest drags me

to my knees until I crouch before the tree, bow until my
forehead brushes grass trampled by grieving family and
friends from the Academy. I groan and try to think of
words, imprecations, a curse to rend the light and living
from my world so abruptly strangled and still. But I can
only moan. My mouth opens upon dirt and shattered
granite. My nails claw at the ground as though to wrest
from it something besides stony roots and scurrying ear-
wigs. The earth swallows my voice as I force myself to my
knees and, sobbing, raise my head to the tree.

It is enough. He has heard me.

Through the shroud of new leaves he peers with lambent
eyes. April's first apple blossoms weave a snowy cloud
about his brow. His eyes are huge, the palest purest green
in the cold morning sun. They stare at me unblinking,
harsh and bright and implacable as moonlight, as languidly he extends his hand toward mine.

I stagger to my feet, clots of dirt falling from my palms.
From the north the wind rises and rattles the willow
branches. Behind me a door rattles as well, as my father
leans out to call me back to the house. At the sound I start
to turn, to break the reverie that binds me to this place, this
tree stirred by a tainted wind riven from a bleak and
noiseless shore.

And then I stop, where in memory I have stopped a
thousand times, and turn back to the tree. For the first time
I meet his eyes.

He is waiting, as He has always waited; as He will always
wait. At my neck the wind gnaws cold as iron, stirring the
collar of my blouse so that already the chill creeps down
my chest, to nuzzle there at my breasts and burrow between them. I nod, very slightly, and glance back at the
house.

All the colors have fled the world. For the first time I see
it clearly: the gray skin taut against granite hills and
grassless haughs; the horizon livid with clouds like a rising
barrow; the hollow bones and nerveless hands drowned
beneath black waters lapping at the edge of a charred
orchard. The rest is fled and I see the true world now, the
sleeping world as it wakes, as it rears from the ruins and

whispers in the wind at my cheeks: this *is what awaits you; this and nothing more, the lie is revealed and now you are waking and the time has come, come to me, come to me. . . .*

In the ghastly light only His eyes glow, and it is to them that I turn, it is into those hands white and cold and welcome that I slip my own, it is to Him that I have come, not weeping no not ever again, not laughing, but still and steady and cold as the earth beneath my feet, the gray earth that feeds the roots and limbs and shuddering leaves of the tree. . . .

And then pain rips through me, a flood of fire searing my mouth and ears, raging so that I stagger from the bed as tree and sky and earth tilt and shiver like images in black water. Gagging, I reach into my own throat, trying to dislodge the capsule Emma Harrow has bitten; try to breathe through the fumes that strip the skin from my gums. I open my mouth to scream but the fire churns through throat and chest, boils until my eyes run and stain the sky crimson.

And then I fall. The wires rip from my skull.

Beside me on the floor Dr. Harrow thrashes, eyes staring wildly at the ceiling, her mouth rigid as she retches and blood spurts from her bitten tongue. I recoil from the scent of bitter almond she exhales, then watch as she suddenly grows still. Quickly I kneel, tilting her head so that half of the broken capsule rolls onto the floor at my feet. I wait a moment, then bow my head until my lips part around her broken jaw and my tongue stretches gingerly to lap at the blood cupped in her cheek.

In the tree the Boy laughs. A bowed branch shivers, and, slowly, rises from the ground. Another boy dangles there, his hair tangled in golden strands around a leather belt. I see him lift his head and, as the world rushes away in a blur of red and black, he smiles at me.

A cloud of frankincense. Seven stars against a dormer window. A boy with a bulldog puppy; and *she* is dead.

* * *

I cannot leave my room now. Beside me a screen dances
with colored lights that refract and explode in brilliant
parhelions when I dream. But I am not alone now,
ever. . . .

I see Him waiting in the corner, laughing as His green
eyes slip between the branches and the bars of my window, until the sunlight changes and He is lost to view once
more, among the dappled and chattering leaves.

Part Two

Stories for Boys

1. Primordial zone of Bohemia

"Raphael . . ."

The sigh came again. For an instant I paused with my head thrown back, the sweat on my shoulders cooling as I tried to recall who it was that moaned beneath me. Then a breeze stirred from the hidden panel left slightly ajar so that other Patrons might watch if they desired, and the chilly air wafted to me the scent of burned leaves and earth. A Botanist: Iris Bergenia, a friend of my Patron Roland Nopcsa and an exceedingly plain woman. The most memorable thing about her the ripe odor of loam clinging to the rough fingers that clutched me. I murmured some mindless endearment and slowed my movements, hoping this might hasten her climax so that I could join my House at last worship. Then, as an afterthought, I ran one hand across her scalp (her hair close-cropped like all the Curators', and none too clean), and when her breathing came fast and shallow I tugged her hair as I whispered her name. She gasped and cried aloud. I pulled out of her and rolled aside on the bed. I moaned as in pleasure, hoping that no one was watching from the Clandestine Adytum to see my grimace of distaste give way to a grin as she continued to squeal and sigh.

"Ah, Raphael," she murmured a little later, reaching to stroke the long russet tangle of hair spilling down my back. I yawned and stretched, mimed a perfect smile as I turned from her to pull on my tunic.

"That was lovely," I said. I found my riband on the floor and braided my hair carelessly, tying the shining bit of brocade around the end. Then I stood. I pressed three fingers against my mouth in the Paphian's beck and stared over her head at my reflection in the ancient ormolu mirror hanging from the far wall of the seraglio. It cast back my image: a slender gold-tipped shadow standing above Iris Bergenia's stolid figure as she yanked heavy leather workboots back onto her feet. I repeated my comment, glancing down at her. But in pulling on her coarse dun-colored trousers and blouson she had also cloaked any hint of the desire that had kept her straining after me since we had met a week before at the Illyrians' Sothic Masque. I made a face. Few of our Patrons had anything to say to us afterward.

Fewer still wanted to look at us and be reminded of their own ugliness of body and soul, forgotten for a few moments in the embrace of a pathic or little mopsy.

"Did you bring the tincture of opium?" I asked, tossing back my braid as I crossed the chamber to light more candles.

"Why—no, I mean—" Iris stammered, her foot hitting the floor with a thud. She gazed at me abashed. "I understood from Miramar it was to be delivered later—"

"*Oh,*" I said, investing the syllable with all the sneering doubt I could muster. As the yellow tapers threw more light into the chamber I was rewarded with her blush. The mere thought that their association with us consisted of anything but raw commerce mortified even the most devout Patron of the Hill Magdalena Ardent. I knew that Miramar would be furious if he heard I had embarrassed Iris Bergenia by this intimation of impropriety. I also knew that there would never be any punishment for Raphael Miramar, favorite of the House Miramar and Roland Nopcsa's pet. "Well, if Gower Miramar is *expecting* it . . ."

I stretched, wondering if the exchange for my favors might also bring us more of the cosmetic madder the Botanists had given us at the last masque. "May I escort you to your friends, Iris?"

"No." Hastily she collected her cloak and carrying

pouch, the tarnished swivel gun that I knew wasn't loaded but which all Botanists carried anyway when they visited our Houses. "I think I remember the way out—"

I walked her to the chamber door, enjoying her discomfort as I embraced her. I shut my eyes and sighed into her ear, felt her shudder as she pulled away from me. She bared her teeth in a false smile. She did have even white teeth, as so many of the Botanists did; Miramar said it was from chewing birch twigs. For a moment a hint of warmth flared in her eyes.

"Roland was right about you," she said. She gave me a fleeting smile.

I bowed my head, affecting modesty, and said, "I'll tell Miramar you promised the tincture would be delivered *soon.*"

Her smile froze. With a shrug she turned and fled.

"Puh," I said aloud. "That old bitch." I walked to the bed and retrieved my rings and the aluminum bracelet Roland had given me last year when I had been chosen cacique at the Masque of Winterlong. It was a lovely bangle, taken from the Hall of Civil Servants in the Museum where Roland lived and where soon, soon! *I* would live as well. For several minutes I stood before the mirror, combing my long hair and braiding it again. This time I bound it with a long indigo riband, pulled the braid taut to display the titanium ear-cuffs that had been another token of Roland's favor, ancient ornaments he had found among the ruins beneath the Obelisk. I dropped the braid, gingerly touched my cheek, wincing at how rough it felt. Most Patrons preferred the youngest children. Those of us old enough to shave were encouraged to do so each morning and evening. But Roland had confided that Iris Bergenia would prefer me unshaven, and so tonight I had forgone my toilet. Despite this the face that glowed between the shadows in the mirror's flecked surface was no less beautiful than the painted effigies in the Hall of Dead Kings. Raphael Miramar, most sacred of the Magdalene's Children, beloved of Paphians and of the Curator Roland Nopcsa.

Tonight I would tell Miramar I was leaving.

I smiled into the mirror, once more made the Paphian's beck to myself. I was turning to leave when a shape shot across the room, giggling.

"Fancy!" I cried, laughing as I whirled to catch her. Candlelight struck the spurs of her shoulders, collarbone, knees; made a golden cerement of her thin white tunic. She squealed as I grabbed her and we both tumbled onto the thick carpet. For a moment I pinned her, felt those sharp thin ribs that I could have crushed like the husk of a tamarind. Then she wriggled from my arms and slid beneath the bed.

"Miramar is waiting!" she said, blowing a dust feather into my face. "Let me out." She peered from the bed-shadows: enormous eyes in a triangular face; golden hair just long enough to be pulled into two tight braids that left her ears pitifully exposed to the autumn drafts that chilled our House.

I settled back onto my heels. "Come on out, then."

"You'll catch me."

"I'll come under there and catch you if you don't."

"You can't, you're too big—" She laughed, grasping one of the bed's heavy carven feet and snaking behind it.

"Huh," I said, prying her fingers loose.

With a shriek she darted from beneath the bed. I caught her before she could flee back into the Clandestine Adytum and hugged her to me, kissing her cheek and inhaling her soft scent, still milky and sweet with childhood. "How long were you there, you little snake?"

She shrugged, flushed with excitement, and straightened her shift. "Not long. An hour—"

"An hour!" I pretended to pull her braids, when from downstairs resounded the harsh strains of the sistrum heralding last worship, and Doctor Foster's voice intoning the opening verse of "The Magdalena."

"Come on," she said, and we ran downstairs.

Only Miramar and Doctor Foster lay prostrate in the fane when we arrived. All of the older children and pathics had gone to a Conciliatory Masque at Saint-Alaban. Since this was Third Day, when Doctor Foster attended to Miramar's castigations, I knew that if I remained I would have the chance to tell Miramar of my decision to join Roland at the Museum. I waited while Fancy stood on tiptoe to reach the font which held civet and attar of roses, tried not to grin at how earnestly she anointed herself before turning to let me pass. My own anointment was cursory, and I was punished for my sloppiness in spilling unguent down the front of my chasuble. Miramar ignored Fancy and myself as he chanted the long verses of "The Duties of Pleasure." Doctor Foster sniffed and rolled his eyes as I took my place beside him, trying not to choke on the cloying scent of roses that mingled with the more bitter reek of hemp burning on the altar.

After only a few minutes I heard Fancy's slow breathing: already sound asleep. How could Miramar and Doctor Foster stay awake through worship, night after night, despite long hours of attendance upon the Magdalene's affairs and the samovars of sedative tea they consumed between Visits from Curators and other Paphians? I yawned and focused as I always did upon the ancient figure of the Magdalene. Swathed in smoke from the blackened brazier, the pale contours of Her face had been smoothed to an eyeless plane by the impressions of thousands of small hands over the centuries. To stay awake I counted the stars painted upon Her blue robe and wondered how many years it had been since She was made. Hundreds, perhaps. Miramar and Doctor Foster maintained that ours was the oldest of all the Magdalenes upon the Hill Magdalena Ardent. It was brought there from the ruined Shrine in the northeast part of the City, in the first years of the Second Ascension. That was before the rains of roses made a wasteland of the northeast, before the aardmen and hydrapithecenes and other geneslaves drove the Curators and the first Paphians from their homes, to dwell in the Museums and Embassies as we did now. The House Saint-Alaban claimed that its Magdalene was older than ours. It had come from the Cathedral that still stood to the northwest upon Saint-Alaban's Hill. But the Cathedral was an evil place. The very earth there was poisonous, contaminated by the rains of roses. Only lazars lived in the ruins now, though Doctor Foster said that many janissaries once

stood guard over an ancient hoarde of weapons placed
near Saint-Alaban's Hill before the First Ascension.

"Only a Saint-Alaban would want to lay claim to an image from the Engulfed Cathedral," Miramar would say
disdainfully whenever the issue was brought up. "If they
are so proud of their ancestry, why don't they return there
to live?" This would anger whatever Saint-Alabans were
present, but the rest of us would laugh.

Perched upon a small ridge overlooking the River
Gorge, our House commanded a view of two others—
Saint-Alaban and Persia. To the south sloped the Hill Magdalena Ardent, shadowing the ornate fastnesses of Illyria
and crowned by High Brazil's minarets and glowing lights.
Many nights as a child I had huddled with my bedcousins
in the upstairs nursery, staring out the beveled windows to
watch Miramar and the older children traipse across the
Bison Bridge to attend masques in those gaslit halls, or
begin the longer pilgrimage to the outskirts of the Narrow
Forest where the Curators dwelled. By the time I was old
enough to accompany our Patrons outside, I had learned
that (alas!) the House Miramar was not as wealthy as the
House High Brazil (that entertained the Botanists almost
exclusively, in exchange for opium and atropa belladonna);
that our own Doctor Foster had been sold to the House
Miramar by the hydrapithecenes who had devoured his
parents, for a vial of tincture of opium and a bolt of water-
proof silk (to which we attributed his predilection for lau-
danum and costly fabrics); that the occasional Ascendant
visiting our Patrons must be entertained without question;
that from the Curators we might demand orchids and tex-
tiles and cosmetics in return for our rarefied lust, but never
ask for learning.

Still, no Curator or Illyrian could have lavished us with as
much affection and as many attempts at luxury as did Miramar. The original gold and indigo mosaic tiles glittered on
our nursery walls, although there were many gaps in the
intricate geometries patterned there. Our clothes were
designed and woven by Curators at the Museum of Technologies, or obtained by them from Ascendant traders. In
seraglios lit by dozens of electrified candles we entertained

our Patrons, and slept in beds that had been imported from the Balkhash countries centuries ago. My room had a balcony overlooking the river, and my own tiny radio-phone patched into the House generator. Late at night, after my last Patron had left, I would lie long awake listening to the pulsing strains of waltzes broadcast from the Museum of Technologies as I pored over the brittle pages of the volumes Roland Nopcsa had given me last Winterlong. Books with titles like *The Ancient Life-History of the Earth* and *The Modern Changes of the Earth: Its Inhabitants Considered as Illustrative of Geology*, and *A Short History of a Great Group of Extinct Reptiles*. And one cold and windless winter's eve I picked up an Ascendant radio signal broadcasting from somewhere in the United Provinces. For hours I listened to a faint sweet voice telling an old, old story of a man redeemed by ghosts, until the signal, ghostlike itself, faded into the dawn.

But there was no radiophone to entertain me now: only the featureless Magdalene with Her plaster hands joined, holding the beads upon which She counted the Decades. Five sets of beads; five Houses. In a whispered monotone Doctor Foster responded to Miramar's Invocation of the Sacred Jade, the secret names of Desire. Fancy's breathing had grown softer still, the smoky air warm and ripe with dreams.

I must have dozed myself. It seemed that the figure of the Magdalene had gathered Her robes tightly about Her thighs. As I watched She writhed as though in pain, a sight made more horrible because of Her eyeless face. Her gown rippled and swelled until it tore apart. Then I saw that at Her feet crouched a boy with fair curling hair and grass-green eyes, beautiful as any Paphian mite. He might have been the twin of those other images of the Magdalene, a boy as lovely as She herself, but his lips curled in a cat's cruel smile, and his green eyes winked malice. In his hands he held the torn hem of the Magdalene's gown, and I saw that She bled from wounds in Her hands and feet. The shining stars upon Her robe turned to tears of blood.

Then I saw that the boy was wounded too. About his neck hung a bit of cord, or perhaps a vine. It had left a red scar around his neck. But he did not seem to be suffering. Instead he smiled to see the Magdalene in pain, although She reached to him with Her white hands, to offer succor or perhaps forgiveness. I knew then it was that boy who had injured her. In a rage I sprang to hit him.

My head banged against the edge of the altar. I fell back grunting. Above me the faces of Miramar and Doctor Foster and Fancy folded together in concern.

2. Convergence of a number of separate and independent probabilities

"Just stay still and drink your valerian," ordered Doctor Foster. "Here, Benedick: give this to Raphael."

"Thanks, cousin," I said, taking the steaming mug Small Benedick held out to me. I waited until he skipped back to Doctor Foster before grimacing and drinking the awful stuff.

To my mortification, they had brought me to Doctor Foster's infirmary. Actually the anteroom of his chambers, dignified by the term *infirmary* only by virtue of a warped wooden shelf sagging beneath a row of very old glass bottles. Inside of them one glimpsed homunculi swimming in the cloudy spirits, or the clenched fronds of bizarre plants, the preserved limb of a carnivorous betulamia. I had fortunately never seen these used in any treatment, indeed had never known him to treat us with anything except tincture of opium or chamomile tea (for pain or overstimulation), or sops of wine or an infusion of valerian (for everything else).

"I'm all right," I said. I glared at Small Thomas and Benedick and the other very young children sniggering at me from the other side of the room. They sat at Doctor Foster's feet. My forehead felt bruised where I had knocked it against the altar, and there was that familiar dull throbbing that often followed worship, from inhaling hempen smoke. Doctor Foster nodded, stroking the coiled yellow hair of Fancy in his lap.

"Yes, well, drink it anyway and try to rest. I gather you weren't going to the Conciliatory Masque, so there's no need to rush out of here." He smiled, tossing back his hair (graying at the temples and starting to grow a little thin on top, despite frequent applications of lilac water and honey). He shifted so that more of the children could lean against his legs, and cleared his throat. Doctor Foster liked to talk and liked to have an audience. Too old to be engaged by Patrons, he was still too clever to meet the usual fate that elders meet, little more than slaves to their younger cousins. Instead he had parleyed his gift for storytelling, along with his (mostly imaginary) healing abilities into a position at the House Miramar that was, if not precisely honored, still eyed affectionately by Miramar and the rest of us. We older pathics had lost our appetite for his tales—*stories for boys and stories for girls,* he called them —preferring the real intrigues of our constant round of masques and the intricate couplings that accompanied them. Still it was soothing to lie upon the swaybacked couch beneath a catskin comforter, breathing the sweet fumes that rose from his narghile as he related old tales of the City of Trees and the tragic love stories that were the Paphians' favorite entertainment.

". . . and so the aardmen took him, and Lilith Saint-Alaban gave herself to them in exchange for his life; but the aardmen killed him anyway, and her too; and their son Small Hilliard died in a rain of roses." Doctor Foster sighed. I started, realizing I must have drifted off again.

Not that it mattered. All his stories ended the same way: tragically, with beautiful Paphian boys and girls kidnapped by geneslaves or devoured by lazars or enslaved by Ascendants and Curators. It made life seem a somewhat more comforting prospect in comparison; except that as we got older we learned that most of the tales were true.

"Now a story for *boys,*" demanded Small Thomas, pinching Fancy as he shook his curls at Doctor Foster.

Doctor Foster drew from his narghile and stared at the

mosaic ceiling, as though he read there some strange history. "What story?" he said at last.

"My story!" said Small Thomas.

"Raphael's story!" said Fancy, kicking him and hugging Doctor Foster. "Please, Doctor Foster!"

I pulled the comforter to my chin and tucked my long braid around my neck. Doctor Foster exhaled a plume of smoke and began.

"I remember the day Raphael came here. Sixteen years ago; the same day that Trahern High Brazil performed his inspired Akolasian gambade for the Curators, and as a result of their overly enthusiastic ravishments died; but it was an extraordinary thing to see all the same." He sighed at the memory.

"Raphael's mother was a beautiful girl, a child really— no older than you are now—" He inclined his head to me. "Miramar wanted to take her in, she was so lovely; but I discouraged him, she had been among the lazars for too long. But she was a Paphian, Saint-Alaban we thought, because of her eyes; so many of them have green eyes. She had two children with her, twins—"

"Twins!" said Thomas. He was very young and had not heard all this before.

"Twins," Doctor Foster repeated solemnly. "Raphael and his sister. We bought them both—you all know how rare twins are, and these were extraordinarily beautiful."

"The Saint-Alabans say twins are holy," said Small Thomas. He was thinking of the Masque of Baal and Anat performed at Saint-Alaban each Autime.

Doctor Foster snorted. "Yes, well." He turned back to me and smiled. I dropped my eyes as the children looked at me, and pretended to pluck at a stray thread on my chasuble.

"So did she die?" urged Fancy.

"The mother? Oh, yes, of course. Probably the aardmen had followed her to our door and were just waiting, hoping they'd get all three of them. Miramar thought I was heartless to push her back out again, but—" He shrugged. "I thought we could take a chance on the babies, they seemed free of contagion. And at first they both seemed fine. After a few months the boy—" He pointed the mouth-piece of his narghile at me. "Raphael: he started talking. But the girl never did."

He paused, one hand dropping to pat Thomas. "She was a head-banger. Frightened the Patrons. I did all I could."

He gestured vaguely at the shelf of physics. I silently thanked the Magdalene that he had never had to do anything for me. He shook his head. "But she wouldn't behave. We finally sold her to the Ascendants."

Benedick sniffled at this. More than one Patron had recently complained of his truculence in the children's seraglio.

"Still, the boy was fine," Doctor Foster continued, tugging Benedick's braid reassuringly. "After his bedwarming he drew more Patrons than any of us: a true Son of the Magdalene!"

He ended suddenly and fell to staring at his pipe, his fingers still laced about Benedick's braid. When it seemed apparent that there was no more story forthcoming, the children started to yawn and fidget. I amused myself by making cruel faces at Benedick until he looked about to cry.

From the pendulum chamber several stories above us came the faint tonging of the hour: well after the children's bedtime. Like Sieur Maggot in a play, Miramar's head suddenly popped around the corner of the door.

"Doctor Foster!" he scolded, clapping his hands so that the long azure cuffs of his robe swished against each other. *"Wicked* Doctor Foster. Come, children! Fancy, you know better than this! Benedick, Magnus Stoat will be joining you after breakfast tomorrow—"

Clucking and chirping like peevish sparrows they left, calling goodbyes to Doctor Foster and Miramar and myself as they scurried to where the waiting elders met them in the hall and carried them upstairs to the nursery. Doctor Foster gave them a desultory farewell and nodded off in his chair. Miramar remained smiling in the doorway.

"Is your head better, cousin?" he asked me.

"Yes, uncle," I said, suddenly nervous. I had almost forgotten the reason why I had stolen this evening at home.

Now it came back to me, and my voice cracked as I said, "Miramar—I—could I speak with you?"

He nodded and motioned for me to follow him to his chambers.

A low brass table had been set with steaming glass carafe and two tumblers. I wondered uneasily if somehow he had been expecting me. Miramar knelt to pour our tea, crushing mint leaves and a cube of raw sugar into each glass.

"To your future," he said, raising his tumbler and quickly downing its contents.

My heart sank; he knew. I flopped onto a pillow.

"Iris Bergenia told me this evening that Roland Nopcsa has offered you his bed in the Museum of Natural History."

I bit my lip to keep from cursing, vowed to humiliate Iris publicly as soon as the opportunity arose. But to Miramar I showed a calm face.

"I was going to tell you tonight. . . ."

He listened with studied casualness, eyeing the tea dregs that had settled at the bottom of the empty carafe. He lifted it and gently shook the damp leaves onto a saucer, then squinting tilted the plate to read them.

"What do they say?"

He smiled. "What they always say: love with a romantic stranger." A flick of his scalloped nail dispersed the dregs into a sodden heap. I met his eyes.

"I'm going with him, uncle."

As I spoke I realized this was not how I'd planned to make my announcement; but there it was. I stared at my feet.

"Mmmm." No surprise. But a wince of regret tugged at his gentle mouth. Miramar sighed. "I could refuse you permission, you know." But his expression showed such sorrow that I knew he would not refuse me. He never had.

"I had hoped you would stay—" he went on, cleaning his fingers on a linen napkin.

"I might come back," I said, and was immediately ashamed. Because that proved I was afraid, had doubts; and I wanted to leave boldly. I bumped against the table and sent a tumbler rolling. With a sigh Miramar picked it up.

"I hope you do. You are . . ." He glanced up at the polished copper ceiling that reflected us floating in a molten sea. "The loveliest of all of us. We—*I* wanted your daughters born here, because never have we had a child so beautiful."

I looked away. Tears glittered in his eyes, and I knew I would cry too and change my mind if I saw him weep. "Thank you, uncle."

"It's no favor I'm doing you, letting you leave us."

I stared at the arabesques in the carpet, but my voice betrayed my resentment. "You think I'm a fool to go," I said at last.

"You've been sheltered and spoiled—we *all* have been," he said gently.

"But especially Raphael."

"Well, yes: of course." He reached to stroke my leg. "But you understand why."

"Because I'm worth more than the rest."

"Because you are more beautiful than any of us; because we love you. But they will not love you out there, Raphael—"

I shook his hand from me. "The Curators—" I began.

"The Curators consider us whores and fools! Do you think Roland wants you for your learning?"

"Do you think I want him for his bed?"

Miramar groaned in exasperation. "Listen to me! You could continue with Roland, use his books, and then return to teach the children here, if you like—"

"Teach whores and fools," I snapped, then bit my tongue. Miramar's face grew taut and he folded his hands upon the brass table.

"Your cousins," he said softly; but I knew the glint in his eyes heralded anger. "Do you think you're the first pretty toy to go among them to *learn?* Do you?"

As he leaned forward the table shook. The empty glasses rolled to the floor. I fumbled for a reply as I straightened the mess, but he cut me off with a brusque wave. "Do you know what happened to the others?"

I started to answer, but his voice rose above mine as he named them:

"Estevan High Brazil: raped and blinded by the Librarians. Lorelei Saint-Alaban, throttled when she fainted while entertaining Nelson Dewars's guests at his birthday ball. Three children from Persia engaged for a Senator's cotillion, strangled in their sleep.

"It is not safe for us to live among the Curators, Raphael. Maybe once it was; maybe before we had our own Houses and our own wealth bartered from them over the years.

"But not now; especially not now." He paused, ran a finger along the rim of the glass carafe. "Last week I entertained an Ascendant janissary at High Brazil. He was there to receive a shipment of opium from the Botanists—"

"You told me," I said impatiently.

"I told you nothing. He was besotted with whiskey and frilite; he talked too much. They are sending a man to govern the City, an Ascendant commander—"

I smiled. "Come now, uncle—"

Miramar poured himself another glass of tea. As he sipped it he looked at me through slitted eyes. "Perhaps it won't happen; perhaps he was lying. But the Curators are worried. If this rumor is true—if they really *do* send a Governor to intervene—at the very least it will disrupt trade within the City, and the black market with the Ascendants."

He drank the rest of his tea as I waited. "And?" I said at last.

"The janissary I spoke with said that they intend to retake the City. There would be no place for us then, Raphael; no place at all."

I thought on this in silence. Finally I asked, "Why would he tell you this?"

Miramar shrugged. "What am I to him? A mindless courtesan, just as I am to the Curators. Perhaps he meant to help me, to warn me to escape. But where could we go? We would have nothing without the City and without the Curators."

"So we should hide here forever as their whores and ponces?"

Miramar pounded the floor in aggravation. "We are priests and merchants!"

"And currency!"

I thought he would dismiss me then. Instead he rocked back on his heels and, after a moment, laughed. "Oh, Raphael. I can hear myself saying the same things when I was your age."

"Then why won't you let me go without all this?"

"Only because I've never let anyone go without a warning. And because I am afraid: for you, for all of us. Roland will tire of you, Raphael. They always do." He cut off my protests by placing his hand against my lips and with three fingers traced their curve. "And also because I love you. I had hoped you would stay to take my place as suzein one day."

His voice was low but free of any wheedling tone. I met his eyes and saw there only affection and desire.

I shook my head, taking his hand firmly in my own. "I want to go, uncle."

He stared at me a long time, those golden eyes blank and inscrutable as the Magdalene's smooth face. "I wonder sometimes if your sister got all the brains. At least she knew enough to keep silent."

His voice was bitter; but I knew it was finished. Miramar sighed and inclined his head as if praying. When he raised it he was smiling, and with a sardonic bow he stood and pulled me to my feet.

"If I may have the honor," he murmured. He drew back the heavy indigo drapes that curtained off his bedchamber from the rest of the suite. "A farewell to my favorite nephew."

"Thank you, uncle," I said, and tears stung my eyes as we embraced for the last time.

3. Introduction of new lifeforms

"You won't like it Outside," Ketura whispered to me much later. She had returned from the Saint-Alaban's Masque, and the two of us lay together in her bedroom. "When I stayed with Flora Pyracantha last year they beat me while I slept, until I left." She licked her lower lip as if tasting old blood.

I yawned. "That's stupid. Didn't they know you're good for better things?" I stroked her breast, but she pushed me away, sitting up and pulling the quilt tight about her bare shoulders.

"Dammit! You should listen to me, Raphael, before going with Roland. They're so different. . . ."

"How?" I yanked away my half of the quilt and slid beneath it. "How are they different?"

Ketura snorted in exasperation, grabbed a long plait of my hair, and tugged me so that I faced my reflection in the mirror. "How do you think?"

I shrugged. "Their hair is short?"

"Don't be a fool." She pulled my hair, hard, and I kicked her away.

"Roland has hair. *Everywhere.*" I laughed and hid my face in the pillow.

"He's still young. When they get older—" She gathered her long red curls and pulled them from her face so that her white cheeks and temples gleamed in the candlelight.

"Like this. They're bald. They're *ugly,* all of them." She shuddered. "I never knew how ugly they were. . . ."

"So close your eyes and think of me. That's what I do." I shut my eyes and reached for her, grinning.

"Idiot!" She pushed me away and I sat up, surprised at her vehemence. "You should learn to fight, catamite, before you think about leaving. . . ."

I grabbed her then, wrenched the comforter away, and bit her shoulder until her mocking voice softened and her hands fumbled to loosen my hair from its long braid.

"Why fight when we can do this?" I murmured.

Ketura sighed and turned away.

"You just don't understand, do you, Raphael? The Curators don't think like that. They don't want us around, really; they just want to use us, and then leave us. Flora used me, and then she grew tired of me, and finally she hated me for being young and beautiful, and there all the time to remind her of it. They all hated me. And these were tribades, Botanists! The other Curators are worse. . . ."

I traced the whorls of her breast and kissed her. "Roland has always been kind to me, Ketura."

"Because you're still young. Because he never gets enough of you. Flora was like that, too: before I left here." She shook her head and glanced out the window. "I have to meet Adolph Drake soon," she said, and flashed me a rueful smile. "Well, you've never needed to have any sense before, Raphael, so I don't suppose I can give you any now. But—" She slipped from my arms and crossed the room to her armoire. "I *can* give you this."

A six-pointed anthemion embellished the wardrobe. She pressed one of its wooden blades and a tiny drawer spat open. For a minute or two she poked through its contents, broken candicaine straws and prophylactic feathers, a handful of old ribbons and the broken keyboard from an ancient computer; then she carefully drew up a small object wrapped in desiccated paper. "I want you to have it."

The paper crumbled as she unwrapped and then handed to me a sort of open-ended bracelet. Drab gray with faint lavender stripes, its smooth surface etched with a network of tiny whorls. It seemed to me a crude and ugly ornament, and I shot her a puzzled glance. She returned the look impassively as I examined the bracelet, hoping to find some brilliant or cantrap concealed within its somber coil. Finally I shrugged and started to put it onto my hand.

"No. Let me show you." She took the bracelet from me and carefully eased it over her own wrist. She raised her face to meet mine. "Now. I want you to hurt me."

I laughed. "You sound like Iris Bergenia!"

"I mean it—do something to cause me pain."

Uneasily I shifted on the bed. "You never used to want that with me, cousin."

"I don't now, either, really. But I'm trying to show you something. Now go on—" She tossed back her mane of fiery hair and glared at me, then pointed to the knout draped over her wardrobe. "Use that if you like."

I took the lash—a pretty whip of light braided doeskin that her Patron Flora Pyracantha gave her at Semhane one year—and raised it, smiling ruefully. When I struck Ketura she gasped: the blow was harsher than she had anticipated. I dropped the knout and rushed to comfort her.

"No!" She pushed me away and raised her clenched hand. "Watch—"

On her wrist the stony bracelet glowed very faintly, the lavender stripes deepening to violet against the luminous shell. One end of the gray loop was open, with a small rounded lip. As I stared it grew brighter still, until— *zzzkkk!* a shining black spine shot out from one of the dark whorls. At its tip a cobalt droplet gleamed like a gem's tear. I breathed in sharply and moved to touch it.

"No: watch." Ketura drew back, still holding her fist rigidly in front of her. As I stared the spine slowly retracted. I turned to her, marveling.

"What the hell is that?"

Ketura regarded me through narrowed eyes. Then she carefully slipped the bracelet from her wrist and handed it to me. "Now you should be very grateful to me for giving you this."

"I don't even know what it *is.*" I held it prudently in my

palm, waited for her to snake it about my wrist. It grew
warmer, as though adjusting to my body temperature. I
touched the gray surface tentatively.

"It's a sagittal: an engineered mollusk. Very poisonous,
very rare. It was made during the Second Ascension."

"That's its shell?"

She nodded. "It lives inside, curled around like a—like a
slug."

"It's poisonous?"

"Yes. If I'd struck you with it I'd have killed you."

"Who gave it to you?"

"A boy I met at the Botanical Gardens during the
Masque of Poppies."

I raised my eyebrows. "A Botanist gave you this?"

Ketura shook her head. "No. He wasn't a Botanist. I
don't know what he was, really. He was beautiful, but he
wasn't a Paphian. Flora told me afterward that she had
never seen him before; no one seems to have known who
he was, or who invited him to the masque.

"I didn't even entertain him; only talked with him in
one of greenhouses for a little while. He gave me that—"
She pointed at the sagittal, gray and cold about my wrist.
"He said that it might serve me for a little while, and if I
tired of it to give it to a friend." She shook her head at the
memory. "Not really the sort of gift we usually exchange, is
it?"

I held up my arm and stared at it. "No, not really," I
admitted. "It's ugly."

Ketura nodded. "I know. I'm sorry; but it seemed like—
well, it seemed like it might be useful for you, where
you're going."

I looked at her coldly. "It's a weapon."

She nodded.

"How does it work?"

She leaned back against the wardrobe, flicking the hair
from her eyes. "It feeds off the dead skin on your wrist.
And it responds to changes in your body indicating fear or
aggression. That's when it sticks its spine out—"

"You knew all that?" I glanced at her admiringly.

She flushed. "No. The boy told me. He explained so that I'd know how and when to use it."

I waited for her to continue, but instead she stood and paced back to her armoire. She rifled a drawer, finally chose a jet-black sheath trimmed with striped cat, and shrugged into it, smoothing the fur until it gleamed. I turned the sagittal this way and that, careful not to touch its anterior lip. After a few minutes Ketura said, "You could stay here and get rich, Raphael. There's no reason for you to leave."

I crossed my arms, keeping the sagittal away from my chest. "You left."

"I wanted to study under the Botanists," she said. "And I'm older than the rest of you. In a year they'll have me in the kitchen, or carrying slops, or—" She shook her head, tight-lipped. "But you—why should you leave? Miramar wants you to stay," she said bitterly.

"As the next suzein."

"You should be flattered." A bone pin sprang from her chignon. I retrieved it and handed it back to her. For a long moment she let her fingers rest against mine, and I felt her fingertips, callused from wielding the knout for her Patrons, the rough skin that never would have been allowed within another House. Then she took the pin and turned away. "I would never have left if Miramar had tried to stop me. But he didn't. He thinks I'm already too old."

I watched her chalk her face and drop two pearls of octine into each eye before she turned to me once more. "Raphael, you just don't know—"

I stood and stalked to the window. "And you think you know it all now, just because you're *so old.*"

"That's not it!" Beneath the chinese lead her cheeks reddened. "It's *dangerous* for us out there. Even among the Botanists—all they want from us now is hurt and humiliation. They hear news of the outlands, rumors of the next Ascension, and they hope they can somehow profit from it. They fear that the world has grown beyond their knowledge, but they know that we are still beautiful! So they hate us, and fear us. Beauty and youth and pleasure are no longer enough. They want pain and death; they no

longer want to share the City with us. Haven't you noticed
it among your Patrons?"

I shook my head. "No. *My* Patrons expect something
other than pain from me."

She sighed. "I suppose so. Only the sweetest sugarplums
for Raphael Miramar." Her tone grew harsh, but the gaze
she turned on me was soft. "I'm just afraid for you,
Raphael; for all of us. What if we are betrayed by the
Curators?"

I began to pull on my clothes. "That's why I'm going to
stay with Roland. To learn; and maybe someday come back
here and share it with the rest of you."

Ketura turned to regard her face in the mirror. One at a
time she drummed three fingers against her lower lip,
then bared her teeth in a snarl. "They don't want us to
learn—"

"Oh, shut up. I hear the same damned lies you do." I
grabbed my chasuble, glaring at my own reflection as I
dressed. "Doctor Foster boring me to tears with his
damned stories for boys and girls! All to frighten us from
ever leaving here—" I tied my hair loosely and stormed
past her without a word.

But at the door I hesitated, glancing at the gray band on
my wrist. "Ketura . . ."

She shook her head, smiling as she turned from the mirror to meet me. "I'm sorry. Maybe you're right. Maybe
Roland Nopcsa really is different." And she kissed me, then
drew back and brushed three fingers against my lip.

"Be careful with that," she warned, nodding at the sagittal and cupping her hand a scant inch from the dark curve
of the shell's edge. "It protects its host; but the venom is
always fatal when it strikes."

She paused, then said, "But you know—"

She stood in the doorway, pulling the domino from her
sheath and draping its dark folds over her face.

"But what?" I urged.

"They're almost beautiful when they die," she said, and
walked down the hall to meet her Patron.

4. A break in the historical record

"Our predecessors here believed in a slow process of evolution. *We* know that new lifeforms emerge suddenly— we see it in the Narrow Forest, and through the work the Zoologists have done with the aardmen and other gene-slaves."

"Like that?" I pointed at the glossy model of an infant protoceratops nosing its way from an elongated leathery egg.

Roland took a long pull from his beer and nodded. "Exactly. Except that we can choose the form of our history, and presumably the protoceratops did not have that luxury."

Above us the skeleton of *quetzalcoatlus northropi* hummed faintly, as a draft from the ventilation pipes stirred its hollow bones. I leaned forward to blow upon the blue-gray cube of pressed herbs burning in the little brass tray Fancy had given me as a going-away gift, watched the smoke coil about the arching claws and rakishly outthrust pelvis of the looming Deinocherius that guarded Roland's bed. As Regent of the Natural Historians, Roland chose his own quarters in the Museum: the Hall of Archosaurs, where we retired each evening to talk and smoke and drink and make love. Miramar was right: my education was not foremost among Roland's concerns.

But it was my oldest dream. To learn the true history of the old world, to memorize the alphabet embedded within the layers of calcareous rock, and so discern in the new damp mud and broken asphalt outside my window the whorls and patterns that would shape the future. And I believed that Roland knew these things, because he was descended from those who had been set here to guard the City's knowledge after the First Ascension.

"What luxuries *did* the archosaurs have, Roland?" I asked, burrowing deeper into the heap of wool rugs covering the bed.

"Oh, the usual," he replied. "Time. A variety of comestibles. Warm sunny days and cool yet pleasant nights: bring a sweater when visiting the Mesozoic." A small potent explosion of laughter rocked the bed as he guffawed, throttling a bolster between his huge hands. "Oh, they had a wonderful life, the archosaurians. Huge and hungry and cruel, lumbering and gentle-eyed. Their footprints remain, and we little mice creep from the trees to drink from the impressions of their toes, and make our homes among their bones."

He gulped the rest of his beer, leaned over the cask beside his bed, and refilled the bottle. "Ah, Raphael. Why would you leave your warm House upon the hill to live here? It's so fucking *cold.*" Those heavy hands around my waist, now, pulling me close so that I could smell his sweat, sweetly sour from the Botanists' bitter lager.

"I came to keep you warm," I said obediently, nuzzling his chest. Roland was shorter than I, but massive: barrel-chested, thighs like tree stumps, hands so big and clumsy-looking it was a marvel to watch him assemble the delicate pinnules of shattered crinoids, until the fossilized sea lilies bloomed again within his brown palms.

"But orchids die in the cold," he said mockingly. "Miramar would never forgive me if his prize blossom withered here."

"No chance," I replied. Roland laughed more loudly and pulled me closer.

"I feel a chill," he said, forcing my head down, and for a while we turned to other matters.

In the night I woke. For six years Roland had been my Patron. I knew this vast chamber as well as I knew my

oom at the House Miramar. But in the weeks since com-
ng here to live I had slept uneasily, waking often in the
ool darkness to start at the sight of the vast silent behe-
moths that reared overhead. I stared at them now, wondering how their bones came to line these halls and clutter
he vast storerooms of the Museum, whereas the remains
f the men who had been here mere centuries before us
vere lost forever.

"You see how we choose which histories to recall?" Ro-
and had remarked once, hefting a mannequin. "Please
note that only Aides and Technicians sleep in the Hall of
Man," he added scornfully.

The Aide helping us move the exhibit glared when I
aughed at Roland's comment. She said, "*We* work our way
up to the best Halls. We *earn* our beds."

Blushing, I shut up. Even Roland was silent for a moment. Then he said, "Raphael earned his place in the
House he came from, Franca."

"It's not the same," she snapped. She was two or three
years younger than I. Her hair had recently been shorn to
indicate her promotion from Docent to Aide. She stared
contemptuously at my long beribboned braid as we hauled
he heavy steel desk back into storage. "They should know
their rights here."

"Raphael has been my student since he was a child.
Allow the Regents their privileges and passions, Franca."
And he winked at her. I looked away quickly, my face
ourning from the complicitous smile they had shared for
hat instant.

But now beside me Roland lay dreaming. His heavy arm
pinned me to the bed as he snored. I sighed and stared at
he ceiling, where bats darted between the Deinocherius
skeleton and the hollow-eyed trachodons. In the darkest
corners of the gallery rats scuffled, nosing fruitlessly
hrough the ancient bones stacked there. I watched the
oats' ceaseless waltz, until once more I fell restlessly asleep
vith their bloodless song echoing in my dreams.

5. The dark labyrinth of the ages

Each dawn we woke to the screech of the Regent's trumpet echoing through the Rotunda. Its clamor aroused Aides and Technicians and Regent alike from the galleries where they slept: the Aides and Technicians to begin their round of chores and maintenance, Roland to join his fellow Regents in their incessant discussion of useless research papers mined from the Museums' Libraries. Although lately other things seemed to occupy their meetings. Roland returned to the Hall of Archosaurs later in the evening, and often was in no mood for me. I tried not to think of Miramar's warning, of the rumors that even a Paphian catamite heard within the Museum of Natural History these last few weeks: that the Curators had taken a stand against the Ascendants. There had been a murder, or murders; would there now be retribution?

"I thought you were going to ban that damned horn," I said, rolling away from Roland to cover my head with a bolster.

"Tradition is stronger even than Regents," Roland replied. The trumpet bleated fitfully for another moment. In the stillness that followed I heard the hum of voices and footsteps and doors creaking throughout the galleries, the muted click and burr of the Museum's generator tumbling to life in the basement. Roland sighed. "But I love to hear them all wake: to think that once the City stirred so each day. . . ."

I yawned and shook back my tangled hair. "Too early! No wonder they fell to the Ascendants without a fight."

Roland shot me a disgruntled glance. "What are you going to do today?" he asked, tossing me a robe.

I dressed, wincing at the rough linen. My own clothes were reserved for masques and the rare occasion when I might meet with other Paphians. "The Devonian." I tipped my head toward an adjoining gallery. "You'll be in the Library?"

Roland nodded. "The Regent of Aviators questioned my defense of *quetzalcoaltus* as the model for the Langley Aerodrome Number Three."

"*My* idea," I said hotly, but Roland cut me off.

"There's nothing I can do, Raphael! I let you in the Library when I can—"

"*Once* since I've been here!"

"It's not my decision—we have to abide by the rules the Board of Regents sets."

I turned to the mirror I'd leaned beneath the allosaurus. It showed a leaner and angrier face than the mirrors at Miramar had ever thrown back at me. I tossed back my hair and glanced down to see my sagittal showing from beneath the cuff of my robe. Its shell glowed faint lilac; I pulled the sleeve to cover my wrist. Roland had noticed it before during an argument, when the gray carapace had begun to gleam warningly. I knew how foolish, and dangerous, it was for me to continue wearing it. But Ketura's words stayed with me. It was the only weapon I had if we were betrayed.

Behind me stood Roland, his robe hanging open as he slapped a roll of papers against his palm. "Why are you fighting me, Raphael?"

I knelt in front of the mirror, sliding open a lacquered cosmetics box (Miramar's parting gift) and drawing out my kohl wand. "Because I want to learn! Because I'm tired of being treated like a child—"

"There's nothing I can do about that, Raphael." He reached for my hand, tried to slide the kohl wand from between my fingers. "But maybe there is something you can do for me. . . ."

I pulled away from him. His surprise flared into rage as I stormed from the Hall.

"Raphael!" he shouted, but before he could follow me I had fled down one corridor, and then another, and another still; until I found myself walking through the immense jaws of an insular shark that served as entry into the Hall of the Deep.

My anger had faded somewhat by now. I almost regretted leaving Roland in a fury. Certainly the thought of confronting him later sobered me: he had a ferocious temper. But I calmed myself by wandering through the Hall, glancing at exotic seashells and sponges and reading aloud the ancient placards that decorated each case.

I had just turned the corner of a great display of dorados and slimefish when I nearly tripped over a stack of empty buckets. Glancing up, I saw that I had walked into an Aide's work area—the same Aide Francesca I had met some time earlier in the Hall of Man.

"Good morning, Franca." I bowed, sweeping the floor with my braid.

"Fran*ces*ca," she hissed, her arms feathered with brushes and long-handled brooms. Small and lithe, with a boy's flat chest and long legs, she reminded me of my little Fancy, moving too fast for her clumsy feet. But Fancy's mild blue eyes never would slant and darken with fury as this girl's did; and Fancy would die rather than crop her yellow hair.

"Excuse me: Fran*ces*ca."

"Don't call me anything, whore." A smudge of a mouth twisted in a face broad and flat as a plate. Years ago I'd given up looking for any shaft of beauty in the Curators' faces. But, because I was homesick and lonely, I watched her hungrily as she turned her attention to cleaning a case full of blowfish. Graceless as a puppy; skin blotched and broken where she'd scrubbed it with the harsh soap they made of lye and tallow. Long narrow eyes the color of wax. Octine might brighten them, and kohl darken those invisible lashes. But nothing for her slab cheeks, except perhaps to daub hollows there with powder.

"Stop staring, whore." She moved up a step on the ladder to reach a gaudy blue marlin. Like everything belonging to the Curators, the ladder was ancient. I swore that the only thing holding it together was Franca's spite.

"Don't talk to me," she warned, brushing a strand of hair from her eyes. "Give me that brush."

I handed her the brush and crouched to watch her. "Why do you cut your hair like that?"

"I thought you studied under Nopcsa for six years."

I shrugged. "I studied Paleontology."

Without looking at me she replied, "Because only whores wear their hair long."

"Whores and sometimes lazars," I corrected her. She shot me a surprised look, then quickly turned back to the marlin.

"Fit company." But after a few minutes she asked, "Why do you wear those ribbons?"

I pulled my braid forward, staring at it with mock perplexity. "These ribbons?" I said, stroking the colored tendrils plaited into my hair.

She nodded. For a moment she could have been a Paphian child at worship, earnest and still.

"This one"—fingering a bit of green and gold brocade—"for my House. And this one from my favorite Patron." Thin worn strips of ugly red plaid, clumsily stitched together.

"Roland gave you that?" asked Franca. She rubbed her shorn scalp, then turned to blow dust from the marlin's painted scales. I flicked my braid back petulantly. I wished she could have seen me at Illyria's last masque, when it had taken me an hour to plait thirty-four ribbons into my hair, and the Magdalene disappeared beneath the flowers tossed by my admirers. I sighed and followed her as she moved her ladder to the next glass exhibit case.

After a few minutes she clambered down again, coughing as she shook a gray cloud from her duster. At the bottom step she sat and stared at me for a long moment.

"Have you seen them?" she said at last.

Puzzled, I shook my head.

"Lazars," she said. Elbows planted on her knees, chin resting on her grimy hands, she looked like an ugly child waiting to hear one of Doctor Foster's stories. I started to laugh, but caught myself.

"I saw a dead one, once," I said slowly. Her eyes narrowed. "Two years ago. Roland was with me. It was after a rain of roses—"

Franca curled her lip. "Only whores call it that."

I shrugged and turned, pretending to examine a shell. She clicked her tongue and explained, "I mean, you never call a thing by its real name. 'Rain of roses,'" she added derisively. "Say its real name: a viral strike."

"Well, this one was dead," I said. "Look, do you want to hear this or not?"

Suddenly serious, she nodded. "Yes. Please."

I moved closer to the ladder. "She was very pale and her hair was tangled—"

I recalled the night: the wind soft and sweet with apple blossom and that faint cloying scent that stains the air for an hour or two afterward. There were six or seven of us—I remember the albino Whitlock was there, from High Brazil. Roland was accompanying us back to Miramar.

Whitlock saw her first. He yelled and ran back, tripping over his gown to tumble onto the broken bricks at my feet. I ran ahead with Roland. I was fearless because I knew he wore a gun, traded from the Ascendants, in a sheath at his side.

"She's dead," he said shortly, staring down the narrow ravine to where the body sprawled beside a rotting stump. "Come on—"

But I couldn't leave. I stared, fascinated: because I found her beautiful.

"She looked like she was sleeping . . ." I said.

"I've seen dead people," Franca said thoughtfully. "Before we burn them. They look asleep, sometimes."

"Well, I've only seen one."

"We have a lot of accidents. Someone gets poisoned in the tannery or a heavy box falls on them. Or someone gets old and just dies. Doesn't that ever happen where you live?"

"No," I said. "None of us ever gets very old."

"But you saw one." Faint admiration shaded her voice.
"A lazar . . ."

I didn't tell her how Roland sent the others running back
to the House; then came after me, pinning me to the
ground where I could see her the whole time, the shadows
of her cheeks, the way her eyes glittered with phosphores-
cence, her hair rippling so slightly where bluebottle
worms seethed within the knotted ringlets. Afterward I
was so weak he had to help me stand. Because I was frightened, he thought. But it wasn't that at all. . . .

"Huh?—No," I said, startled. I'd only half-heard Franca's
question. "I wasn't scared."

And I turned to stare at the ceiling hung with plasticine
leviathans; because I no longer felt like talking.

6. Articulate animals

Roland never mentioned our argument that day. It was the beginning of Autime, and he was busy with the other Regents. Or so he said. I began to spend my days in the Hall of the Deep with Franca, who ignored me at first but gradually began to answer my questions, and sometimes even allowed me to assist her in her duties.

For a week we cleaned the models and mounted fish that hung from the Hall's ceiling and aquamarine walls. "By the time we finish the last one, the others will be filthy again," I complained. Overhead a pod of fiberglass whales hung by invisible wires. Aqua globes encasing electric lanterns cast dreamy waves of light upon walls and floor and the ribbed sweep of the whales' bellies. It made me drowsy. Squatting atop a dilapidated ladder, I yawned often, batting lazily at the suspended hulls of bottlenoses and rorquals with a broom.

"You'll fall," Franca yelled up to me, wiping her forehead with her arm.

"Fall asleep, maybe," I called back. "Come on up."

She scrambled up, pausing halfway to steady herself against the wall. "You don't like this gallery, do you?"

"Not really. There're no people in it."

She laughed, pushing a strand of lank blond hair from her forehead with a dirty fist. I smiled. I had grown accustomed to the Curators' odd uneven features, to the stumbling way they all moved, their loud voices and even their smell: sweat and formaldehyde and the cedar shavings that kept moths from eating the pelts of stuffed lemurs and jerboas. In the rough map of Franca's face I had come to discern hidden places that, if not precisely beautiful, still fascinated me. When struck by a slanting ray of morning light her yellow eyes would blaze suddenly, alarmingly, topaz. The same light might streak her cropped head with bands of gold, and I wondered: If only she would let it grow long, was there enough sun in the world to make it flash like my little Fancy's wild mane? And once, after a day spent beneath a bright skylight, cleaning the convoluted whorls and ridges of a case full of murex seashells and dogwinkles, a faint spray of freckles rained across her cheeks. And somehow this delighted me.

"Well, people put them here," she said. She spat on her hand and rubbed it clean against her tunic. "Besides, what's the use of dead things?"

"Your precious birds are dead," I retorted. "Everything in here is dead."

"But they weren't always dead." She steadied herself with one hand on the ladder. With the other she pointed to the vaulted ceiling high above us, its ancient panes of leaded glass scarcely allowing a hint of sunlight inside. "Sometimes I see real birds up there—they get in, and nest in the ceiling. But the Curators always kill them," she said sadly. "They say they damage the Collection."

I stared at the ceiling, recalling the bats in Roland's chamber. "If you went outside, you'd see lots."

"I can't go outside. Not 'til I'm older." She made a face. "Too *dangerous.*"

"Well, someday you'll see all the birds you want, Franca." I leaned forward and took a strand of her short hair, wrapped it around my finger, then slowly let it fall back against her scalp. She twisted to regard me with those cool eyes.

"And someday you'll see all your dead men, Raphael," she replied, and burst out laughing. I laughed too as she clambered down. She stared up at me, hands on hips, her brooms and brushes stuck under one arm.

"I'm tired of this place," she announced, tossing her tools onto the marble floor. "Let's take a walk."

I climbed down. The ancient ladder shuddered with relief when I finally stepped from the last rung onto the floor. "Outside?"

"Of course not. But—" She nibbled her fingernails thoughtfully. "We can visit the Egyptians," she finally said. "They're dead men: you'll like them. Have you ever seen them?"

"Not really. Roland pointed out the wing once when I first came here." I glanced down the long Hall to the shadowy archways that opened onto passages leading to other Collections. "Won't someone come to check on us?"

Franca rolled her eyes. "Has anyone checked once since we started working together? Come on. Everyone does this."

She tugged at my sleeve. As her fingers brushed against my wrist my heart quickened. "All right," I said, and followed her down the hallway.

7. Some races can boast of an immemorial antiquity

We ascended to the Hall of Dead Kings by a circuitous route: forsaking the cool blues and greens of the Hall of Fishes for the smoke-hued walls of the Hall of Man. The corridor leading from this gallery was long and narrow and dark, lit only by the faint light that pooled from each end of the tunnel. I walked quickly and pulled my worn tunic tight about my shoulders. I knew very little about the Hall of Dead Kings. Roland had been uncomfortable even talking about it.

"They built the pyramids and the great Obelisk by the Narrow Forest," he said as we passed the Hall late one evening, returning from an Illyrian masque held in the West Wing. "We believe they built the Phantom Fighters for the First Ascension as well. The Aviation Regent disagrees." And he had paused at the entry to the Egyptian Wing, staring broodingly at a crumbling tapestry of ivory-colored fiber.

Now I wondered how Franca had disappeared so quickly down the dim hallway, and hurried after her. I shivered a little at the thought of doing something I knew would anger Roland. Lately he had seemed more and more distant from me. More than once he'd snapped about my broken fingernails and callused hands—

"I can find as good as *that* in our own crèche," he'd said, pushing me away. "And can't you get your slutty friends to send you some new clothes?"

I flushed at the memory and pounded the wall with my fist, swearing beneath my breath. Before me the light grew brighter. On the wall I recognized the same tapestry Roland had pointed out, angular figures with the heads of dogs and birds drawn on frayed and moldering cloth. I squinted, trying to make out Franca's silhouette against the bright square of light that glowed a few yards ahead. Finally I reached the crumbling wooden entrance. I passed through this and beneath a second lintel formed of huge blocks of carven stone, and into a room ablaze with sunlight.

I blinked, wondering where Franca was. Then:

"Yaah!" A figure darted from the shadows and grabbed me by the shoulders. I swore and backed away to see Franca laughing breathlessly. "Scared you—"

Grabbing her wrist, I pulled her toward me, until she writhed giggling against my chest. She tried to pull away. I tightened my grip.

"Oww—stop, Raphael, it was a *joke!*"

I did not let her go. For a moment I breathed in the scent of her hair, tangled with dust and smelling of harsh soap and sweat. That and the warmth of her beside me in the sudden sunlight made me dizzy. Abruptly I released her.

"Very funny." I straightened my tunic. "Are these your Egyptians?"

She nodded, trying to catch her breath. "Ye-es," she gasped, and bit her lip. She smoothed out her tunic, like a child running late into first worship. At the sight of me staring she quickly looked away. "Those are the Egyptians."

I turned to see the Hall of the Dead Kings.

8. *"The riddle of the painful earth . . ."*

There were scores of them, the ancient men, in rows stretching on into the far dark corners of the echoing gallery. Even Franca was silenced by the place. "You've been here before?" I whispered. She did not reply, only nodded as she paced from one catafalque to another. I followed her, still blinking a little at the brilliant light that streamed from the arched glass vault overhead. The floor beneath us was black marble, and shot back a pantherish light at the ceiling's spangled glass. The coffins themselves glowed golden and azure and scarlet, their patina of dust giving them a sheen as though draped in velvet. Throughout the vast room were raised huge statues, like sentinels guarding their sleeping lords, and great blocks of sand-colored stone etched with flat figures of animals and men. A heaviness in my chest made me realize I was holding my breath. I inhaled, and smelled sandalwood and rotting cloth.

How many aeons had they waited before coming here to sleep in silent rows beneath glittering columns of dust and sun? The very air was heated with their dreams. Before the first catafalque I stopped, placed my palm upon the smooth wooden plane of its face, feeling the dust of centuries seep into my pores so that when I turned my hand upward I half-expected to see imprinted there its enigmatic smile and onyx eyes. But there was nothing: only faint gray whorls and feathers of dirt, and a beetle's shattered wing carapace. I recalled a phrase from one of Roland's books, referring to the disinterment of the first archosaurs: "The riddle of the painful earth . . ."

I left the first effigy. Behind it, ranks of mummy cases and catafalques seemed to march endlessly. Only the uneven seams where the silvered glass had shifted gave the lie to this vision of infinity, and showed me where a vast mirror covered the far wall of the chamber. Franca drifted down the aisles, her reflection a white shadow slipping between the stone faces.

As if in a dream I wandered from one coffin to the next. Kings, queens, regents; royal embalmers and charioteers. Glass cases held the desiccated corpses of cats, their shriveled limbs bound with twine and stained brown cloth. Ibises wrapped until they resembled misshapen cruets were stacked in hollowed stone vessels. And everywhere those blank fixed eyes, gazing from catafalques and funerary urns, torques and golden breastplates and the gilded skulls of jackals.

"Who were they?" I asked, and started when Franca answered me from only a few feet away.

"They were the first ones here," she said softly. "The Pilgrims. They came over the ocean in airships, fleeing the Old World where they were persecuted. They built the great monuments in the City in memory of their homeland. The Sorrowful Lincoln, the Obelisk, the Library of Conquest."

I frowned. "Are you sure?" I asked, absently scraping a brittle label from a glass case. "I thought they were built by someone else, by Ascendants. . . ."

She shook her head firmly. "No. After the Thirty Wars in the East, the Egyptians came to the City; after their desert was bombed. They all died here in the Long Night, during the Contagions. That's why they're in the Museum—"

I snatched my hand from the glass. "They all died from the Contagion?"

"No. They killed themselves rather than submit to the Ascendants. And their priests hid them in these boxes and brought them to the original Curators. Before we came, before the Second Ascension. We have protected them

ever since." She smiled at me, a child seeking approval for
a lesson well learned.

"Then why is no one allowed here?" I traced a golden
tear upon a wooden case. "If you're protecting them, why
are there no guards?"

She shrugged. "Why are there no guards for your precious Magdalene?"

I paused and bit my lip. "Because no one would harm
the Magdalene," I said at last.

Franca leaned on a stone mummy case, chin resting on
her hands. "Not even the gaping ones?" she said slyly.

I sniffed and made a face. "The Gaping One," I corrected her. "I thought you knew nothing about us?" I
flicked at her cheek and she grinned.

"I saw it in a play last winter. At Saint-Alaban. About a
boy and a girl, twins—"

"Huh. Saint-Alabans: the Masque of Baal and Anat."

"That's right!" She brightened and waited expectantly.
"Do you know it?"

I shook my head. "Superstitious nonsense, taught them
by the Historians. You Curators think we're such children!
Only the Saint-Alabans believe in any of that, really. Most
of us just do those things out of—out of habit, I suppose," I
ended. "The way you keep these damn galleries open and
the cases clean and the exhibits in order. For who!"

Franca shrugged, then burst out laughing. "For the
Egyptians! We're waiting for the Egyptians!" And giggling
she ran down the aisle, pausing to make a clumsy curtsey
to the great cracked mirror.

9. A sudden and awful convulsion of nature

I watched her, grinning. I seldom saw any of the Curators laugh among themselves, although we Paphians shared our own delight at the world's foolishness as well as our joy in the flesh with our sober Patrons. Laughter did not make Franca any less ugly; but the sight and sound of it were rare enough to arouse me.

"Aren't you afraid you'll wake them?" I asked, slipping down the aisle to stand behind her.

"Not me!" She swung around to face me, bumping against a heavy pedestal. I caught her elbow as she steadied herself.

"Is it true what they say?" she demanded. I let my hand rest on her elbow and, when she did not pull away, stroked her arm.

"What's that?" I asked softly.

She tilted her head. For an instant the sunlight made a bright halo of her tousled hair. "That you've had a thousand lovers."

"At least." I let my fingers drift to the small of her back. She stared at me suspiciously. When I did not smile she nodded.

"They said your master wanted you to be the next ruler of your House." I shrugged modestly. "Why would you come here, where you'll never be welcome?"

I looked up, surprised at her bluntness. "I did not know I would *never* be welcome," I said bitterly. "I—I had hoped to learn great things here, and someday share my knowledge with my people. . . ."

She shook her head. "But we would never share our secrets with a whore," she said. There was no malice in her voice. "You have nothing to give us in return."

"Nothing?" I drew her close to me. "Your people take everything we value—our youth and our beauty and our love—and disdain it!" She grew pale and tried to draw away from me, but I took her chin in my hand and twisted her face toward me to kiss her. Her lips were chapped, her mouth tasting of that morning's apples and oatmeal. When I released her she did not move away. "What's all your learning worth to a girl who's never kissed a man?" I said more gently, and reached to take her hands.

Flushing, she tossed her head, looked away only to meet her face in the mirror and quickly turned back to me. "I—well, now I have," she said, staring at her feet.

"Not really," I murmured, and this time she moved against me and her hands roamed awkwardly down my back.

I slipped off her tunic and found a sweet young boy's body beneath, long-legged and starred with moles, only with small round breasts and the slightest swell of hips and stomach. I went slowly, so as not to frighten her. I kissed her and was surprised at her innocent response, surprised and excited, too. Occasionally I glanced aside at our reflections, watching her unravel my braid so that my hair fell about us in auburn waves. And my own response excited me, that I could be so aroused by a Curator. . . .

I held her more tightly, started to remove my trousers. She tried to pull away then. "No—what are you doing?" she said.

"Just wait," I urged her, and tried to pull her to the floor. She pushed at me, then struggled to get away. "No, Raphael—stop, I'm afraid here—"

"What?" I shook my head in disbelief. Then I remembered Iris Bergenia, playing at fighting me in our chamber. I grabbed Franca's hair and yanked her to the floor beside me. "I'll teach you what you need to know about the Paphians," I whispered, holding her beneath me.

"*No!*" She kicked at me and I fell back, then turned and grabbed her before she could run away. Panting, I held her, furious and scarcely able to keep hold of her, I was trembling so from excitement and rage. She stared at me wild-eyed, not angry but terrified. I desired her more than I had ever wanted anyone.

"Now," I whispered. As I pulled her face to mine she kicked at me again. Without thinking I struck her, saw a flash of violet at her neck. She shuddered, and I was stung by sudden remorse. Her mouth opened.

"Raphael," she said thickly. As I stared her eyes widened. The pupils bloated suddenly, then contracted to specks like poppyseeds.

"Franca," I said, alarmed. Her head lolled onto her shoulder. As I started to draw my hand back I felt a small tug at my wrist. I glanced down.

Against the taut skin of her neck my sagittal clung like a leech. I yanked my hand away and raised my fist, incredulous. For an instant I glimpsed the ebony spine retracting, felt the tiny shift of weight as the propodium curled back into its shell. I dropped my arm.

"Franca," I repeated, raising my voice. "Franca. Wake up."

Her mouth tightened. Saliva pearled on her lower lip and began to trace a silvery snail's path down her chin. Where the sagittal had clung a small purplish star radiated upon her flesh as capillaries burst and feathers of blood unfurled beneath the skin. From a vein that only moments before had pulsed visibly a violet thread unraveled, a corrosive needle's flourish to her heart. Heedless of whatever poison raced through her, I rested my cheek against her lips.

She was dead. As if dreaming, I let her corpse slip back to the floor and knelt beside it. "Franca," I whispered over and over, staring wildly about the vast gallery, the silent figures and glowing catafalques now washed in amber light. "Franca . . ."

In the next few minutes her entire body began to flower

with faint mauve petals. From neck to chest the tracery
crept, her breasts blushing as from unseen kisses, her
hands turning dusky blue as blood pooled in her fingertips.
Rosy blossoms stained her thighs as though raining from
the vault above us. Through my mind raced a song, nonsense we sang as children, the lazars' song:

> Rain the rain of roses
> peonies and posies
> Ashes, ashes
> Now fall down . . .

Already the skull shone beneath her skin. I crooned her
name, thinking *How beautiful she is now,* thinking how
angry she would have been at this final betrayal of her flesh
to loveliness, the septic garden that bloomed about her
bones. Then I ravished her.

Quickly, because already her flesh stiffened about me,
and her breasts tasted cold and faintly sweet. As my groans
subsided I let her slip from my arms. Her head thudded
against the floor. I staggered backward, wondering too late
if the poison had now entered me as well. I grabbed a
pedestal behind me and clung to it, weeping, embracing
the cold stone until I could steady myself and turn to her
again.

The canker had burst in her eyes. To my numb face she
now returned a pansied stare. I kicked her tunic over her
face and stumbled to my feet, choking, even as I knew that
I wanted her again, felt my heart tumbling at the sight of
that stark white figure lying among all those calm and
golden sleepers. But I forced myself to look away, to cast
my gaze instead upon the wild figure that stared back from
the ancient mirror: auburn hair disheveled, my face
blotched with tears and dust. I almost laughed to see myself thus: the pride of the House Miramar weeping above
the corpse of a scullion!

And then, echoing from the distant Main Hall came the
braying notes of the call to the first dinner shift. Franca and
I were on the third shift; but soon they would be missing us
at supper. I turned back to her poor corpse, as if it might

rise and give me solace. I bumped against a small catafalque atop a broken marble pillar, jarring its lid so that I
had to catch it before it fell. And so jarred my own mind to
wakefulness.

A full-size sarcophagus stood upright next to the broken
column. I prized it open a crack, enough to glimpse inside
the bound figure of its ancient king. I shoved the lid back
and hurried to another. Its lid was sealed fast, as was the
next one, and the next. But there were hundreds of cases
here, and surely some of them had been robbed or disturbed over the aeons. . . .

In a dark alcove I found it. No doubt it had once held the
remains of some princeling: the lid showed a gilded face
surmounted with enormous lapis eyes and a strangely calm
mouth, slightly pursed as if dreaming fair dreams. Tentatively I rapped upon the lid. It returned a faint hollow
sound. In a moment I had flung it open, to find only the
yellow dust of its decayed wrappings and the curled remains of ant-lions and silverfish.

All about the inside of the sarcophagus were inscribed
odd characters. I hesitated, gripped by a sudden cold fear
of the coffin itself. But then I thought of how she loved
birds, and here were painted birds to fly a soul to peace,
surely: eagles and gyrfalcons and ibises, kites and watchful
owls. I blew the dust from the case, then stood to get
Francesca.

It may be true what Doctor Foster says, that the soul has
weight and matter; because in my arms now she seemed to
weigh nothing at all. I wrapped her worn tunic about her
poor bruised body as a shroud, and wept again to think I
had no finer raiment in which to lay her to rest. I com-
forted myself to think she shared her bed with the dust of
princes. The lid slipped back on as if it had never been
removed. For a moment I stared at the sarcophagus, then
leaned forward and gently kissed the cold impression of its
painted mouth.

At the doorway I paused. Above me hung a scrim of
tattered cloth, stirring slightly from some faint breeze.
More tiny pictographs stalked its borders, but in its center
a small square of newer cloth had been sewed—frayed and

yellowed itself from centuries of wear. I squinted to read what must have been a clumsy translation of an ancient epitaph into doggerel:

> **Here we lie**
> **head to head**
> **asleep in the dark with the dead.**

I shuddered; and passed from the Hall of Dead Kings.

10. An interminable vista is opened out for the future

I retraced my steps to where we had been working. Several Aides passed me as I wandered into the Great Hall. Their scornful glances made me realize how Franca's companionship had not only seemed to make my days easier, but actually served to deflect their hatred and disdain for a little while. The thought of remaining here among them, with the terrible knowledge of Francesca so carelessly interred nearby, filled me with dread. I hastened past the Curators jostling their way to the dining halls below. For a few minutes I considered confessing everything to Roland Nopcsa, throwing myself upon his mercy—he was a Regent, after all, and surely could argue my case against those who would demand my execution.

But then I recalled his recent disappointments with me: his flash of temper at my ill-fitting clothes and my fatigue after a day slogging with Franca through the Museum basements. Others no older than myself had been cast from their Patrons like worthless rags. *Hothouse flower*, Roland had mocked me; but he wanted soft hands and scented hair awaiting him each evening. I glanced at my hands now, the nails broken and begrimed, palms filthy and blistered. To think that I had thrown away all my beauty like this, and doomed myself to die away from my own people!

". . . you! Slut!"

I started, brushing my eyes as I looked up into the cold face of Franca's Supervising Technician. I said nothing but halted.

"Tell your hoyden she's been reassigned. You're to report to me tonight: Nopcsa will be attending the Butterfly Ball at High Brazil this evening," he announced with malicious glee. I stared at his pockmarked face, the jagged spur of a yellowing broken tooth in that crooked mouth, the slouch of his scrawny shoulders.

"Do you hear me?" The Technician swatted the air in front of my face, then stroked my hair. I shrugged his hand from me and began to walk on.

"Whore!" the Technician yelled. "Do you understand me?"

I turned and grabbed him by the throat with one hand.

"I didn't hear a word you said," I hissed, shoving him against the wall. I left him sputtering and cursing in the corridor.

My disquiet at the thought of Roland attending the ball without me faded somewhat when I found our chambers deserted; I would not have to confront him yet, after all. I drew the heavy door shut behind me and collapsed upon the bed.

For some minutes I lay there, shuddering as I tried to contain my tears. Because it was clear to me now that I would have to flee. Roland's attendance at the High Brazilian masque without me would signal to Curators and Paphians alike that I had fallen out of favor. There was fierce rivalry between Houses, and High Brazil and Miramar had long fought over lesser prizes than the favor of the Natural Historians. There were those who would relish news of my downfall, and garnish them in the telling.

Not to mention the thought of the Technician's leering face, and the memory of Franca killed by my hand . . .

I stood quickly and paced the room, gazing up at Roland's beloved archosaurs.

"What would you do?" I whispered, stroking the long obsidian curve of the Deinocherius's tail. And recalling

Franca's mockery of the old things here I wept, knowing that I would not see them again; knowing that whatever reply their ancient hollow eyes might have made to me, I could no longer hide among the dead.

Part Three

After the Rain of Roses

Eyes everywhere. Dr. Harrow's shift into those of her brother Aidan. Anna and Andrew split like an amoeba, grinning as they proffer me a feathered headband. Atop my armoire a boy laughs, his smile strangled by a belt that twists into a garrotte as he falls onto the foot of my bed. Margalis Tast'annin looms above me, his voice soft as he repeats his question, the same question day after day, echoing now through my dreams—

"How do you do it, Wendy? What is it like, what do you see when you make them die?"

I scream and lurch forward, the sheets tangling my arms as I try to stand.

And then light rent the room. A lumiere guttering within a cupped palm tossed black and golden petals upon the hooded face before me.

"Get up," he hissed, dragging me from bed. I stumbled to my feet, dizzy from the drugs they had given me. I tried to explain that the session earlier had left me bruised and unable to dream properly. My tongue caught on my teeth and I retched, tasting my own blood.

"Quiet," he ordered, still whispering. I felt the sharp prick of an ampule against my neck. He missed the vein and I moaned. The figure pulled me to him, covering my mouth with his palm as he drew the hood back to show his face. It was the Aide Justice.

"We're getting out," he said. With a quick motion like someone killing an insect, he slapped another ampule to my neck. "Your acetelthylene."

My spine tingled with a rush of pleasure. I nodded grate-

fully. I had been without proper medication for days now
—I was uncertain how long. My head ached from where
they had shaved it to attach the electrodes and chemical
lozenges they'd used for the endless experiments of the
last few weeks. Only in the last few days, since Tast'annin
had left, had the rounds of questioning and testing abated.
I stripped off the yellow shift they'd given me and pawed
through my wardrobe, tossing clothes onto the rug.

"Hurry." Justice glanced behind him, kicking aside several scarves and a leather blouson. As I reached for my
favorite blue haik he stepped forward.

"No—nothing they might recognize." For a moment he
stared at me, then rubbed my shorn scalp with the back of
his hand. He glanced at the floor and nudged something
with his foot. "Those—"

I pulled on the trousers, a loose white shirt. I crammed
Anna's hummingbird bandeau in my pocket and started
rummaging in the back of the wardrobe when Justice
yanked me away.

"Now." He pulled me after him to the door. He cracked
it and peered out, then tossed the spent lumiere behind us.
For a moment he regarded me as I swayed beside him,
trying to steady myself. Then he clicked the door shut and
motioned me down the hall.

Sudden freedom made me giddy. Paneled walls ballooned in shadow. Beneath me the florid carpet snaked
blue and gold in the rain-washed light. Justice took my
hand and led me like a child, the two of us racing silently
down the dim hallway. Abruptly he stopped and dragged
me into an alcove. He drew something from his pocket. I
smelled his fear and shut my eyes until the piercing desire
to tap him faded.

"I'll kill you now." He spread his palm to show a cobalt
capsule. "Or will you come with me?"

I nodded. He stared at me, after another moment replaced the capsule and turned to the door. When its old-
fashioned latch gave, the door creaked inward onto a long
dark stairway winding down: Andrew's secret passage. I
glanced down, half-hoping that I might see him crouched
on the stairs with his cigarette lighter, luring spiders.

But no. I had seen no one for weeks, no one except for Dr. Leslie and Tast'annin and the janissary medics who slipped into my room when I was sedated. Later they would attach the siphons to my head as I slept. I began to shake and stumbled against Justice. He took my hand and squeezed it.

It was so dark that I could not even glimpse the step I stood upon. A sharp crack; I started and saw a fresh lumiere glowing in Justice's other hand. He steadied himself against the wall and glanced at me.

"They were going to kill you," he said. "They've already killed most of the others. Do you think you can walk?"

I nodded and stroked his face, his skin warm beneath its sheath of sweat. He shrank against the damp wall. I brought my hand to my lips and licked it. In his sweat I tasted blunt desire, and shivered with the sudden thrill of understanding that it was an empty he wanted, as there had been those I treated who longed to sleep with the dead. I stared at him until he looked away and shifted the lumiere to shadow his face. We descended the stairs.

As we fled downward the air grew cooler. The walls roughened from wood to rough granite and moldering brick. I smelled refrigeration; rotting orchids; the drowsy chypre of the sleeplabs. The lumiere's faint light dwindled.

"Do you know where we are?" I asked.

"Not really," he said, slowing his pace to answer me. "But I thought we might gain a little time before they track us here." He glanced at me doubtfully. "But this is only a way out of the building. We can't stay on the grounds—the dogs will find us for sure."

"Where does it come out?"

"The Glass Fountain."

"And then?"

He shrugged, shaking the lumiere in a vain effort to get a stronger light. "It's only the old fence there—I don't think there's a surveillance system. They never worried about keeping you in; it was more to keep the world out. Behind the fence there's the cemetery and the forest. They might be afraid to follow us there." The stairway curved so sharply that for an instant I lost sight of him and heard his voice echo, "Anyway, we have no choice."

"But where can we go?" I coughed, trying to keep up with him. "The forest—they'll find us there—"

He waved the lumiere as though to drive off hidden enemies. "I know. But I read the applications disc for you, Wendy. . . ."

Below us I glimpsed a break in the darkness.

"This is it," Justice whispered. He halted and took my hand, fumbled in his pocket for a moment. "If they catch us, I have these." His fist opened to display five cobalt ampules threaded with jet.

I shook my head. "I don't want them."

He stared at me, fingering his hood.

"I'm not afraid," I said. "They can kill me."

"It's not that." He shoved the ampules back into his pocket. "It's how—"

"It doesn't matter," I said. "He's in my head now. I can't get rid of Him, Justice. She gave Him to me, Justice. Dr. Harrow."

I could not finish. He turned to face another door that opened easily. Lantern light splintered about us as we stepped onto a patio. Justice pulled his hood tighter around his face, then tossed away the spent lumiere.

We hurried down steps that glimmered pink and yellow in the glow of sulfur lanterns. Far above us in the jutting gables and turrets of HEL, lights flickered and died. I heard the mewling whine of night monitors on their circuit through the upper gardens.

"Are you sure this is right?" Justice whispered. I ignored him, finding my way by scent as much as sight: tracing through the boxwood maze a thread of citrus that led us into a tiny circle of dwarf kumquats, and from there seeking out the firs that bordered the very edge of the estate.

"You said the Glass Fountain." I pointed to where it danced and sang in the soft rain, its canopy embracing a circle of rainbow light.

"Can you see behind it? To a fence?"

I squinted through the rain, then shook my head. "We'll have to get past the fountain."

We slid down a small knoll and waited beneath its shadow. A sound rose behind us—the yelping of guard hounds. A moment later the wailing shriek that signaled the release of the mastiffs from their pit beneath the greenhouse. Justice grabbed my hand.

"There!" he gasped. I stumbled with him over a low stone wall. To either side stretched the high impenetrable hedge of lindens and thorntrees that bounded HEL. In front of us leaned a barbed-wire fence, overgrown with thorns and strangling ivy except for a few yards of rusted metal snagged with feathers and a loop of some small animal's vertebrae. Beyond the wire stretched woods and the tilted gray humps of tombstones.

From the hill behind us a mastiff squalled. I whirled to Justice. "You said there was a way out—"

He still gazed behind us like one entranced. I shook his arm and he pointed to the ground where a strand of wire had nearly rusted away. "Under there . . ."

We scrabbled through a few inches of dirt until we scraped broken concrete and gravel. Justice leaned back on his heels, swearing.

I shook my head, took a deep breath, and flattened myself against the ground. A barb tore through my clothes, raking my back almost to my waist. I pushed myself forward, hands and elbows grinding against crushed cement and glass.

I was on the other side. Justice hesitated before he bellied against the slick ground, yelping as the wire tore his cheek. In a few seconds he stumbled to his feet beside me. We kicked rocks and leaves to cover the shallow opening, then stood staring back at the rainbow Fountain, the glittering emerald lawns sloping above us beneath their diadem of watchlights. As the baying of the dogs shook the hedges we fled into the black and dripping woods.

During the last centuries the trees had grown unchecked. Decaying leaves muffled our footsteps. I stumbled on toadstools the size of dinner plates that expelled acrid clouds of brown spores. After a few minutes Justice whistled for me to stop.

"Wait."

The forest fell back around a clearing studded with the domes of mausoleums and kudzu-covered pillars. A stand of young gingkos littered the ground with their leaves, already bright yellow. Tombstones lay everywhere like discarded dominos poking through the undergrowth. I tipped my chin westward toward Linden Glory.

"So why—" I began.

"No—listen." He wiped the rain from a tombstone before leaning against its mossy flank. "Can you hear?"

The dogs' howls grew more frantic, then abruptly stilled. "They can't have given up already. But where—"

Then I heard it. From high overhead a very soft whirring, persistent as the rain. Something huge and black crept across the floodlit lawns of HEL, a shadow like that of a vast cloud.

"Wendy." Justice stared at the sky. Without looking at me he made a strange gesture, crossing his hands at the wrist. "Wendy, it's a strike. . . ."

More lights sprang on in the towers. Shouts and the clang of doors opening. On the lawn I could see the mastiffs waiting, tails wagging uneasily as they stared up. Behind them their keepers ran across the grass. From the highest turret searchlights pierced the night until they found their target.

An airship, one of the great dirigibles called fougas. Immense and nearly silent, its vast hull drab blue except where a white hand surmounted by a crescent moon had been painted near the rear propellor.

The sigil of the Balkhash Commonwealth.

I had never seen a fouga, and started to my feet in amazement when Justice grabbed me. Yelling, he pulled me with him into a mausoleum.

Rotting acorns popped beneath our feet. A cracked marble slab leaned in front of a tomb robbed decades before. Justice shoved this out of our way and dragged me after him. Inside it smelled of decaying leaves. He tore the hem from his jacket, wrapping it around my head. I tried to push him away, but he silenced me and pointed outside.

Against the black sky I saw the fouga silhouetted, hovering over the lawn in a near-silence eerier than any roar or siren. Brilliant streams of light suddenly erupted from its gondola, sweeping across the grounds of HEL and touching the edge of the woods. As we watched, the viral strike began.

A gentle pattering upon the lawn and the canopy of trees. A wind like the promise of spring. A sweet smell seeped through the damp air, the odor of a million roses masking the chemical stench of the mutagens. Watchlights swept the lawn and candled shallow pools where the viral rain had gathered. Beside me Justice stared, his hands on mine cold and unmoving.

Then, as quickly and quietly as it had come, the fouga retreated. Its lights winked out; the shadows crept back across the lawns. Outside, the forest dripped black and still. I crept forward to peer at the stricken gardens of HEL.

On the grass stood the mastiffs, shaking their heads. One had collapsed and was licking its front leg. Another pawed repeatedly at its face, as though to dislodge a burr or tick. Their human keepers staggered nearby. I could hear one screaming, the muted voices of the others moaning or calling for help as they tore off their clothes. A siren began to shriek, too late to warn the denizens of the Human Engineering Laboratory. Justice let his breath out in a shuddering sigh. I turned back and crouched beside him.

"Were they after us? Who were they?"

He shook his head. He also looked dazed. "I don't know. Rebels, I guess. Fougas supplied by the Commonwealth."

"But what are they doing here?" I unpeeled the cloth he had wrapped around my face, coughed at the cloying scent of roses. I leaned against the wall, trying to find a comfortable spot.

Justice shook his head. "Who knows? The Aviator, maybe; maybe they were making a show of force to impress him, maybe—"

"But he's gone. He left a week ago, he went into the City with his guards."

In the darkness I could feel Justice next to me, brushing aside stones and dead leaves. "Maybe they don't know that. Or maybe they do and don't care. Or maybe he's already dead, and this is their way of telling us."

We were silent for a long time. Outside, the siren ceased its bleating. I wondered if anyone would come searching for us now.

"No," said Justice, as though he had read my thoughts. He reached to take my hand. "We're safe, I think. Anyone at HEL will assume we were caught by the rain. No one will look for us, at least not tonight. They're afraid of the rebels; they'll be trying to trace the source of the attack."

"But what of us? Won't the lazars find us out here?"

He made a face. "We'll have to chance it. But I think we're safe for now, at least this side of the river."

He hugged me. "We're free, Wendy. By morning we can leave. I know a place we can go for a few days—"

"But," I stammered, "what will we do?"

I could imagine his mouth pursed in the darkness, thinking. "We'll go to the City," he said at last. "I have people there; they may help us." But he sounded doubtful.

"But what about me: they'll know who I am." I pulled closer to the wall, disliking this enforced proximity. I felt stronger since he had given me my medication, and wished morning would come. I wished he would leave.

"No one knows who you are, Wendy," Justice said softly. "Outside of HEL no one has heard of you or the others."

"Won't they look for you?"

"They terminated me two days ago, but it's been so disorganized that the release code wasn't changed yet. One of the servers let me in. They won't bother with me. I'm only an Aide." He hesitated, then added, "And I'm not an Ascendant."

I flopped back against the tomb wall. "What about me?" I had never been outside of HEL, except for chaperoned visits to the riverwalk and giddy forays to the ziggurat with Anna and a few of the other empties.

"Can you do anything?"

"I can assist in emotive engram therapy."

"Well." He did not sound impressed. "My—*people*—are in the City. They may be able to help. Or there's others might be interested in you." He regarded me critically. "No one would recognize you like this."

"No one knows me outside of HEL," I said. The thought invoked an echo of Dr. Harrow's sorrow and loneliness, and I shivered. He drew me closer.

"You can use another name. Travel in disguise. It might be exciting." He rubbed the nape of my neck, brushing the short hairs the wrong way. "We'll say you're a Curator."

"My name is Wendy Wanders."

"Take another; take a boy's name."

I thought for a moment, then said, "Tell them to call me Aidan." And I stretched out upon the dank marble floor beside him and fell slowly into sleep.

I slept fitfully. Although undisturbed by the rush of wind in the leaves or the faint footfalls of passing animals, I could not grow accustomed to the unfamiliar weight of Justice beside me, the flickering shades of his dreams intruding upon my own. Several times I started awake in terror, seeing a pair of glowing green eyes fading into the confines of the tomb's walls. And Dr. Harrow's voice echoed over and over in my mind, calling my name and her brother Aidan's until finally she faded into silence.

Once, near dawn, I woke to feel Justice's hands sliding beneath my shirt.

"Get away," I said, although there was nowhere for him to go. As I tried to edge from him I could smell his arousal. He pressed me against the wall, his jacket falling about us like a tent. I tried to bite his shoulder, but he shoved me back so that my cheek grazed the marble. Then holding my face in his hands he kissed me, murmuring my name as he ran his hands across my skull. I bit his tongue. With a choked cry he yanked away from me, but not before a little blood trickled into my mouth: enough that his desire exploded in my brain and I shut my eyes, trembling.

Cursing, he touched the tip of his tongue, drew away a finger spotted with blood. In the near-darkness he might have been a stone angel fallen from atop one of the vaults. He turned back to me, his eyes clouded with anger.

"You ungrateful—"

A drop of blood welled onto his lip and I tilted my head to kiss him. My tongue flicked across the tiny cut and tasted what blood remained, the bright flash of his anger melting into disappointment and confusion. He fumbled to put his arms about me, but I crouched against the back of the tomb. Without a word he lay down again, his back to me. I sensed his wakefulness long afterward.

At first light he crept from our hiding place. A few minutes later he returned to wake me.

"Get up," he said. He braided his hair, tying the end with a black silk ribbon. "Even if they think we're dead, we can't stay here."

"But the virus?"

"It doesn't live more than an hour in the open air. But we can't trust Leslie or the others not to come looking for your corpse."

"Will the lazars hunt us?" I stretched, wondering when we would be able to eat.

Justice stood, hands slouched in the deep pockets of his jacket as he watched me tuck in my shirt. "This is probably the best time to avoid them. After the rain of roses they're —sated."

"I have never seen one," I admitted, and smiled. "I'm thirsty."

Justice stared at me as though waiting for me to say something else; to apologize, perhaps. I adjusted the cuffs of my shirt, wishing I'd brought other clothes. After a moment he shook his head.

"Well, come on, then," he said. We left the tomb.

Sunrise misted the eastern edge of the woods, where through the deep green leaves I glimpsed the chromatic haze of the Glass Fountain and the purer emerald of HEL's lawns.

Justice said, "You can go back if you want. Go ahead: see what happens."

"I don't want to go back." I turned from this last sight of my home to follow him. "You didn't have to free me. I'll go on alone now if you want."

"Hah." He snorted, but paused to hold a wiry sumac whip while I passed beneath it. "No point letting you get killed out here after all that trouble." As I passed, his voice rose slightly. "Why'd you bite me last night?"

"I don't like to fuck."

"Then why did you kiss me?"

"I tapped you."

His eyes darkened as he stepped beside me, kicking at mushrooms and damp leaves. "What?"

I squinted to find a path among the ancient trees. "I can read blood."

He stared at me for a long moment. I met his gaze, finally shrugged and turned to make my way through the tangled forest.

We walked in silence until the sun hung high overhead. Justice seemed to find his way by the sun, and by following the river. Occasionally we glimpsed it through the trees, a glitter of blue and gold.

A heavy jasmine-scented steam began to rise from the earth. This came from carpets of white flowers that covered the ground like moss, their blossoms no bigger than my fingernail. As I stooped to watch them the tiny blooms opened and closed like little gaping mouths. When I touched one it snapped at my finger.

"Look, Justice! It's hungry—"

He shook his head and pulled me to my feet. "No, Wendy."

"Are they poisonous?"

"Sometimes. Things change, after the rain of roses."

I followed him. When he wasn't looking I would kick at the mats of white flowers and watch them seethe as we passed.

We skirted the rotted foundations of small wooden buildings, the collapsed tangle of steel walls and cavernous bunkers and commercial ziggurats that during the Third Ascension had been built upon the earlier ruins. On the decaying ziggurat steps I saw copperheads drowsing in

coiled knots and other, larger snakes, blue-black and with
scales so long and fine they looked like feathers. The fallen
steel archways were pied with lizards, golden-eyed and
blue-tongued, waiting patiently for crickets to waken and
warm themselves on the metal. I was hungry. In the trees
ahead Justice waited for me to catch up. I waved to him to
go on ahead, waited for him to turn away so that I could
capture a lizard as it dozed. It was lovely, raised rounded
scales like tiny rust-and-azure studs. I wished I could save
its skin; but I killed it quickly by biting its neck. I sucked
the little blood there was from its body cavity and made a
quick mouthful of the meat in belly and tail. A flicker of the
animal's hunger and heat sparked in my brain: the warmth
of insects and then the quick slash of my own teeth
through its spine. That was all it gave me. I was sorry about
the pretty scales.

I skipped ahead to join Justice and we continued in silence for a time.

"You've never been this far outside before, have you?"
he said at last.

"We had no need to leave HEL."

For what? Dr. Harrow had warned me that the world
outside was a decadent place, and dangerous. Certainly
the ruined City of Trees was no place for a creature depen-
dent upon a carefully administered regime of chemicals
and stolen dreams. But Justice only motioned for me to
follow him to the edge of the forest. We left the cool shelter
of the trees behind.

"Where are we?" I asked, stepping among shattered
blocks of granite.

"Near the Key Bridge."

A path of white stones curled from the edge of the broken road and stretched through the trees. Justice hesitated, squatting on a ledge of tarmac.

"Are we lost?"

He shook his head. "No. But it will be dark soon. That's
the City, there."

He pointed to the far shore of the river. Through a green
scrim I glimpsed broken roofs and towers vying with tree-
tops for the afternoon sun.

"Tired?"

"No." Instead I felt edgy, wide awake. At HEL we would have been dressing for dinner, or stealing things for a secret meeting in our quarters. And a certain uneasiness shaded all my thoughts now: fear of those brilliant eyes and the longing they kindled within me; fear of the loneliness that crept over me whenever I recalled Dr. Harrow's white form lying still on the floor of the Horne Room. . . .

"Good. We'll cross there—" He pointed, and I peered through the thicket. For the first time I saw the bridge spanning the murky river, its ancient fretwork rusted to a filigree of red and black, virginia creeper scalloping the lower struts in waves of green that shimmered in the warm breeze.

We followed the path of white stones. It skimmed the broken ribs of what had once been a road, hedged by tall bronzed oaks and a winding network of ditches now filled with stagnant water. Occasionally the rusted shell of an automobile or velocipede poked from the greenery or lay submerged in the brackish pools like gaunt pike. Once we heard something thrash in the ditch. Justice pulled me after him into the brush, and from there we glimpsed a pale slender appendage like an arm or tentacle gently plying the surface of the black water behind us. Justice watched impassively until it withdrew and the ripples subsided in the scummy pool.

In a few more minutes we reached the bridge. Justice shook his head as though testing the air. Then he turned to me, laughing in relief.

"This is it. We made it."

And as I followed Justice I suddenly felt *Him* again inside me, stirring against the shell of nerve and bone that contained *Him*. I knew that the dark flash that tore through me was not my jubilation, not Dr. Harrow's or Aidan's but *His*, the Other now with me and within me.

He saw the City too, and the sight filled Him with a raging joy: joy and blood-hunger and a thirst for worship.

* * *

But for myself, crossing that river, the sluggish guardian of my childhood—what stirred me at first sight of the fallen City of Trees unfurled before me like a ruined flag, all the more valiant for its tattered heraldry?

The tales Dr. Harrow had told us of the City painted a grimy metropolis, justly forsaken: a cheap bauble not worth preserving. Its people died horrible deaths in the Long Night of the First Ascension—starvation, radiation sickness, plague. Its rulers had already fled west. There they perished in the wilderness or else joined the fledgling alliance that a century later would bring about the Second Ascension. Since then the City was held by the researchers (and camp followers) who had been sent to recover some of the knowledge of the Civil Servants, and then, in the chaos following the first mutagenic warfare, forgotten. They owned the City now: mad watchdogs of useless knowledge and their whores, feasting upon the ruins like fat ticks. And in the streets lived cannibal children and the geneslaves who preyed upon the living.

But always Dr. Harrow gave us a gray city not worth dreaming of, bound by a dead river.

Yet now the river itself seemed to have awakened at the sound of our footsteps, the heavy waters uncoiling to flash silver and blue beneath the bridge. Instead of the mud-colored fish that nudged at our riverwalk in search of crusts I saw huge golden carp, circling slowly to the surface to peer up at us with wise round eyes. And sea-birds whose cries streaked the still afternoon with harsh echoes of white shores, and ospreys and eagles hunting the noble carp, and otters like arrows striking the bright water. I froze.

"What is it?" Justice called, turning to look back at me. I shook my head and steadied myself with one hand upon the rusted ironwork. *Too much!* I wanted to scream; and instinctively crouched and turned to strike my forehead against a piling. Even there the world loomed: a string of tiny scarlet mites threading through the flaking green paint, a tendril of kudzu like a child's beckoning finger. I started to scream.

"Wendy! Stop—" Justice ran and knelt beside me. He

grabbed my wrists and pulled me from the railing so that
my head thrashed against empty air. *"Stop it!"*

I tried to beat myself against his chest and mute the
clamor in my head, the sight of all those things moving and
brilliant in the world. He hugged me tight, until it passed;
until once more I could focus on the shattered concrete I
knelt upon, the raveled hem of his jacket, my knuckles
laced with blood.

"Are you all right?" His face was white. "What *is* it?"

I breathed deeply, the way Dr. Harrow had taught me to
breathe after a seizure; then shut my eyes and concen-
trated, trying to draw up a memory to stanch the horrible
welling of sensation and light. But there was nothing there,
nothing like this river, these birds, this golden haze rising
to veil the heavy green of the eastern shore. Only a faint
comforting memory of dead trees and hills, like a small
cold nugget lodged inside me; and so I focused on that,
until the dead calm soothed me and I could speak again.

"Too much," I whispered, shielding my eyes from the
sun. Justice draped his jacket about me and helped me to
my feet.

"Can you walk?"

I nodded, pulling the folds of cloth about my face. "Too
sudden," I said.

"You've never been outside," he said, as if truly realizing
it for the first time.

"No. I told you." I shook my head. "It will go away—just
too sudden, too much light, all those—" I flapped my hand
at the flickering shapes I could still just barely make out
from the corner of my eyes, the gulls disporting along the
bridge's ramparts.

"I'm sorry. I—I couldn't chance stealing more of your
medication. Can you . . ."

But already I felt stronger—as I always did after capturing a new sensation, if the first violent impressions did not
completely overwhelm me. I took a deep breath, then
lifted my head.

"I'm better now," I said. I stretched my arms and flexed
my hands, feeling my blood quicken. I faced Justice. Far
behind him I could just make out the shattered ramparts

that had been my home. I turned to see the unknown City at bridge's end, just a few feet away. And suddenly I laughed, so loudly that a skein of gulls shrieked and banked away from us. Then I ran the last steps to the far shore.

So we entered the City of Trees. In the growing dusk it looked more strange, the low ruined lines of buildings and verdant trees painted with a brooding light. The air still smelled of summer, wild grapes and honeysuckle and the river's stagnant breath. We picked our way across the rubble of what had once been a road. Now oaks and gingkos thrust through the concrete to tower overhead. Beneath our feet ivy and thick runners of some thorny plant covered the shattered road.

We climbed a gently sloping hill scented with honeysuckle and the rich odors of other, strangely colored flowers. As we left it behind us the river's soft rush fell into silence. Justice seemed more watchful now. Often he stopped to regard the remains of some ancient structure— a metal monument in the shape of a man, a pox of briar roses covering its face; a great machine of some smooth rivetless material still humming and vibrating despite the myriad skinks sunning themselves on its black surface— and he would click his tongue in dismay or curse beneath his breath.

"It changes so fast," he said once. He stared in chagrin at the hollow body of an autobus collapsed in a ditch like some drowned beast, then glanced toward the horizon before us.

I was starting to feel dizzy and ill from hunger and thirst. Worse, the acetelthylene was wearing off. I could feel the effects of being without my medication for so many days: a hollow feeling inside my head and the Voices that, if I listened to them, would call my name repeatedly in soft yet urgent tones. These were the flickering embers of consciousness of all those patients I had tapped at HEL, flaring bits of memory and desire that would not die but were kept imprisoned within my mind by constant medication.

But now they were starting to creep out again, as they did in dreams, or if my dosage was changed, or when I had been subjected to the ruthless probes of Dr. Leslie's janissary medics. I stumbled as I walked, and swatted fiercely at my ears as if that might silence them.

Justice watched me with concern. "Are you all right? What is it?"

I cupped my hands over my ears. "The Small Voices." That had been the name Anna and I gave to them as children; before Anna's favorite Small Voice manifested itself as Andrew, her secondary personality.

Justice stared, baffled. I shrugged and continued to follow him through the underbrush. I was so exhausted that the Small Voices' babble soon grew no more worrisome than the chirping of birds or crickets. After a few more minutes the flutter and squeaking of real birds roosting for the night drowned them out.

We passed a clearing ringed with white trees like birches. The air smelled of warm earth and goldenrod, but also of something foul, fetid water perhaps, trapped in a rotting stump. The sky glowed deepening blue and green. I sighed, feeling the breeze cool against my shorn skull, watched the long slender branches of the birch trees float upon the wind as though reaching for me. I had started toward one of them, thinking I might lie there to rest a moment, when Justice grabbed me and pulled me back.

"No, Wendy!"

I fell against him, and started to push him away angrily when he forced my head around. "Look—"

Against the boles of two trees a pair of figures reclined, as I had imagined myself resting beneath the lacy birches. Their heads had all but disappeared within the loose folds of their janissary's uniforms. Willowy branches had wrapped themselves around them, snaking through flaps of yellow cloth to fasten upon their arms and chest and eyes. One had thrown his arm across his face, as though to shield it from the sun. Crumpled flesh hung from his wrist. Worms had bored small, perfectly round holes through his cheeks. The rest of his face seemed to have slipped from his skull like a mask of thin cloth.

The other gazed rigidly at us. As I stared back her mouth moved wordlessly. A black-winged beetle crawled from it, crept down her chin and onto the peaked collar of her uniform jacket. The net of branches rippled about her, their smooth white outer bark pulsing ever so slightly as they fed.

Justice turned away, tried to pull me after him; but I continued to stare. The scene wavered. Sunlight faded to gray twilight, white ribs and fleshless fingers emerging from black water, another tree whose limbs cracked beneath a body's weight. He falls, turns bald white eyes to stare at me as I scream and look away—

"Shh, Wendy." Justice drew me from the clearing, pushing back vines loud with bees and sparrows until we found a safer spot. "Here, sit . . ."

I found a large stone and settled there, breathing deeply until I felt calm again.

"Betulamia," he explained. He sat a few feet from me, propping his feet on another rock and leaning so that his chin rested on his knees. "But we were safe; they had already fed."

I tore leaves from an oak sapling at my feet. "It wasn't that, really. It—They reminded me of something else."

We rested for a few more minutes. Justice peered through the undergrowth, first north, then west, trying to get his bearings. When we started off again I asked, "Where are we going?"

"There's a woman of my House who lives nearby; if she hasn't left, or been driven out, or . . ."

The woods fell back. Before us opened a wide grassy avenue, speared by small saplings and the green mounds of overgrown autovehicles. To one side it sloped down to the river. A hill continued upward to our left, and there loomed a gold-domed building, its stained marble pillars choked with wisteria and ivy. Sunset ignited the dome so that I blinked to stare at it; but from a narrow barred window at ground level a fainter light gleamed.

"She's there!" Justice said. I let him drag me, stumbling over a moss-grown curb to where a tiny patio building had

been trimmed of underbrush. I squinted to read broken
letters on the dome overhead:

RI S NATION   ANK

On the door itself hung a small hand-lettered wooden
placard, the words spelled out in faded but carefully drawn
cursives:

LAST NATIONAL BANK

Lalagé Saint-Alaban, Prop.

Love Philtres
Tea Readings
Psychotropic Drugs

"What is *this?*" I began; but Justice had already raced up
the steps leading to a set of huge metal doors. A great steel
ring hung there. Justice banged this once, twice. As the
third clang echoed down the empty avenue a tiny slit
opened in the door. An alarmingly bright blue eye peered
out.

"Lalagé!" he yelled. "It's Justice—"

The blue eye disappeared. A harsh grating signaled bolts
being drawn. One of the doors creaked inward.

"Justice!" In the shadows I glimpsed a small figure that
drew up sharply at the sight of me. Justice stepped past me
into the room. I hesitated.

"It's all right, Wen—*Aidan,*" he called back. "It's only
Lalagé."

"Justice," the woman rebuked. She peered at me suspiciously.

"A friend, Lalagé. A *Patron.*"

"Oh, all right," she sighed, and pulled the door back
another inch.

It opened onto a great chamber. The only light filtered
from windows high overhead, touching the room with
glints of green and gold. Tables made of dismembered
automobiles were scattered across the floor, chairs over-

turned or leaning against them haphazardly. Small shapes fluttered around them. There was a strong animal smell.

"Thank you, Lalagé. I wasn't certain you'd still be here. . . ." His voice faded as he stepped farther into the cavernous room.

The woman laughed, turning a series of bolts and locks within the door. "Where else would I go? Too old for the duties of pleasure now. And you can't really picture me in the kitchen at Saint-Alaban, can you, Justice?"

They laughed. Lalagé crossed the room to embrace Justice, leaving me to wander among the tables of a forsaken hospice. The fluttering shapes were birds, guinea hens and peahens and doves. Peacocks dragged soiled trains through the muck. In the shadows a number of small barred chambers protected shattered glass monitors and more empty chairs.

Justice called to me across the room and I joined them, nudging guinea hens from my path. "Lalagé, may I introduce my companion, Aidan."

She inclined her head toward me. Then she smiled and raised three fingers to her mouth, a gesture that Justice imitated: the Paphians' beck.

"A handsome leman, Justice," she said, gazing at me and winking. "Especially for a Curator—"

"I'm not his leman!" I began hotly, when Justice cut me off.

"No, he's not my lover. We're merely traveling together."

"I understand." Lalagé nodded, a smile twitching at the corners of her mouth. Now that we stood in the center of the chamber I could see her more clearly in the hazy light. She was smaller than Justice and myself, very thin, and wearing a shift of some heavy green fabric, once no doubt very fine, now sloppily tied with a black sash and spattered with bird droppings and streaks of dust. But her hands were small and slender (if dirty), heavy with jeweled bracelets and antique rings; and her eyes were carefully painted to play up their oblique tilt and odd color: a dark and clouded blue. Her gray hair—blond once as Justice's—was loosely braided above a pointed foxlike face. And I smelled in her sweat expensive spices—cinnamon, sandalwood, bitter rue. She bent to pick up a bedraggled guinea hen and stroked it gently.

"An interesting traveling companion, Justice." She stared at my auburn stubble. "Someday you will have to tell me of your adventures there in the Citadel." She tipped her head in the direction of the river, toward HEL. "We thought you had forsaken us for the Ascendants."

Justice tossed back his head, avoiding her eyes. "I missed our people. But tell me, cousin: there are no guests?"

Lalagé sighed, picking matted down from the guinea fowl's breast. "Hardly ever now. Outside trade has fallen off. I was supposed to receive more frilite and morpha from the Botanists, but I haven't seen them for nearly two weeks."

She lowered her voice, glancing at the dim vault arching high above us. "There was trouble, Justice. A new Governor was sent here from the Citadel. The Curators were in an uproar. He came here, last week—"

Justice nodded. "In the woods—we saw two janissaries taken by the trees."

"They were in his party. They arrived that night, I fed them, acted innocence, even gave them the last of my morpha tubes. Next morning sent them on their way."

Her eyes glittered. I could smell her cunning like a thick musk. She tossed the guinea hen into the air and it flapped into the darkness. "The Governors will never hear from them again."

Justice nodded, cast me an uneasy glance. "But otherwise, things are as they were? Our people?"

She shook her head and began to cross the room. "They come here seldom. They fear being this close to the edge of the City. I've been lonely this last week; I'll be delighted to serve you both. Come with me."

We followed her, Justice giving me warning looks when I angrily started to question him. Small round tables edged the far wall of the room, some of them still littered with tumblers sticky with absinthium and broken candicaine pipettes. Scrawny roosters and glossy black hens picked among the refuse. I kicked at a shattered morpha tube, the

once-bright label with its grinning Man in the Moon faded
to a pale blur.

"I haven't cleaned in a while," Lalagé admitted. "It
hardly seems worth it, with no Patrons. . . ."

We followed her into a narrow passageway. Runners of
pleated rubber covered the floor, brittle and curling with
age. The hall was lit by elongated tubes stretching across
the length of the ceiling. These were filled with murky
water that sparkled pale blue and green, phosphorescent
algae and diatoms that emitted a faint eerie glow. Fortunately the birds preferred the half-light of the rotunda. I
inhaled with some relief the cooler air, only slightly tainted
with the bittersweet smell of stale absinthium.

"If you wait here for a few minutes I'll make the atrium
ready for you." She flashed me a brilliant smile before
disappearing behind a fringed curtain.

When she was gone I turned to Justice.

"You're a Paphian," I said, pushing him against the wall.
"You've stolen me to be a prostitute."

He winced, shook his head. "No, Wendy. But I *am* a
Paphian." He drew his hand to his mouth and rested three
fingers upon his lower lip: the Paphians' beck, signifying
the three sexes. "But I have no claim on you. They would
have killed you, Wendy. *I* would have killed you before I'd
leave you to them. . . ."

I scented his arousal again, tinged now with the metallic
edge of fear as he edged away from me. I felt a sudden
rush, as though I had received a jolt of acetelthylene.
Where the small nodes bulged from my temples a faint
warmth spread until my hair prickled and stood on end.
And suddenly I felt it, felt *Him*, that overwhelming desire
and terror surging through me like raw adrenaline. I
laughed.

"I was the wrong toy for you to steal, Justice," I whispered. I brought my face close to his, until his shallow
breathing warmed me. I brushed my tongue against his
cheeks, tasted his bitter pleasure. Then I bit his mouth,
until I felt my teeth meet through his soft skin.

With a cry he kicked me away, but not before I kissed
him to draw a sharp draught of blood. I reeled backward,

dizzy at the intensity of his desire, and drew my hand to
my face to wipe the blood from my chin. I started to lick
my fingers; but he grabbed me.

"I did not steal you! I *saved* you—"

But his words echoed meaninglessly as I gave myself up
to a sudden shuddering ecstasy. I struck at him only to trip
and fall. Pain blurred into an image dredged from the last
fevered drop of blood upon my tongue:

My own face, blank and calm upon its soiled pillow. A
golden-haired figure stands silently above me, watching
for hours as I dreamed. . . .

"*Wendy—*"

I blinked to see him standing there still, the pale blue
light tinting his cheekbones and his luminous eyes. But he
no longer wore HEL's yellow robes, and his golden hair
now hung loose and tangled from our flight. I shook my
head, tried to stand. Justice glanced behind him before
pulling me into a sitting position.

"You fainted." He rubbed his mouth ruefully where a
dark welt marred his lower lip. "You really are crazy,
aren't you?"

I stared at the phosphorescent ceiling. My head ached,
and the giddy pangs of desire were gone. I felt only an
indifferent regret for having hurt the boy who'd saved me.

"I'm not safe company for you, Justice," I said at last. "I'll
harm you, whether I want to or not."

He edged closer to me, eyeing the doorway where
Lalagé had disappeared. "I saw your scan on the monitor
that afternoon." He spoke softly, his blue eyes intent upon
me. "You thought you were entering a fugue state."

"I was wrong."

"But something did happen; that's why you came to me
for the scan. You killed them, didn't you?"

I felt a pressure building inside my chest. "I didn't kill
them," I whispered. "I told you that—I told them all that."

"But somehow you drove them to suicide: Morgan Yates,
Emma Harrow, the sleep researcher. All those children.
Why? *How?*"

I leaned forward and gripped my knees. Inside my head
a vision was forming, distinct from the dimly lit room

around us. I bit my lip, feeling sick at the taste of my own blood; thought of tapping Justice again, to somehow draw him into the scintillating landscape that was beginning to loom behind my eyes. Black mountains, an endless plain shot with dead white light. In the air in front of me something else began to form. A spectral figure crouched as if preparing to spring.

I snatched my hand from Justice and pounded my fist against the wall behind me, hard enough to make me gasp with pain. The brilliant interior horizon shivered. The ghostly silhouette disappeared. I sat in a narrow corridor flickering with blue light, staring wildly at a fair young man.

I gritted my teeth, waited for the throbbing in my knuckles to subside.

"Justice," I began. "Dr. Harrow engaged in therapy with me. Did you know that?"

Pupils retracting in gold-flecked eyes: no.

"She— Something went wrong. A long time ago . . .

"She and her twin brother played at—at witchcraft. They invoked something, and—it came. Something strong and dangerous. It killed her brother; it drove him mad, and he hanged himself. But she had this—hypostate—dormant inside of her all that time. When she did my neural implants fourteen years ago, I think the engrams were stronger than anyone ever knew. She patterned me without really knowing it was there, that memory, without *me* knowing. And nothing happened until I was the same age she was when they woke it, and then it—it manifested itself."

"And that's what you think killed Dr. Harrow?" He tilted his head in disbelief. "What of the others?"

"It just waited until I tapped anyone susceptible to it. It latched on to them: Morgan, Melisande . . ."

"A poet and a sick child, a dreaming woman," Justice said slowly. "And Dr. Harrow . . ." He laced his fingers with mine. "But what is it?"

"I don't know. A hypostate. Some terribly destructive impulse . . ."

He stared at me, thoughtful. "Twins, and—well, something. Like Baal and Anat."

"What?" I shook my head impatiently.

"A story, a masque of ours, about twins. At Saint-Alaban. Baal wakes Death, but his sister Anat saves him. It's a story of the Magdalene, really. A fable."

I snorted, and he glared at me.

"Well, if you're carrying this thing inside you, why hasn't it affected *you?* Why aren't *you* dead? Why didn't it kill the other empaths when you tapped them?"

"I don't know. Perhaps because of what we are: maybe we have nothing for it to feed on. But it drove her to despair. The last—what I felt of her—" I licked my lips at the memory.

Justice flinched and rubbed his mouth gingerly. "So it's a separate emergent personality," he said. "Like Andrew—"

"No!" I insisted. "Andrew is *part* of Anna. They induced him when she was little. She was afraid of the dark," I recalled wistfully. "But this is *not mine.*"

"How do you know? All of the multiple personalities at HEL considered themselves independent."

"I am *not* an MP!" I lashed at him. He grabbed my hand, but at that moment we heard the curtains being drawn behind us.

"Ah. Pardon me, cousins." Lalagé smiled. I drew away from Justice and stood up too quickly. I felt dizzy again. Justice grabbed my elbow and nodded to Lalagé.

"He's tired," he explained, glancing at me with concern. "We've come a long way. . . ."

Lalagé held the curtains so that we could pass into another narrow hallway. "Curators tire easily. Don't they, Aidan?" she added sympathetically.

She had changed clothes. Now she wore a loose crimson tunic, no less soiled than the other; but it was harder to see the stains on this one's darker fabric. And she had rebraided her hair into tight coils about her ears. I thought it curious that she would bother to change clothes for two itinerants, until I also noted that she invariably directed her questions to me. Even when Justice answered, her eyes never left my face.

"What is the news of the City?" he asked as we followed her through a twisting hallway. Baskets and heavy sacks lined the walls, Lalagés wealth. It smelled overpoweringly of cumin and coriander and cinnamon.

"It will be a harsh winter this year. The lazars grow bolder every day. The Ascendants I entertained last week boasted of war with the Balkhash Commonwealth."

I would hear more of this, but Justice interrupted. "But what of our Houses, Lalagé? What news there?"

"Oh, such scandals! Salamanda Illyria deflowered her son two nights before his debut to Rufus Lynx, the Regent of Zoologists. Cliantha Persia stole a beautiful child from the Librarians, and in retaliation they took Tarleton Persia. Raphael Miramar left his House to live among the Natural Historians. The House Miramar is losing Patrons without him; but already they say that Roland Nopcsa will dismiss Raphael for that albino boy from High Brazil—"

I yawned, and she laughed. "I forget that the Curators have no patience with our gossip. Come, Aidan—here's something to interest you."

The hallway ended in a barred gate. Lalagé held the door open and we stepped out onto an open patio. Or so I thought at first. When I glanced up I saw that a glass roof soared many feet above us. In its airy reaches flitted numerous butterflies and tiny bright shapes, glowing in the sunset light.

"Hummingbirds!" I ran to where a thicket of bottlebrush grew from a chipped porcelain bowl. Amid the scarlet flowers a dozen hummingbirds darted, flashes of emerald and blue vying with butterflies for nectar.

"I'm roasting a capon for you, cousins, and there are peaches and field salad, and the first plum wine of the year," Lalagé announced grandly. She gestured toward a flat metal chassis salvaged from some vehicle, now set upon stones as a table. "I'll join you shortly." She touched her fingers to her mouth and left.

We sank onto the grass in front of the table. About us fruit trees heavy with plums roared with golden bees longer than my middle finger. They lit upon our table to sip at the overripe windfalls splattered on its metal surface.

I laughed and licked the back of my hand, watched a drone land there and feed lazily upon my damp skin.

After some minutes Lalagé returned. Behind her rolled a very old rusted house server, squeaking and squealing like an ill-behaved child.

"Stop here," commanded Lalagé, clapping her hands.

"Yes mistress yes mistress yes," piped the server, bumping against me. It set steaming platters and chipped plates upon the makeshift table. Lalagé rearranged three unmatched glasses and gave it a kick.

"Welcome mistress mistress mistress," it lisped, grinding over a tree root as it rolled off. Lalagé smiled after it, then sat on the grass between us.

"My pleasure to share my food with you," she said, bowing her head. Justice bowed his in turn, nudging me until I did the same.

The food was very good, surprisingly so. I complimented her, and Lalagé beamed. While we had always eaten the best at HEL, it had been my understanding that our bounty was due only to the good graces and munificence of our Ascendant supervisors. But surely the Ascendants did not provide Lalagé with cardamom and kef and absinthium?

At my audacious question Lalagé stared, then laughed so hard that she inhaled her wine and Justice had to slap her back to stop her choking. She had drunk a great deal by then, as had Justice. I allowed myself a sip for politeness' sake only, though it had a cleaner taste than the water in its rusted carafe.

"He's a comedian!" she exclaimed when she could talk again. She leaned companionably against me. Her hand rustled through the grass and started to glide up my thigh. I moved closer to Justice, trying to hide my disgust. "Are you a Player, then, Sieur Aidan? You are too fair for a Curator!"

"Aidan has not lived with his people for many years," said Justice. He licked a drop of grease from his finger.

"Then why is he shorn?" She ran her other hand up my back to toy with my short hair.

"A sign of respect for his people," Justice explained, clearing his throat as he glanced at me.

Lalagé nodded drunkenly, her voice softening. "Oh, I understand, dear Aidan."

Overhead, twilight deepened. I sighed and let her take my hand as she continued earnestly.

"Our people are of the House Saint-Alaban. And even though they have cast me aside for being *too old*—" She twirled a stray curl from one of her braids, batting her eyes. "Well, as you can see, I've not forgotten how to take care of myself. Not like some elders."

She paused, slightly out of breath. I took this chance to disengage my hand. I tugged a leg from the capon and started to gnaw upon it.

"Aidan is blessed with a memory somewhat shorter than yours," began Justice. He drew me toward him, stroking my neck. I felt as if I were playing a weary round of kiss-in-the-ring with Gligor and Anna. I started to pull away when:

"Help, mistress. Help help help help help," piped the server. It had bumped against the far wall of the atrium, its wheels grinding against the brick.

Another sound came from outside. Muffled voices. Then laughter and the thump of a strong hand upon wood. Beside me Lalagé sat up straight and carefully put down her wineglass.

"Ask who it is," she commanded the server; but it only mewled *help help help help.*

"Damn," muttered Lalagé. When she stood she swayed slightly. "Who is it?" she shouted as she walked toward the far wall.

" 'An ambassador from Witchland and his train,' " quoted a resonant voice. " 'We craveth present audience.' " He also sounded drunk.

Lalagé wiped her hands on her shift. She raced to the wall, stumbling on a stone and sending a peahen cater-wauling. I glanced at Justice, wondering if we should flee; but he only waited until Lalagé was halfway across the atrium, and then drank what remained in her wineglass.

I stood and followed our hostess. In the twilight I could

just make out a heavy planked door in the wall, criss-crossed with metal and set with a listening auricle that amplified the voices of our visitors, so that I heard them shuffling in the grass outside and giggling. Lalagé fumbled with several locks, finally drew herself up, and shouted "Open!"—whereupon the door flew outward. A thump and more shouts and curses followed. After a moment a bedraggled retinue tramped into the atrium.

"Toby!" Lalagé threw her arms around the neck of the tallest figure, who, by his clothes and bearing, seemed to be the leader. Behind her the server squealed piteously, until a plump girl in short skirts and tight crimson jacket kicked it into silence. I drew closer to a tall plum tree.

"We have interrupted a rendezvous!" boomed the tall man. He had a deep voice and a long ruddy face ending in an unruly black beard. He drew himself up and surveyed the atrium grandly, casting Justice a mocking little wave. "How clever of us! We've found a Paphian boy, another Saint-Alaban, too." He blew a kiss, then turned back to Lalagé. "Many greetings, dear cousin! Girls, get out of the *way.*"

He stepped aside so that the others could spill into the court. Four of them: two young girls, one the plump inter-loper who was now pulling peaches from the trees and tasting them for ripeness; the other a tall, heavyset girl with black hair and a mustache. She carried a heavy satchel. A rangy young brown-skinned boy strode in next, somewhere between my age and Justice's. He wore velvet knickers that displayed his slender fawn-colored legs and two enormously knobbed knees, like a pair of blackthorn walking-sticks.

And, finally, stepping demurely behind Toby, a diminu-tive figure in a woman's dress and lace bonnet. I poked my head around the tree to stare at her.

"Why, here's another!" exclaimed Toby, sweeping Lalagé from his path and stepping toward me in one long stride. "My dear cousin, are you poncing?"

I shrank from him, but he pulled me from the sheltering branches. Nearly two heads taller than myself—and I was tall—his hair stuck out in an untidy aureole, adding inches

more to his height. His lanky torso was draped in a long
loose tunic faded to a drab memory of its former glorious
blue and smelling of face powder and sweat. He jammed a
huge hand beneath each of my armpits and lifted me, until
I stared him square in the face.

"A pretty catamite," he announced. He kissed me on the
mouth and set me back on the grass.

"I am Toby Rhymer, boy," he intoned, thrusting his
hand at mine. "A *nom du theatre*, of course. *Née* Toby
Crouch, of the Historians." As I took his hand, Justice
slipped beside me. Toby glanced at him, nodding. "Toby
Rhymer, my dear."

"Justice Saint-Alaban," he said. "You've met my companion Aidan."

"Aidan," said Toby.

"Aidan," a soft voice echoed. From behind him peered
the tiny figure I had glimpsed before. I squinted, trying to
make out the wizened face hidden behind the torn lace.
From within the cloud of white netting I glimpsed only a
flash of intelligent black eyes surveying me calmly.

"That is a woman, sieur," she whispered. Justice flinched
beside me, but Toby only guffawed and pinched my cheek.

"I bet you could play the part better than I ever could,
eh, boy?" He laughed, and gave Justice an admiring look.
"A handsome leman, Saint-Alaban."

I stepped from him to gaze down at the figure who had
recognized me so easily. From the folds of her bonnet
peered a shriveled face, so that for a moment I thought her
a very old woman. But a hag with extraordinarily bright
eyes and a gentle voice. She gazed back at me unper-
turbed, so that I drew even closer, until I gazed directly
into her face and found myself drawing back her silken
bonnet.

I stepped back in amazement.

"Justice!" I gasped. "Look!"

With a sigh the little figure raised her head to Toby, then
plucked back the bonnet with very long slender brown
fingers. Justice drew in his breath.

"A monkey!"

Toby Rhymer shook his head and knelt beside her, drawing his arm protectively about the folds of her gown. "No," he said. "Miss Scarlet is a wonder, a marvel, the prodigy of a prodigal age; a troglodyte with the wit and grace of a Paphian and the brilliance of a Curator, a beacon in these dark and desperate times. In short, An Actress."

She tipped her head modestly, her long lips drawing back to show sharp yellow teeth. "Ah, Toby," she murmured; in her voice the rustle of warm leaves. "He is a showman," she said aside to me apologetically; then fixed me with a piercing look. She said no more; but in her deep-set eyes I read that while she had seen through my disguise she would not betray my secret.

"My dear Miss Scarlet," gushed Lalagé, brushing aside the insistent hands and imprecations of Toby's troupe to greet the chimpanzee. "It's been much too long since I had the honor of seeing you perform."

"How kind of you," murmured Miss Scarlet, extending those extraordinarily long fingers to be kissed.

Behind her the plump girl and her mustachioed companion mocked Lalagé's greeting. Toby glanced back at them.

"Ladies! Perhaps our hostess will not object to your performing ablutions before performing a Bluebeard or Hamlet this evening?" He inclined his head to Lalagé.

"Of course not." She rose and shook the grass from her shift, motioning the girls to follow her.

"Fabian—you will assist Lalagé in serving our meal," Toby ordered. With a wink the long-legged young man disappeared after the others.

"Please forgive my rudeness," Justice began. Toby brushed him aside, taking Miss Scarlet's hand.

"I am not in need of your apologies, and Miss Scarlet Pan rises above such idle speculation. It is Her Way," he said. "May we join you?"

We settled back at the stone table, Toby escorting his little soubrette and seeing that she was comfortable before seating himself. I was unable to resist staring at Miss Scarlet. She beckoned for me to sit beside her.

"I have never known an animal that could speak before," I said. Across from us Justice was offering Toby the last sip of Lalagé's plum wine. "We had macaws and bud-gerigars at HEL, but they only repeated our speech. They had no reason."

The chimpanzee nodded, extending one foot to grasp a peach in her curling toes. She passed the fruit from foot to hand and began to much it daintily.

"I grew up among the Zoologists," she began, pausing to flick a drop of ambrosia from her lip. "As I girl I was quite ill, and underwent a number of operations which resulted in long periods of convalescence. The Zoologists have a cinematograph, film projectors, and video monitors. I spent the months of my recovery watching the spectacles of the last centuries. The experience left me with an undying affection for the glories of the proscenium and the lost and lamented silver screens. I was, in short, stagestruck."

I listened eagerly, sensing within her tale faint echoes of my own fate. "These operations gifted you with speech?"

Miss Scarlet nodded. "Yes." She stroked her throat, extravagantly furred with lustrous dark hair. "I bear scars, here, and—" She caressed her temple, pulling the hair back so that I could discern the faded impression of an incision. *"Here."*

She regarded me curiously. "Do I detect a resonant sympathy within your bosom, Aidan?" She dropped her voice to a husky whisper. "I call you Aidan because your friend addresses you thus; you own another, a gentler name perhaps? Do you too heed the circean songs of Melpomene and Thalia and Calliope?"

I shook my head. Toby Rhymer had now extracted a flask from within the folds of his tunic. He and Justice passed this between them, engaged in their own discussion— which inspired Toby Rhymer to fix me with a very long, searching stare. I turned back to Miss Scarlet.

"I am an heteroclite, like yourself." I bowed my head to display the scars upon my own scalp. "I also was given speech as a child—"

"But as your birthright." Miss Scarlet reached to touch a node upon my temple. I shivered: the touch of that gnarled hand, so like and yet so alien to my own, filled me with a vast and lonely awe. "But all such miraculous venesections have a price. I lost all contact with my family, all pride in my race. When I last glimpsed the faces of my parents it was with the terrible knowledge that they were brute animals, and ever would be."

She pressed her fingers to her jutting mouth as though to stave off the painful memory. "And you, Aidan? What did they take from you?"

"My heart," I said softly. "My soul."

"But surely you have a heart, who travels in such romantic fashion with one of the Children of the Magdalene." She indicated Justice on the other side of the table. "And we all have souls."

"He is not my lover," I replied. "And my soul is not my own."

She edged closer to me, her petticoats rustling as they brushed my knees. "I understand," she said at last. She gazed so intently that I looked away. "There is another set of eyes that sees me through your own. You are possessed by an afreet. A demon."

She leaned back once more, resting her hand upon my knee reassuringly. "Well, Aidan, that is not such a bad thing. Changelings have their own kind of luck—literature teaches us *that* if nothing else!—as well as beauty; and while heartless and soulless they may still assist mortal men and women in their sanguine challenges—"

She coughed delicately, then recited in a soft voice:

> *"They that have power to hurt and will do none,*
> *That do not do the thing they most do show,*
> *Who, moving others, are themselves as stone,*
> *Unmoved, cold, and to temptation slow;*
> *They rightly do inherit heaven's graces,*
> *And husband nature's riches from expense;*
> *They are the lords and owners of their faces,*
> *Others but stewards of their excellence."*

I listened spellbound, hearing in her rich tones the echo of some distant battle, the clash and clamor of a great day dawning to which I would soon wake. Then I shook my head, as though dispersing a dream from my bed in the Horne Room.

"How do you know such things?"

A smile twitched across her wrinkled face as she tapped a finger to her lips. "Science has awakened her brother Magic from his long sleep. The goddess is alive, Magic is afoot. And you and I will follow in their train." She turned from me to take Toby's hand.

It may have been that Miss Scarlet and I spoke for longer than I imagined. Certainly I have since seen hours fly past when she was onstage, and her audiences stir themselves afterward as though resentful that they had been cheated by a performance of mere moments. I was surprised to see that already Lalagé and the Players had returned. The little server squeaked behind its mistress, its hold filled with bottles and globes and a small glass cylinder filled with absinthium of a poisonous green. Behind them Fabian juggled tamarillos and plums, dropping them much to the amusement of the pretty round-faced Player who carried a bowl of fieldcress and nasturtium blossoms. Last of all came the mustachioed girl, balancing on her broad shoulder a platter of salted pigeons.

Fabian tossed a plum to Toby. With a flourish Toby presented it to Miss Scarlet. Lalagé bowed to us, her head held proudly despite the crooked crown of leaves that had displaced the neat braids upon her brow.

"You bring me good luck, cousins!" she called out to Justice and myself. Justice grabbed her and kissed her on the mouth. Toby blew a kiss to Miss Scarlet.

Gitana set the platter on the table, adjusted her spectacles, and wiped her hands upon her thighs.

"Dinner is served," she announced, and flopped onto the grass.

Curiosity was a good sauce for this second meal. Toby and Fabian and Gitana and Mehitabel (I learned her name when Toby bellowed it, demanding more wine from the carafe she hugged between her knees) tucked in with much loud praise for Lalagé's food. Lalagé settled upon Justice's lap to feed him greengages and burgundy streams from the carafe, spilling most of it. Miss Scarlet ate quietly at my side, amassing a small arsenal of plum stones before her.

"An Ascendant among cooks!" Toby tossed another pigeon to Gitana. "Lalagé, why don't you join our troupe? Then we could eat like Governors every day!"

"And I could live like an animal, and sleep in a drafty theater, and wonder if my throat would be slit in the night." Lalagé stumbled to her feet. Mehitabel promptly took her place and began twirling Justice's hair about her greasy fingers.

I averted my eyes. Toby leaned across the table to me, covering both my hands with his huge one (his nails clean and well shaped, I noticed with some surprise, and stained with crimson dye).

"*You* would have no such objections to our life, Sieur Aidan," he suggested, and turned my hands palm-upward. "These hands would welcome hardening—" He brushed my fingertips. "Haven't you ever wanted to see our City by night, when the old moon cuts broad milky avenues through the Narrow Forest, and aardmen swim across the Tiger to hunt swans and lazars?"

"No," I said, and turned to watch Justice.

The new moon had risen. Lalagé had gone to pace among the trees, lighting a series of metal torches that sputtered fitfully before leaping into golden light. After a few minutes the conversation was punctuated by the hiss and sizzle of moths' Icarian flights.

"Ah, but there's better than that!" said Fabian. A handful of candicaine pipettes lay scattered like jackstraws on the table before him. He broke one, inhaled deeply. "There are birds with the breasts of women, and trees that will sing you to sleep—"

"And then suck you dry as a dead leaf," called Lalagé.

Fabian ignored her. "And you should see how the Paphian women treat you! Men, too, I suppose," he added and passed me a candicaine pipette.

I felt a small hand plucking at my sleeve and turned to see Miss Scarlet.

"Would you like to see our show?" she asked softly. She climbed onto the table so that her long skirts spilled

around her. Before I could reply, Fabian and Gitana and
Mehitabel had lunged through the shadows to where their
huge satchel lay by the gate. Toby stood and bowed to
Lalagé', then took Miss Scarlet by the hand and assisted
her down.

"You will excuse us while we prepare the entertainment," he said. As he passed Justice I saw the two of them
exchange knowing glances, and Toby winked broadly.

"Well!" said Lalagé. She smoothed her hair and looked
sideways at Justice, who grinned like a cat. "I suppose I'd
better clear some of this."

"Let me help you," said Justice, carelessly gathering an
armful of chipped plates and the pigeons' carcasses, but
being very careful not to upset a single wineglass or carafe.
He paused in front of me to stack more plates, then dipped
his head to brush my cheek. He turned away, scattering
Miss Scarlet's pyramid of plum stones. I watched them
disappear inside.

By the outer gate Toby's Players giggled and fought for
costumes and scripts. I was alone for the first time since
Justice had freed me. After several minutes I reached into
my pocket and withdrew Anna's hummingbird bandeau. I
turned it over in my hands, then slipped it onto my shorn
head, hoping that when she returned Miss Scarlet would
notice it. I felt my heart stirred by all this cheerful ruckus.
Closing my eyes, I sought within the knots of memory one
that would tighten this thread of feeling.

And found it upon a small raised stage, some fifty years
earlier, a stage lit by hissing gas lamps and smelling of
cheap cosmetics and powder, where a boy and girl in
matching broadcloth tunics and carrying matching blue
books carefully followed marks chalked upon the scuffed
floor, reciting.

> "'. . . I never had a brother;
> Nor can there be that deity in my nature
> Of here and everywhere. I had a sister
> Whom the blind waves and surges have de-
> voured . . .'"

Viola

This a memory of Emma's slipped somehow within my own, a stray cell sailing through me until it bumped another. Then another scene flashed through memory's aperture. Emma's bed, Aidan and Emma and mumbling Molly knocking heads together above the stained counterpane. A rush of displaced thought, like a wind careening through a broken window; and this image too spun off its string to join the others jumbled inside me.

I shivered in anticipation, for an instant thought I lay upon my bed in the Horne Room. But a hand drawn to my forehead touched only Anna's hummingbird bandeau. The flare of memory cooled, coalesced into a firefly dropping through the air, a glowing green scarab. I opened my hand. It lit there, wings blurring as they clicked back into their sturdy casing. I recalled the huge bees hovering in the afternoon air, the trees that had devoured Tast'annin's bodyguard. Fireflies and bees the size of hummingbirds. A talking chimpanzee. Even the Players seemed somewhat inflated, as if they all deigned to imagine one another wiser, lovelier, bolder, and braver than they really were; and by so dreaming had awakened to find it come true.

But now the firefly shakes its wings and buzzes from my hand. In the doorway Justice and Lalagé embrace before rejoining me at table, Justice preening slightly, his long hair tangled and his lip bleeding again. Fabian moves several of the metal torches so that their light falls upon the dark grass before us, then with a bow and a flourish announces:

" 'The Romantic History of Algernon Moncrieff and Gwendolen Fairfax,' as performed by Toby Rhymer, His Troupe, Featuring Miss Scarlet Pan as Lady Bracknell."

And I am a virgin witness as the Players begin their show.

Part Four

Blood at the Butterfly Ball

1. *The fragments of a repeatedly shattered world*

Westering light made a burnished cathedral of the trees when I finally paused in my flight through the forest. In my madness I had fled the Museum, wearing once more the brocaded tunic and ribands that marked me of the House Miramar: these and my sagittal the only arms I bore against the night. And night it would be soon; and I had lost my way.

Rumors that the Ascendants planned vengeance for a murder had alarmed the Regents enough to place sentries at each Museum. But the Technician posted by the North Gate scarcely glanced at me, so intent was she upon a volume of archaic holograms depicting the life cycles of extinct primates. In my Paphian garb I must have looked as though I was to attend the ball at High Brazil that evening. I had passed several high-ranking Curators in the Rotunda, all dressed in sober robes as they made their way to the North Gate to meet the palanquins from High Brazil that would bear them to the masque. I could have followed them, commandeered a palanquin for myself; but that would have meant answering questions, dealing with elders from High Brazil who would not have my name among those they were to receive. And I did not want to face Roland, not yet. . . .

So I left through the South Gate. The sentry raised her

head. Seeing only myself, she returned to her reading. I strode purposefully down the steps, through the broken columns facing the Narrow Forest, and to the edge of the forest itself. Here I hesitated. In the late afternoon light it was easy enough to orient myself to the northwest, where our Houses stood. In the distance the Obelisk pierced the trees' canopy, a somber point among all that glittering greenery. If I steered to its right I would eventually come to the Tiger Creek, or perhaps even a road leading to the Hill Magdalena Ardent. I imagined that I saw the river itself sparkling through the shifting leaves. Before my nerve could break I hurried beneath the trees.

Here the late summer's heat filtered through the leaves to drip in an almost palpable golden broth. Too late I wondered if perhaps I should have worn my Aide's shift—stained and ugly, but woven of lighter cloth. But pride and my determination to confront Roland at the Masque and regain standing among my people had made me choose my own clothes—which quickly grew damp and weighted from the heat. My heavy braid burned against my neck. I winced and shrugged it from shoulder to shoulder, until it snagged on a bramble hedge. I tugged it loose and tucked it into my collar. Almost immediately I snared my sleeves upon the same briars. I pulled the thorns free, careful not to tear my brocade; another step and I was trapped once more. Neither were my boots fit for this sort of travel. The marshy ground soaked the felt soles until with each step I thought I sank to my ankles in muck. But I scrambled on, trying to keep a spur of grief and indignation at my heels.

The late hour held little chance of my meeting anyone else, although there was much traffic among the Museums that bordered this part of the forest. For a short distance well-trodden paths wound between great oaks and wild apples already burdened with fruit: west to the Historians; south to the Weavers and Aviators and Botanists who trafficked with the Ascendants. To the northwest stretched a broken stone road leading to the Zoological Garden, perhaps an hour's walk from here.

I followed this path. I hoped it would bring me to the Tiger Creek, which I could then follow to where it poured into the Rocreek not far from High Brazil. Myrtle and kudzu choked the path; slender apple and cherry saplings sprang from the ferns, heralding new wild orchards. With only a few hours of daylight remaining I walked determinedly, fending off tree limbs and straggling vines as I tried to keep the Obelisk in sight.

I went slowly, swiping at trailing vines and strands of spiderweb heavy with pollen and the striped husks of butterflies. Other trails intersected mine. These seemed to lead nowhere, and were probably known only to the lazars who traveled them on their midnight raids and forays. Certainly only lazars or the great hunting beasts—wolves and wild dogs, cat-a-mountains and eyra and the dog-faced aardmen who figured so prominently in Doctor Foster's most gruesome stories—could slip down those strangled green tunnels.

The ground beneath my foot suddenly shuddered. A strangled shriek made me yelp and jump back, terrified. In the center of the path squatted a couvado toad, fat and round and misshapen as a rotted pumpkin. As I stared it grinned fatuously at me. Then its huge mouth gaped open and, with a gurgling belch, it turned itself inside out, exposing its pulsing heart and vivid entrails.

I covered my mouth with both hands and quickly turned away. Blindly I chose another path that seemed to veer toward the setting sun. I staggered down this, stumbling madly through honeysuckle thickets and rank orchards.

2. The light of imagination is quenched in the darkness of a history so ancient.

The farther in I went, the less clearly marked was the trail. Eventually I found myself in a tiny clearing where a dozen breaks in the underbrush might have been paths leading deeper into the forest. I chose one because pale blue veronica carpeted the earth there. As my feet crushed the soft blue mat of flowers their blossoms wept sweet tears. I hesitated, breathing their fragrance and recalling the name Doctor Foster had taught us for these tiny blooms: lose-all-care. They had a haunting scent, redolent of spring rain and the promise of twilight. But when I started to move again I found that I had forgotten which way I wanted to go. I turned, and sighted a patch of narcissus nodding in the bole of a dead tree. I shook my head, trying to recall which path was mine. Surely I wanted to follow the sun? This way, then, where the light poured through a gap in the trees . . .

But a moment later I knelt among the white narcissus. I did not wonder how they came to bloom there in early Autime, which were harbingers of spring; nor how the faintest of breezes seemed to make them whisper and sigh like frightened children, so that I crooned comforting words to them. I only knew they were the most lovely flowers I had ever seen, and I did not want to leave them.

And I might have remained there until full dark brought

my doom, had not a fire ant climbed and stung my wrist. Its bite seared through my entire hand. I gasped, killing the ant with an ungrateful swat. Then rubbing my eyes I stumbled back to my feet.

Ruddy light now filtered through the leaves. I had long since lost sight of the Obelisk, and hours might have passed since I first entered the woods. My flesh crawled as I recalled Doctor Foster's tales of the evil flowers spawned by the rains of roses: of Philantha Persia's abduction by lazars when she went to hear daffodils laughing by the river; of Botanists lured to their deaths in the Rocreek by sighing hyacinths with the eyes of women; of almond-scented lilies whose fragrance alone brought madness and death. Such stories I had always dismissed; yet here I was now, bewitched by a patch of narcissus! I moved to brush the leaves from my hair, and as I did so saw that a slender green shoot had wrapped itself around my sagittal as I lay dreaming. I cried out and yanked the vine from my wrist. Heedless of the cries of the flowers I trampled, I turned and ran.

I forced myself onward, biting my hand to keep from falling prey to the narcotic fragrance that seemed to rise at my every step. But I could not cause myself enough pain to keep fully awake. Every few minutes I would pause, and only when my head nodded against my chest would I start awake and then stumble on. The ruddy light deepened to violet. A great thrashing of wings and twittering signaled that birds were coming to roost above me. Twigs and leaves and moths fluttered about my head as they made their nests for the night. I paused to brush the leaves from my hair. When I began to walk again it was with heavy steps, as though the earth clung to my boots, reluctant to let me pass. I glanced down, then yelled in disgust.

A silvery track stretched before me. Each step I took brought me in contact with this. My feet were sticky with some gleaming stuff. A few paces ahead humped a slug as thick and long as my arm, its pearly eyestalks waving as it oozed forward with a sound like lewd kissing. At the sight of that monstrous thing all hope left me. Blinking away tears, I floundered from the path and threw myself against a twisted apple tree, hugging it in despair. I glanced down at the sagittal, which seemed to hold my last promise of ease.

"Franca," I choked, and turned so that my back rested against the tree's broad bole. Then I opened my tunic and held my fist above my chest, willing the sagittal to strike. But it was satiated by Franca's death, or my desire was not strong enough to wake it. It remained a lifeless ornament: heavy, cold as bronze. I struck myself with it, bruising my ribs; yelled hoarse nonsense like one gone berserk until I woke the little golden finches and they fled the apple's boughs crying peevishly. And still my sagittal slumbered. It would not strike its host.

Finally I gave up and sprawled at the foot of the apple tree to wait for death. It would come quickly enough, here: I need only sleep until the flowers took me. Or lazars, or aardmen. I glared at the faithless sagittal, then drew it closer to my face. The translucent shell now gleamed like an amethyst held up to a candle flame. I could even see the silhouette of the propodium curled inside, a dark finger gloved in light. I stared at it numbly.

Moths began to hover in the twilight, drawn to the sagittal's dim glow. They drifted before my face like falling blossoms, and it seemed that the beating of their wings somewhat cooled the heavy night air. The night-coils woke as well. The tree I leaned against rustled as the flowering vines stirred, their scent a sweet syrup. I tried to fight this new languor, which felt as if a thicker, slower blood dripped into my veins. But it was hopeless. Within minutes I was yawning, and finally rested my head upon soft ferns.

I dreamed fitfully: of Franca, her pale face framed by falcon's eyes; of Roland panting above me, his hands enchained with light. Once I started awake to see that dozens of white moths had settled upon my chest and face. Their wings opened and shut as they fed upon the nectar that dripped from the night-coils, their tongues unfurling in black threads. I brushed them off, but they only wafted a few inches above me before lighting onto my legs again. With a sigh I fell back to the ground.

Then I must have dreamed; but a dream such as I never

had before, a dream that seemed to show me the dreams of all things that had been, and died; and then all the dreams of dreams; and last of all those of Death himself dreaming of all that was to be—

Of archosaurs rising from their adamant beds to pluck planets from the void; of rivers boiling, and humming trees, and beasts that wept like men; of metal ships that ravished the sun into a thousand stars, and a flaming cathedral rising from the blackened earth; of myriad entombed figures released from their stony beds, and a demonic girl whose eyes burned in a face that mirrored my own; of dying children whose voices rang out like sweet bells, and a cadaver who spoke sagely with Death.

Of all of these, and untold others—myself and Roland and Miramar, and Fancy and Francesca and Doctor Foster, too—all of us, linked in a ronde set to the sound of hollow pipes booming as we swept across the sky.

And then I woke: to a kiss cold as Franca's, so that I tried to will the feathery crush of bracken beneath me into an unyielding marble floor. But the ferns crackled as I groaned and stirred; and the eyes that met mine were not hers.

"Wake, Raphael," a voice said.

I breathed in sharply, shaking the last drunken moths from me. Night had fallen. In the deep blue sky that showed through breaks in the trees I glimpsed a silver spar of moon and many stars. I stumbled to my feet, bracing myself against the apple tree as I tried to remember where I was and what dream had brought me there.

"We are waking now," someone whispered. I rubbed the nectar from my eyes, blinking as I tried to see who spoke to me from the shadows. A flash of terror warned me of lazars; but a lazar would not know my name.

And a lazar would not be so beautiful.

"Who are you?" I stammered.

He dropped from a tree a few paces from me. A glimmer of light hung about him, as though the frail moonlight sought him here gladly. He smiled: a boy a little younger than myself; the most beautiful boy I had ever seen.

"Raphael," he replied. His voice was honeyed, not yet

broken, but mocking as no child's voice should be. That, more than his unearthly beauty, frightened me. "You know me."

For an instant my thoughts careened through all those I had loved, vainly seeking his among pillowed faces in Saint-Alaban, Persia, High Brazil, my own House. But no Paphian would crop his golden curls thus about that white forehead; no Paphian ever had skin so fine that the moonlight seemed to melt into it to glow from within eyes the color of moon lilies.

"No," I said. "I do not know you. I would never have forgotten you."

"Already you have forgotten me," he said. Suddenly it seemed that his face altered. For an instant Franca's features passed over his own: splotches of leaves and mold upon his face the quick reflection of bruises that had blurred her cheeks and breast. I gasped and stepped toward her.

But it was not Franca. Her features rippled and were gone. Instead I found myself reaching for a bloated corpse propped against the apple tree, its hollow eyes wormed with foxfire, its shattered jaw hanging limply upon a neck ulcerated by the rotted remains of a hempen rope. I cried out: and then he stood there once more, still and white and lovely in the fitful moonlight.

"I do know you," I whispered. I shivered uncontrollably. "The Hanged Boy . . ."

He nodded. "That is a name," he said after a long moment. "You may call me by another." Smiling, he crossed his arms upon his pale hairless chest.

"Lord . . ." I began.

"No," he murmured. I could almost imagine that the unblinking green eyes regarded me with pity. He stepped toward me. I was shaking now and crouched on all fours like a dog, my hands kneading the earth frantically as I tried to steady myself.

"Please go." I shut my eyes. "Please, please go . . ."

"No, Raphael," he repeated. "We are waking now. . . ."

He reached for me with a hand that gleamed with a hard pure light, a hand white and cold as bone. His touch evoked the frigid impression of the kiss that had awakened me. And then I knew that I had not really awakened earlier; that in my seventeen years I had never been awake. Only now; because only he could wake me. I felt as though those fingers bored into my skull, probing the soft center of my brain where sleeping thoughts trembled for release. I would have cried aloud, but that cold clenched my jaws shut, gripped my neck in an unyielding vise, froze my eyes so that I stared up at him and trembled at the sight.

Because such beauty as his shrieked for worship. Those luminous green eyes, his face and body radiantly white, that exquisite form . . . I was stirred by desire such as I had never known, save when I had seen the lazar's corpse so long ago, and Franca's that afternoon. And that terrified me more than all else: because I knew that such beauty could not be evil, any more than mine could be; that such beauty would seek and find worship surely as a flower seeks sunlight and rain.

But even as his beauty roused me I saw the livid horror seething within his eyes, the corruption and utter madness of extinction that he expelled as unconsciously as I breathed air. And as I had seen within Franca's broken face a strange and compelling beauty, I knew that from now on I would glimpse within whatever was lovely the foul thing it would become.

And then I did scream, and begged him to take back that knowledge and vision, the awful counterpoint to my soaring dream.

"No," he whispered. His cold mouth pressed against mine. "You must learn: it is all one, Raphael. It is all one. . . ."

At these words I fainted. When I woke he was gone.

3. The birth of yesterday

I thrashed to wakefulness, tangling my fingers in the grass. The moon had scarcely moved across the sky. From the night-coils' tongues still dripped a slow sweet rain. For a moment I thought it might have been a nightmare brought on by those poisonous blossoms, or the ghastly white moths they fed.

Then I saw the jackal.

It crouched a few paces from me, beneath that same tree whence *he* had dropped a short while ago. Like a wild dog, slender, with a long muzzle and pointed ears; but with hair the color of frost, milky white except where a darker stripe crossed its back from tail to head. Escaped from the Zoologists, maybe—they bred them for hunting —although I had never seen a white jackal before.

Perhaps I had grown brash in the face of all the terrors of this accursed place. Because I was not afraid of it.

"Go on!" I yelled, shying a stone at its muzzle. The jackal darted to one side. I would have thrown myself upon it and strangled it, I was that maddened. I grabbed the overhanging limb of a tree and glared. It did not run away. It sank back upon its haunches again, head cocked to one side, regarding me with an alarmingly prescient gaze. I snatched up another stone but it slipped into the shadows to reappear in a moment—so close that I dropped my weapon and tripped in my haste to get away from it.

As I fell, something snaked about my ankle, something

soft yet unyielding. I tried to scramble to my feet and collapsed, my elbows sinking into the loamy earth. When I glanced back I saw that a vine thick as my wrist had crept from the tree and encircled my ankle. It was pulling me backward, as if a hidden green winch cranked me toward the tree. Other vines disentangled themselves and looped to the earth, their pale trumpets opening and closing as if scenting something besides their own sickly fragrance. As the vines humped toward me I saw that the small and ineffectual green thorns protecting each bloom had turned bright red, as an anole's throat blossoms when it sights a foe. They whistled softly as the vines flailed through the air. I rolled onto my back, striking at one as it whipped past my face. Like a serpent it drew back, the wind hissing through the hollow thorns. Other vines lashed about my legs. The trumpet-shaped flowers swelled and disgorged a heavy fluid onto my legs, thick as honey and with a cloying scent. Where it seeped through the fabric of my trousers I felt my legs grow numb.

The first vine tightened about my foot. I felt a prickling where another, smaller loop of vegetation attached itself. As I watched helplessly the vine lashed against my leg, until one or another of the tiny thorns pierced my skin. There was little pain, but I saw a trickle of blood seep from my boot.

That same odd fearlessness stayed with me in these moments. I dug my elbows into the soft earth and pushed myself up, watching as my own blood welled into the vines. They pulsed slightly, the pale jade flesh darkening to evergreen where they fed. The narcotic effect of the thorns kept me from pain. No doubt it dulled my senses as well. When I saw the jackal rushing to nip at my feet my first thought was to kick it away from me, and I twitched my legs uselessly. I watched in mute amazement as, snarling, it darted between the thrashing vines, tearing at them with its fangs and slipping between them like quicksilver. The thorns slid through its silvery fur like the teeth of a comb, catching nothing but air. The dog leaped and snapped a thick vine in two. The pieces fell, squirming, and I realized this was the vine that had held me fast. I yanked myself free from the myriad tendrils clinging to my tunic and rolled away. The jackal spun about and followed me through the writhing vines.

In the darkness one path shone brighter than the others, moonlit. I stumbled toward it only to find the jackal blocking my way. I turned and ducked under a tangle of ivy; the jackal was there in front of me.

"Go *on!*" I yelled, pulling a rotted branch from a tree and brandishing it. The animal sat back and cocked its head. Behind us the night-coils thrashed and hissed harmlessly, out of reach. "Damn you," I swore.

I was almost as angry with myself as I was fearful of the animal, because hadn't it just saved me? Jackals were wild dogs, and dogs were rumored to be friendly toward humans sometimes. Miramar had often told of how as a child he had tamed a wild dog that could do tricks. I had seen him weep to recall it. Doctor Foster verified that they had an ancient and noble history before the concatenations that had resulted in the aardmen and other geneslaves. Miramar swore that dogs could understand human speech.

But wild dogs hunted and indiscriminately fed upon humans, as did the aardmen. I slashed the air with my stick, glancing around me for signs of other predatory plants or beasts lurking in the moonlit trees. The jackal cocked its head, following me with its slanted eyes. It did not appear hungry. When I took a step forward it rose and followed, tail twitching.

"What do you want?" I stopped and faced it head-on. A small glade tufted with pale myrtle reflected the starry break in the trees above us. The jackal halted, then threw back its head and cried.

Not the barking or howling I had so often heard in the distance, but a mournful yodeling that had the varied cadence and intonation of speech. Behind us the night-coils grew still and the wind died. The jackal alone cried out, as if calling to the very stars. At that sound the hair on my arms and neck stood up. My dream rushed back upon me: the dream of the Hanged Boy, whom the Saint-Alabans call the Gaping One.

He who is also named by them the Lord of Dogs.

"What do you want of me?" I repeated, but I lowered my stick. "I am not of your people." My voice cracked like a boy's, and I felt foolish.

The animal remained poised, its muzzle pointed starward. I looked up to see what it watched there. Through the break in the leaves I saw the new moon. Many stars: the Polar Star; the hunting stars Cerebus and Sirius; uncounted others, nameless and no doubt dead to any eyes but mine. As I stared, a faint point of white tracked slowly across the sky, one of the Ascendants' sad lights doomed to count the clouds forever. I watched until it disappeared behind the leaves. Still the beast watched the sky. I sighed, turned to go. With a low growl the jackal warned me, and I glanced up.

From the center of the sky welled a brightness, a silver rent in the firmament. It grew so large that I gasped, thinking the heavens would be torn apart to show the blinding void that hides behind the fastnesses of space. But no. It swelled until a second moon burned there, tear-shaped, sliding through the darkness and leaving a trail of fire in its wake as it streaked across the sky. Then it disappeared in a molten glare, tail glowing like a dull ember.

"Sweet Magdalene," I breathed.

For thus had each Ascension been heralded, by new moons appearing in the heavens to flame and burst like mafic-lights. And suddenly I heard from every point of the City distant cries and clamor. From very far off came the screams of sirens, the thrumming of fougas, and faintest of all the boom of congreves being launched across the river.

I turned, stumbling against the jackal. It grabbed my trouser leg with its teeth and tugged insistently. By now I had no doubts but that I had somehow fallen into an adventure such as Doctor Foster had so often recited to us. As easily as a serpent shedding its skin I sloughed off any reservations I might have had a day earlier about following a ghostly animal through a forest where gods walked and the flowers thirsted for the blood of men.

"Where you will, Anku!" I said. That had been the name of Miramar's tame dog. This one fairly danced upon hearing it, tossing its head back and letting forth once again that weird wailing song. Then it darted into the woods, its white flanks gleaming through the tangled brush. I followed, steeling my heart against the echo of distant sirens and airships. I ran with wild delight, daring them to hunt me who ran with Death's dog.

4. *Organic beings of a different character*

Through the woods we plunged. It seemed to me that days had fled since first I entered that place, but the moon had scarcely crept across the sky. It was still early evening. With Anku racing ahead of me I ran, head held low to keep him in my sight. The trees seemed to shrink from our passage. Beneath my feet mandragons puled as I crushed them in spurts of white froth. Neither these nor the cries of the betulamia, slender trees like birches that reached to embrace me, could frighten or impede me now. Somewhere ahead of us the river slumbered and the Houses of Eros guttered with golden light. Somewhere Roland embraced another pathic and coursed the first slow steps of the pavane that began each Paphian masque.

At the thought I clenched my teeth. A new kind of lust stirred me: a sudden fierce need for pain and harrowing, a raging desire to wrench the veil of flesh and tendon from Roland's face and slake this fever with his blood. About my wrist the sagittal burned with a pulsing violet light. I laughed and raised my fist so that it lit the path before me. Anku turned, his white teeth glittering.

The trees thinned to a copse pricked with flashing fire-flies. Anku bounded through the tall grass. I hesitated, blinking in the brighter moonlight that spilled onto the coppice. A few yards ahead the shallow reflections of stars glimmered across the Tiger Creek. I whooped in delight and raced across the field to splash in the shallow water.

Already Anku waded there, drinking and shaking his muzzle. I sloshed to where the water flowed knee-high, gazing
upstream to see if I could locate the Hill Magdalena Ardent hidden behind the dense foliage. And yes, if I
squinted I could just make out the more refined silhouettes
of ruins and even a pale glimmering that was surely the
lights of High Brazil.

At that sight my heart leaped with an overwhelming
desire to see my people: Miramar and Ketura, Small
Thomas and Benedick, even old Doctor Foster.

And Fancy. Most of all, little Fancy, who danced through
all my dreams and alone remained a kind of light to me
when I was most desperate. Even now, when about me
reared the black spires of the Narrow Forest and lazars
hooted in the distance, the thought of Fancy, somewhere,
(missing me perhaps?) waking from her evening nap to
dress for the ball calmed me as nothing else ever could. All
the madness that had befallen me could be kept at bay by
the knowledge that she sang and slept and danced there
upon the Paphian's hill; as if I was like the princess in the
story, who could not be killed by fire or sword or swivel
because her heart was hidden safely elsewhere. The bitter
longing that had hurried me through the woods melted
into a gentler need: for the comfort of those like me; for
laughter and lovely things; above all for forgiveness for
having valued wisdom above the varieties of love.

When Anku nudged me I started and nearly fell into the
shallow water. I kicked him away from me. He growled
plaintively, but suddenly I wanted no more of him, no
more of this forest or of the Curators and the evils they had
awakened in me. I was turning to wade upstream, to
where I thought the Tiger ran into the river, when I saw
the figures lined upon either shore watching us.

In the moonlight they might almost have been en-
chanted trees, betulamias or bitter alders: thin figures with
spindly arms upraised, silent, their eyes black in haggard
faces. Four of them upon one bank, three on the other.
Most were smaller than myself. Even in the dim light I
could see that they were children; but more than children.

Lazars.

Beside me Anku stood alert. I glanced down at him. The
eyes that met mine were so obviously fired by some uncanny intelligence that I shivered, standing in the middle
of that warm and languid river. I lifted my head and met
the gaze of the lazar who seemed the eldest. A girl, flanked
by two boys upon the farther bank. Her long hair burned
almost white by the sun, face dark as though stained by
some dye. About her shoulders hung the remains of a yellow janissary's jacket. A carcanet of braided human hair
hung around her neck. The boys beside her were very
young, seven or eight years perhaps. One of them had
flaming red hair, and was making faces at the group on the
other bank. When I caught his eyes he giggled and hid
behind the tall girl. The others were young as well, so thin
and dirty I could not make out if they were boys or girls,
with their rags and tattered hanks of hair tied about their
waists. None of them bore a weapon, save their eyes—
huge and glittering and feverish: *starved.*

Still, they were so young and thin, and really they were
only children, after all. I smiled, and took a step forward.

In an instant they were on me. I had a sideways glimpse
of the two little boys springing from the sward before I fell.
One of them clung to my back, kicking and screaming as
he dug his fingernails into my neck. The other wrapped his
arms around my knees. Then he butted me in the groin
with his head. I doubled over in pain.

And panicked. They were lazars, not children: diseased
ghouls. I tried to flee, but tripped and fell into the river. I
felt the first boy clambering up my back until his weight
forced my head beneath the water. I tried to knock him
away, but now the air was shrill with their cries. I inhaled
water, choking; felt other hands swarming over me. Then
another sound, a hollow roar booming through the rush of
water in my ears. A shriek, abruptly cut off. The knot of
squirming hands withdrew. I rolled a few yards down-
stream, gagging and trying to wipe the water from my
eyes as I staggered to my feet.

In the river six children now stood, the water roiling
about their ankles. Anku half-crouched in the shallows
among them. At his feet lay the red-haired boy, blood

streaming from his torn throat like a tangle of his own bright hair. Coughing, I splashed upstream. Anku lifted his head, dipped his dark muzzle into the river until it was washed clean. Then he bounded to join me.

Three of the remaining lazars grabbed the dead child by his hands and dragged him to shore. The others drew closer to the tall girl. One wept silently, thumb in her mouth. Her eyes met mine beseechingly and I felt a stab of regret, that she looked to me—the oldest one present—for comfort. I turned to face the tall girl.

"Let me go," I called to her. Anku pressed close against my leg. "I only seek passage to High Brazil. I must attend a Masque there—"

The girl took the hands of the two beside her and for the first time spoke. "They are hungry." The children began to cry.

I glanced at the near shore. The lazars who had dragged the dead boy there now crouched beside him. A third child fumbled at the sopping rags she wore until she withdrew something that gleamed. I averted my eyes.

"You have him now," I said. "Let me go."

"He is too small," the girl replied. Her tone was surprisingly deep for one so young. She drew the two beside her closer, patting their heads in that absent manner that children have when they are imitating adults.

"Shh," she said, glancing at the shore. "He sleeps now. Go help Tristin."

Tristin. A Paphian name. I bit my tongue to keep from crying out at this awful thing: to think of one of my own cousins meeting such an end! And yet it happened to some of us every time there was a rain of roses. Children and older Paphians (but mostly children, because they could not run as quickly) were caught outside before they had a chance to flee. And I had never admitted to myself that the lazars hunting and dying in the streets were very likely lovers I had been paired with on the Hill Magdalena Ardent.

The oldest girl pushed away the two little ones. They splashed across the river to join the others, looking back fearfully at Anku.

"A star fell tonight," the girl said after a moment. She scratched her chest, adjusting the torn yellow jacket until it closed about her hips. "In the Cathedral we saw fougas." She cocked her head, listening to the dying echo of sirens.

"So did I." I looked over my shoulder to make certain there were no others gathering there. Hugging my arms against my chest, I took a step toward the far bank. The girl regarded me with those piercing black eyes and kicked at the shallows.

"You are a lazar," she said at last.

"No," I said. "I am a Paphian. I go to the Hill Magdalena Ardent, to High Brazil for a Masque. Let me pass—"

"You dress like one of us," she said, indicating my torn clothes. Anku tilted his head to watch us. The girl pointed at him with her thumb.

"That is a dog." She said this as though expecting me to refute it.

"Of sorts. It's a jackal."

"We had a dog," she said wistfully. "They ate him. I was too small so they took me. From the Zoo."

"The Zoo," I repeated. I glanced to the northwest, where on an unseen hill hidden by white oaks the Zoologists lived. A Curator, then. I looked back at her, the dark frets of her ribs shadowed beneath the torn jacket, her gaunt blackened face; the white scars on her arms where the rains had fallen. Thirteen years old, maybe. "What's your name?"

"Pearl." She moved closer to me with a slow uneven gait, as though immeasurably fatigued or sedated. I backed away. Behind her I could see the others swarming over the boy's corpse, some of them heaping sticks and branches on the shingle beside him.

"Your skin is so white," she said. She stretched a hand to touch my chest.

Anku growled, but the girl only glanced at him. I shrank from her touch. She shrugged and shuffled a few steps off.

"Let me pass," I said. Anku's eyes followed Pearl as she drew nearer. "I'll kill you otherwise—"

She regarded my raised fist with its dimly glowing sagittal and shrugged. "I am pledged to Death already," she said. Grinning, she bared her teeth at me. Then she tipped her head and stared at me more closely. "I think you too are promised to the Gaping One."

She made a mocking bow, then coughed. "I will tell the Consolation of the Dead that I have seen the Gaping Lord's chosen one playing with a white dog in the river." Anku's growl grew louder. He crouched as though to spring. Pearl laughed and shambled a few meters off.

"Who is the Consolation of the Dead?" I called after her.

She smiled, flashing those yellow teeth again as she shook her head. "Our master," she said as she trudged onto the shore. "The Lord of the Engulfed Cathedral."

She turned and waved. "The little ones are afraid of that dog," she called. "So they will not kill you. And I am no longer hungry. I go very soon to meet the Gaping One, the Lord of Dogs. I will tell him I saw you here."

Her laughter was bright and clear as any Paphian child's, and she raised a hand in imitation of the Paphian's beck. "I was a Zoologist's favorite daughter. Now I have the plague that softens the bones until they melt into the skin like butter. Still—"

She made an awkward pirouette, stopping at the river's edge. "I like the face of your dog."

Laughing, she kicked water at Anku, who sprang snarling at her. But already she had stumbled back onto the shingle, where the younger children greeted her with mewling cries and pulled her into the circle of their bonfire's glare.

5. Well-preserved fossils

Anku and I crossed the Tiger to the shore nearest the Hill Magdalena Ardent. Behind us the lazars' shadows drowned the smaller flare of their bonfire. In a few minutes they were lost to sight.

After a short time the hill we climbed began a downward slope. I recognized in the near distance the first of our Houses, Saint-Alaban's ornate spires and minarets rising above the black spirals of cypresses that lined its curving drive. I half-ran, half-skidded down the grassy hillside to where the rutted Old Road was still maintained by the Curators for their occasional passage through the City. I paused.

Hunching against a stump, I smoothed my tunic over my knees, flicking shards of bark and dead tendrils from my leg. The sight of the robe's tattered hem reminded me that I was scarcely attired for a masque. I touched my hair, tried to untangle the mass of knots and torn leaves. No wonder Pearl had mistaken me for lazar.

And then with a grim smile I decided that I would enter the Butterfly Ball as such. It would make it that much more difficult for me to be recognized, for who would expect the catamite Raphael Miramar to appear thus—uninvited, as well!—gaunt and unkempt, yet fair and murderous as the Gaping One himself, guarded by a laughing dog and the hidden prong of a poisonous whelk? I laughed, tearing off a narrow piece of fabric from my tunic to bind back my hair;

and thought blood thoughts. I called Anku and headed for
the road.

I had traveled this route before, though never by moonlight and never alone. The Hill Magdalena Ardent rose
before me, broidered with a road paved white with
crushed marble, the tilted remains of lamp posts strung
with globes of *ignis florum*. All afternoon the elders must
have been busy, releasing the swallowtails and sambur
moths in whose honor the Butterfly Ball was held each
Autime. Sambur moths do not feed in their adult state.
They live for only one night, to breed, and it was this brief
transit from chrysalis to shattered husk that we celebrated.
The butterflies drifted across the road, their hind wings
dragging across the broken stones and staining them with
their faintly luminous pigment. But the moths flitted everywhere, drawn especially to the greenish globes. The
slow retort of their wings caused their brilliant eyespots to
blink drowsily, so that the night seemed to cloak a great
invisible Argus.

A sambur moth with branching coral antennae fluttered
so near that the hairs on the back of my hand prickled at its
wings' breath. I raised my sagittal, concentrating the pulse
of my heart and its attendant furies until the shell began to
gleam. I opened my palm. Drawn to the sagittal's violet
glow the moth landed there. It crept across my hand to my
wrist. For a moment it stopped, feathered antennae
quivering. I thought of Roland betraying me, of my rage
and lust at Franca's corpse, and felt my blood quicken.

The black spark of the sagittal's single tooth shot out,
stabbing the moth's thorax and impaling it. Then the spine
withdrew. The tiny legs stiffened against my skin, the hollow abdomen released an atom of air as a breeze stirred its
frozen wings. I blew upon it, and watched it float to join
the exhausted legions of its kind who crawled across the
white road. Beckoning Anku, I stepped between the dying
butterflies.

At the hill's summit glittered the House High Brazil,
myriad globes and candles strung about its eaves, prismatic reflections shimmering across the famed Hagioscopic Embrasures. Numerous palanquins littered the oval

drive, the elders who had drawn them now dozing or playing *go*. Their soft voices and the click of stones moving upon the wooden boards made my head swim with nostalgia. I hesitated. Only the gentle press of Anku's muzzle against my thigh stirred me to walk from the half-lit road into the drive.

A louder click as all the stones fell at once and a dozen pale faces turned to gaze at me. I swallowed, then tossing back my hair I touched three fingers to my lips in the Paphian's beck. The elder nearest me regarded me shrewdly, kohl and the heightened shimmer of octine giving a faint cast of ardor to the ruins of a lovely face.

"You have traveled far to join us, cousin," he said.

Another elder rose to greet me, a woman with faded yellow hair and a tooth missing from her quick smile. "Pass slowly among us," she said, laughing, and stroked my arm as I entered their circle. Other hands reached for me. I tried not to shudder at their limp touch, the awareness that the sight of me candled a faint flame within their sunken faces and caused their hands to linger upon my waist.

"Not so far," I replied. The woman gave a little gasp. Glancing back, I saw that Anku trotted a few meters behind me. "We walked from Miramar. The animal is tamed—"

"I remember Gower Miramar's dog," said another voice. I turned to see Delfine Persia rising to greet me with a crippled bow. "As I remember you, Raphael."

"Delfine?" I forced myself to smile and extended my hand, letting three fingers brush her lower lip. As a child I had been Delfine's favorite. She had been old then, perhaps thirty, but with skin still glowing and firm and soft brown eyes that followed me hungrily as I pranced about her seraglio. I had not seen her in many years. Her face had grown bloated, her dark hair streaked as with cobwebs; the gentle eyes betrayed by kohl that caked in sagging creases beneath brows plucked in two fine arches. The soft arms were now muscled from bearing palanquins and her bare shoulders showed the marks of much labor.

"Sweet child, to remember my name." She laughed. Cupping my chin, she tilted my face toward her own. "But how you've changed!" For an instant an expression flickered across her face, something between dismay and triumph. She touched my hair, grimacing as she tugged a dead leaf from my brow.

"An unusual costume," remarked a man whose pocked face was not much older than my own. His eyes glinted raw malice. "Whose guest are you?"

"Roland Nopcsa's." I heard several of the others whispering among themselves before the elder who had first greeted me turned to speak.

"Roland Nopcsa arrived this afternoon and engaged Whitlock High Brazil for the evening. I am of High Brazil and bore them here after their matinee castigations at Illyria." He stared at me with some sympathy. "Perhaps another will vouch for you—"

"I'll vouch for myself, then," I said.

The youngest elder laughed. "Not here, Miramar! Look at him—" He flicked disdainfully at my torn robe. "He's been dismantled in favor of Whitlock. I heard Godiva Persia say so at balneal this morning."

A murmur passed through the group. I glanced at Anku resting in the shadows. I drew myself up and turned to Delfine.

"I bring this dog to Nopcsa as a gift to win back my favor."

Delfine laughed. "So Gower Miramar won Jellica Persia at Semhane that year with a spotted eyra!"

An effete man with the Illyrian calyx tattooed upon his palm giggled, peering into the shadows where Anku's eyes glowed carmine. "Another albino! Whitlock will be furious—"

I laughed suddenly at the thought of Whitlock's discomfiture (although I had been fond enough of him when we were paired at Winterlong). The elders too seemed delighted at this unexpected entertainment. I wondered how long it had been since any of them had been allowed to attend a masque as anything but servitors. Not long enough for the pocked Persian to grow accustomed to being a slave: that I gathered from the venomous looks he continued to shoot at me.

"But this is Whitlock's House nonetheless, and not Miramar's," he hissed, tugging at a plait of jet-black hair that remained the single aureole of his beauty. "And look how he is dressed! Poor auspice, to mock the Gaping One on Her Hill."

"Oh, Balfour is just jealous, Raphael," said Delfine. She let her hand slip between my legs in the caress called *carnassial*, for which she had been noted in her youth. "Whitlock is his cousin-german. *I* think it's a wonderful idea, and so original—an albino jackal! Wherever did you find it?"

"I captured it beneath the Obelisk."

"Escaped from the Zoologists, I imagine. I never realized you were accomplished with animals, too," said the Illyrian admiringly.

"He was a gifted child," said Delfine with pride. As her face drew nearer to mine I could smell the sickly odor of gingko negus upon her breath.

"Do you remember *me* from Winterlong, Raphael?" a new voice piped. Clammy hands clutched at my shoulders.

"And me?" said another as she stroked my cheek.

"You never forgot dear Delfine, did you, my cherub?" Her rough hands scuttled across my thighs.

"Of course not," I said. Carefully I disentangled myself. I wobbled a few paces to where Anku lay and leaned against a lamp post. I stared into a globe of glowing orchids as I tried to steady my trembling hands. I drew a deep breath.

"You are all too much of a temptation for me, friends!" I raised my head to look at them. Delfine with one arm draped about the Illyrian's shoulder. A trio of gouty *paillards* ogling me from behind the Illyrian. Balfour glaring as he twisted his braid about his scarred hands. And behind them others shambling toward the light, their leering faces stripped of all beauty and warmth to betray the harsh ligaments of a lifetime of unslaked desire. I felt my knees buckle beneath me, but before I could falter Anku leaped to his feet and let forth that weird yodeling cry.

A reluctant sigh from the elders. One by one they settled back onto the drive. Delfine stooped to retrieve the scattered ovals of her game and cast me a final longing glance. Only Balfour remained standing, staring at me defiantly.

"I hope you are banished for interjacence," he said. Low peals of laughter greeted this, and he turned and stalked into the shadows.

"Forgive our hasty departure." I bowed. "But I must try to mend this breach between my mentor and myself—"

"Fare well, Raphael," said Delfine, touching her lips. "Remember me at the Butterfly Ball!"

"Remember me! Remember me!" the others joined in with soft voices. The dust beneath them stirred as their fingers fluttered to mark the Paphian's beck.

"I will," I called back haltingly; "I will—" And with head bowed I hurried toward the marble steps of High Brazil.

6. Primitive colors

Once it had been the Antipodal Embassy. Elaborate carvings in the marble facade still displayed the writhing faces of capuchins and marmosets and uakaris. The main doorway's lintel was the painted effigy of a serpent whose opal eyes each year were wrested from their sockets to glitter for this one evening upon the brow of the Butterfly Ball's cacique, chosen at midnight by the masquers. But it was early yet. The fiery stones still gleamed in their sockets and the torchieres burned brightly—although the elders guarding the door were already drunk, and demanded the right to fondle each costumed reveler before granting entry. For a moment I paused in the shadows. Anku whined softly at my feet as he watched the steady passage of glittering figures, boys and girls stumbling beneath the weight of jeweled and feathered headdresses and flowing silken wings.

"Hush," I whispered. I nudged him with my foot. "Well, you're a pretty prize, at least," I added, and stooped to ruffle his white fur. His steady growl grew louder. When the two guards had turned their attention upon the willowy figure of Aspasia Helen, I walked into the brilliant light of the torchieres.

". . . seven years old, and only *this* big!"

One of the elders whooped as Aspasia pinched him, a flurry of glitter powdering the air. At the sound of my tread upon the steps she looked back. For an instant puzzlement clouded her impish features. Then she squealed and nearly tripped over the sinuous drapery of a pair of wing spurs made of pale green silk.

"Raphael!"

Her arms circled my neck and I buried my face in her shoulder, feeling faint at the scent of jacaranda and the clean soft pressure of her skin beneath my mouth. I whispered foolishly, overcome at finally being here once more; and clung to her so long that I heard the guards snickering.

"Raphael," she murmured, and pulled away from me. Peering more closely at my face, she drew back, brushing at the threads of blue and lavender *mille-fleurs* woven across her breasts. "Is that your *costume?*"

I started to reply when she gave a little squeak and clutched my arm. "And what is *that?*"

"A jackal," I explained. I grabbed Anku's ruff and pulled him against my knees. "A favor for Roland Nopcsa."

"Is he tame?"

"Perfectly." I patted Anku's head reassuringly.

"He doesn't sound very tame," said Aspasia. She stretched out a white beribboned hand. Anku sniffed her tentatively, then licked her wrist. "Oh! Tickles—" She glanced at me sideways. "What happened to you, Raphael? We heard you'd gone among the Curators—"

"I've come back." I could see a crowd from Saint-Alaban starting up the drive, the elders groaning as they set down their palanquins. "Are you going in now?"

"Well—yes," she replied, still doubtful. "That's *such* an odd costume—"

"I'll walk with you, then." As I took her arm I turned so that the guards could not catch more than a glimpse of my face.

"Hey," one of them began as Anku pattered past. But already the Saint-Alabans crowded the steps behind us in a roil of jasmine and crinoline. We slipped inside unchallenged.

A rush of scent—jasmine, ylang-ylang, *carcasse d'amour;* sandlewood and galingale; the heady reek of opiated cedar burning in copper braziers. We paused before a wide curving parapet overlooking the Great Hall. Aspasia detached

herself from my embrace. Below us the marble floors flickered beneath seething waves of masquers in butterfly
garb. Senators and Curators threaded their way cautiously
through the room, holding the trailing sleeves of their
sober habits above the ground. The black domino of a
Persian malefeants with her whip pied the pastel train of a
score of moth-winged children trying very hard to perform the steps of a salacious maxixe. High overhead the
ceiling seemed to dance as well, as thousands of courting
samburs wafted in the dim vault and macaws and brilliant
finches chased the poor exhausted amorets above the ballroom floor.

"The Botanist Edmund Blanche has engaged me for the
kursaal with Beata Helen and an Illyrian spado," said Aspasia. She gazed at me wistfully, then dabbed at a spot on my
cheek.

"If I were you I'd clean up a bit," she added. "Really, the
animal is enough, without all this—" She grimaced, waving
her hands at my torn clothing. "Perhaps later, after
they've chosen the cacique . . ."

She kissed me. Her small tongue traced the curve of my
lower lip before she nodded and brushed her fingers
against my mouth. Before I could say goodbye she disappeared among the revelers.

"Well, Anku," I sighed. A pair of tall queans, not twins
but dressed and carefully painted to resemble Gemini,
unlaced their hands long enough to pass me one to each
side. One laughed and showered Anku with the shattered
remnants of many butterfly wings. He growled as they
tripped giggling down the steps.

"Well, come on," I said crossly, cuffing the jackal's head. I
now had to admit to myself that my plan for vengeance
(such as it was) had, in theory, scarcely even taken me this
far. I had imagined some sort of confrontation upon High
Brazil's outer steps, with Roland called in to arbitrate, and
myself lunging at his throat to destroy him with my sagittal. That, or a reconciliation between us, which seemed so
unlikely that it remained in my mind a vague impression
of parted thighs and murmured endearments. To find myself suddenly back among the Paphians' Court, invisibly

armed and under the protection of a sentient beast, made me feel more foolish than otherwise. I sighed and leaned against the marble baluster.

A polyphemus moth drifted by my face. I watched it sail above the crowd, dipping and rising on eddies of laughter and music until a finch not much larger than itself shot from the shadows to spear the hapless insect. I thought of Francesca, who would never see the aviaries of the Zoologists; who would never look upon the fabled beauties of the Hill Magdalena Ardent. Closing my eyes, I tried to draw up the image of her standing beside me in the Hall of Dead Kings, invoked the brush of her hand against mine.

Then her image shivered. The frail wraith I'd conjured broke into a thousand bits, insubstantial as the butterflies brightening the air. A sudden sharp odor , as if a censure below had overturned to scorch some rich fabric. My wrist burned as though clamped by red-hot metal. The fluttering afterimage of the polyphemus moth arrayed itself into livid eyes writhing across white breasts and arms, its twitching antennae worming from a gasping mouth. I cried out; and opened my eyes to find myself clutching the balustrade as though to leap into the crowd.

"Impetuous boy," a voice said behind me. I glanced back at a tall black man striped like a tiger swallowtail. He carried a small boy not more than six years old, a pretty child with enormous cocoa eyes and skin like watered milk. From his feverishly bright eyes I guessed it was the child's first masque.

"Hello, sweetheart," I murmured. I reached to stroke the wisps of brown hair that curled about his face. But as I did so the boy's eyes grew wide with horror. The rosy cheeks ballooned and burst like an overripe love apple. I staggered back against the balustrade, splaying my hands against the haze of blood; and looked down to see my legs spattered with peony petals and dried crescents of orris.

"Moth bit!" shrieked the little boy, his face crimson with laughter. The black man laughed too, but with a sideways glance, first at my face and then at my feet, as if he too half-expected to see blood.

Baal

"Pretty thing." He nodded at Anku. His dark black eyes met mine. "Are you all right, cousin?"

I swallowed and tried to smile. Anku growled, his tail swishing against the floor and dispersing the rosy petals. "I'm waiting for someone," I said. I turned as though to search for a face in the glittering throng.

With a chuckle the man turned as well, his little charge battering his shoulders and casting in farewell another handful of petals.

I waited until they disappeared and gave a soft whistle to Anku. Quickly I walked toward the main stairway, trying to calm myself and staring resolutely at the floor awash in crushed blossoms and struggling moths. I was not unfamiliar with hallucinations, the dulcet visions of gospel mushrooms and the headier drowning stupors of opium tincture and hempen tea. But now I was the unwitting channeler of Death's dreams and Death's desires. I tightened my grip upon the banister, and then went on my way.

At the curve of the staircase three Paphians blocked the steps. An Illyrian traced the blue veins of her companion's throat with one white hand. With the other she tugged a spent tab of frilite from her temple and tossed it away. She lifted her torpid eyes to gaze upon me, extended her hand to pluck at my tattered hem. "Look, Johannes," she murmured. "He has come for you: Baal-Phegor, the Naked Lord. . . ."

Before I could pass, the one she called Johannes blinked and with great effort lifted his head.

"Ah," he mumbled; then choked and with a strangled yelp drew back, smacking his head against the banister. This stirred the third in their menage, a very thin young girl with black hair and the slanted ebony eyes of Persia. For an instant, wonder and fear stained her sharp features with a piquant flash of crimson. Then:

"It's a *costume,*" she said, annoyed. She turned to display shoulder blades incised with threads of gold from which tiny black feathers fluttered. "You idiot, Johannes." With a petulant yawn she reached for him; but he pushed her away and continued to stare at me wide-eyed.

"A costume," I repeated, nudging Anku to continue.

Johannes shook his head as Anku pattered down the next two steps. When I started to follow he raised both hands before his breast and crossed them at the wrists, palms opened to me. The Persian girl tittered.

"He's a Saint-Alaban." She giggled as I stepped over her long legs. "*So* superstitious!"

The Saint-Alaban turned on her and in a flurry of squeals the three resumed their sally.

We wandered through the crowd, Anku and I. The revelers scarcely noticed me; even Anku received few surprised glances. From one dim corner of the hall a sweet sound echoed through ripples of laughter and the clamor of pipes. I followed this to a recess where water purled from a marble fountain. Drowned moths floated on its surface like blossoms. I swept the poor dead things from a brass spigot shaped like a peccary's head. Dipping my face in the scented water, I washed away the grime, then unbound my hair and let it fall into the basin. Afterward I dried myself as best I could, leaving my hair to dry wild and tangled about my shoulders.

"Here," I called to Anku. Filling my cupped hands with water, I bowed to let him drink greedily. "Supper next."

A passing couple glanced at me and tittered behind their velvet dominos. I stared back at them coldly. The taller of the two (a spado, I guessed by his hairless, somewhat fleshy face and sweet childish voice) paused to gaze at me from gray eyes half-hidden in the folds of his domino.

"Ill-met, young Lord Death," he said. He tilted his head to indicate my tattered clothes and the looped vine dangling from my neck. His partner clung limply to his arm and glanced at me sideways, a painted fantoccio draped in scarlet.

"An original conceit," she murmured, her husky voice deepened still more by chloral. "The Saint-Alabans will forfeit their place in the masquerade rather than be judged alongside a likeness of the Hanged Boy."

The spado nodded and stretched a hand to graze my cheek. "Will you join us in strappado, Hanged Boy?" he asked, lips parting to show a ruby placebit glimmering in a front tooth. One long pale leg slid from the folds of his domino to rub against my thigh.

I shook my head but did not move away, liking the feel of his smooth limb against mine. "I am looking for a Curator," I said.

"Many of us will find Patrons tonight," the woman murmured, leaning forward to gaze at her reflection in the sparkling basin. "There's luck in threes—come with us." She took my hand and pressed it between her legs, so that for a moment I felt only heat and the gentle sweep of velvet falling about my arm. Behind me I heard a faint growl. I looked back to see Anku watching from the fountain.

"A jealous companion," laughed the spado. From beneath his domino he drew a long quirt of braided hide. "Come with us, Boy." He prodded me gently with the cord. "My Patron is Constance Beech, a Botanist. She will be delighted to introduce you to her fellows. Come with us."

From the echoing hall erupted shrill laughter and cheers. I peered vainly into the swirling shadows to see what this heralded.

"They've brought out the **ORPHEUS**," said the woman. "Oh, do come dance!"

"The Curator I am looking for is a Naturalist," I said quickly, grabbing her hand and pressing it to my breast. "A Regent. Roland Nopcsa. Do you know him?"

She shook her head and turned to her companion. "A Regent. Constance might know him." She slipped her hand back into the folds of her mantle.

The spado nodded. "*I* know him: he engaged me once as Inquisitor for an esclandre. Constance attended the excruciation with us." He tapped my shoulder with his quirt. "But he has engaged Whitlock High Brazil this evening, Boy! You know that, eh?"

His cool gaze met mine. I lowered my face so that he would not see the color that flooded my cheeks. "Yes indeed," I said. "Whitlock and I were paired at Winterlong—you remember us, perhaps?"

The spado regarded me through narrowed eyes, nod-

ding slowly. "You had a different look, then," he said at last.
"I know you now. The favorite of the House Miramar.
Raphael." He turned and grasped his partner's elbow.
"See, cousin! This is the boy I told you of, the Miramar—"

"But he is not so young, Nataniel," she protested, tugging at his domino. "And we're late—we'll miss the cacique's judging if we don't hurry."

"No, you are not so young," the spado Nataniel agreed.
He raised the butt of his whip to my chin and tilted it back
an inch. "Eighteen?"

"Seventeen!"

"Seventeen, then . . . but seventeen has bright empty
eyes gazing ever forward, and already yours are full of old
dreams and brooding on the past."

I started to make a sharp reply, but the spado only raised
his quirt to gently tap my lips: once, twice, thrice. His eyes
were keen and bespoke *Silence.*

"I had a summer's folly with Roland Nopcsa once, Boy
Miramar," he said. A glance at his companion showed her
more intent upon the Great Hall than upon either of us.
"He took rather more liberties with a promising young
chaunter than perhaps he should. My House—Illyria, but
you knew that, eh?—my House was not pleased with
Nopcsa's inspiration, although they did gain a fine soprano
for chanting the "Duties of Pleasure." A dedicated ear for
fine music, Sieur Nopcsa . . .

"I hear he has engaged the Exiguous Hagioscopic Chamber this evening for a private recital with Whitlock prior to
the bestowing of the cacique's jewels."——

"Indeed," I said, and snapped my fingers in Anku's direction. "Where might a lover of music find the Exiguous
Hagioscopic Chamber?"

Nataniel drew the hem of his domino away from Anku's
anxious tread and pointed across the hall. "Through the
archway carven with the image of a jaguarondi seizing a
great fish," he murmured, then extended his arm to embrace his companion. "Come then, Dido! This boy will not
join us, but the gynander Anstice Helen has as pretty a face
and she is waiting."

The two of them bowed to me, Nataniel kissing his three fingers and reaching to brush Anku's muzzle as he passed.

"Fare well, Miramar," he called softly. "Tell Nopcsa that Nataniel Illyria taught you a song to sing him: *'Toujours Jeune.'*" They disappeared into the shadows.

7. Somewhat dubious affinities

I paused, wondering if I should go now to confront Roland, then glanced after the spado and his partner.

At the far end of the hall a great press of dancers had gathered. In their center reared the luminous pilasters and glass pipes of High Brazil's great electrocalliope **ORPHEUS.** High above the throng glowed its metal cabinet. Bright figures—dancers in dark glasses, women wearing silver headbands, autovehicles spinning on metal wheels—flickered beneath the elaborately lettered scroll still gleaming with bright blue and yellow metallic paint:

THE ECHO MUSICAL MACHINE COMPANY
OF
NORTHERN AMERICA

Beneath the scroll was a winking face, twice man-size, chipped silver headband upon its wooden brow, lips pursed to blow into a pair of great glass pipes. A frieze of tipsy letters spelled out **ECHO ORPHEUS** beneath the figure's chin.

Another wave of cheering swept the room. Rubbing my eyes, I glanced down to see Anku crouched between my legs, staring moodily at a tiger swallowtail. When I looked up again I saw that someone had lifted a woman in white domino and black mask above the crowd. To rollicking cheers she clambered up the side of the calliope, clinging for support to bas-relief leaves and the backs of fantastically carven vehicles, until she swung her legs over the gaudy face of Orpheus and raised her arms triumphantly. Amid shrieks of laughter she pelted those below with flowers.

The electrocalliope bellowed so that my ears ached. I wondered how the woman could bear it. Still I found myself moving closer to the front of the crowd, staring at her. Anku slunk beside me. When he occasionally brushed against my leg I could feel him shuddering from the noise and smoke, and I let my fingers droop to touch him reassuringly.

We reached the edge of the melee. Behind us revelers cavorted in the ceaseless spray of smoke and flowers. Before us was the expanse of peach marble adrift in petals and quivering wings, surmounted by the **ORPHEUS**. A rowdy crowd of boys from Persia and my own House—with a pang I recognized Small Benedick and Small Thomas—had clambered onto the balcony abutting the machine. They waved their arms as if conducting the calliope. I stared enraptured at the metal mouth releasing puffs of hempen-scented steam that rose to sear clouds of moths. Only Anku remained unmoved, imploring me with soft urgent cries to move on.

The carnival anthem rolled to a finish. A rush of steam and cheers; then the first piping notes of "The Saint-Alaban's Song." Drunken voices began chanting. Beside me a tall Illyrian sank to her knees beside a Botanist. At their feet a girl with Saint-Alaban's red ribbons braided through her hair plucked absently at their robes as she sang:

> "O Saint-Alaban
> We now must say goodbye
> We've lost our hearts and lovers
> and must go—
> we don't know why . . ."

I pushed away Anku, tired of his insistent whining. I applauded with the rest as the boys from Miramar tossed a

crown of lilies at the girl atop the **ORPHEUS.** To a volley of
cheers she plucked a single scarlet blossom from the
wreath of flowers. Setting the crown firmly upon her head,
she straightened. Then, surveying the crowd below, she
searched for a deserving recipient among us. Laughing
with the others, I waved and urged her *To me! to me!,*
trying to catch her eye.

Abruptly her gaze fixed upon me. Other faces began
turning to me, laughing that the game had reached this
end. Between my feet Anku stirred, growling. He stared at
the figure above us as she raised the red lily, then tugged
her mask free of its braids and ribbons to reveal her face:
dead white, pitted with blackened holes whence crept
writhing threads of spiders. I stepped back, my eyes still
riveted to her. Her hands had been chalked to hide the
bloody grooves where she had prised free the lid of the
sarcophagus. White powder flaked from the raw bruises on
her arms. Ghostly moths lit upon her thighs with slowly
beating wings. As I stared, she touched three fingers to her
lips. Then with a grin she kissed each of the lily's garnet
blades and laughing tossed it from the pensive brow of the
ORPHEUS: a poisonous shaft tumbling through the air,
cleaving the tremulous wings of moths and grazing a half-
dozen eager fingertips before it began to tumble toward its
mark.

"To me, Raphael!"

A shriek as I staggered against the Botanist hugging my
side. Something white and snarling whipped past me, tore
at her sleeve so that a net of blood trammeled the falling
blossom. In mid-air Anku seized the crimson lily, shearing
the bright petals so that they swirled and shriveled into
tattered shards. Red mist obscured my vision, clouded the
faces of those fighting to restrain me as I tried to flee that
horrible giggling figure with her bleeding legs splayed
about a winking face.

The crowd suddenly gave way. I stumbled to a marble
bench, clutched my head and wept.

"Raphael!"

I forced myself to look back. Atop the **ECHO OR-
PHEUS** the woman stood, shielding her eyes from the

smoke as she scanned the hall, calling my name over and over as though her heart would break.

Not Francesca.

Ketura.

"No," I whispered. Behind us, Paphians and Curators danced and sang as if there had been no rent in the shimmering fabric of their carnival marquee. Only the forlorn figure clinging to the **ORPHEUS** sought the ghost of Raphael Miramar at the Butterfly Ball.

"There is little time," a voice said behind me. I started and glanced at Anku, terrified that this would begin my final plunge into madness, to hear my jackal familiar speak. But Anku stood alert, his tail switching as he stared at something behind me. I whirled to see a slight figure shadowed by another column. He was naked save for a wreath of ivy about his neck and a mask of leaves behind which his green eyes glowed.

"Your sister has awakened," he said, and stepped into the light. Anku leaped toward him, to collapse whimpering at his feet. The Boy stooped to stroke the jackal's throat.

"My sister is dead," I stammered.

"She was asleep," he said, and with a last flourish to Anku stood facing me. "As I was. As were you."

"What do you want with me?" I whispered. Behind us the ball continued unabated.

"To bring the Final Ascension," he said, laughing as though he had answered a simple riddle.

"But I am no Ascendant!" I pressed myself against the marble pillar as if its solid embrace might steady me. "I am a Paphian, a courtesan—we are whores and children!"

He made a swift cutting motion with his hand.

"Desire is my child; and cold Science," he said. As he spoke his fingers moved in and out, in and out, as though choking an invisible enemy. "But her frigid heart will melt and your fever will rage to shake the stones from their buildings, Raphael Miramar."

"I do not want such power," I said, trembling.

"Power?" he repeated. "You have no power."

K. Lear

"Then leave me in peace!" I cried. "I want nothing of your Ascension!"

At this foolish temper Anku stood whining. I lashed out at him, my foot grazing one silvery flank. The jackal only blinked and settled back onto his haunches, head cocked to regard me reproachfully.

"Ah, see, Anku," said the Boy, raising his leg so that he stood on one foot like a dancer. "We are as flies to this wanton boy: he would kill us for his sport." Then he laughed, and I looked away, frightened.

"Raphael!"

I turned to see Ketura scrambling from the ORPHEUS. A flash of shame burned me as her gaze held mine: neither blaming nor accusing, only asking how I could have betrayed our friendship by fleeing her. Then she dipped from sight and I ducked behind the column once more. A few meters away the Boy stood with his back to me. He faced a high archway which held as though fixed in pale amber the image of a jaguarondi, its teeth piercing a young inia. Beneath this frieze Anku lay with his muzzle resting upon his paws, watching his master.

Sudden resolution emboldened me. Glancing back to make certain I was not seen, I walked to the Boy, grabbed his shoulder, and wrenched him toward me as I demanded, "Come with me, then!"

"Where, cousin?" an indolent voice replied agreeably. He turned to me, slanted green eyes widening beneath a broad white brow and a feathered cap that hid his hair.

It was not he.

"Forgive me," I stammered, dropping my hand. "I mistook you for another."

Before he could respond I fled beneath the arch, Anku darting to follow me. My heart pounded so that I feared I might stop breathing, so painful was that ceaseless hammering inside my chest. But after a few steps the air felt clearer, flensed of smoke and scent and sound. I breathed deeply, until I felt as though a ponderous weight had been lifted from within my lungs, and looked around to see that I had entered one of the branching hallways that snaked through the first level of High Brazil. There was a low

murmur as of many voices, but I could see no one. Tiny
electrified candles glimmered from brackets set behind
translucent petals of jadeite and peridot. These cast pale
green shadows upon the alabaster floor and walls, a marine
glow that soothed me yet made me feel more alert, as
though the beryl light revealed shapes and designs nor-
mally hidden from sight. Cool draughts flowed from unseen air shafts. To either side were many narrow doorways.
Each was surmounted by a scholiast in the likeness of a
gynander with brightly colored phallus in place of a
tongue, and breasts whose nipples were ocular sensors that
rotated as they focused upon me. We passed doors of
scented wood inlaid with plasma crystals and heated copper coils exhaling the narcotic haze of veronal. Doors of
prismatic glass cast back not my face but the holographic
images of other Paphians, their fingers tracing the outlines
of painted lips and eyes and genitals as over and over they
beckoned unseen guests. There were doors of interlocking
metal gears that snapped and spun ceaselessly, allowing
only glimpses into the twilit seraglios beyond, where sultry
figures swayed. As I approached each room its scholiast
would click and whir, the gaudy phallus unfurl as the automaton turned to fix me with its hollow eyes and pipe in a
pure breathy voice:

*"Welcome cousin. This is the Chamber of Equivocal Pu-
rity."*

*"Welcome sisters. Inside sleeps the Ensiform Concilia-
trix: rouse her to battle with your embrace."*

*"Welcome cousins. The Adytum Intrigant is engaged for
the Spados' Private Bath."*

*"Welcome cousins. Step carefully into the First Eleva-
tion of the Entresol of Unctuous Sighs."*

Anku ignored this prattling, pausing only to sniff at the
postern whose scholiast murmured, *"Welcome cousins.
Circe High Brazil awaits within to change women into
swans, men into swine."* Faint grunts and moans of pleasure seeped from beneath a door scaled with the hides of
many pangolins. The freshly flayed pelt of a young lamb
hung from the doorjamb, blood slicking the marble beneath it. Anku leaped to tug at this. I cuffed him and hissed

for him to follow. He did so with a disapproving growl, slinking at my heels.

"Welcome errant brothers. Join us in the Chamber of Lashes and Gentle Lapidation."

"Welcome rhapsodists. Retire to the couches of the Anodyne Cubicle."

"Welcome cousin. The Exiguous Hagioscopic Chamber is engaged for Dolorous Palpation."

The scholiast's phallic tongue retracted into its mouth with a click. To each side of the automaton rose slender windows of glass: glowing purple, deep scarlet, jonquil yellow. Archaic figures were depicted within the panes. For several minutes I studied these curious representations of men and women, shining vehicles, and slender aviettes. Anku sat at my feet as I pondered how to enter the chamber.

From inside came a sudden soft explosion of laughter; then muffled voices.

"Roland," I whispered. Memory of the day's terrors faded. I felt honed to a spike of raw feeling, suddenly knowing exactly where I was, and why; and what I hunted. When I moved my hand a spidery glint of violet crept from beneath my fingers. Anku whined.

"I would enter the Exiguous Hagioscopic Chamber," I announced to the scholiast. I gazed up at it fearlessly.

The ocular sensors extruded. Squinting, I could see the array of lenses inside the metal nipples circle and reverse as they sought to focus upon me, the pinpoint of light that revealed the periscopic aperture within the mechanism. The phallic tongue unfolded, flecking the air with metallic dust.

"The chamber has been engaged for private excruciations," the hollow voice intoned.

"I am an expected guest of the Curator Roland Nopcsa and Whitlock High Brazil." I glanced at Anku. The scholiast's sensors shifted to regard him. The voices inside the chamber grew louder, as though arguing, then silent. "This animal is a gift for Roland Nopcsa."

Loud whirring from the scholiast. The cool air pouring

from the air vents made me shiver, so I moved from the wall. The sensors followed me.

"Whitlock High Brazil and Roland Nopcsa have re-quested no assistance for the evening's excruciations. The chamber may not be engaged."

"I do not wish to engage the chamber!" I said. "I bring a gift for Roland Nop—"

"The chamber may not be engaged."

"But this—"

The scholiast's jeweled navel suddenly dilated. I shut up and backed across the hall and to one side, kicking at Anku to alert him. From the scholiast shot a needle that sprayed the air with a fine mist. Anku whined. I covered my mouth with my sleeve to avoid breathing the sedative essence.

The needle retracted. The painted breasts swiveled. The phallus furled back into the cold steel mouth. Before the sensors could focus upon me again I slammed against the door. It swung inward as easily as the postern to my room at the House Miramar. I felt Anku's soft fur against my legs as he slipped beside me and the door shut behind us.

8. The traces of the existence of a body

"Magdalene," someone whispered. The sound was magnified in the bell of a vast chamber that seemed to encompass all of High Brazil. I stood surrounded by shafts of violently tinted light: orange, violet, turquoise, burgundy columns rising to explode against a ceiling of brilliant stained glass. The far end of the chamber appeared to open above the Great Hall, where masquers reeled and shouted in eerie silence, heedless of us watching from the seraglio above. I gathered that this chamber was located directly behind the wall of prismatic glass that overlooked the east end of the Great Hall. I shut my eyes to blot out the sense of vertiginous space in a room that I knew could not possibly be this huge. When I looked up again it was into the face of Roland Nopcsa regarding me with muzzy brown eyes.

"Raphael?" he said thickly. " 'Sat you?" He pawed at the air. I stepped backward, lost my balance, and fell onto a pallet heaped with satin coverlets and the remnants of a feathered costume.

"Raphael!" exclaimed the voice I'd first heard upon entering. "Magdalene save me, I'm glad you're here! He's a madman." From the tangle of bolsters and sheets a figure half-rose to greet me. Slender, with skin so translucent it shimmered with the pulse of blood in his veins, blue-green and violet. The marks of bruising kisses lingered upon his shoulders and throat.

"Oh, Whitlock!" Ignoring Roland, I crawled to where Whitlock hugged a pillow to his frail chest. "What happened to you?"

He dropped the pillow and wrapped his arms around me, cool and insubstantial as a wraith's. He blinked often as he spoke, those weak lovely eyes always seeming to focus on someone else, slightly to my left.

"He's shattered my poor splendid wings," he said, laughing. Dabs of silver arched across each cheekbone where bijoux tears had been artfully wrung. I kissed him, recalling our pairing at Winterlong: my auburn locks braided with his shining hair. He looked no less lovely now for his bruises and disarray, only achingly fragile.

"S' dog?" rumbled Roland, staggering as he waved his arms toward Anku. "S' dog, Whitlock."

Anku had trotted to the far end of the chamber where the floor seemed to open onto the Great Hall below. Glitter and dying moths beat the air relentlessly, always just inches out of reach of the jackal's quicksilver jaws. The figure of Anku himself blurred as he leaped close to the edge of the room, then grew sharper and clearer as he fell back to the floor.

"Obfuscating oriels," Whitlock explained. "I *hate* them, they give me vertigo. But *he* likes to think that all of *them*" —he indicated the silent crowd beneath us— "are *watching.*"

"Raphael," Roland repeated. He plopped onto a pile of cushions, splaying one heavy thigh across a crimson comforter. "How'd you get in?"

"Oh, *I* sent for him, Roland," said Whitlock, kicking a pillow so that it sailed and landed with a thump against Roland's leg. "We make such a striking couple. I finally had to dose his wine," he added aside to me. Ruby flashed to ivory as he rolled his eyes. "I never had your constitution, Raphael. Curators *exhaust* me. What's it like *living* with them?"

"Awful," I said. "I've left."

"Good for you." He smiled and kissed my cheek. Dear Whitlock! "You know, Lemuel paired me with Aspasia Persia for The Glorious—she's lovely, reminded me of Ketura

from your House, that red hair and those legs!—and I kept
thinking of last Winterlong when . . ."

He chattered on, while beside him I sat nearly stupefied
with—

What?

Relief? Indecision? Fear?

All of these; and a twisted desire for Roland, who now
stood staring down at the masque. His hands rested against
some invisible barrier at the room's edge, and he mumbled
to himself while Anku lay watchfully a few feet away. And
I felt desire for the sweet and faithless Whitlock beside me,
giggling as he recounted his own exploits at recent castigations, punctuating each anecdote with quick childish kisses
and toying with the cosmetic cylinders and ribbons and
gleaming candicaine straws strewn on the floor about him.

". . . and, Raphael, tonight Iontha High Brazil said she
heard congreves launched across the river, and Gamaliel
and Swan Illyria saw lazars gathering near the Tiger!" He
paused, and plucked a cherry from a silver serving platter.

"Lazars," I repeated. I took a deep breath. "I saw
lazars—"

"You, cousin!"

"Yes—by the Tiger." I continued to stare at Roland. I
wondered whether he was too drunk to identify me later if
I simply left now; or if I should confront him with my
dismissal.

"But you were alone! How did you escape?" Whitlock
grabbed my hand.

"Oh—" I stammered, quickly but gently moving my
hand from his grasp. When I glanced down I saw the sagittal gleaming very faintly. I slipped that hand into the folds
of my tunic, with the other pointed toward the far end of
the room where Anku lay. "The jackal—"

"But lazars—!"

I turned and laid a finger to his lips.

"Whitlock," I said. "When did Roland first engage you?"

"Nopcsa? Months and months ago. Right after you went
to the Museum." He gazed up at me, cabochon eyes glinting with surprise. Then he clapped both hands to his small
mouth and glanced from myself to Roland and back again.

"Raphael! I'm so sorry—I had no idea—you didn't know!" There was the faintest note of glee in his apology.

"No, I did *not*," I said. Suddenly all of my anger and hurt and spite flooded me again. I glared at my former Patron, naked save for a loose undershift of white cambric now stained with wine, peering at Whitlock and myself. "I am not accustomed to such treatment."

"Ah, Raphael." A twinge of malice quivered in Whitlock's smile. He tipped his head toward Roland, then reached for an atomizing tube. There was a soft hiss staining the air with sandalwood. "You are too proud, you know. *All* of us are accustomed to 'such treatment'—only Raphael Miramar ever thought he was above it. To dare live among the Curators! Didn't you know he would hate you for it?"

I winced. I recalled Ketura's warning, Franca's callous wonder that I had ever imagined the Curators would accept me as anything but a common whore.

"I wanted to learn from him—" I began, when Roland suddenly called out.

"Whitlock! They're gathering the suzeins for the judging —" His expression clouded as he saw me standing above Whitlock. "Miramar," he said.

He no longer sounded drunk. He strode across the room to his paramour. "Who let him in?"

Whitlock flinched, then tossed back his white hair pettishly. "Raphael and I were paired a—"

"Who let him in, you pasty slut?" Nopcsa kicked at the pile of blankets.

Whitlock stumbled to his feet, wrapping a sheet around his thin shoulders. "Best go, Raphael," he said, and stooped to gather his costume. "*I* don't know who let him in, Roland. Perhaps the scholiast was tampered with."

"Who let you in?" demanded Roland. "How did you know we were here? How did you *get* here?"

"I crossed the Narrow Forest," I replied. "I've brought you a gift, Roland. Anku!"

Like smoke seeping up through the floorboards the jackal materialized at my side. Whitlock eyed him nervously, tugging on his robe as he shifted from one foot to the other. I could feel Anku quivering as he stared at the Curator.

"An albino jackal," Roland said, stroking his chin and eyeing Anku. Suddenly he began to laugh. "Miramar, I always thought you were too clever for a whore!" He stooped and snapped his fingers at the jackal. Anku's ears flattened against his skull but he did not move.

"A peace offering," I suggested.

"An albino?" said Whitlock, somewhat plaintively. I shrugged. My head had begun pounding again. About my wrist I felt a steady pulse of heat come and go, come and go, in rhythm with the rush of blood through my veins.

"As pretty a consort as ever you've had, Roland," I said. I hoped my excitement and fear would not betray me. But I felt a little ashamed as well, and dared an apologetic glance at Whitlock. He was regarding me curiously. I saw his glance slide from my face to my arm and then fix upon my wrist. I gripped the glowing bracelet with my other hand. At my feet a wan pool of violet reflected from the sagittal. And to my horror the gaze Whitlock cast back upon me mirrored my own. His blinking eyes darted between fear and wonder as he looked from the sagittal to my face and back again, shaking his head in disbelief.

He knows what it is!

For an instant I held his gaze, thinking *Do not betray me!* as I stood there calmly, and even Anku's breath stilled as he waited with me.

Then—

"Well, Roland," Whitlock announced with that same lazy note of petulance, as though he were only half-awake and none too pleased about it. With calculated slowness he bent to pick up a crown of azure and yellow macaw quills. "*I* must go to the judging—"

"Take me," I said to Roland. I turned to confront him, almost near enough now for us to embrace. "Leave him and be my escort."

Because suddenly, more than anything—more than vengeance, more than surcease from pain and exhaustion, more even than I longed for his love and desire for me to return—I simply wanted everything to be as it had been. I wanted to enter the Great Hall with Roland and lower my eyes as he guffawed at the sight we made together, as he had done at so many masques and balls. I wanted to have Gower Miramar as my lover and confidante and suzein once more, and Fancy my beloved cousin beside me, and Ketura with her explosive laugh and temper to match. . . .

"I won't leave again, I promise," I pleaded. My hand had fallen upon Anku's head. My fingers kneaded his fur as I raised my eyes to Roland's. "Just let me go with you now."

He stared at me for a long time. Like a moth that alights upon one fair blossom and then forsakes it for another, desire for me lingered upon Roland's dark face; and then was gone forever.

"You're too clever for yourself, Raphael," he said at last. Disdainfully he kicked at Anku, missing the jackal but sending a small tide of silks washing across the floor. "Some whore's trick to curry favor with your people! A white dog—"

Anku growled and slipped to the other side of the room.

Roland glanced at Whitlock lining his eyes with kohl and smiled. "I have a prettier pet than that already, Miramar. Hurry up, Whitlock." And without another glance at me he turned and began to pull on his tunic and Regent's sash of red and black.

I watched him, stunned that he had rejected me—really rejected me!—so easily, without so much as an argument over my hair or torn clothes, without even acknowledging that I had braved the perils of the Narrow Forest to come here, and risked humiliation by my own people in order to break into this garish seraglio and offer myself to him.

"Roland . . ." I began.

He paused at the far wall and tugged at one of a dozen multicolored ropes of braided velvet that looped from the ceiling. A clear sweet chime. Then a tiny door opened in the wall. A brazen face blinked verdigrised eyelids. Its speaking mechanism ground resolutely, as though it had been unused for many months.

"Speak cousin," it finally pronounced in the same chilly tones the scholiasts affected.

"Bid the elders come and remove an uninvited guest from the Exiguous Hagioscopic Chamber. Inform Lemuel High Brazil that the catamite Raphael Miramar has committed a crime of interjacence."

"As you wish," the brass head replied. The tiny door snapped shut.

"Roland!" Whitlock gasped. The kohl wand snapped shut in a flurry of black powder. "That's *banishment*—you *can't!*—"

Roland snarled and slashed at the air with his hand. "Do you want to go with him?" He turned, grabbing blindly at the dangling ropes. Chimes pealed and tinkled. From a dozen alcoves soft voices rang from brazen throats. "Summon Lemuel High Brazil!"

"No!" Whitlock cried, cowering on the floor. A tremor of pity for him cut through my own fear and indecision. Before I could say anything he shrieked, pointing.

"Raphael!"

I turned, too late to avoid Roland's arm swinging to smash against my throat. I fell to my knees, gagging as I tried to catch my breath. But Roland grabbed my shoulders and yanked me back up, his crimson face swimming before mine.

"Whores and lazars! You all feed off us—" His hands gripped me so that I cried aloud, and he laughed. "Not so strong and well fed as you were, eh, Miramar? You won't last long once you're banished."

And he tore at my tunic, pushed me to the floor, and with one hand tight about my throat twisted to turn me onto my stomach as I struggled. Roland cursed and smacked me with the side of his hand. My head reeled. For a moment I lay once more beneath the apple tree in the Narrow Forest, the figure grunting above me not Roland but the Hanged Boy, hands like a rope tightening about my throat, pain ripping through me and a voice braying such triumph and utter desolation that I screamed. . . .

"Raphael!"

This *is what awaits you this and nothing more and it does not end no not now no not ever no come to me come to me—*

"Raphael, *please!*"

And there above me crouched neither Roland nor the Gaping One but Whitlock, Anku panting at his side. From Roland's neck a broken ampule protruded.

"—*dead*, Raphael, I killed him, sweet Magdalene, oh save me he's dead!"

I tried to speak but my bruised throat could not form the question. The clamor in my ears softened, the roaring broke into discrete notes that I gradually realized were words, the voices of scholiasts pronouncing the same message over and over again:

"*We summon the suzein of the House High Brazil.*"

"*Raphael Miramar has committed a crime of interjacence.*"

"*We summon the suzein of the House High Brazil. . . .*"

The muted cadence of the masque below faltered and then stilled. With a clang the brazen voices of the scholiasts announced my name one last time and fell silent.

"Whitlock," I began.

"Shh!"

His fear bled into taut concentration. I raised myself to lean upon one elbow, reaching for Anku. Behind the jackal I glimpsed Roland's bulk, a maroon coverlet tossed across him so that only his hand could be seen. Within that ominous silence this alone seemed right: that Roland should lie there dead, and that I should sit a few feet away and be glad of it. I felt my shoulders heave beneath the weight of some kind of vicious glee and turned to Whitlock as if he might explain to me this sudden violent humor.

But he was not looking at me. Nor did he stare at the man he had killed protecting me. Head cocked to one side, he gazed at the ceiling, pale ruby eyes blinking as though he strove to read our names there among the velvet ropes and spiderwebs. And now Anku mirrored Whitlock's posture, sitting on his haunches and staring upward, ears pricked.

"What—" I demanded, hearing nothing at first; then bit off the end of my sentence. From far within the labyrinth of High Brazil a bell began to toll.

"That is the tocsin," said Whitlock very slowly, as though

somehow it might not really *be* the tocsin until he had pronounced the word.

I nodded, dazed. By some extraordinary effort I got to my feet. "The tocsin," I said.

Whitlock turned to face me. "High Brazil is beset by lazars," he said, and stumbled to the windows overlooking the Great Hall.

Now I could hear it clearly: three long repeated notes, deep and dreadful, a sound I had grown up fearing from Doctor Foster's tales. The tocsin sounded once a year to announce the Masque of Winterlong and so allow us all to hear its hollow song, and afterward begin our games of go-bang and snapdragon.

But this was not Winterlong. This was the Butterfly Ball, and the warning tocsin sounded now when we should be hearing the laughter of the judges pronouncing the masque's cacique.

"That's impossible," I protested. But in my head rang other words: *I have gone mad; I am dreaming.* Whitlock fumbled with a curtain at the wall's edge until his fingers found a switch. A soft click. The obfuscating oriels shimmered. The chamber grew dim.

"Look," my friend whispered. "It has begun. . . ."

I stepped around Roland's corpse to join Whitlock. As we stared down I saw upon the entrance balcony a grinning line of emaciated children, one beside the other, hands linked as though for some harrowing antic. They had torn the ropes of flowers from the balustrades and hung them about their necks in imitation of the Paphians. Some of them wore the remnants of actual costumes. I recognized Aspasia Persia's beaded cobwebs now adorning the matted curls of a boy with fiery eyes and livid face.

"They must have taken her outside," said Whitlock. "We will be eaten alive." He pointed at the **ORPHEUS**, its glass pipes now silent. The masquers ringed tightly the calliope's gleaming bulk, as if it might shelter them from the murderous children.

Upon the parapets more and more lazars gathered, and at the top of each stairway, and within the embrasures, their skeletal arms and legs outstretched like mayflies impaled upon the varicolored glass. But they moved in utter silence, as though waiting for a signal to begin their play.

Suddenly I heard a piercing cry. From the crowd huddled about the **ORPHEUS** darted a willowy harlequin, his costume billowing behind him as he ran toward the main steps.

None of the lazars pursued him. He cleared the top step. It seemed he might escape, go free to summon aid, when a bowstring twanged. The figure halted, jerked back and forth like a teetotum. Then he toppled and rolled down the steps, a scarlet streamer unraveling behind him upon each white stair.

A moment more of silence. Then from the main balcony rang a strong familiar voice.

"Greetings, cousins!"

Whitlock started as I turned and began to look among the spectral children ranged across the House, until I saw her.

The yellow janissary's jacket slipped from her thin shoulders as she balanced atop the balustrade on one foot. A grinning child at each side waited to catch her if she fell. She raised her arms, crowing with delight at the terrified revelers huddling below. Laughing she cried, "The bad fairies have come to the ball!"

She turned to face our side of the Great Hall, her eyes probing the blank faces of the Masquers. Then she stiffened, and slowly raised her head to where Whitlock and I stood in the Hagioscopic Embrasure. Her eyes fixed upon mine. With a swagger she tossed back her tangled hair. The janissary's jacket slid back a little more upon her narrow shoulders as she cried for all to hear.

"Ill-met by moonlight, Young Lord Baal! Many thanks for the invitation! My master bids you come now as his guest to the Cathedral. But I go to meet your lord: he waits for me below. Look for me in the gray lands among the gaping ones—"

Then she leaped, spinning so that her wasted smile flashed one last time from within that tangle of white hair. On the floor below masquers scattered, giving voice to the first wails of horror and despair as the girl struck the marble and, like a child turning in her sleep, tossed one broken arm across her smiling face and lay still.

"Baal . . ." whispered Whitlock. His eyes showed fear, but he did not pull away from me. "She named you Baal? How did she know you, Raphael?"

I shook my head. "The river," I said. "They think I am the one the Saint-Alabans call Baal or the Hanged Boy—"

A wave of sound overtook the Great Hall. Shouts and wails and bleating cries mingled with the gleeful yelps and laughter of the lazars as they watched the hapless revelers try to flee. Several of the children who had stood beside Pearl now turned their eyes upon the embrasure where Whitlock and I stood. I could see them talking excitedly and pointing to us.

"The Hanged Boy," Whitlock repeated, licking his lips. He nodded slowly, his ruby eyes filling with tears even as he smiled. "Ah, Raphael—it has come, then."

"What?" I cried. "What has come?"

"Like the Saint-Alabans always told us. The Final Ascension, the coming of the Hanged Boy—"

"I am not the Hanged Boy! I'm Raphael Miramar— you've known me your whole life!"

Smiling, he leaned to kiss me gently upon one cheek. "Ah yes. Well. I know, dear heart." He gestured toward the far balcony. "But they see us, there—they will come for you, and kill me.

"I don't want them to kill me, Raphael. . . ."

He drew my hand to his face, pressed the sagittal against his neck as he raised his mouth to kiss me. "Take me, Raphael," he murmured. "Let me die now, with you, and take some memory of beauty with me."

I tried to push him away, but he only smiled and crushed me closer to him. "They're right, you know," he whispered between kisses as we sank to the floor. "You were the most beautiful of us all, Raphael. Let me die now with you. . . ."

Without wanting to I tangled my fingers in his silver hair and kissed him, groaning. A shimmer where my sagittal cast a violet nimbus about his lovely face. Then he drew my hand close until the bracelet rested against his throat and he arched against it.

A sound soft as night falling; the clouded blur of the spine darting into Whitlock's skin. He shuddered. For an instant his eyes fixed upon me, soft and ardent.

"Remember me at Winterlong," he sighed; and was dead.

Part Five

The Players' Book

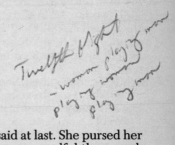

"Too much red," Miss Scarlet said at last. She pursed her long lips so that she looked even more soulful than usual. With one finger she dabbed at the inner corner of my eye, drew her finger away blotched with the rouge I had too vigorously applied so that my eyes would stand out boldly before my audience. "Just two little dots, there and *there*—"

I shut my eyes as she touched me. I felt the impression of her finger setting the cool dye upon my face and knew again that strange surge inside me, a fingerling of joy that only came at times like this, as we readied ourselves for a performance. From the House Miramar's tiny stage down the hall I heard the shuffle and laughter of those taking their seats: the suzein of the House Miramar and his guests, Botanists who had traded hemp and roses for the Miramars' last masque. In the room where Miss Scarlet and I costumed ourselves bowers of roses bloomed in cracked bottles, showering the slanted floor with their petals. One perfect bloom peeked from within the folds of Miss Scarlet's peignoir. She had tucked it there until she might wear it in Act Three of our play, when as the widowed Olivia she sought to court me in Viola's disguise of young Cesario.

A discreet rap at the heavy oaken door of our chamber.

"Near time, Master Aidan," called Mehitabel. Even after these many weeks I could still hear the bemusement in her voice. A young actor so shy he would disrobe only before a chimpanzee! "Miss Scarlet—"

"Is it a full house?" the chimpanzee asked. Her hands

trembled as they fastened the last button upon the back of my long and carefully torn skirts.

"Not quite," said Mehitabel. "But *very* well dressed! And the suzein has already invited you and Toby to supper afterward. I hear Miramar has a very good cook," she added, then drummed her fingers in a farewell upon the door.

Miss Scarlet sighed. She stepped from the little stool she used to help me dress, holding up the hem of her peignoir like a demure young bride.

"Would you tend to my coiffure, Wendy?" she murmured, settling herself on the floor in front of me. I squatted behind her, careful not to let my skirts graze the floor awash in flakes of eye-paint and powder and stray hairs fallen from wigs. With one foot Miss Scarlet reached for a pillow and slid it to me. I sat upon it and began to groom her.

With a purr Miss Scarlet shook herself free of my hands and nodded. "Now for my wig," she said, sighing luxuriously and stretching her long toes to pick up an ebony kohl wand. "Thank you, Wendy. I think I hear the overture?"

This a delicate reminder not to miss my cue. The overture itself consisted only of Gitana's unpleasant brayings upon an archaic solar melodeon. I nodded, straightened my wig, and scratched her head in farewell, then slipped into the hallway.

"Hello, goodman divel," a voice called from behind folds of velvet. Justice stepped forward to join me in the darkness. The heavy soft drapes fell back behind him to obscure the little proscenium.

"Hello, Justice," I said, shrinking from the touch of his hand upon my elbow. He winced; then nodded and tossed his long hair.

"Put my braid under the cap," he said. He handed me the Captain's livery he wore in the first scene. I did so quickly, listening to the nervous giggles of Gitana and Mehitabel as they struggled into their boys' tunics (they always missed their entrance) and wondering where Toby was.

"Ah, Master Aidan," came his sonorous voice suddenly

at my ear. One huge hand descended upon my shoulder
like an owl roosting there. With the other he dismissed
Justice, snapping his fingers and pointing to where Fabian
struggled with a lightpole. "You make a fetching Viola."

I bared my teeth, then bowed my head so that he would
not see. I felt the Small Voices stirring inside me, the Boy
who woke hungrily at any sign of anger or unease. My
heart quickened; the blood tapped hard and fast against a
node beneath my left temple.

"Thank you, sieur," I whispered, shrugging myself
deeper into the folds of Viola's tattered scarf. From those
assembled before the stage came murmurings more stri-
dent than they had been earlier. The performance was
starting late. Toby straightened, his shoulders brushing a
flat as he pulled taut the folds of the cape he wore as
Orsino.

"Gower Miramar has asked myself and Miss Scarlet to
dine afterward. If he is pleased with your performance he
will no doubt request your company as well. He has a taste
for young men."

A soft threat therein. I had sworn chastity before Toby
Rhymer and the others, save Miss Scarlet and Justice, who
knew my secret. For I had seen that the Players were often
expected to perform more than once each evening. Besides myself, only Miss Scarlet refrained from these en-
gagements, drawing back her lip with the merest hint of a
sneer as she withdrew her gloved hands from the kisses of
her admirers—Paphians, mostly, and the occasional Zoologist.

"I will join him at dinner, if he wants. But not afterward," I replied. But my heart hammered at the thought
of encountering new blood that evening.

"Time, Toby!" hissed Fabian from the wings. He shoved
the melodeon into Gitana's arms as Toby strode onstage to
arrange himself languidly as the lovesick Duke, raising his
face to catch the dimpled light from an electrified follow-
spot. Gitana plunked the melodeon's keys desultorily, rolling her eyes so that Mehitabel collapsed giggling beside a
papier-mâché boxtree. Toby's arm lolled behind
Mehitabel. I watched him pinch her until she grimaced

and turned her pretty blank eyes on the audience, as Justice tugged back the proscenium curtain upon Toby's sighs.

> *" 'If music be the food of love, play on!*
> *Give me excess of it, that surfeiting,*
> *The appetite may sicken and so die . . .' "*

I caught the amused glances of several of the audience as Gitana's melodeon gave a melancholy wheeze. I counted seventeen of them, mostly Paphians in gaudy drag. A small audience. Most of the Hill Magdalena Ardent was at High Brazil that evening, attending the Butterfly Ball. But Miramar hoped to impress his Botanist guests with our command performance, and so obtain more of last spring's small harvest of saffron.

The mingled stench of the Paphians' perfumes did not discourage the lewd ministrations of the Botanists, all women of surpassing plainness. In the center seat smiled a tall Paphian, very thin, with an ascetically beautiful face counterpointed by sumptuous robes of violet sateen aglow with azure lumens. He would be the suzein, Gower Miramar. Beside him sat a very homely Botanist in sober brown. Her hands twitched in her lap, seemingly to keep them from caressing the child seated next to her. A very small girl in a violet dress, her golden curls caught up in an elaborate coiffure braided with feathers and triangulated shards of glazed eelskin. For some reason she fascinated me. A flicker of feeling like a lizard's tongue brushed against my heart.

Why her? I thought, trying to slow my breathing. I had not seen her face before. Yet something woke in me, some hunger or desire perhaps of the Boy eager to feed. She could not have been more than six or seven. Yet there was something in the way she tipped her head to listen to the Botanist's smug whisper, a certain hauteur to her child's bearing and the stiffness with which she held in her velvet lap an elaborate dorado fan. The fan seemed to twitch of itself as the Botanist's suggestions took a more lecherous turn. In all of this I sensed a refined quality which belied the pale triangular face with its huge and innocent amber eyes. A strange excitement seized me, compounded equally of hunger, fear, and lust. I stepped into the folds of the proscenium curtains, the better to observe this strange child and allow myself to be engulfed by the emotions she roused. But just as the sharp taste flooded my mouth Toby careened into me as he made his exit and prodded me with his walking-stick.

"Now, boy!" he ordered. He pushed me from the velvet folds onto the momentarily darkened stage behind him.

The spotlight a lance through my eyes. A dazzling film of blood for an instant obscures my sight. Before me stands Justice, the Captain once again. From the audience a very soft sound, like a child starting from sleep only to plummet back into dreams. Then my own voice strained with desperation and loss as I tugged at the Captain's sleeve:

" 'What country, friend, is this?' "

Justice's eyes avoid mine so that I will not see his pain and desire there, even now, even alone with me upon a stage before a score of opium-besotted courtesans and their sniggering Patrons.

" 'This is Illyria, lady.' "

I drew the scarf more tightly about my face as my voice rose:

" 'And what should I do in Illyria?
My brother he is in Elysium.
Perchance he is not drowned. What think you?' "

Justice countered:

" 'It is perchance that you yourself were saved.' "

I cried:

" 'Oh my poor brother! And so perchance may he be!' "

clever conflation of twin-based plots

Another sound from the audience. A single high voice called out in surprise and distress. I caught the shape of a name. So profound was the sense of loss in that sweet tone that I turned downstage and searched the rows of seats to see who was so moved.

The seat beside the lecherous Botanist was now empty. The suzein glanced about anxiously. Then I saw at the lip of the stage the little girl who had sat near him. Her coiffure bobbed as she tried to clamber onto the stage, her golden eyes fixed upon me.

"Raphael!" she cried. As she reached one hand toward me she slipped. Before she could fall she was caught by her frowning Botanist Patron, who carried her to the back of the theater, scolding her loudly.

From offstage came Toby's bellowed whisper, "Justice!" I glanced back to Justice, who was also staring after the protesting child.

I coughed. Justice turned to me and faltered:

" 'True madam, and to comfort you with chance . . .' "

The scene wound on until the Captain led me offstage to disguise me as young Cesario. I shrugged off Justice's hand and hurried to where Miss Scarlet waited with my costume change.

"The Paphians are taken with you," she whispered, helping me step from skirts to trousers as she teetered in Olivia's high-buttoned boots. But a shred of uncertainty wafted through her voice. She twitched her nose worriedly. Over the reek of white lead powder and rouge I caught the fulsome smell of her unease.

"What is it?" I grabbed her arm and felt through layers of crinoline the hair and muscle strung like rope. "What happened to that child? Did you recognize her?"

"No," said Miss Scarlet; then, "I don't know, Wendy." I stooped so that she could remove my wig and tousle my short hair so that it resembled a boy's. "They seem to sense something. Miramar—"

"The suzein?"

She nodded. "He didn't take his eyes off you."

"I will not traffic with Paphians," I said. But Miss Scarlet shook her head, indicating silence as she glanced behind me to where the other actors fussed with their costumes.

"That may be so; but you draw them to yourself all the same, dear friend." She sighed, fastening the last lace upon my jacket. "Be quick now, or you'll miss the cue."

I strode out beside Gitana, herself still attired as a man-servant (her downy mustache helped). I paused upstage to allow the audience a moment to note the effectiveness of my masculine attire. That delighted gasp of amused recognition I was accustomed to by now; but then I heard a sharper intake of breath from several in the audience. Suddenly I felt my knees shake, knew the vertiginous approach that meant I was flashing onto something else, *someone* else, and who was it this time?

Emma Aidan Melisande?

Morgan Justice Scarlet Pan . . . ?

Or *Him,* the heavy thing I bore like a dart lodged immovably inside my head, leeching all those others into Himself until He might devour me as well? I began to shake, caught Gitana's alarmed stare, and realized that for the first time I had dried up. Behind me Toby had already made his entrance.

" *'On your attendance, my lord, here!'* " I stammered as Gitana scampered offstage. Toby smiled. He cuffed me with grim playfulness as he walked upstage, nearly knocking me to the floor.

" *'Stand you awhile aloof, Cesario,'* " he commanded.

I caught my breath and balance, made a low bow and let the blood rush to my head. Then I straightened to continue with the scene. As we bantered, the Voices inside my head crept back into their secret places, small creatures with patient claws. A pulse of adrenaline. I spun on my heel to exit and dared a direct glance at the audience, aimed my sight at the center row where the suzein sat—

Bolt upright, staring at me with utter amazement. As I stepped offstage I heard his voice from the front of the house, repeating softly but insistently a name:

Raphael.

* * *

"You are his very likeness."

The tumbler the suzein handed me glittered green with sweetmint tea. We were gathered in the Pandoric Seraglio of the House Miramar. A number of television monitors were set about the chamber, hundreds of years old and recently acquired from the Historians. Through their cracked glass flickered candlelight, and in some of them little figures had been set, dolls and small automatons, robotic hands encrusted with rings and armillas, dried nosegays of roses and lilies-of-the valley. I could smell the opiated fumes rising from the narghile in Toby's hand. Beside the suzein three leaden-eyed Botanists sprawled upon pillows. Seated near me were Miss Scarlet (refusing like myself all refreshment save plain tea and a plate of sweet loquats), Justice, and Toby Rhymer.

"Master Aidan is an almost supernaturally talented young man," said Miss Scarlet, drawing back her long upper lip to show yellow teeth. She inclined her head to Gower Miramar, plucking a loquat from the platter and offering it to the suzein.

"Thank you, Miss Scarlet," replied Miramar. When he moved, the azure lumens on his robes blinked to detail the constellation known as The Capitol. Behind him our shadows fluttered upon the seraglio's tapestried walls, were trapped within the gold-shot eyes of the ancient monitors. A small room, oddly shaped so that the soft and richly hued cloths fluttering from the ceiling made it seem we were embarked upon some strange vessel. Miramar crumbled a leaf of sweet-smelling herb before his face and inhaled before continuing.

"Ah, Miss Scarlet! Aidan's talent I have no doubt of—a lovely performance, sieur," he said, turning to me. "I have always respected Toby's craft, his attention to the details of an ancient art. Among other things, encouraging young men to play the feminine roles originally written for them."

Miss Scarlet sniffed. I had to keep from smiling at the

remarkable conceit of a girl disguised as a boy disguised as
a girl traveling incognito upon the stage!

"But you know I am not Raphael Miramar," I said again.
Across from me a young Botanist snored. "You are certain
of that."

"I am," said Miramar; but he looked disturbed. His
glance lingered again upon my throat, where earlier his
long fingers had sought a birthmark that was not there.
"Your learning proves you grew up among the Librarians
after your parents' death—" (This was the story Justice and
I had created to explain my erudition, if not my beauty.)
"But you are certain you have no surviving family? No
sister?"

I laughed, dread uncoiling inside me like an asp. "No,
sieur! No sister—

> " *'I am all the daughters of my father's house,*   ~Viola~
>   *And all the brothers too—'*

And I am certain I have no brother."

Miramar sighed. "Well, it is very strange then. The favorite of our House left here two months back: Raphael,
whom you so closely resemble that I thought you must be
that other child I sold to the Ascendants many years
ago. . . ."

My fingers tightened upon my tumbler. It was as if some
great and terrible vista was opening before me; as though a
mountain that for my entire life had reared above my
home had suddenly one day begun to tremble and fall into
ruin.

A brother, I thought. From beneath the layers of scarred
brain tissue that buried my past something stirred,
thrashed as in wakefulness and then fell back into the
abyss.

A brother; a twin brother. Emma and Aidan Harrow,
and now myself: another twin. Another girl torn from her
brother . . .

No wonder I had been Emma's pet. No wonder it had
not been difficult to pattern me with the intricate spires
and helices of her tortured consciousness; no wonder I had

driven her to madness and suicide, when through me she could not reclaim the boy she had loved and lost but never escaped from.

It can't be true, I thought; but inside me a Small Voice (Dr. Harrow's perhaps; but I could not be sure) said: *It is so.*

Abruptly I remembered where I was and drew myself up to gaze at Justice across the table from me. He blinked, once, twice, and gazed at me with wonder.

Say nothing! I tried to command him with my eyes. But already he spoke, phrasing a question with stunned slowness.

"You sold her to the *Ascendants?*"

"Yes," said Miramar. Next to him Toby Rhymer tapped a generous stream of brown powder from a small vial into his tea. Miss Scarlet sat very straight beside him on two pillows, her black eyes fixed upon mine. "There were two children—"

Miramar hesitated. Toby quaffed his drink and belched loudly, then with eyes closed leaned back against the tapestried wall. The Botanists slept on, their snores stirring the fragrant air with a faint tepid odor of earth and fish emulsion. Only Justice and Miss Scarlet and myself waited for the suzein to continue. He glanced at each of us in turn, seeming to measure one against the other.

"Well," he said at last. His gaze settled upon me. "It was some time ago—*years* ago, oh—!" He turned his palms upward in a helpless gesture. "We are no good at these things, keeping track! Doctor Foster would know; but he is at nocturne castigations. But there *were* two children, a boy and a girl. Twins. I took them in, because they were very beautiful. The mother I left to the lazars. She was scarred from childbirth. And she was mad, she talked of visions, of seeing the Magdalene and— Oh, it was such a long time ago, I can't remember it all.

"The little girl was mad as well. At least Doctor Foster thought so. She couldn't talk, not to be understood. Just nonsense with her brother. Raphael Miramar, my dearest child." He sighed and stared at me.

"Even your eyes are much like his," he said after a moment. He beckoned me closer. "And not just the color:

those same wild gray eyes. Even as a child Raphael had wild eyes, always looking into corners and finding the oddest things. . . ."

With a dismissive gesture he flicked his fingers. He turned to Miss Scarlet and added graciously, "But your eyes as well are profound, and a lovely shade of brown."

Smiling, she accepted the compliment, her black lashes fluttering as she replied.

"Ah yes; but Aidan does have a powerful vision, a rare and marvelous gift for charming his audiences. It is evident from the claques who are turning out to see him. We have not enjoyed such a success since I first joined the troupe." She regarded me with that stare holding within it the long shadows of barred cages and moon-tossed trees. "And they *are* lovely—

> " *'Eyes I dare not meet in dreams*
> *In Death's dream kingdom these do not ap-*
> *pear . . .'* "

She quoted softly, to herself. Miramar nodded, his fingers playing with a braided tassel hanging from the wall behind him.

"I do not understand why he left," he said at last. He stretched his hand across the table toward me, as if I might answer the question half-asked. "He was the loveliest of us all. . . .

"You must have some understanding of that, Aidan: to command by a look alone, by looks alone—?"

"I have never sought to command," I said. But I felt the flare of that raging Small Voice I knew betrayed my words.

Because I did seek power; and had found it upon the stage. There I might command by my eyes alone, where rapt faces turned upon me, *me*, ME!—not Emma Harrow or Toby Rhymer or even Miss Scarlet Pan, the Prodigy of a Prodigal Age—but myself, Wendy Wanders, the idiot savant, the reclaimed autist, the wild girl of the Human Engineering Laboratory.

"—not meant as an insult, my dear young sieur, please forgive my clumsy words—"

I snapped my head back up from where it had bowed,
perilously close to striking the edge of the table I clutched
with white fingers. "Forgive me," I whispered. Miss Scarlet eyed me with alarm, but Gower Miramar continued
heedlessly.

"No, it was rude of me—there is no question but that you
are a different sort entirely from that poor sick child and
even from my beloved Raphael. *He* lacks all discipline,
save in the amatory arts; and he is too easily distracted, too
easily seduced by dreams of power."

He paused to pour a stream of green tea from the samo-
var into Miss Scarlet's glass.

"Thank you," she said. "But what became of the girl?"

Miramar refilled his tumbler, held it before a candle so
that emerald rays sprang from the faceted glass. "One day
Doctor Foster met an Ascendant woman at a masque, a
Physician. He was more involved in trade with the outlands then, Doctor Foster. She had accompanied a group
of Physicians from the Citadel; they were being entertained by the Botanists. They were looking for research
subjects, they had brought things to trade for them: a generator, cilla ampules, prosthetics.

"She told him of her work. I would imagine she even
asked his advice. He is a very brilliant man, our Doctor
Foster. . . .

"She believed it might be possible to cure this child. At
the very least she would be well cared for. She was so very
beautiful, I didn't have the heart to let her die.

"We sold her to the Ascendants."

He stared at me for a long moment, shaking his head.
"She was a lovely girl; but she banged her head and her
ears bled all the time. There was nothing we could do."
And he shrugged and drank the rest of his tea.

From across the room I could feel Justice's excitement.
Miss Scarlet raised an eyebrow: she feared he would betray
me. I was afraid myself that this news would prove too
much for me to absorb at once. I leaned across the table to
take Justice's hand. I hoped that the suzein would not see
how my own shook.

"My dear friend, this pretty story has tired you!" The

words sounded so false that I expected Justice to rebuke me. Instead he only trembled as I stepped around the sleeping Botanists to sit beside him.

I glanced up at Miramar. "Can you arrange for a palanquin to return Justice and myself to the theater on Library Hill?"

Disappointment creased his face. "I had planned for all of you to spend the night, as my guests. After matins I've arranged for a Sapphic burletta—not the same sort of entertainment as you offer, young sieur, but we consider ourselves artists too."

I began to protest, when I glimpsed Toby Rhymer regarding me with one eye slitted open even as he feigned sleep. Beneath the table Miss Scarlet's foot curled about my ankle.

Beware! She mouthed the word.

I nodded, then raised Justice's hand to my lips and kissed it. My tongue darted between his fingers to taste desire salted with a brackish haze of opium; a sluggish remnant of exhilaration from our play; and fear.

"Perhaps you are too genteel for our entertainments," Miramar suggested, a slight downward tug to his butterfly mouth.

"I would not dream of refusing your hospitality," I demurred. I allowed myself a look at Toby. His raptor's eye caught my own. For a moment he held it in silent struggle before releasing my gaze and once more pretending sleep. "It is just that I fear my companion has drunk too much of your Lethian cup—"

I cast Justice a look of grave fondness. With a slight twitch he nodded, rolled his eyes, and then laid his head in my lap. Toby sniggered, though his eyes remained shut.

"Oh, we are accustomed to much worse than that!" laughed Miramar. "Many of our guests fall prey to sleep before they ever succumb to our charms!"

I let my hand linger upon Justice's forehead, then said, "I am tired as well. Can I find my way to a room by myself?"

"I will accompany you," Justice said quickly. I started to object but caught Miss Scarlet's slow nod as she stared across the table.

"Of course," I replied. As I stood, Toby made a great show of yawning and rubbing his eyes.

"So early to bed? To bed at all, Sieur Aidan?" This with a leer at Justice.

"Even Aidan and Justice must sleep," said Miss Scarlet. "Leave them alone, Toby." She tugged at a lock of his hair, still gray with chalk powder from our show. Toby turned a fond glance upon her. He extended one arm to enfold her to him, until she stepped from her chair to stand upon his knee.

"My dear Miss Pan," he murmured, burying his face in her soft ruff of dark fur. "Forgive me. Miramar, perhaps we will retire to our chambers as well."

Miramar rose and drew back a curtain to show us the way from the Pandoric Seraglio. One by one we stepped over the legs of the sleeping Botanists, Toby escorting Miss Scarlet last of all.

"They will sleep forever," Miramar snorted as the curtain fell back to hide them. "They smoke and talk of their poppies and sleep, smoke and sleep and talk some more. They are worse than the Historians for dull talk."

Justice stepped ahead of me to walk beside Miramar. He nodded as the suzein prattled on about recent scandals, the success of certain liaisons and the expected failure of others.

"Your favorite, Raphael Miramar," I heard Justice ask. He cast me a backward glance. "I have been away for so long, everything is news to me—he left to join the Curators?"

Miramar sighed, beckoning us to follow him up a narrow stair to the next level of the House. "Yes. I begged him not to, his Patron is notoriously fickle. It's rumored he has taken a new pathic as his favorite, and will support him at tonight's judging at the Butterfly Ball. Whitlock High Brazil, a young . . ."

I yawned and let Toby and Miss Scarlet pass me, so that I would not have to listen to more of this endless chatter. The hallways we paced seemed endless as well. Flickering tubes of luminous diatoms did little to dispel the darkness.

Near dawn by my guess; but I had seen neither window nor timepiece since our arrival.

The aura of constant twilight was heightened by the thick and intricately woven tapestries covering the walls and the many doorways we passed. One showed the bomb blast of the First Ascension, a brilliant star rising north of the City. Another had two panels. The first showed stiff-jointed men and women in white coats and robes. Some held beakers and complicated optical devices; others sat in front of screens where even smaller figures performed. A woman prodded a four-legged body stretched upon a table, a geneslave with eyes sewn shut. Other women stared earnestly at the sky, where so many dirigibles, zeppelins, gliders, helicopters, balloons, and airplanes soared that it was a miracle none collided. Behind them gleamed Museums not yet overtaken by kudzu, an unbroken Obelisk. The same backdrop was in the next panel of the diptych. Only here gaudy Paphians cavorted in front of the Museums, and coupled with the white-robed Curators on the steps of the Sorrowful Lincoln.

As I went down the hall other tapestries showed similar scenes. In many of them the Paphians' Magdalene figured: diverting flames from the five Houses; keeping aardmen at bay so that a group of children could safely cross the river; healing lazars so that they jumped and ran once more. Over and over again the same blue-clad woman, eyes closed because she is asleep, waiting for the hour when the Gaping One will wake her to do battle. She was usually shown alone, but one tapestry had her upon a stage with a figure much like herself, the two of them grappling or embracing while myriad Paphians and Curators watched their masque. Beneath the figures tiny words were stitched into the cloth: *Puissant Baal is dead.*

For some reason these made me think of the small girl in our audience that evening. Her face pale, wistful to the point of yearning. I thought of her calling out to me; of Miramar too naming me *Raphael;* of a brother, *my* brother, somewhere in this City, and did he dream of me as Emma Harrow had dreamed of Aidan? I was seized with

ELIZABETH HAND

the overpowering desire to know more of him, but I could
not risk betraying myself to the others in our company.

Without thinking, I quickened my footsteps.

"Excuse me," murmured Miss Scarlet. I had trodden
upon the trailing hem of her taffeta gown, so caught up in
my thoughts that I did not notice the others had paused in
the hallway.

"Sieur Aidan and Justice may have this room," Miramar
announced. With a flourish he swept back a fringe of indigo cloth to display a narrow door inlaid with rare titanium discs and metal gears. "You will be shielded from the
sistrum sounding first worship, and there are no windows
to let the sun in."

As Justice began a lengthy paean of thanks I interrupted
him.

"Suzein Miramar," I began, stroking my fingers across
my open palm to signify I was interested in obtaining a
doxy for the night. Behind me Justice choked audibly.
Toby Rhymer snorted and loomed past me with a broad
wink, on his way to a familiar chamber for the rest of the
night. From beneath her lacy mantilla Miss Scarlet cast me
a piercing glance as she minced behind him.

"Do not sleep too late, Aidan," was all she said in a low
voice. They disappeared down the hall.

"Ah!" Gower Miramar exclaimed, nodding polite goodbyes before turning to me with a radiant smile. His interest
now lay with myself alone, although he beamed at Justice
glowering at my side. "Sieur Aidan, you at least do not
disappoint me! I pride myself on the luster of our House's
reputation—with all respect to you, Saint-Alaban, may
your House never gray. But from Master Aidan's demeanor I guessed he is unaccustomed to our ways. I would
relish the opportunity to share with you both the ministrations of Lais—"

He pressed three fingers to his mouth, with his tongue
traced the outline of one finger. I shook my head; I had
been misunderstood.

"You are too generous, Suzein. But my own taste is
rather more—" I struggled for the right word, looked help-

lessly to Justice. He regarded me for a long moment before coming to my aid.

"Aidan is shy," he said. He leaned against the wall and toyed with a velvet cord that hung there. I looked at my feet, trying to appear awkward: not too difficult under the circumstances. Fortunately Miramar had the grace to regard me with something like sympathy rather than affront at my unintentioned insult.

"He is—inexperienced with women?" suggested Miramar. Justice flicked me a look. I nodded at Justice; he nodded at Miramar; and Miramar nodded to himself.

"He might perhaps like a young boy?" The suzein raised one finely plucked eyebrow to Justice, the experienced merchant steering a recalcitrant customer to the appropriate wares. Again Justice glanced at me; I shook my head. We played out the same guise of innocence, Justice fingering the velvet tassel, Miramar pretending thoughtfulness as he touched the blinking lumens upon his sleeve and changed their pattern from that of The Capitol to The Veil, myself trying not to demand that the suzein produce Raphael's elfin friend upon the spot.

"Ah. Maybe a young girl?" said Miramar with a sudden show of insight. He extended his hand as if admiring the new light pattern upon his sleeve. "A very young girl, perhaps?"

I nodded, looking directly at Miramar and so breaking the chain of pretense that bound us. "Yes," I said. "The ones who accompanied you this evening: they are available?"

"They are all abed," Miramar said thoughtfully. "No, wait—Arethusa has been engaged by two Senators for dousing—".

"Is she the fair one?"

"No—that would be Fancy." Miramar's glance suddenly grew sharper. "Fancy . . . Did you know she was the special intimate of Raphael Miramar?"

"I couldn't help but hear her interrupt my performance," I said. "But so what? You said yourself he was the loveliest of all of you. If I so resemble Raphael Miramar, then certainly I may request an intrigant deserving of my absent brother."

I grinned; but it seemed that I had been too bold. For a long moment Miramar regarded me shrewdly.

"You are not what you seem," he said at last. A flash of anger in his dark eyes. "Do you know who you travel with, Saint-Alaban?"

Justice stood up straight, sleep's last softness gone from him now. "I do."

"Who is he?" Miramar's eyes narrowed. That dim fragrant hallway seemed suddenly to have shrunk into another place, a closed inquisitory chamber like that where I had spent so many hours in my last days at HEL. I took a step nearer to Justice.

"Who is he, Saint-Alaban?" repeated Miramar. "A rebel? An Ascendant delator?"

"He is not a spy," said Justice. "I told you, he is what you see: my friend, a Librarian now traveling with Toby Rhymer's troupe. Miss Scarlet can vouch for him."

From the belled cuff of his robe Miramar withdrew a sheaf of anaphylactic lozenges. He peeled one from the rest and applied it to his temple without offering one to either of us. "I only want to know who I am doing business with," he said. "Fancy Miramar is a particular favorite of Constance Beech the Botanist."

And worth her weight in opium because of that, I thought. I drummed my fingers against my lip, facetiously imitating the Paphian's beck, and waited for Justice to reply. His blue eyes sparked angrily for an instant. He let his breath out slowly, then laughed.

"You drive a hard bargain, Miramar! All this for one little mopsy? A pretty girl, but really! Come on, Aidan—" He made as though to pull me after him into our chamber.

Miramar sniffed, then smiled. A flush crept from the edges of his scalp. The lozenge was beginning to have its effect.

"Ah, well, forgive me! Doctor Foster will no doubt examine me and suggest I join the elders after this Winterlong: I am growing old and suspicious.

"But we hear frightening tales these days. Some weeks

ago a drunken janissary told me of an Ascendant coming to govern the City. Since then we've heard that a band of Ascendants was attacked near the river; that another group was captured by the Curators and killed. They were searching for someone, prisoners escaped from the Citadel. And there is talk of lazars gathering in the Cathedral under a leader. They have grown bold these last few weeks. A group attacked Mustapha Illyria's birthday party and bore off three boys. And last week we entertained Zoologists who told me of aardmen trying to lure children from the Zoo, and betulamia devouring a Botanist near the Gardens."

"I've heard none of this," said Justice. "I told you, I have been gone . . . but surely this doesn't bear on our plans for the evening?"

Miramar sighed. "No, no. It's foolish to worry about all this; leave that to the Curators. Good sense is bad business, after all! It's just I've had no word of Raphael for so long, and I worry." He made the Paphian's beck and bowed, turned a smiling face to us once more.

"So your bashful friend will engage Fancy Miramar for the rest of the evening?"

There followed several minutes of bargaining in low voices. The two Paphians spoke as much with their hands as their tongues as I waited. After another minute or two they kissed. It was done.

"She will be here?" I asked as Justice stepped beside me. A few feet away Miramar stood smiling. The lumens on his robe blinked faster and faster as they responded to the lozenge's quickening of his blood.

"Well, yes. Wendy, he—" Justice stared at my feet. "He won't take payment."

"Well, good. We have nothing to trade." I tugged at the door handle.

"No—I mean, he'll only take one payment. He wants a kiss; he wants you to kiss him."

I began to argue but he cut me short.

"Because you resemble Raphael—well, don't do it then, Wendy." I sniffed as he put his hand anxiously on my shoulder: jealous! "We can go to bed, it's late—"

"I want to see the girl."

I turned to Miramar. "Well, Miramar, you demand small payment for the special intimate of Raphael Miramar and Constance Beech." I tilted my face to his.

He kissed me so violently that I recoiled, twisting so that his hands would not feel my breasts. The lozenge's acrid taste lingered on my tongue. I shut my eyes and tried not to respond to his desire, its memory of a face so much like mine that I felt queasy, as though I tasted my own blood. I clutched at Miramar's sleeve. His laughter rang out, flecking the air with that bitter smell.

"He *is* an innocent!" he said, eyes flashing delightedly. "How gratifying to see that I can make you dizzy with a kiss, Sieur Aidan! No, he is not Raphael Miramar," he said to Justice. "Kisses like a Curator, doesn't he?"

Justice smiled wryly. I untangled myself from Miramar's embrace and stepped away, noting that Miramar's lumens now glowed a brilliant violet, pulsing like a warning beacon.

"I will wake Fancy," he said as he turned on his heel.

Once inside our chamber I set to warming the room's single diatom lantern with my hands. Its cool light flared to a brighter blue to show us our sleeping chamber: a long narrow room overhung with more tapestries. Justice stood by the door staring at me, waiting for an explanation. I met his gaze, felt a surge of desire stirred by his anger. I turned away from him.

"I should have taken my own chamber," I said, staring at the bed that stood at the room's center: wide and sumptuously pillowed, canopied with drapes of viridian velvet. I felt uneasy, as though on the edge of a seizure, and empty, the way I had felt after the janissaries siphoned me.

"This is dangerous, Wendy," Justice said, drawing closer. "This girl: she'll know you're not Raphael Miramar."

"I don't want her to believe that I'm Raphael Miramar," I said. "I want to tap her."

"You can't do that!"

"Why not? I won't hurt her: just a moment, just long enough to learn more about him—"

"You already heard what Miramar said. There was a girl, they sold her to the Ascendants—"

"*I* was that girl!" Suddenly I felt more frightened than I had since I first saw the Boy; but also enraged, as though everything since that moment had been a betrayal. I grabbed him in a fury. "Sold like a fucking animal *by a whore!* Sold to the Ascendants so that I could be patterned with some monster, so that I could be melted down for *this!*"

I pointed at my head, screaming as my entire body shook. I was on the verge of a seizure. When Justice tried to restrain me I struck him, sending him reeling.

"*Where is that boy?*" I shouted. "Raphael Miramar— what kind of a brain does *he* have, the suzein's favorite, *why wasn't he sold?*"

Justice stared, terrified. I fell to my knees, my voice strangling as I brought my head back and then smashed it against the floor.

"No, Wendy!"

I heard him cry out, but only dimly. Already it calmed me, that warm wave of enkephalins rushing through my mind in response to the pain I could not feel. I struck my head again, and again, until finally I lay exhausted, my cheek resting against the floor as I breathed heavily. From the other side of the room I heard Justice weeping.

Minutes passed. I heard another, softer sound. I glanced up to see Justice standing by the open door, turning to look from me back to a small figure silhouetted against the hall's dusky glow.

"Fancy," I said thickly. I thought she might be frightened, to see me crouched upon the floor like this; but it was obvious she had seen many stranger things in her few years. Still blinking with sleep, she smiled up at Justice, then peered into our chamber. She had yet to recognize me.

"Thank you," Justice called after some figure retreating down the hall. He was careful to shield the doorway so that no one might see inside.

"Miramar said I have been engaged by a gentleman. You are he?" The girl stood on tiptoe, arms outstretched so that

Aidan Arent (Hannah)

he might lift her. Justice stared down awkwardly, then with a sigh closed the door and shook his head.

"No. This— you have been engaged by another gentleman. Aidan Arent, a Player. There." He gestured to where I lay upon the floor.

Still smiling, Fancy turned, taking a few steps to follow the shadow of his arm upon the carpet. When she saw me she stopped.

"Raphael!"

I braced myself, holding one hand out to keep her from me.

"No, Fancy," I said, struggling to my feet. But already she hugged my legs. I could feel her entire small body vibrating with excitement. "Aidan, my name is Aidan. You saw me earlier this evening—"

"Raphael," she repeated. Her face pressed against my thigh. Her eyes were shut tight against my denial. "I miss you."

"No, Fancy," I began, then sighed. I felt calmer now. "Come sit here," I said more gently. I settled back upon the floor. Fancy clambered into my lap, still not meeting my eyes. From across the room Justice watched us impassively.

"I am not Raphael Miramar," I began again. I took her chin in my hand and forced her to look at me. "See? I'm *not*."

"You look just like him." She reached to touch my hair. His would have been long, braided in a heavy russet chain. I nodded as she stroked the small raised node upon my temple.

"But I'm not him."

"You're not him." Her voice no longer held much doubt. She squirmed in my lap, her little hands stroking my thigh. I thought suddenly that she might discern my disguise— she was, after all, a prostitute—and shifted until I had her perched upon my knees. She raised her hand to trace the line of my chin. "Are you his twin?"

I shrugged. "I don't know." A child; what matter what she knew or thought of me, really? "I'm a Player, I travel through the City with Toby Rhymer's troupe. You saw us tonight."

"You were that lady—" She frowned, stuck a finger in her mouth.

"That's right: Viola. I was in disguise. I pretended to be a lady in the play. Do you pretend things, Fancy?"

She nodded solemnly. "All the time. Miramar teaches us to pretend lots of things." She tilted her head and smiled across the room at Justice, then lifted her face to mine as for a kiss. I turned away, then looked down at her hand upon my knee. A small scab on her wrist, like a star.

"Did you cut yourself?" I asked.

She nodded. "With Constance. She set the pinion too tight."

I raised her hand to my lips so that I could kiss the broken skin. "Fancy, I want you to pretend something for me, something about your friend Raphael. Can you think of him, remember doing something with him?"

"Pretend for you? Like a game?" Her eyes widened. "I will do whatever you wish, sieur."

I looked at Justice. He was pale, squatting by the door on a large pillow, but he returned my gaze unblinkingly. I turned back to Fancy.

"I want you to think of Raphael." I bowed my head and whispered the words, lifting a coil of her golden hair to display one tiny ear. "Don't pretend I'm him, just *think* of him. Of something that really happened."

"Like when he was cacique at Winterlong last year? That really happened. I should think of that?"

Against my cheek her warm breath. Her long hair sweet with some floral soap, that sweet warm childhood smell still perfuming her skin. It made me dizzy, to imagine that *he* had sat with her like this, the small trembly weight against his thighs, her hands caressing his cheeks. . . .

"Yes." I grabbed one of her hands and held it tightly, squeezing my eyes shut as I emptied my mind to tap her. Perhaps Justice was right; perhaps it was too dangerous, not for this child (I cared little for her, a mere courtesan), but for myself.

But I would know, I had to know something of him—

Because since I had heard Miramar's tale earlier it was as though I had discovered myself to be a changeling, the goblin barter of some malevolent agent. And in learning this I suddenly felt I had lost everything I knew of Wendy Wanders; and only *he* might somehow make me whole again, Raphael Miramar, my beautiful brother—

"Does he look like me?" I asked in a low voice.

"We-ell." She closed one eye to scrutinize my face. "His hair is longer, and he has a strawberry mark, *there.* And Raphael smiles more. His eyes don't cross like yours." She grazed my forehead with a finger. "It's not all bruised there, either."

"Show me," I whispered, drawing her face to mine. "Think of him, don't think of anything else. Kiss me."

Her mouth was so tiny that I had to hold her chin steady so that I could find it, probe gently with my tongue; and how clumsy I felt before her quiet obedient response. I recalled Miramar's cutting aside to Justice:

"He kisses like a Curator . . . he is not Raphael Miramar. . . ."

Think of Melisande, I told myself to keep from trembling. *A girl, she's just another little girl, a whore besides. . . .*

Sleep a soft fur upon her tongue. Her milk teeth small and sharp as a kitten's. I shivered as she bit my lower lip, drew back murmuring *No* so that she would not break the skin.

"I'm thinking of Raphael," she said.

"Good girl. Now shhh . . ."

I covered her mouth with one hand. With the other I took her wrist, brought it to my mouth. She giggled as I licked the rough skin, then frowned when I bit very gently where Constance's pinion had left its own cold kiss.

"Ow."

I moved my hand to cover her eyes. I didn't want to alarm her, didn't want panic to overwhelm the subtler impressions I sought. From the star upon her wrist blood welled.

"Raphael, remember Raphael," I said. I bowed to lick

the blood from her hand, rubbing her arm so that it would come faster. "Raphael."

There was barely enough for me to taste, but it was sweet, nothing of salt or sweat or tears in her smooth skin. I moaned and squeezed harder on her wrist, until she cried out, arms flailing.

It is enough.

Winterlong . . .

There are the candles, twelve of them shimmering upon a high stone shelf, high high above me. Jada passes me the silver tray blued with negus flame and I try to snatch a snapdragon, wrens' hearts burning crisp and red on their bed of green holly. Blue flame licks my fingers, I cry out and lick them and Jada makes a mean face, I hate her. Miramar is watching me from his big chair, he laughs so hard his gums show and he looks ugly.

—Here, Fancy, don't cry!

He grabs Jada's wrist, plucks a snapdragon from the tray, and tosses it in his palm 'til it cools and then he pops it in my mouth. I like the burnt ones best. Where is Raphael? My dress itches, it scratches my stomach. Quistana Illyria picked it out. I hate her. Constance gave her an electrified eel lamp and seventeen grams of tristain for Winterlong but she kissed me when Miramar wasn't there and I told Raphael before he left. Constance keeps smiling at me and now Quistana is mad and Jada and her are both sitting on Constance's lap but she keeps smiling at me. Where is he?

Knock knock knock. Benedick and Small Thomas yell.

—Here is the Mayor!

They run to the door. Benedick knocks over the big thing with all the presents on it and Ketura picks them up, she looks so sad since she got back. The one wrapped in blue silver with the featherbells is mine from Raphael. It's a mirror made of faëro eggs. I peeked.

—The Mayor, the Old Gray Mayor! yells Benedick. He goes to pull the door open but Neville Warnick grabs him.

Pygmalion

—*Ho ho ho little boy, I wouldn't do* **that!**

Benedick starts to cry because Neville is taking him to the Lustrous Chamber and he'll miss the guise. I want to cry too because Raphael isn't here yet. Small Thomas opens the door instead.

They are all there, the mummers in disguise for the Winterlong masque. Doctor Foster has on a big hat but I know it's him. One of the Curators pretends to be afraid of him but Miramar tells him Shush, Listen.

—*Who in this House will let the Winter in?*

That is Galatea Saint-Alaban dressed as the Old Gray Mayor. She wears a black tuxedo and a horse's head from the Zoologists. Mandala Persia showed me once where they keep the bones.

—*Who will let me in?*

—*Not I,* Miramar says very loud.

—*Who will let the Winter in?* That is Doctor Foster, he makes the Dead Boy in the masque better after he dies.

—*Not me! Not me!*

I yell too, I am laughing too even with Jada and Quistana, it is not such a bad dress. Malva Persia is dressed just like Aspasia Persia, when he walks in everybody laughs. He looks so funny! He lifts his dress and he has bells on, the Mayor pretends to bite him and he screams just like her.

—*Who will let the Winter in, who will let the Winter in?*

But nobody does. Old Nick comes, he was behind Malva. He kisses Ketura and gives her a golden hat but he gives me a peacock mask and throws comfits in the air.

—*Send her on, send her on, we won't keep the Winter here!* everyone yells to Winter the Old Gray Mayor.

—*Take her to Persia, take her to Illyria, take her to Saint-Alaban!*

—*Take her to the lazars!* says Small Thomas, *Take her to the la—*

Constance Beech kisses him so he will shut up.

—*I will be back!* screams the Mayor. The bones clack and she takes off her top hat and paper snow comes out and her teeth snap clack-clack-clack. I know she is Galatea Saint-

Alaban but it is scary anyway. I wish Raphael was here, I wish so hard I close my eyes. I open them, here he is.

—Fancy!

He smells so good, like opium and silver powder.

—They made me cacique! I can't stay, Whitlock is paired with me, Miramar is late too and why are the masquers still here?

He grabs me and throws me in the air, I sit on his shoulders and pull his hair and everyone is looking at me because I am his favorite and he is everyone's favorite, Raphael, they say Raphael! The Mayor goes snap and bites at his hair, he yells because his costume is getting messed.

—They're waiting for you for Winterlong! he says. Hurry up! I have to go back—

No one hears him, they are singing now. Doctor Foster takes the Mayor by a white rope and hits her, not hard. They hurry because they have to go to Illyria and Persia and Saint-Alaban last of all for the Masque of Winterlong. Everyone starts singing.

> *We will walk, we will wander*
> *Farther on and over yonder*
> *Not a song not a word*
> *nothing more is spoken*
> *Hang the boy and raise the girl*
> *'til Winterlong is broken.*

—Don't go, Raphael.

—I can't stay, Whitlock is waiting! Hurry, Miramar!

—I want to come!

—You're too little.

Constance Beech frowns at me.

—I want to come, I want to come!

—Let her! Raphael smiles, he takes me in his arms and swings me around and kisses me, his hair falls in my face and I see his eyes looking at me, gray eyes shading to green and he shakes his flaming hair and it falls in my face and it is him, Raphael Miramar, I can see him now and it is me, I am seeing my brother—

I scream, thrash, and tear at wires that are not there.

"Go!" Justice is shouting. Something falls from my hands, another voice cries out, but it is too late, he is gone—

A door slams. Later it slammed again.

"She's gone. I had their Doctor give her something. Maybe she won't remember." Justice's face was dark with anger. "How could you be so careless? Didn't you hear Miramar? The Ascendants are looking for someone, they may still be searching for you. If they hear of this—"

"You told me they think I'm dead. Leave me alone." I stumbled toward the bed. Before I reached it he was there behind me, pulling me to him as I tried to push him away.

"Then *why not me*, Wendy? Why her and not me?" His voice cracked as he sought to caress me.

"Justice, don't—" I rolled away from him.

I shut my eyes and tried desperately to retain that image of a face so like my own. A hundred tree-strung candles cast golden light upon his hair as he turned from me, from the child Fancy, the smell of him like jasmine and opium, burning wax and balsam, his pale gray skin, his eyes—

"Yes, Wendy!" Justice murmured in my ear, mistaking my silence for compliance. I pushed him away, his lips leaving mine with a sigh.

Too late. Already the metallic taste flooded my mouth and my heart pounded, as it had each time he had approached me thus backstage. Then it had always been furtive, a stolen embrace with blood bartered in exchange; his swollen mouth in no need of rouge because I bled it each evening, but slowly so that I could taste his own desire and climax as he moved against me.

But it infuriated me now, when I had for a moment glimpsed my brother's heart and past. I punched him in the ribs.

"Leave me," I yelled. "Go *away!*"

Justice gasped. Clutching at his stomach he sat up, tears glittering in his eyes. "Why?" His voice tripped into a fit of coughing. "Why, Wendy? Why won't you let me? I understand—"

"You don't understand, or else you'd leave me." I kicked aside a pillow so that I could slide beneath the blankets.

"Emma and Morgan and that other woman are *dead,* Justice. It killed them, *I* killed them—"

"But you slept with other empties at HEL," he protested, yanking back the coverlets. *"They* didn't die. And you just took that girl—"

"She knew something," I said. "About me; about my brother. I care nothing for her, nothing at all. And you understand nothing, Justice, or you'd be afraid even to touch me."

He knotted the blankets, avoiding my eyes. I felt a sudden pang, pity mingling with my anger. "Don't you see, Justice? It kills them sometimes—what I see, what I am—and I . . . I don't want to hurt you."

Still he refused to look at me. I waited, then said, *"Why* am I so important to you? You could have anyone in this House, in this whole forsaken City. Why do you want me?"

He pushed the blanket from him and looked up, his hair falling into his eyes. "Because you are beautiful. Because they hurt you at HEL. Because I love you."

I thought of how he had saved me; of him standing over me in the Horne Room, watching silently through the night while I tossed in the bed with the Ascendants' machines hooked into my brain. And I thought of tapping Fancy, her joy as she greeted Raphael; her delight when she first saw me and thought I was he. Raphael Miramar, beloved of the House Miramar.

And who loved Wendy Wanders? Who even knew who I was, except for Justice and Miss Scarlet?

But I couldn't risk returning their love; could only imagine it, really, for I had nothing of my own to give. Only nightmares and despair and suicide.

I laughed harshly. "Love? Your people are whores. You want to use me, just as Dr. Harrow did—you're no better than any of them!" But I knew my words were not true.

Pain and yearning so distorted Justice's face that I looked away.

"Oh, Wendy . . ." He took a deep breath, shook his head before going on. "It's not just that you are beautiful—"

"But you are beautiful, Justice. All of your people are beautiful! Any of them would welcome you as a lover."

In the soft light his eyes burned a vivid sapphire blue. Angular face rounded just enough to keep its lines from gauntness, smooth brow raked with that golden hair above slanted deep-set eyes. I had seen how other Paphians gazed upon him with presumptive pride, as if in his even features each recognized his own. But to me they all seemed too much alike; only something in Justice's face marked him, lines left by his time at HEL, the relative hardship of our life with the Players.

"Beauty is too common among your people for it to move me," I said at last.

He sighed and wrapped a blanket around his knees. "There is a saying we have: 'Empty vessels are the loveliest.' That is why we love children, innocents, anything that is young and new, before the world changes it and it begins to die. Maybe that is why I love you."

"But I am no innocent, Justice. And I think I am Death itself sometimes."

He reached to stroke my hair where it had grown back to cover the nodes and scars upon my temples. "You are not Death, Wendy." He drew me closer to him. "But even if you were . . ."

I shut my eyes and let him touch me, felt an odd dizziness that frightened me. I opened my eyes and took his chin in my hand, brought his face close to mine, kissed him until I drew blood once more from his broken lip. He cried out and drew back, but not soon enough.

Giggling, I fell upon the bed, exhilarated by the taste of his dismay, those few drops burning like some hot liquor upon my tongue.

"Oh, it's lovely, lovely!"

A blurred glimpse of his face, Justice shaking his head, his mouth moving though I cannot hear the words. And then it comes . . .

* * *

Strands of blood and saliva entwine within my mouth. Fire flares back to my temples so that the blood dances beneath my skin. I shut my eyes tightly, the better to see what sings there so bright and clear—

Eyes, eyes, eyes dancing, green as the highest branch upon the tree, eyes so clear that they show no pupil, nothing but the reflection of what He sees before me, Justice's white face dancing now too as he tries to hold me and suddenly I am clawing at him, grunting deep in my throat as my nails tear his face and—

With a cry Justice rolled across the bed, and I wailed to lose my dream. I scratched at my own face, dragged my fingers across my cheeks until I felt something warm, jammed my fingers into my mouth and gagged: because it was my own blood I tasted, the shining strands snarling into clotted chemicals. On the other side of the bed Justice wept.

My stomach stopped heaving. The shrieking in my mind stilled. I raised my head to see Justice crouched on the corner of the bed.

"Why won't you let me?" he cried. "I could make you happy!"

I held my head in my hands, pressing my thumbs beside my eyes to stop the pain raging there. As he reached for me I spat at him, pointing to a thread of blood trailing from my lip.

"That makes me happy," I snarled.

But as I spoke I reeled back as though I had been struck. My sight dimmed as something black and huge and cold loomed in front of me. I began to shake uncontrollably and choking reached for Justice.

"No—stop Him—"

But it is too late.

* * *

"Baal is dead," a Small Voice wails. "I have killed my brother: puissant Baal is dead."

My hands fall back helplessly; Justice's face ripples as though reflected in dark and quickly moving water. A cloud across the surface. From the depths rises another face, leaden-hued, soft and pallid as a salamander. As He turns to smile at me the skin droops from his cheeks. From His neck floats a rope—no, a vine—but then it too falls away, its flaccid curve tracing the outline of His mouth. His smile widens to show white broken teeth, swollen tongue, the waxen tendril of a feeding maggot.

Another Voice whispers, "No. Baal is risen; his sister Anat we take now—

> *"With sword we cleave her,*
> *With fire we burn her,*
> *In the field we doth sow her.*
> *Birds eat her remains,*
> *Consuming her remains,*
> *Devouring her remains.*
> *Puissant Baal died;*
> *And behold, he is alive.*
> *And lo, Anat we take now."*

His grin is hideous. I scream, try to escape those livid eyes but He is there reaching for me. His hand beckons me and all He has to do is touch me and I will lose all this, this room and earth and the warmth of air and blood, He will take me as He took them, all of them, and I feel Him, He is inside me the blink of His eyes His mouth opening to rend me my beautiful brother in the dark—

His eyes close, his mouth snaps shut, his lips furl into new green leaves spilling from a tree where stranger fruit grows. Another boy, yellow hair plaited about a leather belt, smiling, smiling as he always does seeing me in the mirror: Emma, Aidan, Raphael, my brother, we three there . . .

The face that rears to gaze upon me with hollow eyes rimmed with bone is not his: not Aidan's or the laughing Boy's. I scream because as the belt slips from the neck it leaves no scar, no burning flesh, but instead skin soft and smooth as Justice's had been beneath my nails. The swollen eyes that stare from the corpse are my own.

"*Wendy. Wake.*"

Dr. Harrow's voice rings clear and strong enough to pull me from a profound stupor. Beside me Justice stirs, then moaning turns to hug a pillow. I sit up, keeping my eyes shut so that the vision is not disturbed.

I know she is not really here, not in the Paphians' chamber where I have finally collapsed. She is a Small Voice now, but it is Emma Harrow I hear and not my own thoughts.

"Dr. Harrow," I whisper. My hands tremble as I pull the coverlets to my breast. I can still taste the bitter residue of my brain's own bile. "Dr. Harrow—please help me. I have entered a fugue state. Please—"

She laughs. A starburst of pale yellow light as the threads of her consciousness leap neural chasms.

"*You live in a fugue state now, Wendy.*" Her voice fires along my locus ceruleus so that I begin to sweat in fear. The neural threads twist and spiral into a brilliant trail. Her sour laughter plunges into the utter darkness of regret.

"*Too soon, too soon,*" she sighs. "*And now swallowed into the void. Poor Wendy wanders alone now. . . .*"

"No!" I try to follow the faint spark of her consciousness as it soars and plummets through endless canyons. "Don't leave me! Help me, Dr. Harrow—"

"*Help you?*" In my mouth a faint sweetness as of old apples. "*You killed me, Wendy—*"

"Not me!" The sweetness roils into norepinephrine's cloying honey. She leaps into flame, white and blinding. I start to cry out, to press my face into a pillow so that I will not see the room and wake to lose her again. "The Boy, Dr. Harrow—who is that Boy?"

"*Ahhh . . .*"

Two Voices now, two bright flecks in my spinning firmament.

"My brother—"

"My sister—"

Faint as first light the Boy's bleak consciousness touches the rim of my temporal lobe. I groan in disappointment and terror. Already I can feel Dr. Harrow's retreat into my corpus callosum, those gray mountains.

But Dr. Harrow lingers a moment longer. Axons whip and slash against the Boy's first firings. I derive a numb solace from her presence, unclench my fingers from the pillow and draw a deep breath. Something had stirred her to wake me; something she would warn me of. A moment longer and she will be gone and only the Boy will remain to torment me.

"Dr. Harrow—"

A sigh echoes through the gray chasm. *"Wendy,"* it breathes. *"Oh Wendy it is cold, He is so cold. . . ."*

I shiver at her anguish, but another urgency forces me on. "A brother, Dr. Harrow. Do I have a brother?"

Her consciousness wavers. A pulse of noradrenaline. Emerald novas burst to send her spinning into the shadows. A last cry soars through my mind's abyss and I shout in pain as a blocked pathway erupts into crimson flame.

"There is a Boy," she cries at last. *"Our brother—Baal—"*

My head pounds from the effort of trying to hold her another moment. *Who is Baal?* my mind shrieks. Aidan? Raphael?

Her consciousness a crimson streak as she spirals into the void—

"He is our brother, the dying god—we woke Him and now there is no peace until He is slain—

'But oh, my offense is rank, it smells to heaven;
It hath the primal eldest curse upon 't,
A brother's murder!'

"Find him, Wendy—"

She is gone. I am alone with Him, the One she woke, the One who slumbers within my tangle of dendrites and neurons and axons: the One who uses me as a flail to reap His harvest, His tribute of souls. The God in the Tree, Dionysus

Diomysius Dendrites

Dendrites. The Gaping Lord. My hands pummel the bedcovers as He strives with me. My fingers curl helplessly, then flex and open as the blood pumps into them.

I feel Him, the cold and iron pressure of His limbs within mine, my blood streaked with the raw fluids He has released within my brain. A roaring as of some vast beast freed from its prison. A cry that I know is Justice's as he wakes, as I claw and scream and tear at the sheets.

"No, Wendy!"

I do not see Justice as I fight Him, try to keep Him from seizing Justice like an animal, until finally I fall back onto the bed, grunting as I rip the comforter into shreds.

"Find him, Wendy!"

Her last words echoing as above me Justice hovers, in his hands some heavy object that smashes against my forehead. I hear a howl of frustrated rage, and plunge into unconsciousness.

Somehow Justice and Miss Scarlet engaged palanquins to bear us back to the theater. Justice pleaded I was ill. I recall only Gower Miramar leaning over me in our small chamber, and a fleeting impression of sunrise striking the minarets of the House Miramar as the elders carried us off.

I slept fitfully through that entire day and night, waking often from terrible nightmares. Like shades flickering in a cinematoscope the faces of Justice and Miss Scarlet would reveal themselves to me, first one and then the other as momentarily I awakened, struggling to lift my head before collapsing back upon my pillow.

When finally I did wake it was late morning. Sunlight bloomed upon the peeling wallpaper of my tiny room. I turned to see Miss Scarlet sitting primly upon a child's rocking chair she had dragged from the prop room, her lips moving as she read silently from Mrs. Fiske's *Memoirs*.

"Miss Scarlet," I whispered. When I touched my forehead I felt a bump there as big as Miss Scarlet's fist, and recalled Justice's face as he struck me in the Miramars' chamber. I tried to raise myself, and knocked against a

"being dead doesn't excuse it"

half-full pitcher of water on the nightstand. Miss Scarlet
caught this before it could fall. She put it back upright,
carefully reserved the place in her book with a tattered
strand of velvet ribbing. With a sigh she set the volume
upon the nightstand.

"How do you feel?" she asked.

"Awful." I flinched as she brushed the hair from my
forehead. She nodded, poured me a glass of water, and
waited until I drank it before saying anything more.

"You could have killed that child. You could have killed
yourself," she said at last. I shut my eyes and started to turn
from her. "No!—listen to me, Wendy!"

I opened one eye, then shrugged. With a groan I pulled
myself up to stare back at her angry face. "I'm listening," I
said.

"Perhaps you do not care about putting yourself in danger; but you have no right to endanger our lives as well.
That child was hysterical. *Justice* was hysterical. He
thought he'd killed you. He had to lie to the suzein about
what happened, else Miramar might have taken action
against us all because you harmed the child.

"That was ill-conceived, Wendy. You heard Miramar:
Ascendants have crossed the river. They might be looking
for you. A strange, cold young man resembling a Paphian
favorite, driving a Paphian child to the edge of madness—
this may sound too much like a runaway empath who
caused the suicide of the Ascendants' most renowned researcher."

"They think I'm dead," I protested weakly.

The chimpanzee trembled with indignation. "Being
dead doesn't excuse it! You could have killed her—"

"I don't care," I said, exhausted. I pressed my palms
against my eyes. "Please let me sleep—"

"Dammit, Wendy!"

In her excitement she had climbed onto the seat of the
little rocker. It swayed precariously as she swung her arms
to punctuate her sentences, bits of the decayed fabric of
her dressing gown pocking the air with flecks of oriental
green and black. "You have to care!" she exclaimed, one
long arm plucking at my bedcovers. "You must care, about

everything; else how will you become a Great Artist? How will you become Truly Human?"

I groaned. "I don't want to become *anything* right now. Right now I'd like to sleep, or maybe eat. Where is Justice?"

She blinked painfully, as if she had been slapped. "Not care?" she repeated, as if she had not heard me. "Not care?"

I rolled my eyes and turned onto my side. I could hear her breathing deeply ("from the diaphragm," she would say) as she sought to calm herself. I pretended to be asleep, although I knew this would not fool Miss Scarlet, who declared she could smell sleep, and daydreams when one should be preparing for one's entrance.

But perhaps she decided it would be better to wait for this imperfect vessel to knit itself back together before attempting to fill it again. The bedstand shook as she brushed against it, retrieving her book. Then I heard the soft rustle of a page being turned. She cleared her throat.

> " *'Great acting, of course, is a thing of the spirit; in its best estate a conveyance of certain abstract spiritual qualities, with the person of the actor as medium. It is with this medium our science deals, with its slow, patient perfection as an instrument. The eternal and immeasurable accident of the theater which you call genius, that is a matter of The Soul.'* "

The muted kiss of her volume's brittle pages as they met each other once again. "Goodbye, Wendy," said Miss Scarlet. The door clicked shut behind her.

The house was dark that evening. Fabian visited me briefly. He told me that while we had been performing for Miramar and his guests, the House High Brazil had been beset by lazars. Many were dead or taken prisoner, Paphians and Curators alike, and there was talk of gruesome things, children beheaded by other children in the darkness, the living corpse the Saint-Alabans named the Gaping One seen frolicking with a jackal familiar at the ball; captives led to be human offerings to Him at the Engulfed Cathedral. The City was in mourning.

After he left I lay long abed, half-expecting to be visited again by Miss Scarlet, or Justice, or even Toby himself. At the very least by Gitana or Mehitabel. But no one came. A distant clock clanged somewhere within the theater. Still I waited; still no one came. It seemed I was being ignored, or left to recover in solitude. Finally I decided to go out.

I met no one in the halls, though from far off I could hear the swish and clatter and shouted expletives that accompanied fencing practice in the gymnasium. A reassuring sound, whispering that normal life was going on somewhere despite the massacre, despite my madness. I went through the Grand Hall, passing quickly down the center of the ancient carpet with its worn arabesques. As I hurried I passed rotting cabinets holding portfolios so ancient that the very meanings of the words they contained had changed over the intervening centuries. It was with some relief that I reached the massive oaken doors that led outside.

Shadows stretched across the wide sward in front of the theater, to wither and die before reaching the boundaries of the Library facing it. A score of skittish sheep belonging to the Librarians grazed upon the theater lawn. Occasionally Toby called them into service as decorative additions to certain pastoral plays in our repertoire. For the most part they just wandered aimlessly across the grass. I nodded at the young Librarian perched across the way upon the ruins of a marble pillar. A re-engineered swivelgun rested in his lap as protection against lazars or aardmen. I exchanged a melancholy greeting with him and headed for the Deeping Avenue.

Already the sun had dipped behind the Library's copper dome. As I crossed the common I heard the rush of hawks settling for the night, and the moans of owls as they made a few half-hearted forays into the twilight. An undeniable glamor hung over this place, the Library grounds a disor-

dered but still lovely tangle of rosebushes and cherry trees
given just enough attention to keep them from utter abandon, while magnolias and white oaks lofted high above
them. From here I looked down the long sweep of the
Deeping Avenue to where the Narrow Forest overtook it. I
could just make out the blackened finger of the Obelisk
rising from the trees. Behind it the sun glinted upon the
distant river. In places I saw where the Deeping Avenue
was still kept clear. There were little orchards of apple and
cherry trees, and pasture compounds where the Curators
grazed sheep. White blocks like salt spilled upon a smooth
green table were wooden beehives splitting beneath their
load of honey. I saw the tulip poplar allée leading to where
the Regents' few and splendid horses lived in the circular
Horn Building, and the red turrets of the High Regent's
Castle, still proud and tall despite its broken towers and
shattered windows.

But for the most part the view down Library Hill was of
trees massed between the ruins of once-elegant marble
buildings, and the crumbling bulk of vast gray edifices that
had never been lovely. Only in decay had they finally
achieved a sort of truce with sky and rain beneath their
heavy kudzu beards.

I sighed, and stopped to climb a ragged pine tree whose
branches spoked out to form a comfortable vantage point.
It was October, what the Paphians called Autime, but the
air still smelled sweet and warm. Only the browning leaves
of the oaks seemed like fall, that and a faintly chill northern breeze that stirred the evergreen boughs.

I braced myself against the pine's bole and stood, the
breeze ruffling my hair. Its touch made me think of cold
granite, stony earth; a pale face half-hidden by new green
leaves. But I shook this melancholy from me and turned to
face due west, to the river, and felt the last bit of sun slide
down my cheeks.

Since I had entered it nearly two months ago it never
failed to stir me, to see it thus. The City of Trees, the
Senators' abandoned capital, the forgotten City by the
River. To go out upon the stage gave me great joy; but it
was joy shot through with despair and feverish longing, as I

re-defines "human" as loss, not fullness (Laser

felt myself buffeted by the waves of desire that my audiences tossed back upon me. I felt no triumph in my performances, as did Toby; took no ordinary pleasure as did Gitana and Fabian and the rest, with the surety of an evening spent in lovemaking afterward. And I could not be like Miss Scarlet and treat the theater as a temple, or a laboratory. She found acting a form of alchemy, a crucible in which to purify the raw lusts and loves and everyday fevers of humankind and then, having cooled them in the detachment of rehearsal, fortify herself onstage with this elixir of human memory.

No. The joy of the theater was for me the joy of longing, of yearning for that humanity which I could simulate but would never truly possess or understand. I did not yet understand that it is longing and loss, as much as anything else, that makes one truly human.

But to look like this upon the City of Trees *was* to understand something of men and women, of how they had lived once long ago, when the avenues were roads that stretched white and smooth and as yet unmarred by trees, and the Obelisk stood whole, and Senators ruled from atop Library Hill. It made me feel empty, somehow, and alone. But emptiness and solitude eased my heart like nothing else, they were so rare to me.

And so for a few minutes I felt as though the City belonged only to myself. That it was my secret, somehow, and my creation. As the Small Voices were mine; as were the memories of Emma and Aidan and the poet Morgan Yates and the courtesan Fancy Miramar. Small voices; random neural firings; stolen memories. But they were mine now, as I imagined this City was mine, to savor and horde and protect against the One who would steal them from me, the One who sought to drive me to despair and death as He had those others. I shook my head, then raised my fist to the dusky sky and laughed.

"You will not have me!" I cried aloud. But only the wind called back.

I thought then of an ancient poem Miss Scarlet recited sometimes when we traveled across the City to perform. She would gaze upon the ruins of Library Hill, its glory now dust and rubble beneath the greenery, and say, "The Ascendants may have abandoned the City, but the gods have not, and we have not. We hold her still, Wendy, people like you and me. We wait for the day when the Magdalene will wake again, and walk here as the lazars say the Gaping One does now. While we can still believe in Her and hope, the City is ours. They will never wrest Her from us again, not with inferno or rain or fear. 'We are not to despair; we are not to despair.'"

Then she would recite, and afterward we would both be silent. Because it was the very ordinariness of this vision that we loved—

The dream of small lives no longer led. Of a light left burning upon a well-swept porch, and small machines clattering along the dusty avenues. The smells of scorched coffee and cheap wine hanging above a sordid little cafe. The thrum of trains moving beneath ancient avenues now enthralled by starving children and the relentless usurping trees.

I leaned back against the pine trunk. As the first star blinked in the pure and empty sky I recited softly.

Auden

> "'. . . *Even now, in this night*
> *Among the ruins of the Post-Vergilian City*
> *Where our past is a chaos of graves and the barbed-*
> *wire stretches ahead*
> *Into our future till it is lost to sight,*
> *Our grief is not Greek: As we bury our dead*
> *We know without knowing there is reason for what*
> *we bear,*
> *That our hurt is not a desertion, that we are to pity*
> *Neither ourselves nor our city;*
> *Whoever the searchlights catch, whatever the loud-*
> *speakers blare,*
> *We are not to despair.'"*

Part Six

The Skeleton Transcendent

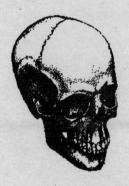

1. Catastrophes of different kinds

Lazars woke me from a black and dreamless sleep in the Hagioscopic Embrasure.

"It is him," said a child's voice. So vast was the void that had swallowed me I could not for some moments discern their figures moving about the room, although my eyes were open and gray dawn slanted from slits in the varicolored ceiling.

"Yes," another voice lisped. "He killed Peter in the river last night. I saw him."

"We must take him," the first voice said, but doubtfully.

"Yes," the other agreed, and fell into thoughtful silence.

They did not kill me, though I lay for many minutes waiting to feel their small knives in my throat, their teeth. I heard them stirring about the room, kicking at oddments that rolled across the floor, and imagined what broken toys they played with: Whitlock's cosmetics, candicaine pipettes, a flask of absinthium emptied of its green liquor. I groped at my side for Whitlock's body, felt nothing there. I whispered Anku's name: nothing.

The voices sounded very young. Finally I could stand it no more. I sat up, blinking.

At the edge of the obfuscating oriels several figures squatted. One swept the floor with a cosmetic brush, drawing something in the powders and ointments spilled there. The others watched her with no great interest. Their voices were soft, curiously inert, as though nothing remained in the world to amuse or frighten them.

Surely not this empty chamber. Nopcsa's corpse was gone, and Whitlock's. Of Anku I saw nothing.

"Where is my familiar?" I asked.

Every head turned to stare. Then they raced to my side, giggling and shoving at one another. They gathered in a circle around me, grinning: all of them filthy, with stained hands and hair clotted with blood and dirt. They smelled of rotting meat.

"He's awake! Where's Dr. Silverthorn?" wondered a little girl of five or six. She had painted her cheeks with rouge and eye-powder and stuck her ratty hair with feathers. She turned to face a boy taller and older than the rest, maybe thirteen. "Oleander?"

I repeated, "Where is my familiar?—the white jackal."

The oldest boy pushed the girl out of his way. Great open sores erupted everywhere on his arms and face. The rest of him was hidden by some dead Paphian's costume, all sequined sighs and tears. "Your dog brought us here," he said. "But he ran away. We didn't hurt him, I swear." He smiled, twitching at the sleeves of his costume so that sequins rained to the floor. "I'm Oleander."

"And I'm Bellanca," piped the little girl as she slipped beside him. Beneath a shift of torn indigo linen her swollen stomach bulged. What remained of her blond hair fell free of its confining ribbons, wispy feathers about sunken cheeks. She smiled. Then, to my horror, she raised three fingers to her blackened mouth. "Greetings, cousin," she lisped sweetly.

My heart sank: more Paphian children.

"I thought that was your dog," said another child smugly. I turned to recognize one of the lazars I had met by the Rocreek, a plain boy with intelligent eyes burning in a scarred face. He would have been a Curator. "A boy took him away—"

"A boy?" I repeated stupidly.

He nodded. "Like you—" By this I could only imagine he meant another Paphian. He continued respectfully,

"He wore flowers in his hair and said you awaited us here. Are you ready to go now?"

I stared at them dully, counting five. The boy Oleander. A girl his age, her scalp smooth and bald as a stone, who opened and shut her mouth constantly, as though gasping for air. The child Bellanca and another small girl who drooled and said nothing, and the boy I had met earlier with Pearl's troupe by the Rocreek.

"I'm Martin," he announced shrilly, poking at his thin chest. "She's Octavia," pointing at the silent girl.

I said nothing, imagined killing them, either with my sagittal or my hands. But I felt no desire to kill them, or do anything to save myself. Because hadn't I led them here, hadn't I betrayed my people to them? How many of those at the masque had been murdered or captured by lazars? And Ketura among them, and Fancy too perhaps—

"Wait," I said, beckoning Martin. "I'll go with you; but tell me, was there a woman, or a little girl, did you see a little girl—"

"Lots," Martin said helpfully. "I saw some, they took some—"

Oleander frowned. The sequined rags made him look foolish, and the others seemed to pay him little attention, but he obviously felt that he must act the leader. "Shut up, Martin," he ordered. He tapped a long-nosed gun tied about his waist with a leather thong. He turned to me, drawing himself up and scratching at an oozing cut on his thigh. "You are Raphael Miramar? The one they call the Gaping One?"

I hadn't the strength to argue. "Yes."

"Well, you're to come with us. <u>Tast</u>— The Consolation of the Dead says so. Please." His voice cracked. He coughed, glancing to see if the others had noticed. The silent drooling Octavia had wandered to the edge of the chamber and glanced down at the Great Hall. Bellanca and Martin were dabbling with the ruined cosmetics. The remaining older girl yawned, her slack mouth working as though she would say something to me, but no words came. Before I could move away she shuffled toward me, hands reaching for my hair.

"Get away!" I scrambled backward, terrified of her scabbed hands, the slack curl of her mouth. But she did not listen, only continued to gape like a dying fish as she tried to touch me. I cried out and swiped at her. A flash of violet as I struck her arm. She gazed at me curiously, her fingers brushing against my hair.

"Pretty," she said thickly. She sank to her knees. As the other children watched she died, her face and hands erupting with crimson petals.

Oleander stared at the girl, then turned to me. "What did you do to her? To do that? The colors." The others lifted their heads for my answer. Bellanca stuck her thumb in her mouth and gazed at me with wide eyes.

I stammered, "She was— I didn't want her to touch me!"

"She was looking at your hair," explained Martin. "She lost all her hair, she was just looking at your hair—"

"Shut up!" I whirled to raise my fist at them so that they could see the sagittal glowing there. "Take her—get it out of here!" I kicked at the girl's corpse and stumbled away from it, shielding my eyes.

After a minute I heard Oleander command them, "Do it." The smaller children scuffled for a little while, dragging their burden. The door wheezed open and shut. When they returned I stood panting in the center of the chamber, glaring at Oleander as he fingered his swivel nervously. He cleared his throat.

"You—we're supposed to—you're still to come with us." He raised his eyes and smiled, looked more sober as I bared my teeth at him.

"And if I don't?" I snarled, when from the chamber entrance rang the scholiast's harsh voice.

"Flee, cousins. The House of High Brazil is beset by lazars. Flee, cousins. The House—"

A crash. The scholiast fell silent. The door swung open to show a tall slender figure silhouetted against the pale light.

"Dr. Silverthorn!" Bellanca cried. She and Martin ran to greet him. Oleander bit his lip, drew the gun from his makeshift belt and pointed it at me. From across the room Octavia made a thick clucking sound and waved. Her fingers had rotted, flesh and bone, all the way to the second knuckle.

"Dr. Silverthorn," began Oleander. He shifted the gun from one hand to the other. "It's him. That boy. The one he told us about."

The figure stepped into the light where I could see him for the first time. I gasped and looked away.

"I understand that the Consolation of the Dead wishes him to be returned alive, Oleander," he said, disdain icing the words *Consolation of the Dead*. A thick voice—he had difficulty forming the words—but kindly and intelligent for all that. "Will you put that damned thing away and let me see him? And where is Angeline?"

Sheepishly Oleander tucked the gun back into his belt and stepped away. I heard the other children whispering as they surrounded the newcomer and plucked at his clothes.

"He killed her, Dr. Silverthorn. I saw it—"

"That one, the one he told us—"

How can they bear to touch him? I thought as I tried to calm myself.

Because in that brief instant I had seen a horrible thing: a man of bones whose clothes flapped about him like gulls taking flight, with a nearly fleshless face drawn into the hideous grimace of a skull picked clean of skin and sinew.

2. Parts of the nature of a skeleton

I stared at the floor, trying to keep my heart from racing. That awful face! I heard the scrape and rattle of his feet upon the floor, the crackle of his stiff clothes as he moved slowly among the remaining children.

"Dr. Silverthorn, can we go home now?"

"Dr. Silverthorn, did you see the party?"

"Dr. Silver—"

"Shh, children," he hushed them. A rustle as he crossed the room. He finally stopped a few meters from me. I heard his breathing, a thick glottal sound as though he choked upon the air. Still, if the children did not fear him I could at least make a show of boldness. I turned to face him.

He stood there, a shrunken scarecrow of a man all in white, his long tunic stained with dirt and grass. White gloves covered his hands, a loose white scarf wrapped his throat. Only his face was not hidden: pink and white and gleaming as a piece of fresh meat, the veins and capillaries stretched like vines across the tendons and smooth solid bones of his skull. My eyes filled with tears.

"Ohh . . ." I cried. In spite of myself I was moved to pity at the mere sight of this stranger. "Why have they done this to you?"

He shook his head very slowly, as though if he moved too quickly the tenuous strands that held him together might tear. "But don't I know you?" he murmured as though he had not heard me. He stretched out one gloved hand to brush the tears from my cheeks. "Wendy Wanders?"

I shook my head. "No—I am Raphael Miramar."

My tears stained the tips of his gloves. He drew his hand to his face and stared at the damp cloth, then turned his gaze back upon me. Once perhaps those brown eyes had been tender; perhaps even now they regarded me with pity or wonder. But with no flesh upon his brow, no lashes to droop across those swollen orbs he could only stare rigidly, a fine sheath of flesh flicking up and down when he blinked. "Raphael," he said, shaking his head. "Yes, of course—the Aviator told me, the children spoke of you, they saw you by the river. . . ."

With a soft creak he swiveled his head to look behind him, to where the children waited. "Poor things, they are tired," he murmured, then returned his attention to me. "But you are not Wendy?"

"No," I said. I was torn between wanting to look away from him and wanting to stare in repelled fascination and pity. I fixed my gaze upon his hands. A clear liquid seeped from beneath the gloves and stained them as my tears had. "Who are you?"

He sighed, the sound unnaturally harsh as it hissed from his lipless mouth. "Three weeks ago I was Dr. Lawrence Silverthorn of the Human Engineering Laboratory. Three days from now I will be dead." His clothes rustled as he shrugged and pulled from beneath his tunic a large black leather bag. He removed a narrow vial and began to rub a clear ointment on his face. "Antibiotic," he explained, smearing it across the planes of his cheeks.

"We heard that Wendy was alive," he said absently, as though once more taking up a long story. "A trader from the City said he had seen her performing with a wretched group of actors. We thought we might escape as she did, we thought we might find help here. . . ."

He glanced up at me and laughed silently, mirthlessly. I hugged myself to keep from shaking at the sight; but I would not look away. "They kept some of them alive for a month while they tried to synthesize the bioprints," he

went on, clumsily replacing the cap on the vial of ointment. "After that they killed them. Their heads in vats
while they pried their brains out. I hid Gligor and Anna in
my room. At the end they ran out of anesthesia. All of your
empath friends, Wendy, except for Anna and Gligor. All of
them dead; all the children."

His teeth clicked as he shook his head to indicate the
lazars. "You were right to run away with that Aide. But you
are not Wendy?" he asked again, confused. He glanced
around the chamber. "Where is Angeline?"

"Dead, she's dead, Dr. Silverthorn," Bellanca cried. "He
killed her. Can we go home?"

He started at the sound of her voice, then nodded. "Of
course. Yes, of course, Bellanca. But lie down first, rest for a
few minutes. All of you, rest." He turned to me. "You did
kill them, then: the albino boy and that other man. How?"

He stared as though he perceived me through a thick
wall of glass. I held up my fist. The sagittal's fierce radiance
had faded to a faint lilac, almost gray. "This," I said. "A
sagittal. I did not mean to." I bowed my head.

Dr. Silverthorn nodded. "A sagittal. I have seen them.
They were prototype geneslaves developed during the
Second Ascension, for—" His jaws moved as he turned his
face toward mine, teeth bared in a horrible leer. "But you
already know what they are for."

He continued to stare at me for a long time. Finally he
dipped his head to pore through the contents of his bag. I
glimpsed the soft white globe of the top of his skull, blue-
veined and shining dully. "Ah—here, boy."

I moved to avoid the hand he reached toward me. He
only stared with those cloudy eyes, continuing to stretch
out a gloved palm holding a small round patch of blue
cloth. "I am not contagious," he said softly. "None of us are
—but nobody here knows that, do they? They pick you off
like little flies and you let them die, you let yourselves die.
You ignorant fools." There was no malice in his voice, not
even a hint of it. All feeling might have been stripped from
him as well as flesh and nerve.

"Here: this is a mild stimulant, it will make it easier for

you to come with us." I shuddered as he touched my neck
but this time did not move away. He pressed the patch
beneath my ear and drew back. "Now: look through this
and find a vial with clear yellow capsules in it and give me
one. Please."

He handed me the bag and waited while I fumbled
through its contents, strange bottles and instruments like
swivels and flares, oddments similar to those I had seen
Doctor Foster employ, but new and gleaming as though
they had never been used. I found the bottle he wanted
and handed him a single capsule.

"Thank you," he said, swallowing it with difficulty. "It's
hard for me to get those out with the gloves. And I can't
use the others now: no skin left for them to adhere to. Soon
not even these . . ."

After a moment or two his eyes seemed to glitter more
brightly, and he flapped his hands. "Well! But I'll feel better now." He dropped the bottle into his bag and patted it
closed. "Are you ready to come with us?"

My head had begun pounding, but not unpleasantly. I
paused.

My tunic hung from me like a tattered standard. The
sagittal was a cool weight about my wrist. Perhaps I might
fight my way free of here. Perhaps I was strong enough to
run, hide within the endless chambers of High Brazil, and
after a day flee to the House Miramar. But then I recalled
Whitlock's face when the lazar Pearl had greeted me as
Baal. Remembered the malicious eyes of the elder Balfour,
and how the Saint-Alaban had cried aloud in fear when he
saw me at the Butterfly Ball, and how even Ketura's face
had twisted in terror when she met my eyes.

There would be no going back for me now. The Hanged
Boy had marked me as His own, and it was as it had always
been in Doctor Foster's tales. The old miser must go with
the ghosts; the magicians must search for the beggar king;
the metal boy find his human father in the belly of the
mosasaur.

I would follow the Gaping One's children to find Him
again. Then I might be free.

I got my boots and pulled them on. Then I stared at Dr. Silverthorn defiantly.

"Where am I going?"

He grinned, baring his teeth. I heard his jaw snap as he replied, "Where we are all going: to die a horrible death."

3. A brief and paroxysmal period

I can hardly bear to relive our trek across the City. At the fringe of the Narrow Forest a path led to the northwest, where no one but Zoologists and lazars ever traveled. That was the road we took. In the distance I saw the spires of our Houses upon the Hill Magdalena Ardent, and black smoke billowing from the minarets of High Brazil. A little while earlier I had watched numbly as flames swept the Great Hall. But Dr. Silverthorn had hurried us outside.

"It is better this way, boy," he said as we passed the ruins of the Butterfly Ball, ribbons and streamers and the empty husks of moths all given to embers now in the blue light of day. "Let them burn, let them burn!" We fled down the Hill and passed into the Narrow Forest.

Fever and fatigue plagued me despite Dr. Silverthorn's stimulants. He insisted upon pressing another patch to my temple, and had me feed him more of the yellow capsules. For hours I stumbled through the forest, prodded by Oleander or helped by one of the smaller lazars when I felt I could go no farther. Dr. Silverthorn's chemistries only fed my hunger and terror, until a sort of delirium overcame me.

"Here, Raphael," someone murmured. Dr. Silverthorn prodded at my chin, tilting it back as he held out a broken shoot of a thick reddish vine. "Drink this." He poured the liquid into my mouth: thick and speckled with dirt and insects, but sweet and cool nonetheless.

"It will give you strength for what is to come," he said. "I tested the water here when we first escaped: pond water, rain water, still water in tree stumps. Did you know it all has abnormally high levels of biotoxins?" He tossed aside the broken vine and started clambering along a twisting path amidst the greenery.

"So you are poisoning me." I stumbled after him. "Is the Gaping One worth anything to your master dead?"

He paused, steadying himself against a slender tree like a white birch, but with filaments of green and yellow dangling from its limbs instead of leaves. They drifted to caress his skull, drew back to float upon the still air. "No," he said, surprised. "I am not poisoning you. It won't kill you. That's what's so strange, that it doesn't kill you. At least not immediately. I took samples of Gligor's blood, before we were—detained. And the toxin levels were high, so high; and it—*changed* him, it does seem to change things." He looked down at his gloved hands, the sleeves of his white robes hanging limply from arms as thin and fleshless as the limbs of trees. "But it doesn't kill you outright."

"Dr. Silverthorn!" Bellanca's voice shrilled from somewhere far ahead and out of sight.

"We're coming," he called. He waited for me to draw alongside him. "You don't think that's odd," he said after we had been walking for several more minutes.

I slapped at a green fly biting at my leg. "No," I said. "I know nothing of the Ascendants and their poisons."

He nodded very slightly, almost regretfully. "No. Of course you wouldn't. But it's very strange. We had no idea, back at HEL, what it's like in the besieged sectors."

I snorted. Through the mesh of leaves I could see the children in the distance, hacking at vines with sticks and pelting one another with the harmless yellow flowers that grew from rotting stumps. "Is that what you call our City? The 'besieged sector'?"

He stopped in the shade of a great sycamore tree and clicked open his black bag, held it out for me. I found one of the yellow capsules and waited for him to swallow it before we went on.

He said, "One of the besieged sectors. Just one."

After a few minutes he added, "There will be many more in the days to come."

I bit my lip to keep from sneering at him. His words infuriated me. All that I had heard of the Ascendants was proving to be true: that they were monstrous, that they had nothing but contempt for my people and even for the Curators whose knowledge was so far beneath their own; nothing but contempt for the entire City they had all but forgotten in the pursuit of their distant and endless wars. I followed him in silence.

But after a while a sort of peacefulness descended on me. The warmth and sweet odor of the afternoon, the buzz of the great gold and crimson bees in the trumpet flowers, even the silent wings of passing butterflies all conspired to drain me of my anger and even my fears, for a little while. The children too had fallen into a drowsy silence. One or another would run a distance ahead, to lie upon a cool bank of moss and nap until the others woke her. Only Dr. Silverthorn seemed untouched by the torpid vapors that drifted here at the edge of the Narrow Forest. He talked ceaselessly the whole time, to himself if no one else was listening. As the afternoon wore on and its languid air dissipated he recited one nonsensical tale after another to the children, now restive and anxious to reach our destination. And he told me things that sounded as mad as those stories he amused the lazars with.

"At the end Emma told me there was a twin boy," he said once. His teeth chattered with excitement, and he stroked Martin's head as the boy paced alongside him. "If we'd only known before!" The gaze he turned upon me was brilliant, the dark eyes glowing. "To think of what we might have learned!"

And later, "If only I'd known. I would have saved her if I could. We might have revived her, you know; although they weren't going to do anything with *her* brain, not after cyanide! She was a brilliant doctor. I quite hated her when she was alive."

And, "I didn't believe they'd come after us, you see. They sent fougas: our own people sent fougas after us. They caught us crossing the river. Anna nearly escaped

but ran back for us. And Gligor went quite mad. He tried
to pluck his eyes out, to kill himself. And I should have let
him, you know. I should have let him." He fell into brooding silence.

As nightfall drew near, even Dr. Silverthorn began to
seem uneasy. He walked faster, waiting impatiently for the
smaller children to catch up with him. I had grown weary
of his endless chatter, and fell back to walk alongside the
sober Oleander.

"Where are we going?" I asked him, hoping for a more
satisfying answer than that Dr. Silverthorn had given me
earlier.

Oleander looked at me in surprise, then made a steeple
of his hands as he replied, "To the Engulfed Cathedral."

I stopped in the middle of the path. "The Cathedral?" I
repeated, stunned. "You mean Saint-Alaban's Hill?"

"That's right." He dropped his hands, pulled a leaf from
an overhanging limb. When he bruised it between his fingers it released the sharp scent of lemons. "Saint-Alaban's
Hill, that's what the Paphians call it. We always said the
'Engulfed Cathedral.' Once great fields of lavender and
dittany-of-crete grew there."

"But why?" I asked. "Why the Cathedral?"

"Because that is where we live," said Oleander. "We
have to return there. Tast'annin says so."

"But no one has ever lived there," I said, stumbling after
him. "It's haunted." I clutched at the tattered collar of my
tunic, drew away a handful of feathers that I cast into the
shadows.

"This entire City is haunted," a hollow voice said into my
ear. I cried out and backed into a thorny hedge of roses.
Beside me Dr. Silverthorn peered from the thicket. He
cackled at my alarm, and the children with him. "You must
walk faster to get there before dark," he scolded. "Else you
won't get the full effect."

But it was nearly another hour by my reckoning before
we reached our destination.

Saint-Alaban's Hill: the viper curled at the foot of all the
Saint-Alabans' superstition, the legendary ruin whence the
Gaping One would rise to confront the Magdalene to be-

gin the Final Ascension. In all my seventeen years I had
heard nothing but evil of Saint-Alaban's Hill and the Engulfed Cathedral. I prayed silently for the Magdalene to
deliver me from what was to come.

In the shadows before us the remains of stone buildings
started to outcrop among the trees. Beside some of them
deep shafts plummeted into the earth, cavernous pits lined
with metal and smooth rock, veiled with wild grape vines
and honeysuckle. The lazars and Dr. Silverthorn hurried
through these glades, but I picked my way carefully: it
would be easy to mistake those thin treacherous cloaks of
greenery for solid earth and tumble into darkness.

By this time I was so drained and starving and heartsore
that the thought of being *anywhere* was enough to give me
some hope. In a few minutes we had caught up with the
others. The children were exhausted. Poor Olivia wept
silently, and tried to brush away the tears with her broken
hands. Even Martin grew peevish, fighting with Bellanca
as they picked their way ahead of the rest of us as we
climbed the long hill that Dr. Silverthorn said would bring
us to the end of our journey. I was too tired to imagine
speaking. But Dr. Silverthorn never stopped talking. I was
to learn that the capsules affected him thus; also that silence terrified him, as did sleep.

"Soon enough!" he shouted when Olivia sank to her
knees beside the ruins of a great stone building, its columns fallen now and threaded with the violet blossoms of
twilight glory. "We will all sleep soon enough! But not
now." He stooped and pressed a small blue patch to her
neck. When she whined and clawed at it he grew angry,
dragging her to her feet though the exertion nearly toppled him.

"See, Olivia? There it is, we are almost there—"

He gestured wildly to where sunset streaked the clouds
with scarlet and purple. At first I thought he pointed only
at this lurid sky. From here I could see nothing but trees
and the overgrown humps of decaying buildings, and far
away the Obelisk shining faintly golden, marking where
the Museums stood and the Curators would now be
mourning their dead. But when I turned back and started

Cryptd Hill

walking once again I saw that something besides clouds did rise above the pinnacle of Saint-Alaban's Hill: a shape so huge and black and brooding that I had thought it was part of the Hill itself. Now I wondered how it had not soiled my dreams all these years, that awful shadow stretching across the entire City of Trees.

"Is that it?" I asked, clutching at Dr. Silverthorn's flapping sleeve.

Dr. Silverthorn grinned and clapped his gloved hands. "Ah, it's almost worth it, isn't it?" he exclaimed. The brazen light pooled like blood in the hollows of his face. "*Etiam periere ruinae:* the very ruins have been destroyed. 'There were giants in the earth in those days, mighty men which were of old, men of renown.'"

"You are mad," I said, pushing him away. "Oleander, is that it?"

The boy leaned against a tree to catch his breath. He pulled a twig from a branch, tossed it in the direction of the Hill. "That is the Engulfed Cathedral," he said. "Where we are going."

I cursed and pulled myself free of the brambles. Dr. Silverthorn and Oleander waited for me, the boy helping to tug from the offending thorns what remained of my garment. When we began walking again the sky showing through gaps in the trees was a deep blue, fading to green upon the horizon. A few faint stars had already appeared. My head ached from the stimulants Dr. Silverthorn had given me. I pulled the remaining pads from my temples and tossed them into the weeds as I scrambled to keep up with my two companions. From far ahead of us rang the high voices of the children. After a moment I heard other voices answer them, although I still saw nothing. We seemed to be in a small depression near the top of the Hill. I could no longer discern the monstrous silhouette that loomed high above us, but I felt it there brooding in the gathering dark: the Engulfed Cathedral.

Of the Narrow Forest I had heard many tales, and of the poisonous rivers that circled the City. But the Cathedral was so ancient, so tainted with the memories of its sanguine cult of worshippers long dead, that even the Saint-

Alabans did not speak of it except with restrained dread. It was said to be haunted. Aardmen dwelt there, and wolves, and in its noisome reservoirs hydrapithecenes drifted, but nothing human. Even the lazars feared the Cathedral. Or so I had always heard.

But someone else lived there now: the one the lazars feared as the Consolation of the Dead, and whom Dr. Silverthorn regarded with less respect. But frightened as I was of going to that place and meeting him, I was still more terrified of being lost and alone again among the trees. I missed my unearthly companion Anku, who for a few hours had given me courage and even a kind of hope. But Anku was gone now. I had no hope left but to follow the lazars.

I sighted the cadaver's white form slipping through the trees like a mist.

"Dr. Silverthorn," I panted.

He paused, waving the children ahead. They ran on, Oleander glancing back at me with an expression compounded equally of pity and envy. At the edge of the woods Dr. Silverthorn waited for me alone, his hand outstretched to point at a sweep of gray lawn before us.

"We are here," he said, his voice curiously empty. Nearly impossible to affix any subtlety of expression to that skeletal face, but a certain flatness and resignation colored his speech. "I am sorry, Raphael Miramar, to bring you to the end of the world."

I stepped from beneath the trees to join him.

4. Conceptions of celestial space

The last upward slope of Saint-Alaban's Hill stretched before me like some horrible vision of the underworld.

Nothing grew there. Blasted trees twisted black and leafless from the ground, their limbs raised imploringly to the merciless thing towering above us. Other trees were strewn across the earth, dwarfed by the Cathedral. Only when we approached them did I see that they were huge, indescribably ancient, and the more horrible for not having decayed in the years since some cataclysm had toppled them. As we passed I heard a low sound coming from their ebony trunks, a faint yet ominous humming.

"Do not go near them." I jumped at Dr. Silverthorn's soft voice as he plucked at my arm. "They are infested with parasitic animalcules that replicate the forms of whatever living thing they touch."

I pressed near to him, choking back a cry when I tripped against a stone, terrified lest I fall and the very earth devour me, barren and starved as it was. "Why have you brought me to this haunted place?" I whispered.

He shrugged. "I must serve something. The Aviator Margalis Tast'annin is the last man to have commanded me. I obey him." He tilted his head toward the Cathedral. "Once they worshipped a god of blood and light in there. Now Tast'annin would raise the effigy of the Hanged One and revive a cult of blackened bones."

His feet made no noise as he walked, as though the

parched ground sucked all sound and light and color from the living world, leaving nothing but the screwed black forms of dead trees and other, pale shapes scattered across the stony slope. The distant figures of the young lazars darted in and out of the shadow of the Cathedral in eerie silence. Only the dull buzzing of the trees and Dr. Silverthorn's hissing voice could be heard in all that empty space.

"Not haunted: hunted, more likely," he wheezed, his thoughts running back and forth down strange alleys where I could not follow. He darted suddenly to one side, his feet seeming to pass right through the sharp stones that choked the earth so that I marveled he did not wince in pain. But the layer of flesh that enabled him to feel had been the first portion devoured by the rain of roses.

"Wait!" I called after him. "Don't leave me, Dr. Silverthorn—"

He halted, staring back as though I was mad. "Leave you? Me, nothing but bones, leave you who are nothing but a body! No, no—" He pointed to a gleaming patch of white, luminous against the dark earth. Human skulls were piled there, but sloppily, as though children at play had grown weary of their game. And with a sinking feeling I realized that this was the truth of it: I had come to the lazars' home, the playing fields where skull and knuckle-bones were used as shuttlecock and dice; where soon no doubt I would be as much a part of the bleached landscape as the petrified trees and leering brain-pans scattered everywhere.

"As ye are so once was I; as I am so ye shall be," Dr. Silverthorn intoned. He kicked and set a small skull rolling, his harsh laugh ringing out like a raven's croak. "I won't leave you, Raphael: you are to be my eyes and ears, and I will be your guide. I have done as I promised the Aviator; but I will try to help you." He cocked his head, clacking his jaws in a manner meant to be reassuring. "And you may be surprised, Raphael: you may not find yourself as alone as you think."

My heart leaped at that, imagining that I might find some of my bedcousins here, or others from the Hill Magdalena Ardent. But the cadaver gave no reply to my questions.

"Not now, not now," he hissed, and pulled me after him. "We must hurry, before he closes the south gate."

High above us swept the huge black towers: higher than Illyria's fortresses, than the House Persia, than High Brazil; greater even than the Library Dome or the ancient Obelisk. Flickering waves of color sometimes passed across one or another of the granite facades. I rubbed my eyes, convinced the unnatural darkness of the place was playing tricks upon my vision, before I finally realized that what I was seeing was firelight showing through immense embrasures of colored glass, like those at High Brazil.

As we drew nearer, strange patterns were traced upon the iron earth. Paths marked out in bones and skulls formed serpentine patterns, narrow tracks that stretched straight to north and east and west. They glowed eerily in the twilight, as though the bones themselves had absorbed hoary traces of the sun. It should have been horrible. And yet I found the bones almost lovely, the strict formality of their carefully assembled fulciments now tossed into disarray: torso, shanks, hands, and ribs displayed so clean and pure and shining, as innocent as driftwood cast upon a riverbank.

"Labyrinths," explained Dr. Silverthorn. "Ley lines. To make this place more powerful." He stopped, regarding a convoluted maze of femurs and delicate finger bones, with a small figure made of sticks propped in its center. "Old things," he said, shifting his black bag to the other shoulder. "There are many old things here. He is a fool to wake some of them."

We had left the buzzing trees behind us. Gaps of blue-black sky showed between the broken towers overhead. On the eastern horizon faint light gleamed where the moon would rise shortly. We were near enough now to the Cathedral gates that I could hear the children playing in the twilight, a shrill fanfare of laughter and tears and shouts echoing in its cavernous inner space as they raced or stumbled in and out of hidden doors. Someone called to my companion. He raised one spindly arm in a feeble

wave, grinning as his name was taken up by the others,
singing:

> "A man of skin and not of bones
> is like a garden full of stones!"

Dr. Silverthorn pointed to a wide path, a dark avenue
lined with larger bones and tattered ribands and bits of
finery. I followed him in silence up this main approach,
trying to ignore the lazars tuneless warble:

> "And when your skin begins to crack,
> It's like a knife across your back;
> And when your back begins to smart,
> It's like a missile to your heart;
> And when your heart begins to bleed,
> You're dead, and dead, and dead indeed!"

The path ended abruptly; or rather, the bones that had
marked it were scattered everywhere, kicked aside in
some mindless game or argument. Past the ring of bones
was a circle of scuffed earth. A few feet from this a set of
granite stairs led up to massive gates set with iron hoops.
Between the oaken doors, and to either side, and in the
portal above stood carven figures of men and women, and
figures like stern yet radiant men with the wings of herons.
"The South Transept," Dr. Silverthorn said. He gazed up
with glittering eyes. "The Cathedral Church of the Archangels Michael and Gabriel."
I hesitated as he started up the steps. I was absurdly
afraid: not of the Cathedral or what it contained but of
those stone creatures. Ethereally beautiful, each face tilted
skyward, as though divining some magnificence there.
They seemed older than anything I had ever seen, older
even than the archosaurs, although I knew this could not
be true. And something in their faces, the pitiless eyes
gazing at the stars, put me in mind of the Hanged Boy.
"Who are they?" I asked.
Dr. Silverthorn rested his bag on a stair. He shook from
the effort of walking, coughing as he tried to catch his

breath. "They are Saints and Angels," he said. "Saints and Angels and ordinary men."

I stepped beside him. A numbing cold rose from the stones around me, as though through the centuries the granite had hoarded nothing but winter. When I touched the base of one of the pillars I found it covered with a sheen of ice.

"It is an anomaly," confessed Dr. Silverthorn.

I withdrew my hand, staring up at the face of one of the winged creatures. "Were they real?" I wondered. "Were they Ascendants?"

Dr. Silverthorn looked at me, his swollen eyes bulging. Then he laughed. "Ascendants! Are they *Ascendants!*" Overcome, he leaned against the pillars, gasping for breath. I turned away in embarrassment.

After a moment he recovered himself. "Forgive me, Raphael! It was just—the idea! A pleasant idea, actually. Your sister, now; she would never mistake an Angel for an Ascendant!" He peered at me curiously. "You have never heard of Angels?"

I shrugged. "I've heard the word, I thought it meant a pretty child. Not a man with wings."

He stared at me, surprised. I could see him taking in my long hair and worn tunic, the remnants of glitter and beads clinging to me like evidence of some grand debauch. "Well, it does, that's right; I suppose it does. The wings: well, they were usually pictured with wings, that's all. But it was also one of the—beliefs of the old religion. This was the Cathedral of the Archangels—they were the most powerful of the Angels, the ruling Angels one might call them. This place honors two of them. Michael and Gabriel."

He grew quiet, then said, " *'There was war in heaven: Michael and his angels fought against the dragon; and the dragon fought and his angels, and prevailed not.'* " He stroked a pillar sadly. "This Cathedral was completed a hundred years before the First Ascension."

Silence except for his labored breathing. It was nearly full dark now. The sound of the children playing had all but died out; I imagined they had gone indoors. I stood next to Dr. Silverthorn, both of us staring up at the implacable stone faces for several minutes. At last he sighed and climbed the remaining steps to the transept gate. He placed one hand on the door and turned to me, and said, "When people first found dinosaur fossils in the cliffs, they thought they had discovered the remains of Angels and dragons."

He waited for me to push open the massive door. I paused, the gate's iron ring biting my hand. "I have seen one," I said. "Walking in the Narrow Forest, one of them spoke to me. But he did not have wings."

Dr. Silverthorn nodded. "Yes," he replied after a moment. "I believe you may have seen one."

With a creak the iron-bound door swung inward, and we entered the Cathedral.

5. *An exceeding barbarous condition of the human species*

The smell assaulted me first: bitter smoke from uncured wood, roasting flesh, human excrement, burning wax. Over all of it the reek of incense of turpentine smoldering in countless braziers, many of them toppled to the marble floor so that their contents had spilled but continued to burn, igniting whatever material was near at hand: cloth, twigs, hair. I blinked, covered my eyes against the smoke, then my nose to keep out the stench. The marble beneath my feet was slick with putrid water. I forced my eyes open, lest I slip and find myself awash with the filth clotting the floor.

A dim expanse swept before me in every direction. It stretched upward to the very stars, since chunks of the ceiling had collapsed to leave great ragged holes open to the cool sky. Were it not for this, the Cathedral's inhabitants would probably have suffocated from the smoke and foul air. Bonfires burned everywhere, each surrounded by little groups of chattering children feeding graying embers or livid flames with green sticks and bark. In the lurid light they looked like one of the dioramas at the Museum, naked tousled silhouettes squatting before ill-tended fires, rocking back and forth upon their heels as they sang or talked or ate. Many of them sprawled in the filth, panting or seeming scarcely to breathe at all: the ones who would

die next. The sight of them eating sickened me, no matter
that it had been nearly two days since I'd had anything like
a proper meal.

"Look at them," said Dr. Silverthorn softly. "Dying of
gangrene and evil humors and sarcomas and sheer igno-
rance, just as they did a thousand years ago. Refugees of a
war fought with rocks and sticks and rain; a war they have
never even heard of."

From the bonfires shrill voices called out to us. They
greeted Dr. Silverthorn by name, but fell silent as I followed him toward the center of the great space, where
most of the fires were clustered. Marble benches stood
here and there, some of them pulled free from their moor-
ings and tilted or thrown to the floor. I wondered who
could have done that: not plaguey children, surely. The
benches were seats of privilege. The oldest lazars sat there
crosslegged, some of them with crowns of twisted
branches and dead leaves upon their brows. They snapped
at the younger children, bullying them to bring morsels of
food toasting upon twigs and water (I hoped it was water)
from a large standing basin near the middle of the vast
room. As we approached they stopped their playing and
arguing and turned to stare, the oldest ones standing upon
the benches and letting their younger favorites join them.
I pulled my torn robe tight and held my head up, trying
hard not to look foolish, though I knew I was as filthy as
they were. They twittered and pointed and called to one
another through the smoky air—

"Look—look—"

"He has come, the Doctor found him, the one Pearl said,
the one, the one—"

"He is here, look, look—"

Giggles and curses; scuffling behind us as they scrabbled
across the floor to stare. I felt their small hands touch my
ankle or arm, countless children circling me like starveling
cats.

"Raphael! It's me!"

In a patch of orange light Oleander popped up, grinning.

I smiled back. "Oleander! I'm glad to see you—"

And grew quiet; because I *was* glad.

"I told him, Dr. Silverthorn. Tast'ann—" He lowered his voice. *"The Consolation of the Dead,"* he continued, walking between Dr. Silverthorn and myself and eyeing the other children scornfully. "I told him we had found him, you and me, I told him we found Raphael Miramar, the boy they call the Gaping One."

Dr. Silverthorn nodded wearily. He handed his bag to Oleander. "Are we to have an audience, then?"

Oleander shook his head. "No. He took more of those pills you gave him, he is making the Saint-Alaban children perform 'The Masque of Baal and Anat.' I think he forgot he told us to bring him."

Dr. Silverthorn snorted, then waved his hand to indicate that Oleander was to open his bag.

"One yellow and one green one, please," he said. We had crossed the center of the Cathedral and stood before a door opening onto a dim passage. The air blew fresher from this portal. I breathed gratefully, glancing back at the children scurrying through the nave. They had already forgotten us, all but Oleander.

"Tast'annin will remember about Raphael," Dr. Silverthorn said after he had taken the capsules. "He has a plan. Worse: he has a vision. Always be wary of men with visions."

He grinned as he said this, a skull ogling us from the shadows. "Well, Oleander, let us show Raphael to his chamber."

The passage snaked along the outer wall of the Cathedral, branching often. Stone staircases loomed out of the darkness, a deeper black where they plunged or climbed to secret bays and chapels. Set high up along the smooth gray walls were empty recesses and narrow windows. Some were shattered; some held black traceries that I imagined would show elaborate scenes in colored glass, come daybreak: if day broke here. Oleander kicked through the debris and found a taper which he lit from a smoking pile someone had left beside a door. With him leading us we descended into the Crypt Church.

The air was better here: not the fresh air of trees and sun

but cool and still nonetheless, redolent of ancient stone and hidden water. We met no one.

"The children are forbidden here without permission," explained Dr. Silverthorn. He nodded at Oleander. *"He* is a clever boy; a sort of favorite of the Aviator's, he runs errands and goes where he pleases. As do I; though nothing will hold me back soon, I will go wherever I wish." A low whistling laugh, air seeping from throat and chest and mouth. "But Oleander races through here like a mouse in the walls. And there are other mice, too, mice in cages, rats in traps."

I shuddered. I had seen small things scamper across the floor, disturbed by the taper's uneven light; but I did not like to imagine what he might mean by *mice in cages, rats in traps.* Everywhere faces glowered at me, white stone figures and flowering columns and bizarre animals, plinths upholding those whom Dr. Silverthorn had named as Saints and Angels and ordinary men. They observed us impassively, dignified in spite of the decay of years and the occasional spray of graffiti rippling across their severe faces. Oleander walked a few feet in front of us, his broken face pitifully young. He might have been a handsome boy, before the rain of roses; a Botanist for sure, but with a Paphian father I would guess.

"How long have you been here, Oleander?" I asked him.

He shifted the taper to his other hand, shaking wax from his fingers. "I don't know. A few weeks? We were caught outside, some of us, we were working on the boxtree hedges at the Botanical Gardens. The older ones ran. They left me and a few of the others who couldn't run fast enough.

"I tried. I tried to take care of them: the little ones. They died soon, except for Lily. My friend Lily." He was quiet, stopping to scratch one foot. He sighed. "Then she died too. And I went off alone. I found some others, in the woods; I know about plants, so we did all right for a little while, eating things. Then we came here, we heard there was a man here who took care of them, I mean he took care of us, people like us, lazars. He hadn't been here long; only a little longer than me."

We followed him silently for several minutes. Then he turned back to us, smiling. "But that was before Dr. Silverthorn got here; and it's better now, isn't it? He has medicine and it helps us, I feel stronger than before. He says we'll get well, if we have medicine and the right things to eat."

"That's right," said Dr. Silverthorn. To me he turned empty eyes that my own thoughts made seem reproachful. In my mind I heard his voice again:

You let them die, you let yourselves die . . .

Oleander woke me from my daze, pulling at my arm. "Down this hallway." We entered another passage. This one opened into a wider space where I glimpsed numberless archways leading who knew where, columns carved to resembled huge trees of stone, gates of iron twisted into grape arbors and latticework, statuary fallen from their pediments to stare up at me with cracked faces. In the distance I spied ghostly lights that seemed to dance in the air. When we grew nearer these resolved into banks of tiny colored candles, blue and red and white, burning fitfully on iron tables set against the walls.

"This is the Crypt Church," explained Dr. Silverthorn. "He makes offerings here. But there is a place where you may rest undisturbed, and Oleander was to bring you food?"

He turned to the boy, who stopped, embarrassed, and fumbled with his free hand through his pockets.

"I forgot," he mumbled. "Wait—there's this."

I took a handful of dried fruit, apples maybe, and swallowed them so quickly I nearly choked. A few minutes later I was rewarded for this gluttony by feeling my insides cramp up painfully; but by then we had stopped.

"Sleep here," said Dr. Silverthorn. He pushed open a tall iron grille and pointed to a chamber within—how large I could not tell in the taper's smoky light. Oleander stood aside to let me pass, my heart heavy: I felt as though I were being imprisoned.

"Am I to die here alone?" I asked bitterly. I bumped against some hard object and swore, rubbing my knee. "No light, no food, no water?"

Dr. Silverthorn shook his head. "We can do no more for you now: he will be calling for us, and it is best for you not to meet him until you feel somewhat stronger. Later I will bring you food and water, and light too perhaps. But for now you should sleep—" He pointed to the floor, where something flat and white had been rolled out as a sort of pallet. "There. And I will give you something to make it easier for you to rest."

He beckoned me to him. I waited, trying not to weep from sheer terror and exhaustion. I took the capsule he had Oleander give me, watched helplessly as they turned and the boy pushed the heavy iron gate closed.

"Until the morning, then," Dr. Silverthorn said. Oleander waved. The two of them walked away, the taper fluttering in and out of sight among the arches and columns until the darkness extinguished it completely and I was alone in the Crypt Church.

6. *"The dark backward and abysm of time"*

I woke—morning? midnight? but it was always midnight there—to find that someone had set a number of candles around me, burning yellow tapers that smelled foul despite the aromatics that had been added to the sulfurous tallow. By their jaundiced light I could finally see my room: a vault really, with a low arched marble ceiling. Its whorls and florid patterns were blackened from smoke and age and seemed to quiver in the light. Besides the pallet I lay upon there were only a number of small wooden chairs for furniture. These were very old, covered with cushions of frayed and rotted embroidery showing strange things: a bearded man covered with birds, wild beasts sleeping at his feet; a storm-tossed boat filled with animals; a white-robed figure surrounded by playing children; a very old man pulling something from a sack. While chairs and cushions alike seemed centuries old they were clean, not covered with dust or mildew as I might have expected. I dropped the last cushion, then paced the length of the chamber. I stopped to rattle half-heartedly the ornate iron grille that kept me imprisoned before stalking to the other end of the vault.

Here in a high curved recess stood an altar. Small shelves cut into the elaborate marble had once held icons of some sort, like those I had seen elsewhere in the Crypt Church. But the statues were gone now. In their place stood clumsily made dolls of bone and fur, leaning haphazardly against the heavy candlesticks. Dripping tallow threatened to set one of these pathetic images afire. I took candle in one hand and icon in the other, holding the taper to regard it more closely. A kind of animal, or a man with an animal's head. Blank eyes scratched in a smoothed piece of bone and colored with dirt or blood. The whole thing held together with wisps of straw and fur and hair. I shuddered and replaced it in a shallow alcove where it was in no danger of catching fire.

Beside these little creatures I found offerings of bones wrapped in neat bundles, and smaller figures made of braided human hair. Other things as well, oddments and bijoux that might have fallen from a hundred hidden pockets. A braided riband, its russet and silver brocade marking it as a Paphian's favor from some curator. A smooth round marble that, when I investigated, proved to be a prosthetic eye: its solid black core responding to the warmth of my hand and dilating as it sought to focus upon me. There was even an untidy bouquet of shrunken blossoms like desiccated human hands, gathered who knows where—beneath the Botanists' glass domes, or within the shadows of the Narrow Forest, or by the dank green shores of the river. Perhaps the flowers had clutched and fought as they were plucked from the damp earth, to be brought here and forgotten. But everything was child-sized, toylike, including the nosegay of dead blossoms: some small fist had held them last. I turned away suddenly, the pain in my stomach that had begun as hunger now knotting itself into queasiness. A black fear gripped me: that I had been brought here as just another offering, another odd yet lovely thing stolen from the dead and left to languish here.

"Raphael. You are awake—"

I whirled to see a spidery figure standing behind the iron grille. Clean white garments covered his limbs, and he held a lantern above his head. Beside him slunk a hunched form. I heard the clatter of keys and then Dr. Silverthorn's command, "Put the food there and leave us."

The gate swung inward. The hunched figure placed something on the floor. It made a soft guttural sound, then slipped into the darkness. When Dr. Silverthorn hung the lantern from a corner of the gate I saw that the doors remained open.

"You are not a prisoner," he said, bowing his head in greeting. It could not have been more than a day since I had last seen him, but already the contagion had progressed. His fine ointments did little now but cover the soft globe of bone and skull with a sheen of gold. "You are here so that the lazars will not disturb your rest. They fear this place, and will not visit it unless Tast'annin forces them to." His mouth opened wider in the goblin grin that was all that remained of his smile. "This was called the Children's Chapel, once." He indicated the objects on the floor. "That is food for you: just bread and water and some dried grapes, I'm afraid. Mostly they eat human flesh here, and die from it: that is not fit nourishment and I will not offer it to you."

I fell onto the pitiful repast like a starved animal. When I finished I turned back to my visitor. He had not moved from his place just outside the gate, and seemed to wait almost shyly for me to invite him in.

"Won't you sit?" I asked, pointing first to a chair and then to my pallet.

"No, thank you." His voice a harsh whistling sound, grating against bare bones as it sought to escape him. The white robes stirred as his breath leaked from lungs and throat. "It is too painful for me to sit now. It has penetrated my marrow. Better to pace and let the virus move with me, exhaust it so that it may sleep later and give me peace." His breath erupted into hiccuping gasps, and he dropped his black bag on the floor between us. "If you will, Raphael . . ."

I found the vial and handed him a restorative. A very few yellow capsules remained. I averted my eyes from the spectacle of this cadaver attempting to gulp the pill, waited several minutes until his breathing slowed and I heard the clicking of his feet upon the floor. "Thank you," he rasped.

I turned back to him. "Do I have an audience with the Consolation of the Dead?" I asked bitterly. "Or have you come to tell me that Death himself awaits me even now?"

"He will not kill you, Raphael. At least not yet. And yes: you are to meet with him this morning."

Guttering candlelight flared in his eyesockets. For an instant shadows fleshed the solemn curves of his skull so that I had a glimpse of what he had been a month earlier: a young man, slender, with quick fey motions and eyes that were deep-set rather than sunk into gaunt hollows. When he stepped closer to the glowing altar the vision was gone; I continued my conversation with a spectre clad in pale cerements.

"I have come to bring you to him, and because I am lonely and curious—you see, I *am* still a man!—I would know more of you before I die; and I want to warn you."

I nodded and settled myself on a chair, leaving him to pace as he spoke. Occasionally he paused to pass trembling fingers across his face, as though to reassure himself that something still remained there of his corporeal being.

"You said you knew of your sister? The empath Wendy Wanders?"

"No," I said. "Only that I had a sister; Doctor Foster and Gower Miramar told me that. It was no secret to us. I assumed she was dead."

"She is not. She lives; at least she lived to escape from the Human Engineering Laboratory two months ago, assisted by a Medical Aide named Justice Saint-Alaban. A Paphian: do you know him?"

I pried a splinter from the bottom of my chair and began to clean my fingernails with it. I believed he spoke nonsense. Yet his words disturbed me if only because they reminded me of Doctor Foster's tales, the stories he had told us at Semhane and The Glorious and Winterlong, where among the lashing tails of aardmen and the Gray Mayor's crimson eyes flitted this other shape, small and wailing and with blood threading from her temples: my nameless twin sold to the Ascendants. "My House does not often consort with Saint-Alabans. They are heretics. I am not surprised one served the Ascendants."

"Well, he did: served us rather well until he ran away with our prized madcap." A hooting gasp that might have been laughter as he reached the altar and stopped to stare at its offerings.

"A thieving Saint-Alaban. Well, that doesn't surprise me either," I said. But it was curious, to think of a Saint-Alaban among the Ascendants; to think of any Paphian among the Ascendants. I wished I had questioned Ketura more carefully about her meetings with them during her time outside. "But they must be dead by now—"

"I told you: they are not." Click of his bony feet upon the floor as he began to pace again. He paused to lean against one of the ancient chairs. "Have you heard of a troupe of actors in this City?"

"Many Paphians perform. I acted in masques all the time." I winced as the splinter dug too deeply beneath my thumb, flicked away the mite of wood, and glanced up at my visitor. "Our great festivals are masques—"

He tapped his foot impatiently. "No. These were traveling Players, they lived in the ruins of a theatrical library and performed ancient plays. They had among them a trained monkey that could speak—"

I nodded and sat back hard in my chair, excited by the sudden memory of bright and archaic costumes, a beast that recited poetry like a courtesan.

"Toby Rhymer! Yes, of course I know them. Toby Rhymer and the talking troglodyte, Miss Scarlet Pan. I wept once when she performed: oh, it was lovely!" I hesitated. "There was a boy from Persia who joined them, Fabian—"

The folds of the skeleton's gown flapped as he interrupted me, shaking his gloved hand. "Your sister is with them! I am certain of it."

I frowned. "How could she have found them? Surely she and the Saint-Alaban would have died, alone in the City— lazars would have caught them, or the rain of roses, or—" I did not want to admit to this learned Ascendant that I feared the aardmen, so I gestured in the smoky air. He shook his head, candlelight pricking the roiling wet shadows of his eyes so that they glittered shrewdly.

"They did not die. I do not know if Wendy Wanders *can* die: although many patients she touched at HEL did. Perhaps her Paphian savior is dead now too: my guess would be that he is." He sucked in his breath and laughed hoarsely. "But she is alive: I know it.

"After her escape we began to hear stories, hearsay about a boy in the City, an actor commanding audiences and calling himself Aidan Arent." He paused, waiting for me to show some recognition.

"You must forgive me," I said. *"My* last few months were spent among the Naturalists, who have little use for Players—or Paphians either," I added bitterly. "That name means nothing to me."

"He is described as being seventeen years of age, with tawny hair once close-cropped but now growing longer, gray eyes, a surpassingly beautiful face and voice. He possesses a supernatural ability to charm and terrify his audiences. And despite the fact that he usually takes the feminine roles in performance, a number of Paphians in his audiences have remarked upon his startling resemblance to a favored catamite now feared dead, one Raphael Miramar.

"Knowing Wendy, and having seen you, I can attest that this at least is true: you are her mirror image."

I sat in silence, oddly disinterested. It was as though he spoke of someone besides myself. And of course he *did* speak of someone other than me; although perhaps it was that this Player, Aidan Arent, sounded more believable than did Raphael Miramar. I shook my head but said nothing.

Behind Dr. Silverthorn the candles burned more and more brightly. The tallow melted into smoking pools upon the altar. Rivulets of flame ran down its marble facade as the burning fat dripped to the floor. In front of this flickering display Dr. Silverthorn glowed like a taper himself, the brilliant light glowing through his robes so that the bones beneath showed stark black, and I could see inside his chest a small dark shape like a fist clenching and unclenching. When he spoke again his voice rang loudly, though it still rasped like a saw through his throat.

"Some of those who have seen Aidan Arent perform have said he is the Gaping One."

I stared back at him, shaking my head. "That's impossible."

He grinned, carmine light dancing from his teeth. "Why? Because *you* are the Gaping One?"

"Of course not!" I said, but he went on as though he hadn't heard me.

"The Mad Aviator thinks you are. That's why he's brought you here."

I stood, bewilderment and anger vying inside me, and stalked to the gate. In the distance I could see the little candles in their banks of dusty glass holders. The wavering shadows made it look as though figures darted back and forth in the murky light; but I heard nothing there. "Why are you insulting me?" I demanded hoarsely. "Isn't it enough that you brought me to this crypt—"

"If Tast'annin hadn't ordered the children to capture you, you would be dead now."

"Better that than this!" I grabbed the iron bars and bowed my head, grief striking me like a stone. "Better you had killed me!"

He shrugged. "Better I had died after that viral strike, the way Gligor did. But I did not, and you did not. I have only a little time remaining; perhaps you have longer, perhaps you have less. But you have power, Raphael; and not all your friends are dead.

"In the evenings I go among the prisoners here and minister to those I can, to ease their last days. The Consolation of the Dead would have it that way," he said with soft irony.

He walked toward me. I backed against the gate, frightened by how quickly he moved, the light in his eyes extinguished to malicious darkness. "There is a little girl imprisoned here. She was captured yesterday near the House Miramar with a party of mourners. I saw her last night. When the child heard where I had been she described you, and asked if I had seen Raphael Miramar among the corpses at the Butterfly Masque. I told her you were here, and alive."

"Fancy," I whispered. I had not forgotten her; rather had spent the last hours refusing to think of her, making a

gift of her memory to those minor deities Grief and Exhaustion. "Where is she?"

"Here. I can tell you no more than that. As I said, my
allegiance is to the Aviator. If he is pleased with you; if she
does not succumb to madness or illness or the lazars; if *you*
do not fall prey to this place: well then, he may treat you
kindly, and treat her kindly, since she is your friend.

"The children told him of meeting you by the river.
Pearl was another—*favorite* of his." He grimaced at some
unpleasant memory. "She too thought she had met an
Angel walking in the forest; and this gave the Madman an
idea.

"He has many interesting ideas."

He stood near enough that I could smell the sweetness of
his decay, the bitter chemical residue of the antibiotic
ointment. He reached for me, his gloved hand moist and
cold as it gripped my chin, firmly as though it were held by
metal forceps.

"How odd," he murmured. Through the thin gloves,
damp and already starting to rot into strings of dirty cotton, the blades of his fingers cut into my chin. I was still
terrified of contagion, but feared even more his anger and
the plunge back into solitude if he left. "You look exactly
like her. . . .

"She was so beautiful, our Wendy; but mad, we all knew
she was quite mad. All of them were by the end. It was one
of the secondary effects of the Harrow Project, because of
course they were all grossly flawed children to begin with;
and who could endure such a life, living constantly the
nightmares and hallucinations of others day after day after
day, and never waking from your own dreams? But we
made of them the walking vessels of our madnesses and it
made them more lovely and then grotesque, the gynander
Merle sprouted more breasts, Taylor's eyes turned from
gray to white and finally calcified like granite pearls,
Gligor began to smell of carrion and butterflies flocked
around him in the garden, Anna woke one day to find in
her bed a shriveled homunculus with her own face and
withered male genitals. . . .

"But Wendy only grew more beautiful and deadly, although of course she could not see it, she was incapable of recognizing anything but pain and horror and fear and she embraced those, oh she did. Emma Harrow was a fool, not to see what was happening to her prize changeling, that stolen child now stealing with no thought or reason the fancies and desires and finally the very hopes of all she touched, leaving only despair in their place. . . ."

I listened fascinated to his ravings. He let go of me and began to pace, three steps and then back, three steps and back, as though some imaginary cage about him was shrinking to the size of his ribs. In my mind a strange picture took shape, the image of this creature called Wendy Wanders: a girl so like me she could pass for a boy and fool my own people into thinking they saw me upon a dusty stage. But with this grew something else, a sensation so hard and bitter it was like an unripe fruit I had swallowed to rot and fester inside me: the idea that all of the horrible things that had happened to me had happened by mistake. It was not Raphael who should have seen death and dishonor and abandonment, but this other thing, this awful simulacrum called Wendy that had somehow broken free from the Ascendants' prison, and in so doing had loosed the rage and grim delight of the Gaping One upon the City.

Then I felt inside me a terrible rage building, a desire for havoc and bloodshed like that which had possessed me in the Narrow Forest when I ran with the white jackal to seek my Patron's death. But to Dr. Silverthorn I displayed nothing; only nodded and stared as he paced, while about us the candles burned to oily smears upon the altar.

"Do you see? Do you understand now, Raphael? There is a reason for this, there *has to be a reason for this*—"

For the first time I heard raw desperation in his voice, glimpsed the ravaged man clinging to some hope inside that cell of bone and diseased flesh. I turned to see his eyes glowing like the flames that sprang like pale irises from the marble. I started to nod, thinking he merely wanted me to reassure him. But then I saw that he was waiting for me to answer, waiting for me to *explain* it to him, as though I saw within the wreckage surrounding us some magic spindle that could be spun to turn all this horror to a final good.

"Do you understand, Raphael?"

"I—I think so," I said slowly. "I would like to, anyway. It's just so strange, to think of it; to think of *her*, alive somewhere, as if—"

As if I were not, I thought; *as if only one of us could be within the City of Trees.*

But she had been alive all along! She had not died, as Doctor Foster and Miramar had told me. Dr. Silverthorn waited for me to go on. I shrugged and opened my hands in a helpless gesture.

"What do you want of me, Dr. Silverthorn?"

He lifted one arm, the sleeve of his white robe hanging from it like a sheet from a broomstick. "You will bring her here," he said, and dropped his arm. I shuddered, half-expecting it to clatter to the floor, but he only regarded me with a grin as though he read my thoughts and then laughed. "You said you perform in theatricals: well, the Consolation of the Dead wants you to act the part of the Gaping One for him. And you must do it, you must! The entire City will hear of it, the Players will hear of it—and she will come with them to see you. Then you can use her to destroy him—"

"But why?"

"Because she is Death, Raphael: those she touches dies, I have seen it!"

I shook my head. "But this is all madness! My sister alive, and you say she is monstrous; and a madman ruling here though I've seen nothing, nothing but yourself and lazars! And why does he want this, why me to act as the Gaping One?"

"To amuse him; to bloat his pride and sickness; to lure your people and the others of this City here: because who could resist it, the chance to see a beautiful demon in a ruined Cathedral! He is mad for glory.

"He was promised a position of power: here, in this City. A puppet Governor, ruling an abandoned kingdom! The Ascendants promised him this, because he was a *Hero*, you see; and they had their own reasons, they wanted to see if there was anything left here worth devouring: dogs sniffing at corpses and rubbish.

"They plan to strike against the Commonwealth. They wanted to reclaim the City, establish a garrison here and seek the lost armory. Margalis Tast'annin was a brilliant strategist, a leader of the Archipelago Conflict. He was to retire from fighting, and NASNA had pledged him this City of fools and whores; what other cities are left to rule?

"But he was betrayed by the Curators—whether in collusion with rebels or not, I do not know. I think not; I think the Curators truly feared him. They gave him over to the aardmen. And the aardmen tortured him; they unmanned him; but they did not kill him.

"In the end they pitied him."

He shook his head. "Foolish creatures! but it is in their slavish nature to obey men, as it is in mine. He ordered them to free him, and they did.

"He will be avenged upon the City now. He claims to have found the ancient weapons stored beneath Saint-Alaban's Hill. He was a *military* Hero. He seeks to bring the Final Ascension."

I shook my head. "This is sheer lunacy! One man against the City—and for what cause? *I* have never heard of him before."

"He was an Ascendant, as I was."

"Did you know him?"

"I knew of him. Margalis Tast'annin was a NASNA Aviator, a Hero of the Archipelago Conflict and many skirmishes with the Balkhash Commonwealth. He came to HEL with Odolf Leslie after the Wendy suicides. They were the ones who authorized the new diagnostics, the new—*methods.* I met Tast'annin briefly. He was interested in the new biosyntheses from the empaths, the aggression resonators in multiple personalities.

"You see, they had many plans, these new Governors. They had some *new ideas,* they had *new alembics,* they were going to make *new things* from the old materials. They have already made many new things, each skirmish brings new terrors and new chemicals and new microphages—"

"There really is a war, then?"

Dr. Silverthorn stared at me, his jaws grinding silently. "No," he said after a moment. "There is no real war. There is no one left to lead real wars. Only madmen in the middlelands and scientists at the fringes of those cities that are still standing. And for the rest, nothing but foot soldiers and freaks: guerrillas and gorillas."

He laughed again; his breathing grew labored. I noticed his glove-clad hands shaking and was terrified that he would die here before me. But no. He gestured wildly until I realized he wanted his bag. I hurried to give it to him, waiting while he dumped its contents on the floor and scrabbled among vials and silvery gavelocks, knocking bottles across the room until he found a metal container, an atomizer of some sort that he sprayed into the hollow cavity of his throat.

"Aaugh," he groaned, heedless of the atomizer falling from his hand. "So soon, so soon . . ."

My heart ached to watch him: to feel one's body decay thus! "Did they do this to you, Dr. Silverthorn? The new Governors?"

His voice was dull, perhaps from the effects of the atomizer. "No. My colleagues did this. The Doctors I worked with at HEL. When I escaped with Anna and poor Gligor they sent a NASNA fouga after us, they alerted the avernian janissaries, and Gligor was, they—"

"God, to watch him die like that! To think of anyone dying like this—"

He drew his hands to his ruined face in an agony of grief and horror and hopelessness. And then I began to weep, because I was exhausted by my own sorrows; because he had been kind to me even while bringing me to my death; because he could no longer weep himself.

I have no idea how long I sat there, slumped in that cold vault with the pitiful offerings of geneslaves and dying children all about me. But eventually my sobs gave way to silence, a cold ache in my chest that was dreadful because it bespoke utter emptiness and despair. I lifted my head to see Dr. Silverthorn standing above me. The last bits of burning tallow had died. From somewhere in the bowels of

the Crypt Church a chilly blue light threaded its way into
the Children's Chapel to touch his cerements with an
ashen pallor. The sight of him filled me with a sort of
detached terror: the silent skeleton staring blankly into the
winding fastnesses of the Engulfed Cathedral, his white
shroud stirring softly to some subterranean air. I knew he
would do me no harm; indeed that he had meant to help
me, and at the least had warned me that my sister now
walked in the City of Trees. But his very presence was a
horror to me. I breathed as quietly as I could and said
nothing, hoping that he would leave. Still he remained
there, watchful and silent, until I wondered if he was waiting for someone.

After a very long time he spoke. "He is walking," he
whispered.

I started to my feet, looking fearfully out the open gate
into the Crypt Church. Dr. Silverthorn said nothing, only
continued to stare with those great dead eyes into the
darkness. Holding my breath, I strained to hear footsteps
or voices. Nothing. In the hallway the corpse candles in
their little glass holders burned a steady blue, wisps of
black smoke rising to disappear far overhead. The gray
curves of the walls receded endlessly, like the inert coiled
heart of a nautilus. Beside me Dr. Silverthorn stood still
and somber as one of the ravished caryatids in the transept
above us. I decided this was another of his imaginings, and
started to cross the room to the altar when he grabbed me,
the bones of his fingers surprisingly strong and cold about
my wrist.

"Wait," he said. "Can't you hear him?"

"I hear nothing."

He shook his head, still watching the hallway. "The
stones shriek as he passes them, and in their crypts the
bones of the dead shiver into pale dust; but to the living he
is silence itself! It is a wonder."

He mused for several minutes, his fingers cutting into
my hand until I could bear it no more and moved away.
"I'm sorry, Raphael," he said. He still did not look at me.
He ignored my physical presence completely now, except
for the moments he had held my hand.

After a little while he said, "I thought I would have more time. But it is coming fast now—"

"What is?"

"My sight is blurring," he announced, as though he had not heard me. "I'm surprised it lasted this long," he added matter-of-factly. "But I am seeing other things. Come with me, Raphael—"

Abruptly he stood, his hand clawing at the air. I gasped at his face. His eyes had finally collapsed like melting wax. He could no longer see. Soon he would be dead.

I took a deep breath to steady myself. Then I took his arm, flinching at the touch of raw bone beneath the fabric. "Where are we going?"

"To walk a little while, before he comes to claim you. My material eyes are dead now, but I have other ways of seeing. I would have you guide me, Raphael; and I will tell you what I see, and perhaps it will comfort you when I am gone."

7. Delicate details of internal structure

We passed into the dark corridors of the Crypt Church. I
carried the lantern and Dr. Silverthorn's black bag, lighter
now than it had been the day before. My companion's arm
rested upon mine like a nearly weightless splint of wood.
We walked slowly, my footsteps silent upon the cold stone
floor, Dr. Silverthorn's joints creaking alarmingly, so that
more than once I saw the tiny shadows of rats racing away
at our approach. Dr. Silverthorn laughed at this, and I
wondered aloud how he could see them if he was now
blind.

"There is no longer a veil of flesh between myself and
the world," he said. He halted and pointed to one side.
"What is there?"

I shrugged. "Nothing: a gray wall of many stones. The
narrow passageway continues there, and . . ." I squinted.
"There are some kind of statues up ahead, but here the
wall is empty."

He tilted his head to me. His sockets held only ruined
jelly, like the tallow smeared upon the children's altar. A
little longer and even that would be gone. "But they are
lovely!" he whispered, letting go my arm to gesture at the
blank expanse of granite, smooth except for where names,
thousands of names, had been incised in the stone. "Can't
you see them?"

I peered at the wall, stretching my hand to touch its
surface, cold and faintly damp, as though I might find

there the impression of what he saw. I felt only the engraved letters, and the grit lodged within them. "I see
nothing," I confessed ruefully. "What do you see?"

"Wonderful things," he murmured. "Many sleeping
faces, ancient men and women dreaming of the morning. I
think that I recognize some of them. Perhaps I may find
Gligor here. . . ." His voice trailed off and his hands
dropped to his sides. I realized that he referred to the dead
who had been interred within the Cathedral walls.

"You see revenants." Shivering, I stared at the wall, as
though they might start to pour from there like smoke.

"No," said Dr. Silverthorn. "They are not revenants.
They are but sleeping, it is but a long sleep, not to be
feared. If only I had known . . ."

He continued on. With each step I felt him drifting farther from me. It seemed now that he could see through the
veil that separated us from the immaterial world, that he
walked between the two. He spoke of flowers within the
granite walls, and faces peering from empty niches; of
many voices raised in song in the great nave above us, and
black engines buried in the fruitless earth. The minutes
passed dreamlike: the whisper of cloth against my skin the
only evidence that I did not walk alone, the whisper of
cloth and a soft voice intoning wonders into my ear.

We turned a corner. Far off in the darkness faint yellow
lights bloomed. I could no longer hear Dr. Silverthorn's
harsh breathing. His voice had dwindled to a rustle, nearly
inaudible; it might have been a voice inside my head.

"He comes," whispered my guide. The sleeve of his robe
trembled as he tried to point at something. "There—they
bear him to meet you."

I squinted. My eyes had been playing tricks on me all
this time, giving life to stone and imagining trapdoors in
every crevice. It was several minutes before I finally saw
that the misty lights in the distance had grown more distinct, formed themselves into bobbing globes. They *were*
drawing nearer. In a few minutes more I saw that they
were some kind of torches carried by moving figures; that
the figures were weighted beneath something black and

solid; that they were indeed bearing something, or some-one; that they were coming now to meet me.

"Dr. Silverthorn!" I dropped his bag. My voice cracked; sweat broke out on my neck as I groped for his hand. It was not there. "Is that him? Tell me!"

Dr. Silverthorn had slipped a few feet away, caught be-tween the ruddy light of my lantern and the torches' smoky glare. He swayed at their approach.

"Greetings, Margalis." His voice was surprisingly loud and strong, echoing through the space about us. "You have come just in time. I was preparing to leave you."

The soft thud of heavily padded feet upon stone; a stench of smoke, and of the bier. I forced myself to hold the lantern high enough to cast its glow upon them.

They were aardmen.

They carried a litter of wooden beams wrapped about with rope and cloth, and upon this lay a man. But all I could see were those others: six of them, their spines arched so that they seemed to lope even though they pro-ceeded slowly, vestigial tails switching behind them as they bore their injured master. Large eyes set beneath deep brows, jaws jutting from faces a little too large or too small; long curved yellow teeth rising from blue gums. Ears pressed against sleek dark skulls, pricking up as they drew near, nostrils dilating as they scented me and their tails lashing excitedly.

"Stop here," commanded a clear voice. They halted, growling softly as they swept their heads back and forth, snuffling, their bright eyes fixed upon me. "Is that him, Lawrence?"

Dr. Silverthorn stepped beside me. "This is the Paphian boy named Raphael Miramar, whom you asked be brought to you."

The insistent voice said, "But is he the one the girl told me about? The one she met by the river, the one she called the Gaping Lord? Boy!"

He turned, gesturing in the dark behind him. Someone else stepped into the torchlight: no, not one, but two slight figures—the boy Oleander, and, winding about his feet, my white jackal familiar.

"Anku!" I cried. He sat back upon his haunches, tipped his head to stare at me with glowing eyes. Then he raised his muzzle and yelped once, sharply. Beside him Oleander shifted from one foot to the other, trying to keep out of hand's reach of the man upon the bier.

"That's him," the boy stated. He moved anxiously from the jackal and into a pool of ocher light. "*Tell* him, Dr. Silverthorn."

The other propped himself up on his elbows to stare at me. He would be a very tall man standing: big-boned but thin, with sandy hair fading from a high brow and eyes of a piercing clarity, even in this eternal dusk: almost transparent eyes. Later I would see that they were palest blue, like periwinkles whose color had been washed away by dark water. The aardmen had broken his face. Seams stretched across his taut skin from cheek to chin to forehead, ragged scars like cracks in parched earth. One eye had been drawn too near the bridge of his nose and bulged slightly, and the corner of his mouth pulled upward, as though he were perpetually stifling a smile.

He did smile, now. "I can see him, Oleander," he reproached him. "It is him. What a beautiful boy." He motioned for the aardmen to set him upon the ground. They did so, still growling. The Aviator eased himself up, standing unsteadily with one hand beating the air until Oleander hastened beside him to help. Anku remained where he was, observing the aardmen from red slitted eyes.

At my side Dr. Silverthorn trembled. I would have embraced him, given or taken comfort; but I knew that any slight breeze would undo him now. I took a deep breath and stood as tall as I could, and addressed the Consolation of the Dead.

"I am Raphael Miramar; some call me the Gaping One."

My words sounded idiotic. I cleared my throat and bowed my head, trying to think of something else to say, something that might make him fear me. Nothing came. I added, "You may let this man go now, he has done what you sent him to do."

The Aviator shook his head, pointing at Dr. Silverthorn.

"I have never kept him against his will. Have I, Lawrence?"

Dr. Silverthorn lifted his head: a barren skull at last. "No," he said wearily. But when he turned to me there was something nearly exultant in his naked gaze; and I knew that he saw past me, past all of us, into those shadows that had finally engulfed him.

"Raphael: remember he is only a man—" he said. "Remember that the dead but sleep—"

Then his jaw rattled, chopped his words into harsh phrases— "Why, they are here! Gligor—Emma—"

A clattering, stones shaken inside an empty gourd. The others watched in silence as the skeleton tottered beside me.

He asked, "Is it like this, then, in the other kingdom? Is it?"

I shivered as he clutched my arm. "I don't know," I whispered. "I don't know."

But he could no longer hear me. He turned so that those black pits seemed to stare into the darkness and pointed to the empty air before him.

"There, Wendy," he chattered. "Is this what you showed them? Emma and the rest, is that what they saw? Oh tell me quick—"

He cried out, so loudly that I yelled and pulled away from him. For one instant as he raised his empty face the torchlight ignited it, made of him a burning mask both terrifying and radiant, transformed him so that I gazed where he pointed—

And I saw it too, glimpsed what he perceived in the blank air: the shades that waited behind the veil, a fissure opening upon blazing heavens and the ranks of sleeping dead: the skeleton transcendent, beneath its skull the promised country unfolding before an endless vernal dawn.

" 'Look at the stars!' " he cried. " 'Look, look up at the skies!' "

And then he collapsed. When I knelt and reached for him in the darkness I grasped nothing, nothing at all save a brittle handful of bones and shrunken cloth.

"Oh no . . ." I drew the hem of his robe to my cheek and buried my face in it. "Don't leave me—"

For many minutes I wept, mourning my patient suffering guide gone to join those other wraiths in the Cathedral's abyss. But finally my tears stopped. I wiped my face upon his robe, groped among his scattered bones until I found one, smooth and light and longer than my hand; and tucked it into a pocket of my robe, to bury later I thought, to inter as was proper for a man of charity and learning.

I sank back upon my feet and raised my head to look at the other waiting there. Beside him Oleander and Anku stood in silence.

"You are mine now, Raphael Miramar," he said softly. His foot nudged at the pile of bones and cloth before me. For a moment I thought he too might draw something from there to remember him by, tibia or rib or skullcap of the scientist who had served him for a little while. But he drew back his foot. His fingers clamped around Oleander's neck. With a voluptuary's delicate smile he pushed him toward me.

"Prepare him, Oleander. When he is ready bring him to me in the Gabriel Tower."

He turned, with a gesture commanded the aardmen to lower the stretcher. Anku danced at his side, leaped after him onto the bier, and crouched between his legs. As the Aviator settled back a groan escaped him, of pain or perhaps of sorrow. Then he cursed, and I heard him strike one of the aardmen as they struggled to lift him again. His last words echoed back to us from the depths of the Engulfed Cathedral.

"Feed him and bathe him and anoint him as befits the one who will serve the Consolation of the Dead in raising the Gaping Lord."

As they bore him into the darkness the aardmen began to howl.

Part Seven

A Masque of Owls

There were no more dark houses after that one.

"Aidan, we have *never* been so in demand," said Mehitabel one morning. It was a few weeks since the massacre at High Brazil. Paphians and Curators alike seemed to want to forget the horrors of the Butterfly Ball, the continuing outrage of children and elders captured by foraging lazars and aardmen growing more emboldened as the autumn passed, the whispered tales of an Ascendant demon holding sway over the Engulfed Cathedral. We Players seldom had a day off anymore. Scarcely a night passed without its masque or burletta or private soiree.

Mehitabel tugged her hair thoughtfully. "Maybe it was like this when Miss Scarlet first joined the troupe; but I wasn't here then."

"Is that when you first saw them?" I asked.

"Oh yes!" She took a bite from a slab of meringue hoarded from an Illyrian moon-viewing several days before. "She was wonderful, just wonderful. That was when *I* decided to become an actress."

I raised an eyebrow. "Really? What changed your mind?"

She swallowed, stared at me open-mouthed. Then she burst out laughing, covering her mouth as she rocked back in her chair.

"Oh Aidan!" she giggled. "You know I do my best."

Silly Mehitabel! She really was a terrible actress. She got by on her looks, and a certain look she used on stage and off, a way of tilting her head to one side and letting her hair fall into her face so that one was torn between the desire to brush it aside or give her a slap. All the Players confided in her, mostly because she would have been crushed if they had not: she brought all her secrets to us, laid them out like so many pretty stones she had found and waited for us to admire them. None of the others had the heart to turn her away.

Neither did I. Although she aggravated me, although I found her gossip tiresome and could no more imagine tapping in to her simple memories than I could imagine tapping a block of wood; still I couldn't ignore her, or tease her cruelly as I once had.

"I don't know what it is," I said to Miss Scarlet that afternoon. "I know she is a perfect idiot; but I can't seem to help it. When she needs help with her lines, or her costume, or—well, whatever it is this time—I can't just send her away anymore."

Miss Scarlet continued to stare at the page in front of her. I tapped my foot, waiting for a reply. When none came I crossed her room to the window.

"And what is with Justice now, he spends all his time with her, 'reading lines.' Reading lines with *Mehitabel!* He knows she's awful, he knows they are coming to see *me*—"

I stopped, fearing I might have insulted Miss Scarlet, once the Prodigy of a Prodigal Age; of late busier playing mentor and adviser to Aidan Arent, the City's newest sensation. She raised her head and smiled, her dark eyes peering from within her wizened face with an odd expression.

"Why should it matter then, who he practices with? Perhaps he feels uneasy reading with you, your talent so surpasses his own." She glanced back down at her book. But after a few moments she looked up again and added, "Perhaps you are jealous, Wendy. Perhaps you are growing a heart."

I ignored her, drumming my fingers on the windowsill. Outside, the earth was gray and brown. The Librarians' sheep grazed upon an untidy pile of straw dumped on the lawn, their shepherd shivering in his homespun jacket. It would be Benedick tonight for the Historians (they loved battles; battling lovers would do if necessary); then tomorrow a smaller role in *Watt the Butler,* and the following week *Titus Andronicus*, and Juliet after that; then *A Midsummer Night's Dream* for the Zoologists, hosting a Masque of Owls for the Illyrians. Finally a brief hiatus while the Paphians readied themselves for the great feast of Winterlong, twelve days and nights of merrymaking that would culminate on the eve of Winterlong itself, shortest day of the year, when we would perform—Toby was beside himself to think of it—*The Spectres' Harlequinade* for the masque of Winterlong at Saint-Alaban.

"Never before have the Paphians requested that we play for them at Winterlong! Never!" he had gloated. Already he could see the bartered riches that would come of it, plastics and woolen cloth and the intricate bits of hardware that the Paphians used as ornaments but which I knew were the remains of archaic computers. But looking out at the bleak lawn this wintry afternoon I wondered about Toby's optimism; about the wisdom of people who could continue their meaningless research and revels while rumors of human sacrifices and hidden weapons brought to light fled across the Hill Magdalena Ardent.

Terrible things had befallen the City in the past weeks. The bizarre murder of a young girl in the Museum of Natural History; its Regent slain at the massacre at the Butterfly Ball when the House High Brazil burned to the ground. A figure seen at the ball, a beautiful boy clad in torn red tunic and with a vine draped about his neck, he who the Saint-Alabans name the Gaping One or Naked Lord. A burning star in the northern sky that heralded the Final Ascension. But still the round of masques and balls did not cease, only proceeded to a more somber music, dark pavane rather than sprightly reel.

"Fancy: gone," Justice murmured after I had told him Fabian's news. He buried his face in his hands. "And your brother—I met an Illyrian spado who claimed to have seen him at the Butterfly Ball. He is dead now; so many of us are dead."

A mist crept over me when he said this. I closed my eyes, tried to plumb the darkness inside me, find something that would give the truth or lie to his words. Nothing; but I could not believe it was so.

apple tree hanging

At last I said, "He isn't dead."

Justice raised his eyes. "How do you know?"

"I don't know. But—"

"It doesn't matter," Justice said bleakly. "So many are dead now, how could it matter?"

And mere days after that a viral strike: and then another.

"They are searching for someone," Justice had muttered. We stood in the theater's upper story, watching the fougas' searchlights slash through the dusk.

"The Aviator," I whispered. From the Deeping Avenue echoed screams; a party of masquers had been caught in the rain of roses. I shuddered. Justice put his arm around me. From his grim face I knew he was not thinking of the Aviator but of me, wondering if they still might search for an escaped empath whose dreams could kill.

But the fougas had withdrawn after these two strikes; although many died in the streets, and the lazars' gleeful wailing kept us all from sleep for several hours. Since then more rumors raged through the City of Trees. Everyday life took on the shocking and explosive nuances of the tales we enacted.

The morbidly superstitious House Saint-Alaban enjoyed an unprecedented wave of popularity in light of the City's recent misfortunes. Death became the fashionable theme at masquerades. Red, the Paphian hue of mourning, colored everything from hair to dominatrice's hoods. The Botanists were unable to meet the demand for a particular shade of crimson henna. Scarlet love apples adorned every dish we ate for two solid weeks, and every invitation to a ball was writ in sanguine ink. An Illyrian eunuch inspired his Librarian Patron to compose a long poem entitled "The Coming of the Gaping One." When recited at the Illyrians' Semhane Masque, three Saint-Alabans fainted. A fourth was found dead afterward, hanging from an apple tree.

Fashion began to reflect these macabre preoccupations. Paphians my own age or younger emulated the startling deshabille of the ill-fated Raphael Miramar as he had last been seen at the Butterfly Ball: deathly pallor enhanced by powder of lead, crimson tunics carefully torn; fillets of

twigs and vine woven upon their brows and hempen ropes
worn about the neck in lieu of the customary wreaths of
blossoms or bijoux. Raphael Miramar himself had become
a sort of romantic figure in death, mourned by his many
friends and lovers. An ardent cult sprang up around his
memory; a violent tango was named after him, and a dangerous means of achieving sexual gratification by use of a
rope.

Fin-de-siècle thinking, a renowned Librarian christened
it all. The phrase was enthusiastically parroted by the
Paphians, although few of them recognized the language it
came from; and no one could have guessed what century
this was, or whether or not we approached its end.

My star continued to rise amidst all this confused speculation. My amazing resemblance to Raphael Miramar had
of course already been remarked upon. Now it became our
stock-in-trade. Paphians from the remaining Houses
flocked to each performance at our theater. A masque was
no longer considered proper entertainment unless we
were there in attendance, and we turned down countless
invitations to perform.

Throughout I enjoyed the attention of myriad admirers.
I eschewed Raphaelesque garb save onstage, as when I
played Lear's Fool. I preferred my own restrained taste in
clothing, although I did indulge in accepting gifts of feathered caps and bandeaux from the Zoologists, once they
learned my fondness for these. The *mode Raphael* was
risky for me, since it involved a certain amount of exposed
flesh.

"You should be more careful, Wendy," Justice scolded
late that night. Our performance for the Historians had
been an enormous success, but afterward I had grown
cocky waiting for my curtain call. Inspired by his recent
triumph, Fabian and I staged a mock duel backstage. He
had playfully torn my blouse with his sword. I took my bow
with the ripped cloth flapping, my hair tangled, flushed
and grinning from our game. The Paphians in the audience had cheered madly. Some even rushed the stage. I
made a scarce retreat down the trapdoor before they
could capture me and adapt my wardrobe further. Miss

Scarlet had been aghast at this unprofessional behavior—
"*Quite* unlike you, Aidan," she had remarked sternly—but
Fabian and the rest of the troupe seemed pleased that
Aidan had dropped his prim hauteur for a few minutes.

Justice of course sided with Miss Scarlet. "What if they
had caught you?" he demanded.

He and I had taken to sharing a room, twin sleigh beds
drawn up against opposite walls beneath curled photo-
graphs of unconvincingly histrionic thespians. This ar-
rangement kept me from being bothered by my admirers.
It also put off the questions of others in the troupe regarding my amorous tastes. Since our visit to the House Miramar, Toby Rhymer had regarded me suspiciously: with
more respect, perhaps, but also with skepticism, fueled by
envy of my success.

"Our dear Aidan is more than what he seems to be," he
often said, affection vying with malice in his tone.

But as a roommate Justice, like Miss Scarlet, was above
reproach. He wanted only to act as my friend and conscience (but still hoped to take me as his lover). I found that
I liked his company: sober and intelligent for a Paphian,
and relatively chaste. After that evening at the House Miramar he had made no more overtures toward me. His
intrigues tended to be brief: a very young sloe-eyed refugee from Miramar; an Illyrian gynander with a jealous
Naturalist Patron; this continuing flirtation with
Mehitabel, under Gitana's reproving gaze.

Now he sat curled up on his bed, weaving colored wires
and tiny bulbs of glass into his braid.

"Do you think you could do that to *my* hair?" I asked. A
Historian had given me a brooch after my performance, a
flat square of plastic embellished with letters and numbers.
"I'll give you this—"

"No," he said, glancing up and shaking his head. "Your
hair's still too short. Aren't you listening to me, Wendy?
What would have happened if they'd caught you and
found out they'd been fooled all this time?"

I held the brooch to my breast. I decided it was ugly, and
tossed it to the floor. "*I* don't know," I said. "Does it matter?"

of respons. bility

"It should. It wouldn't go very well for the rest of us, I can tell you that. People don't like being made fools of."

I felt flushed from that intense rippling joy that remained with me after a good performance: better than my acetelthylene had been, better than almost anything except tapping new blood. "But it wouldn't be *my* fault, Justice. It would be Aidan's! I'm not responsible—Wendy *can't* be responsible."

He gazed at me, wrapping a wire around one finger. "Is that what you think, Wendy? Is that what you really believe—that this is like the Human Engineering Laboratory, that Dr. Harrow's out there somewhere to protect you and save you if you go too far?

"Because you're wrong. Terrible things are happening. If the Ascendants are really looking for you then you're in danger all the time, and so am I, and Miss Scarlet and probably every single other person in this damned City. And if the man in the Cathedral is the same one who ordered the purge at HEL—"

I knelt to retrieve the brooch, so he wouldn't see my face.

"At the very least, Wendy, you shouldn't make it harder for those who love you and are the only wall between you and the dark."

I put the brooch in my pocket. I sat on the floor for a minute, then reached for the bottom drawer of my bureau. I withdrew a feathered bandeau, the one Andrew had given me at HEL. I stared at it a long time without speaking; because I felt ashamed, and angry, and frightened.

Because something terrible *was* happening in the City: something terrible was happening to *me,* but it was not what Justice or anyone else might imagine in all their gory nightmares.

No: I felt within my head a new thing burgeoning, jealous and implacable and tender and bewildering by turns. Even my dreams had changed. They held not the faces of Dr. Harrow or Morgan Yates or the other subjects at HEL, but those of myself and Justice, or Miss Scarlet, or others I met each day in the City. And as I stared at the bandeau a terrifying thought came to me: that after seventeen years I

was changing, that something had changed me: something
even Emma Harrow had never dreamed might happen to
her sacred monster.

A few weeks later an emissary from the Zoologists arrived. It was the morning of our performance at the
Masque of Owls. We were sitting at breakfast together in
the oak-paneled dining chamber, picking over the remnants of one of Gitana's peppery frittatas.

"Someone is at the door," Mehitabel announced.
Through the dirty panes of leaded glass I glimpsed something moving, too big to be a person. A palanquin, maybe,
or a cart delivering goods in payment for past performances on the Hill Magdalena Ardent.

"Then why don't you let them in?" Gitana said through
clenched teeth. She poked Mehitabel with her bread knife
so that the plump girl shrieked and bumped cozily against
Justice.

"Well, all right! 'Scuse me," she said, winking at Justice.
Gathering her skirts above her knees, she flounced down
the hall. The others yawned and chatted as they finished
breakfast. Toby droned on (to himself, apparently) about
the virtues of performing for the lazars.

I could see Mehitabel's eyes widening as she peeked out
the window.

"Toby . . ." she called doubtfully. When she glanced
back at the dining room I was the only one who met her
gaze. "Aidan?" she asked, her hand on the doorknob as she
waited for my advice. I nodded. With a flourish she flung
open the door.

"Hey, girl!" a voice bellowed from outside. Mehitabel
shrieked softly. *"Hey!"*

"Aidan," said Mehitabel weakly.

I went to see who was there. For an instant the morning
sun dazzled me so that I could make out nothing.

"Hey, boy!" the voice yelled again at me. "I've come to
see Toby and Scarlet Pan. They here?"

Blinking, I looked up to see a monstrous figure on the

lawn, two-headed and horned with four glowering eyes. It took a moment to sort out that this was a tall young girl astride a great antlered beast, and that she was growing impatient.

"Agh!" she shouted, and swung down from her mount. A faint jingling of many little bells as it shook its great dark head. "Is everyone here an idiot? Scarlet!"

Behind me a soft voice said, "Jane?"

"Hey, girl!"

I turned to see Miss Scarlet in the doorway, still holding her demitasse. Her expression brightened from disbelief to delight, and she shoved her cup into Mehitabel's hand before running to throw herself into the arms of the strange girl.

"Oh, *Jane!"*

I stared bemused as the girl Jane caught her up and swung her into the air like a child. Miss Scarlet wrapped her wiry arms around her neck and the tall girl swung her around, laughing.

"Scarlet! D'you miss me?"

Now the others had joined us outside. Mehitabel peeked from behind Justice's shoulder. Gitana stood finishing her tea, while beside her Toby shook his head at the commotion.

Fabian walked to the animal Jane had ridden and waved me to join him.

"It won't hurt you," he said. "See?" He tugged its bridle. The animal nodded complacently.

I stepped beside him. "What is it?"

"A sambar." He reached to stroke its muzzle: a creature like a great heraldic stag, russet brown with darker chocolate markings on its legs and back and a thick stiff mane of nearly black hair growing on its throat. I brushed it tentatively with one hand. It regarded me with intelligent liquid eyes and dipped its head. I heard that soft chiming again and saw that its antlers were wrapped with fine aluminum wire and strung with myriad tiny bells. Its saddle was a simple pad of woven cloth, once vivid red and green but now worn and much patched, though bright with bells hanging from its braided trim.

"Isn't it beautiful?" Fabian murmured as he stroked the sambar's muzzle. The animal snorted softly into his cupped palm. "They take such good care of them."

"Who does?" I asked. I hardly listened for his reply. Instead I watched with some dismay as Miss Scarlet climbed upon Jane's shoulders, behaving for all the world like a trained monkey and not the Prodigy of a Prodigal Age.

"The Zoologists," said Fabian. His frosty breath mingled with the sambar's as he looked up from warming his hands in its thick fur. "Who do you think Jane is?"

"I have no idea," I said, and turned to go back inside.

"Aidan!" Miss Scarlet cried as I passed. "Come meet my old Keeper!"

I started to pretend I hadn't heard her. Then, "Yes," I replied stiffly.

"This is Aidan Arent," said Miss Scarlet, smiling to bare her teeth. "He is my newest friend."

Jane shrugged Miss Scarlet higher upon her shoulders and extended her hand. "Jane Alopex," she said. Her gaze swept me appraisingly, a long cool look: as if I were an unusual specimen. I stared back at her. She was a tall girl my own age, stocky, with thick straight black hair cut short to frame round brown eyes and a ruddy freckled face. Strange for a Curator to look as though she'd ever seen the sun. Odd too to hear her brazen laughter. Her clothes suited her: a long green tunic embellished with gold braid over breeches of brilliant sky blue tucked into high black boots, so well polished despite obvious years of wear that they creaked when she moved. She held on to my hand and continued to stare at me through narrowed eyes for a long moment. With alarm I recalled my first meeting with Miss Scarlet—*"Sieur, that is a woman . . ."*—and wondered if these Zoologists and their charges were gifted with some kind of special sight that would enable Jane Alopex to see through my masculine attire.

" 'Aidan errant,' " she repeated with a sardonic grin. " 'The one who wanders.' We've heard of you in your travels."

My own smile froze. I glanced up at Miss Scarlet perched

et now twins — Caliban & Ariel

upon this girl's shoulders; but my friend was laughing and waving at Fabian, heedless of my concern.

"My travels are over. I live here now," I replied. I slipped my hand from Jane's, shrugged in what I hoped appeared to be a careless boyish manner. "Maybe you know my partner, Justice Saint-Alaban?"

Jane Alopex threw back her head and laughed. "It'll be a cold day in hell before I know a Saint-Alaban!" she said, but without rancor. "Are you a courtesan then, young errant?"

"I am as you see me: a Player."

A flicker of respect shot through her brown eyes. "Huh," she muttered, and began looking around at the other Players. "Well, I'm here about the performance tonight in honor of Rufus Lynx's birthday—our Regent," she explained, and then tugged at one of Miss Scarlet's still-slippered feet. "Hey, Scarlet! Did you hear that? There's been a change: he wants that other show, the one with the magician and the shipwreck. *The Storm*—"

"The Tempest," Toby corrected her. He elbowed me aside and stared down at Jane, who stood her ground and grinned. "But we haven't rehearsed that; the arrangements were for *A Midsummer Night's Dream.*"

"Well, Toby." She lifted Miss Scarlet to the ground. "What of it? The Regent says there's enough fairy-dust in the City these days without your Players adding to it. He likes that other story better, he says. 'This isn't Midsummer,' he says, 'there's a storm brewing and we might as well welcome it.' So I'm to ask if you can do it, this other play, *The Thunderclap*—"

"The Tempest," Toby repeated, glaring and indifferent of Miss Scarlet at his side, a beaming black imp. He turned to me and demanded, "Well, Aidan? Can you do it? Ariel and Caliban?"

I shrugged. "Of course."

He snorted. He had revised the play so that I could take both parts, Caliban and Ariel; favorite roles of mine. His own alchemist Prospero and Miss Scarlet's tender Miranda were also sheer joy to watch. It was of the others he was thinking, the lesser parts unrehearsed.

"Humph," he said again. He stroked Miss Scarlet's head. She took his hand and murmured, "Now, Toby."

Toby glanced over at the rest of his troupe, ticking them off one by one. He sighed. "Tell Rufus we'll do it; but we're underrehearsed. I don't want to hear any complaints—"

Jane Alopex waved her hand. "No complaints, no complaints. A birthday masque, that's all. To cheer him up; to cheer us all up, dark days behind us and darker ones ahead, hey Scarlet?" She gave that short barking laugh again, twisted her head to flash me a wink. I shoved my hands in my pockets and walked away, uneasy.

I started to find Justice; but he was engaged in laughing conversation with Mehitabel and Gitana. So I waited while Fabian cooed to the Zoologist's sambar, and Mehitabel and Gitana made sniggering remarks about our visitor as she haggled with Toby over the arrangements for Rufus Lynx's command performance. A caracul pelt apiece for Toby and Miss Scarlet and myself, furs of lesser worth—coyote and raccoon—for the rest, and a vial of civet musk we could trade with the Botanists later for perfume. All of us to share in the feasting afterward, and an extra pair of snakeskins for Toby's trouble, not to worry about missed lines or cues—

"We'll never notice," Jane Alopex assured him. Toby scowled.

"All right then!" exclaimed Jane, clapping her hands against her breeches. "I've got to get back, else they'll think the aardmen got me." She laughed, striding across the sward to cup her mount's muzzle in one strong hand. "Eh then, Sallymae: you ready to go home?"

The sambar tossed its head in a jingling of silver bells. Fabian grinned. "Toby, I'll send a pantechnicon for everyone this afternoon. Not afraid of our animals, are you?" she called out to Mehitabel, who giggled and hid her face in her sleeve. "Who's for going back with me now? Scarlet?"

"I would be delighted," replied Miss Scarlet, smoothing her bare head. "But I'm not even dressed yet!"

"Well, hurry up then," said Jane impatiently. She blew into the sambar's ear and scratched its chin.

Miss Scarlet bustled past the others, pausing to remind Gitana of the change in costume.

"You'll be certain to bring the blue gown, not the silver one? Toby—?" She turned to pat his knee. "You don't mind, do you? It's been so long since I visited!"

"Of course not, Miss Scarlet." I imagined he was still tallying up his share of the night's proceeds. "Just don't forget your nap."

"Anyone else?" demanded Jane Alopex. Fabian started forward eagerly, but before he could say a word Jane turned and pointed at me. "What about you, errant? I bet you've never been to the Zoo."

"Oh, yes, Aidan!" Miss Scarlet exclaimed. "Come with us —you'll love it, the trees and all the birds singing!" She clasped her hands and fluttered her eyelids.

"I will come if Toby permits." I looked at him questioningly. Out of the corner of my eye I saw Justice and Mehitabel walk back inside, arm in arm. I turned back to Toby. He tapped a finger against his nose, then nodded.

"All right. Aidan may accompany Miss Scarlet this time. Fabian, I need you and Justice to dismantle the flats for *Tempest.*"

Fabian checked his disappointment and shrugged. He saluted Jane Alopex's sambar and spun on his heel to return inside.

And so we set out, Miss Scarlet and Jane Alopex and I. Miss Scarlet rode astride the sambar, clutching the edge of its cloth saddle to steady herself. Jane Alopex and I walked alongside, myself glancing back several times to see if perhaps Justice had returned to watch me leave; he had not. This amused Jane Alopex greatly.

"Such a pretty catamite, Aidan Arent! Wasting yourself on a foolish Saint-Alaban. I could find a better boy for you at home."

But her laughter belied this: the Zoologists loved nothing and no one so much as their animal charges. No Paphian would ever look lovelier to Jane Alopex than Miss Scarlet Pan. And nothing Miss Scarlet had ever told me of her upbringing—the long rainshot afternoons in the Infirmary watching ancient films and videos; learning human language from a captured aardman tamed for this sole purpose; her heartbreaking decision to leave the Zoologists and join Toby's troupe—none of this prepared me for the slavish devotion Miss Scarlet showed Jane Alopex, or the condescension with which the Zoologist treated her former charge.

"Don't tug too hard on that, Scarlet," she scolded; and, "Sit farther up on the saddle and it won't rock so." And, "You know, that's rather a bright yellow for your eyes, you should have one of those red things made like they're wearing now." After each admonition she turned and winked at me. But otherwise I found it quite pleasant to travel through the City with Jane Alopex at my side and Miss Scarlet chattering from atop her mount.

Light streamed through the bare limbs above the grassy avenue as we walked down Library Hill. A few rosehips still brightened the roadside, and the sun took a little of the cold edge off the morning, but the air smelled of smoke, fires burning in distant woodstoves. Soon it would be true winter. Jane tried to draw me into conversation but I was quiet, thinking of Justice walking arm in arm with Mehitabel.

"What news of the Cathedral, Jane?" Miss Scarlet asked after a time. We had reached a spot where the Deeping Avenue continued on to the Museums, but it seemed we were to turn here. Jane tugged the sambar's bridle, leading it to the right. Through the thick mesh of dead matted kudzu ran a small track, barely high or wide enough to allow the animal easy passage. Jane laid a hand upon its steaming flank to steady it. Miss Scarlet looked concerned: not frightened but distracted, as though the scene called for a change in demeanor and she was unsure how to act. Jane reached into a deep pocket and withdrew a heavy pistol, ancient but shining where she had recently oiled it. She held it up and stared down the barrel before tucking it into her belt.

"It's faster this way," she explained. "Perfectly safe, really; but these days . . ." She shook her head. "We see strange things in our part of the City."

"The Cathedral?" asked Miss Scarlet again.

Jane Alopex nodded. "What have you heard?"

"Only the rumor that a deranged Ascendant lives in the ruins there, and commands the lazars bring him captives for sacrifice."

Jane chewed her lip. After a moment she slapped the sambar's flank so that it lumbered on again, shaking its antlers free of tangled vines. Miss Scarlet lurched forward, caught herself, and dug her paws into the sambar's mane. Then she straightened the stiff folds of her skirt and fixed Jane with a stare. The girl looked away and sighed.

"It's true, then!" Miss Scarlet exclaimed, alarmed. "Have you seen him, Jane?"

Jane Alopex shook her head. She stepped aside to allow the sambar onto the trail, eyeing a yellow creeper whose serrated leaves twitched slightly as the stag trudged past. "No. I've been on duty in the Herp Lab; the anacondas are shedding, and I'm saving the skins. But some of us have seen things—

"A star, a sort of brightness in the sky like an explosion the night of the Butterfly Ball. You must have heard about it; the Paphians said it heralded the next Ascension. Isidore Myotis saw it, he was tending a live birth among the flying foxes. A nova, he said; but we've heard it was something else. . . ."

Absently she pointed her pistol at a dead tree limb and fired. An explosion; the tree limb crashed to earth. The sambar snorted, rearing back in fright. Jane turned to stroke its muzzle. "Ah, there, Sallymae, I'm sorry."

I paused to finger a charred bit of wood. Atop Sallymae Miss Scarlet rubbed her hairy chin.

"What do you think it was?" I asked.

Jane Alopex pursed her lips. "That's rather a blunt question to ask a Curator, Sieur Aidan," she said. She gave me the same condescending look she'd given Miss Scarlet earlier. "It seems to me that you're rather adrift in our City, young Arent. Unfamiliar with our ways of doing things, if you know what I mean."

I flushed, but she cut me off before I could protest. "No: if Scarlet likes you, I guess that's good enough. Uppity actors don't bother me, really. And I've heard of Aidan

Arent, of course. The Paphians are quite mad about you."
Grinning, she flicked at my hair; but there was a glint of
shrewd intelligence in her eyes.

I followed her in silence as she led Sallymae down the
path. Miss Scarlet pulled her shawl closer against the chill,
then twisted to look down at me.

"Something is happening in the world," she said at last
to Jane. "I spoke of this with Aidan at our first meeting. You
and the other Zoologists may think it's nonsense, but I fear
the Saint-Alabans are right: Final Ascension or not, something is coming."

Jane squinted at the weak sunlight. "Well, you may be
right, Scarlet. Last week we heard that runagates from the
Citadel escaped and entered the City."

I stopped in the middle of the trail. A small astonished
sound escaped me. I looked up at Miss Scarlet. She stared
back in amazement, but quickly composed herself by grabbing her mount's mane.

"When?" she asked with breathless innocence, rocking
as the sambar loped down the path. "How many?"

Jane shrugged. "Three of them, two weeks ago. *Escaped
research subjects,* is what I was told."

Three! And two weeks ago. Not Justice and myself, then
—but who?

As Jane stared at me I realized I had muttered aloud.
"Who told you?" I asked. I pretended to be having difficulty clambering over an ivy-choked log, and paused to
collect my wits.

Jane frowned. "Now why would you ask me that? Why
would you even want to know, unless you were an Ascendant delator?" From her expression I could tell she was
measuring me up, trying to decide if it was possible that
the Ascendants had chosen such a careless informer. She
finally shook her head.

"No: you're too stupid to be a spy. And too obvious—
who'd trust you?"

This thought seemed to cheer her. "Well, Aidan Arent,
since you're so bold as to ask, I'll tell you: an aardman told
me. I caught them poaching in the Zoo. I let one go free, in
exchange for news; nothing like aardmen for news.

"He told me that three refugees escaped from the Citadel. Fougas pursued them and one died in the strike. The other two fled into the Narrow Forest. They were tending to the corpse of the boy who died when the aardmen took them. A man and a girl. The aardmen thought he was a Scientist, the girl they said was a witch. A witch!"

She laughed a bit too heartily. "The aardmen give allegiance now to the one in the Cathedral. He has commanded them to bring to him, alive, anyone they capture in the City. They brought him the Scientist and the girl. They told me that the Scientist will certainly die from his injuries. The girl I know nothing more of, save that they took her to the Cathedral as well. The aardmen said that she scratched and fought like a wolf."

"Anna!" I exclaimed; then bit my tongue.

Jane yelled a command to the sambar. It halted and began to graze upon the yellowing grass. Miss Scarlet took a sudden interest in the hem of her shawl.

"Scarlet," asked Jane Alopex with measured calm. "What do you know of this?" She grabbed my arm and pulled me close to her.

"Only what you've told us," the chimpanzee replied. She looked up, her face clouding. "And rumors, just rumors. What we heard from the suzein Miramar: a shooting star in the north, a runaway Paphian favorite the Saint-Alabans says is a demon incarnate. None of this other, I swear—"

"But Master Aidan seems quite disturbed by this news. Although, as a matter of fact, it doesn't even seem like it's *news* to him."

She tightened her grip on my arm, waiting for me to explain. Her face was quite pale: I had taken her by surprise. She tapped uneasily at her pistol. I wondered if she knew something more, something worse than this. I closed my eyes, my head whirling, and tried to imagine myself somewhere far away: back in the Horne Room, or in my little chamber at the theater. When I remained silent Jane snapped, "Well, say something, dammit!"

"Anna," I said at last. "The girl's name is Anna."

"Or Andrew," I added a moment later.

Miss Scarlet began to fan herself with her shawl. Jane stared at me as though I spoke an unknown tongue. Finally she said, "How do you know that?"

I said nothing more; only opened my eyes and stared at my hands. When it became clear I would admit to nothing else, she let go of me. The sambar shook its head, bells jingling gaily in the cold air. Apart from that there was silence.

"Well, Scarlet," Jane said at last. "You've met up with bad company this time. 'Actors,' I always said; 'she'll get herself into trouble if she leaves us for *Actors*.' And I was right: this is a bad business, Scarlet."

She turned to me, pointing her pistol at my feet. "And you, sweetheart: either you're mixed up in this trouble past all help; or else you're a fool.

"The aardmen brought the Scientist and the girl to the Madman in the Cathedral." She spat. "Paaugh! The aardmen are idiots, and the Historians cowardly fools who didn't have the courage to kill the Aviator themselves; and now look what they've brought on to the City! They gave him to the aardmen, so if there was ever an investigation it would look like the aardmen had devoured him. And of course when they took him prisoner the aardmen botched it. They tortured him and castrated him—"

Miss Scarlet gasped.

"—but then he convinced them to free him. He told them he was actually an emissary of the hanged god, he told them he had been sent here to rule not by the Ascendants but by the Gaping One, the Lord of Dogs; and the aardmen would be punished horribly if they did not free him.

"They let him go; they escorted him to the Cathedral, and now they pay him homage. All this the aardmen told me when I caught them sniffing around the civets' cages. I killed one of them, just to let the other know I meant business. Then whimpering he told me the last part of the story:

"'*He looks for someone,*' the aardman said. He was

afraid to tell me; terrified the Aviator would find out and
kill him. 'He is searching for one of their subjects, a girl
kidnapped from the Citadel. He wants to find her and
return her alive to the Citadel. For further processing,'
said the aardman.

" 'She has powers, this girl; she deals death with her
mind, and contorts the dreams of men so that they go mad.
Even the Ascendants feared her; and now they fear to lose
her, fear that in the City she will find followers, and turn
upon the Citadel and destroy them.

" 'But this Aviator is already mad, he has no fear! He
wishes to avenge himself upon the City, and the Ascendants: upon everyone he feels betrayed him. To this
end he seeks the girl. He would use her power to destroy
anyone who will thwart him. And he preys upon the weak-
ness of the Paphians, he claims that he will raise the god
that they call the Gaping One. The aardman said he raved
about ancient weapons in the earth that he will turn upon
the City of Trees. He uses the lazars to work the earth
beneath the Cathedral, seeking an arsenal buried there
after the First Ascension. And still the lazars flock to him,
and the aardmen. He will make an effigy of the hanged god
to frighten your stupid whores, and they too will worship
him.'

"So the aardman told me."

She finished, wiping her brow. She seemed surprised to
see the sun still shining and Miss Scarlet and myself there
beneath the trees with her. I had begun shaking as Jane
Alopex told her tale. I heard tiny sounds like insects boring
into my ears. I clasped my hands and paced back and forth,
back and forth, trying to think my way clear of this, trying
to force back the Small Voices.

"Why doesn't someone kill him?" I asked.

"Someone? *Who?!* There are no warriors in this City!"
Jane exploded. She pointed her pistol at a rotting log,
clicked its release. Nothing. "See? Everything is hundreds
of years old, nothing works when it should! I had to slit that
aardman's throat to kill him because my other weapons are
useless; and you think I'm going to creep into the Cathe-

dral among a thousand lazars and aardmen and capture a
NASNA Aviator by myself?"

She waved the pistol furiously above her head. It went
off and a shower of bark rained onto us.

"Yes, of course, I understand," I said hastily. I looked up
at Miss Scarlet, hoping that she might come forth with
some revelation, some word that would gainsay all that
Jane Alopex had told us. But she only shook her head, as
though she had perceived this a long time coming. Jane too
stared at me, her eyes glittering.

"If he finds the ancient arsenal he will destroy us all," she
said at last. "It is as the Saint-Alabans and lazars are saying,
it has come at last. The Final Ascension." She slipped the
pistol back into her pocket and turned to her mount.

I watched as she stroked its dark flank. Atop it sat Miss
Scarlet, chewing on the fringe of her shawl. I thought of
Justice and the others back in the theater. Tiny figures
they seemed to me now, brightly colored and moving with
jerky slowness, as though some great hand tugged and
twitched at invisible strings. Words roared in my head, the
Small Voices gathering force like some shrill whirlwind:

> *I can't be responsible, I'm not responsible . . .*
> *Find him, Wendy!*
> *Something has happened, something is happening in
> the City—*

And over them all a soft chanting, a child's voice repeating again and again:

> *hang the boy and raise the girl*
> *'til Winterlong is broken—*

The roaring grew louder, became the voice of something huge and black, something pressing against my temples until I thought the blood would burst from there.

Then suddenly there was silence, utter silence.

And it came: the terrifying pulsing in my head that signaled the beginning of a seizure. I sank to my knees;
clutched at my head as the air swam before me in motes of

gray and black and I thrashed against the earth, trying to smash Him, rend Him, push Him back, His white hands reaching for me and eyes glowing like flowers, like stars, like great suns exploding above the City's ruined spires—

"Scarlet! Stop him! What *is* it?!"

Other voices shouting but I could not stop, could not turn, He is there and He is too strong for me, I feel Him within me and the rage burns through my eyes, He has come at last, o come to me, come to me—

"Aidan!"

A flash of crimson light; then nothing.

Gradually I heard voices again, and wind. It was the wind that told me I was not hallucinating. I blinked and sat up groggily, groping to feel the bump where I had knocked myself unconscious. Jane and Miss Scarlet squatted a few feet away, staring at me with drawn faces. Behind them the sambar munched upon some purple thistles.

"Aidan!" Jane exclaimed. "What happened? Are you all right?"

I rubbed my forehead, grimacing. "I think so," I said. Miss Scarlet twittered in relief and ran to my side.

"Oh, poor Wendy," she cried, her words tumbling back to the Zoologist before I could stop her. "She's been so overworked, Jane, Toby won't listen when I—"

"She?" Jane Alopex stood, dead leaves falling from where they'd stuck to her breeches. *"She?"*

Miss Scarlet gasped and covered her mouth with her paws, then drew up her skirts to hide her face.

Jane stared at me in amazement. Before I could move she jumped beside me, grabbed my shirt, and tore it open. I recovered myself in time to slap her and yank my shirt closed; but not before she had seen beneath it. She collapsed back onto her haunches and cursed so loudly that the sambar started, looking over its shoulder with mild questioning eyes.

"Sweet mother of us all! It's *you* they're after."

"Don't hurt her, Jane," begged Miss Scarlet, running to Jane and throwing herself upon her. "Please, please—"

Jane didn't move, only continued to look at me in astonishment. I stood a few feet off with my hands clenched at my sides.

"*She* couldn't hurt me!" I sneered. To prove it I shut my eyes, drawing up those last images once more, the Boy ghastly white and laughing, that rush of ecstatic pleasure and terror as He turns to me—

"No, Jane!"

Abruptly I was knocked down again. I grunted, opening my eyes to see Jane straddling my chest, holding her pistol like a bludgeon. I hissed in disappointment: had she broken my concentration, or was I losing control of the thread that bound me to Him, subject now only to His whims and desires and not my own?

"Tell me your name," Jane ordered. She nudged my cheek with the butt of her pistol. "Your *real* name."

I twisted to see Miss Scarlet plucking at Jane's sleeve. She gazed at me. Then, suddenly defeated, she fell back and clasped her paws.

I turned back to Jane and recited, "I am Wendy Wanders, Subject 117, neurologically augmented empath specializing in emotive engram therapy." As I spat the last word I shoved Jane from my chest and sat up. We glared at each other across the grass.

"Oh, stop, *please*," Miss Scarlet pleaded. She knelt beside Jane, a small pathetic creature in crinoline and lace. Jane let out her breath in a long frustrated sigh, then stuck her pistol back into her pocket.

"All right. But *tell* me—"

We did. Or rather, Miss Scarlet did, embellishing my tale so that even I held my breath at certain points, and wondered had it really all been so dramatic—the horrifying tenure at HEL, followed by dangerous flight and pursuit and finally success with Toby Rhymer's Players, not forgetting my bosom friendship with that acclaimed thespian Miss Scarlet Pan?

Jane listened dubiously.

"Well," she said at last, when with paws joined Miss

Scarlet had beseeched her to help and not betray me. "This is all a little hard to swallow, isn't it?"

At Miss Scarlet's offended expression she quickly added, "But *very* nicely told, Scarlet, very nice! But—well, suppose she *is* the one they're searching for."

She indicated me with a nod. I had for the moment become stock character in Miss Scarlet's picaresque and not a participant in this discussion. "How am I to know that? And what is she going to do? If this Aviator is drawing the lazars and aardmen in to a search for you—"

She turned to me again. "Aidan Arent is too well known now in the City. Even if I don't breathe a word—and I won't—once a secret's out it's out, if you know what I mean. Someone else is bound to discover you, and then . . ." She circled her throat with her hand and made a choking sound.

We sat in silence for a few minutes. The sambar snorted, munching grass. Pale sunlight laced through the trees. A cricket sawed in the thickets, waking to the scant warmth. Miss Scarlet stared with sorrowful eyes into the forest, and I brooded on the Ascendant in the Cathedral who had vowed to find me, and cursed the labyrinth of chance and careless science that had brought me here.

Finally Jane said, "What exactly is it you *do,* Wendy?"

A cunning thought came to me: a means to escape. I looked up at her and asked, "Do you want me to show you?"

"Wendy!" Miss Scarlet said; but Jane had already nodded.

"Come here," I said, drawing her to me. She lifted her face to mine. I pushed the hair back from her eyes, stared into them for a long moment. Still a little suspicious of me (rightly so, Jane!) but bold and unafraid. Then I kissed her. She pulled back, embarrassed, but I held her chin and brought her mouth to mine, my tongue probing between her lips until she sighed and closed her eyes. I waited until I felt her breathing quicken, then nipped softly at her lip, once and again, until blood mingled with the sweet salt in her mouth.

Bewilderment; a fiery burst of amazement and I behold

her confused spectrum of desire and fear, liquid rolling eyes and a rich odor of the stable. Jane's consciousness surprisingly powerful, a heated core burning through me so that I groan with pleasure, fall back as it flows over me, the warmth of sun and thick matted fur beneath her fingertips, undiminished awe as she watches a cinnabar fox being born, the damp scrawny mess of a hatching finch, a viper's demon face breaking through a leathery shell with its egg tooth—

I recall myself, force my will upon the serpent's triangular head until the black agate chips of its eyes slant, grow pale and green and glowing and its shining scales take on the contours of fluttering leaves. Before me the Boy shimmers into sight, face and body rippling as though seen through waves of heated air, His eyes alone steady and unwavering, green tunnels leading into darkness.

I pull back to consciousness, sit up drunkenly to peer at Jane's face twisted into a look of blank yet intense concentration. Her eyes fluttered open and she blinked, trying to bring me into focus.

"That, how did you, what—" she stammered, swaying. Miss Scarlet clutched her arm as Jane reached for something not quite there, leaf falling through autumn light or whirring emerald-hinged beetle. Marveling, she brought her hand before her face, then suddenly doubled over as though struck.

"Aaah—" she groaned. She twisting to stare at me, choking on her words. "Take him!—make it *go!*—"

I stared at her coldly: she was but another of those bright figures moving through a gray landscape. Her pleas faded to a whisper of despair, the sigh of wind in leafless branches. Then I heard Miss Scarlet's shrill voice, chattering and keening and it was *that* I could not bear, it was that which finally drew me back—

"Help her, Wendy! Please—"

I turned from her, bowed my head to meet Jane's eyes. Dull now and exhausted, their light extinguished as she contemplated what *He* offered her, the wasted fields and stony ground that would give birth to no more birds, no more serpents or sambars or black-eyed vixens. Only livid sky to see and ashes to taste for eternity, only this and nothing more.

"Look at me," I said. I squeezed my eyes so tightly closed that tears welled from them. I summoned Him, forced Him to turn that implacable gaze from Jane to me, His glittering emerald eyes staring without anger or surprise, their reserve broken all the same as they froze upon me.

"Leave her," I commanded.

He stared, cold and pitiless as a great cat disturbed at its repast. Then, slowly, He smiled, gnashing His small white teeth as He acceded me this small triumph; and faded into nothing.

The remainder of our trip to the Zoo was subdued. Jane crept back to consciousness, shaken as a child waking from a nightmare. Like a child she recovered quickly, although her eyes darted distrust as she walked beside me, and she held herself a little distant even from Miss Scarlet. Miss Scarlet was quiet upon her antlered mount, the sambar the only one of us unshaken, if silent as the rest.

My own thoughts were bleak ones. I felt a growing sense of shame at what I had done, and an odd bewilderment: because how was it that I was feeling shame? How was it that I felt anything and everything these days, until it seemed I was a roiling caldron of joys and terrors spilling over to scald those who loved me, those whom Justice had named as the only wall between myself and the dark?

Was that how I had pushed Him back, the Boy in the tree? Was it as Dr. Harrow had dreamed: that exposure to sensation, to real human emotion and not the refined chemistries of HEL, had rived new channels through the scars in my brain, so that I now began to feel what I had distilled from the hearts of others for all these years?

And could it be that feeling these things made one stronger, not weak and stupid as Anna and Gligor and myself had always thought? Strong enough that my own tongue might one day drown out the Small Voices, and my own eyes lock with the Boy's and force Him back into the empty lands beyond sleep and dreaming?

But I did not know any of this; only guilt and sorrow and apprehension of the long night ahead. To ease the trek I went over my lines, and found myself repeating what Miss Scarlet had told me when we first met:

> They that have power to hurt and will do none,
> That do not do the thing they most do show . . .

Pondering these words, I came to the northwest part of the City, where I had never been before: where ancient gates rose from the trees and rubble to enclose the Zoological Gardens, and where if one stood upon the yellowing turf beneath the Regent's Oak one might glimpse in the near distance the black cusp of the Engulfed Cathedral stabbing at the sky.

All was in an uproar when we arrived. A spotted cat, Rufus Lynx's namesake, had escaped. It was to have been led by a very young Paphian girl (looking much relieved by the turn of events) to the center of the grass-grown amphitheater where our play would progress, and there presented with pretty ceremony to the Regent as the festivities began.

"Mmm! Jane Alopex! Mmm, they were looking for you in the Paradise Aviary, mmm mmm—"

A short heavyset man puffed up to greet us as we entered the Zoo barricades, waving back the two gatekeepers who hurried to his side.

"Rufus!" exclaimed Jane Alopex, dropping the sambar's bridle and wiping her hands on her breeches.

"Yes yes, mmm, hallo, Rufus Lynx, mmm, Scarlet Pan, yes, h'lo, mmm, Aidan, yes yes yes—"

Nodding, he shook all our hands, not excluding the abashed Jane's. The Regent was nearly bald, with a soft fine fringe of dark hair that might once have been red and stuck out in uneven peaks about his pink skull. This, along with his habit of humming to himself and his saffron tunic, gave him the manner of an agitated cockatiel. He wore muck-stained boots and bright trousers spattered with dirt and flecks of birdseed, and barely came up to my chin. He expressed vague pleasure at meeting Miss Scarlet once again, but scarcely seemed to see me at all. He was intent only upon recapturing the fugitive lynx.

"Now Jane, mmm, come along, it's frightened the nesting hoopoes into the rafters and Fauna Avis seems to think you're the only one can get them down again, mmm mmm."

He took Jane's arm and started to walk off with her, leaving the sambar to the care of the two gatekeepers. Jane patted it goodbye and waved at Miss Scarlet, then gazed at me coldly. But after a moment she grinned wryly. "I'll find you and Scarlet later," she said, and sauntered off.

This left me alone with Miss Scarlet. The early afternoon's cool breeze licked at my neck and I shivered.

"Come, Wendy," Miss Scarlet said in a low voice, slipping her small hand into mine. "I'll show you where I grew up."

We started along a neat little path of crushed tarmac, weeds and dead plants trimmed from its borders. In the near distance several odd buildings poked through the mesh of leafless trees and tall wild grasses. On the paths between these raced figures clad brightly as Jane Alopex, carrying buckets and trays and brooms in a rumpus of activity such as I had never seen elsewhere in the City.

We passed a red-roofed pagoda with a wrought-iron stork standing one-legged at each end of its peak. Two real storks stalked splenetically between these effigies, ugly and bald and with beady eyes as bloodshot as a Senator's. When they met in the roof's middle they paused, flapped their wings and clacked their bills together dolefully before continuing on their brooding perambulation.

"The Bird House," explained Miss Scarlet. She waved at the storks, who glared down disapprovingly as we walked past.

Next was a stark glass and steel structure that gleamed coldly in the sun. Amorphous figures fluttered in some of its dark windows. In others tiny furred faces pressed close against the glass to stare out at us with wide mad eyes, baring their teeth and scrabbling at the glass as we went by. Miss Scarlet grew tight-lipped at the sight of them and quickened her pace, head bowed. After this a gentle slope rose before us, topped by a mock gothic cathedral with stone geckos and chameleons instead of gargoyles perched upon its eaves.

"You look uneasy," said Miss Scarlet. She nodded as we passed a young boy pushing a wheelbarrow full of stones. "Which is understandable."

I grimaced. I was not accustomed to having others know what I was thinking. Miss Scarlet laughed, her fingers tightening about mine. "When I first met you, Wendy, your face was blank as a block of wood. But now!"

She stopped and drew herself up, her dark agile face contorting as she mimicked my expressions: alarm, fear, wonder, pique, delight.

"I don't look like *that*," I said, offended.

"See for yourself." From the satin reticule at her waist she withdrew a tiny mirror set in a sheath of aluminum. I grabbed it and tilted it before my face.

"I look exactly the same," I pronounced. But as I squinted at my reflection I noted with surprise the new constellation of freckles arrayed across my cheeks. I pushed back a wisp of hair at my temple and rubbed the fleshy nodule hidden beneath. It felt smaller, less swollen. When I tipped the mirror to peer at it I saw that the scar tissue had indeed grown smoother. The node itself seemed to be shrinking. Turning to inspect its mate on the other temple I saw that it was no longer than my thumbnail. I let my hair fall back to cover the scars and returned the mirror to Miss Scarlet. She replaced it, then stroked her throat wistfully.

"I don't suppose mine will ever disappear," she said. She indicated a curving grass-grown pathway that crept over the hill. I followed as she clambered up, holding her skirts to keep them from dragging in the high yellow grass. "The Zoologists don't have the sort of refined instruments that the Ascendants used with you. I'll bring these scars to my grave."

I winced as a long briar tendril whipped back into my face. "Mine weren't supposed to heal." I slapped the dust and clinging seed pods from my trousers, straightening as we stood at the top of the little rise. "And for all I know they're not healing at all. I've had no medication for months now. Maybe this is terrible for me. Maybe I'm *dying.*"

I pressed a finger to my temple, biting my lip as I realized I felt nothing: no customary ache as though I grazed against bruised flesh, no tremor of pain or longing triggered by the random firing of nerves. I was afraid then, to think that I might be losing my sole conduit for the only emotions I had ever known, those channeled into me at HEL through Emma Harrow.

"But maybe it is good for you, Wendy," said Miss Scarlet. She pulled a burdock sticker from her skirt and popped it into her mouth. "Maybe the medication made you sick. Maybe now you can begin to get well."

I shuddered at the thought of being so exposed to raw sensation. "No! I hear Voices. I see faces in the air. I had a seizure this morning and almost killed your friend Jane. I will never be well, Miss Scarlet." I smiled bitterly. "I am as you see me: a Player only."

Miss Scarlet nodded. She raised a finger as though to make a point but then stopped. "Well, perhaps. But I will show you something while we wait for Toby and the rest. Just don't tell him that I missed my nap."

I smiled and motioned for her to lead on.

Before us swept the curved gray buttresses of the faux gothic Reptile House. Lizards and serpents of chipped green enamel clung to its crumbling walls, half-hidden by a sheath of virginia creeper gone crimson since the first frost. On the lintel above the main entrance stood a stegosaurus of red sandstone, its lumbering gait captured by some artisan centuries earlier. Crouching at its tail was a little carven mouse, winking slyly at onlookers below.

"At least it's always warm in here," said Miss Scarlet as we passed through the entrance.

I sighed gratefully as a blast of heated air rolled over me. It was dark inside, illuminated only by squares of greenish light coming from glass cages set into the walls. An overwhelmingly pungent smell pervaded the chambers, rotting flesh and rotting vegetation; but the floor was immaculately swept and the glass fronting the cages was so clean that more than once I paused to prod it with my finger, just to be certain there was something between myself and the cages' sluggish inhabitants. The place was empty, although brooms and mops and nets stacked in corners seemed to caution that its Keepers would return soon.

"They're busy getting ready for this evening," said Miss Scarlet. She stopped in front of a large cage. She eyed its inhabitant with loathing—a serpent coiled about a dead stump. "Are you warmer yet, Wendy?"

I nodded, stooping to stare at a speckled viper. It regarded me balefully, black tongue flicking in and out, then without warning lunged toward us and struck the glass. I stumbled backward, tripping over Miss Scarlet, then laughing a little breathlessly helped her to her feet. A small bloody streak smeared the glass. On the floor of the cage the viper lashed back and forth, trying to find us in the darkness.

"Did you see that?" I exclaimed, pushing my hair from my eyes. "I've never seen a—"

I turned to see that my friend had collapsed against the wall, heedless of the brooms that had toppled beside her. "Miss Scarlet! Are you all right?"

As I knelt beside her she nodded. "The snake," she said faintly. "I can't bear them."

I helped her to her feet and looked around for someplace to sit.

"Really, I'm fine, Wendy— Here, turn at this corner, I wanted to show you something in here."

We hurried past a huge display area covered by a glass roof, where crocodiles like immense and idle machines floated in stagnant pools. Crested white herons stepped nimbly from one plated back to another, dipping their bills to spear fish from the dark water. Miss Scarlet looked away and held her breath until we were safely past, but I glanced back, marveling that they never moved.

"The Herp Lab," Miss Scarlet muttered, almost to herself. "This way, if I remember it right. Or not?"

She stopped in front of a case which held a pair of bloated golden toads, each bigger than my head but with lovely round jeweled eyes wise and tender as an aging courtesan's. "Yes. This way."

We rounded a corner into darkness. No cages here. The only light trickled from chinks in the ceiling high above.

"They used to leave it open, we'd come in here, Jane and I and some of others—Jane was a clever child, she taught me how to run the old machines—"

She halted, quite out of breath, and gestured toward a tall arched door, oak inlaid with stained glass. Very old figured metal letters spelled out HERP LAB/AUDI VIS AL FAC ITY. I was surprised when the knob turned freely in my hand, and Miss Scarlet laughed in relief.

"Oh! I was so afraid it might be locked—not that anyone would dream of stealing anything, but—*you* know, *policy* changes."

I nodded as we stepped inside. The door creaked loudly as it shut behind us. As if in answer a chorus of bell-like voices chirped from a corner of the room.

"Peepers," said Miss Scarlet. Cages filled this end of the laboratory, some of glass, some of metal or plastic, some crude shells of wood and wire mesh. The room had a dry sugary smell, no longer merely warm but hot. I wiped my brow and blew down the front of my shirt. Miss Scarlet looked comfortable, in spite of her heavy crinolines. Holding up her skirts, she crossed to the far side of the lab, fastidiously avoiding looking into any of the cages. Against a windowless wall a number of very old machines were arranged on metal shelves, most of them sheathed in silver or black metal, a few with their intricate inner anatomies exposed to show wheels and gears and shining levers.

"You're in the Nursery," she called, waving me to join her. I could scarcely see her head poking above the uneven rows of cages. "But they store projectors and videos and cinematographs here, too. Come see."

I walked slowly, pausing often to peer into cages where ruby-throated anoles stalked each other up and down pale bamboo shoots, and agamas blinked beneath the heat lamps as they guarded leathery eggs, and where in a cool dim corner the deceptively big-voiced peepers proved to be only three tiny frogs now silent at my approach: translucent throats deflated, their mottled brown backs crossed with red as though someone had X'ed them with a fingernail. I passed them and stopped in front of a narrow cage labeled HOGNOSED SNAKE. Half a dozen eggs lay in a depression in the sand, eggs the color of spoiled milk, the approximate shape and length of my thumb. As I watched one shifted very slightly. I thought of Jane, recalled her joy at witnessing the birthing vipers. And suddenly I wanted to stay to watch them, to lose myself among all these new small lives. I felt a violent pang as I recalled Jane's accusing eyes, and remembered sadly the lizard I had killed the morning I escaped with Justice from HEL.

"Wendy!"

I started. Miss Scarlet stood atop a wire chair and beckoned me, brow furrowed. "Ugh! You can't be mooning over those things! You're worse than Jane."

I shrugged and crossed the lab. Several yards of empty space divided the Herp Lab from where the machines were stored. A single diatom lantern was suspended from the ceiling, its silvery filaments casting bluish light over the silent machines. The air smelled pleasantly of cedar.

"Hog-nosed snakes," I said. "Hog-nosed snake eggs, actually."

Miss Scarlet rolled her eyes. "How revolting! I despise serpents—I don't suppose you can smell them, else you would too."

"I never saw one before," I said. "Except in pictures. So many things . . ."

My friend nodded, patting my arm. "Well, we haven't an awful lot of time left before the others arrive." She coughed discreetly. I turned to see that she had drawn her chair in front of a cinematograph. Pinpoints of red and green light shone at its edges. After a moment pearly sparks began to glimmer across the dull black screen.

"Wendy?"

She dipped her head to indicate a chair beside hers. From their corner of the room the peepers began to chime once more. We settled into our chairs and stared at the screen brightening before us.

I glanced at Miss Scarlet and saw that she was sitting bolt upright, her face rapt with an expectation so intent it might have been dread. The little screen cast greenish highlights across her smooth black face. She began to rock back and forth with excitement.

"What is it, Miss Scarlet?"

A louder, sweeter music drowned out the peepers' song. Words flowed across the black screen in an elegant script, yellow and green and white, names it seemed; but they meant nothing to me.

"It is one of their histories," she whispered. She clasped her hands together. "A very old story, I first saw it oh so many years ago and that was when I realized I was not the first, just as when I saw you I knew that you were another, Wendy—"

Colors swirled about the screen, formed vague lines, then took shape. A midnight sky speared by stars, tiny buildings clustered in a valley between dark and snow-capped mountains. A high voice singing to itself, so achingly sweet that I shivered and knotted my hands together. It was like one of the Small Voices, piercing me with a yearning that could never be fulfilled. I leaned forward to stare at the screen. A square of yellow light swelled into a window looking in upon a solitary old man and a room filled with toys and clocks, and unnoticed among these automatons a tiny figure, singing.

"What are they?" I said. Not real actors, surely? I had seen holos and videos and even films before, but never anything like this, never such colors and faces, no more alive than the Paphians' scholiasts but strange and lovely all the same: and moving and speaking like human beings.

"It is an ancient history of those who were here before the First Ascension," whispered Miss Scarlet. "It is one of their lost Arts. It has survived to show us the world as it truly was then."

When I started to ask another question she put a finger to her lips and shook her head. "Watch, Wendy," she said; "and you will understand why I dream that one day we may become Truly Human, you and I."

So I watched and listened to a story like nothing I had ever seen before. Oh, histories I knew; but even as Dr. Harrow taught us of these she had cautioned us:

"There are too many histories now. Once there was only one, and the world was a simpler place. But now every Ascension has its Historian, its Poet, its Savior, its Traitor." Memory of her bitter voice rang in my ears as she said, "Choose carefully the history you want, Wendy: it will determine the world you live in."

The world on the cinematograph was not the one I had chosen. But as I watched the strange images race across the screen I knew it was Miss Scarlet's world: one where the animals spoke, and the cruelty and kindness of humans was punished or rewarded; where audiences showered gold upon a marvelous fantoccio that danced and sang, and a man could love a creature made of wood. And as I untangled the threads that strung the tale together—selfishness and lies, laziness and arrogance and too late the bittersweet knowledge of love—I realized why she had wanted me to see this.

"She thinks it's like me," I thought, mortified.

And, shrilling like the peepers, the Small Voices whirred inside my head, *It's you, it's you, it's you.*

Something moved behind me. I turned to see Jane Alopex shutting the lab door, shaking her head so that I would remain quiet as she crossed the room to join us.

"Look," Miss Scarlet said as the girl pulled another chair beside hers and sat. The long black hairs on her neck stood up out of her high collar. I smelled the ripe odor she gave off before a performance, fear and arousal and anticipation all at once.

"I see," said Jane, letting the chimpanzee crawl into her lap. I looked back at the screen. A woman in long blue robes floated there. She reminded me of the images of the Magdalene I had seen at the House Miramar, except that she had wings. I wondered if the Magdalene was that old; if

before the First Ascension Her followers had worshipped
at the Cathedral as others did now.

The blue lady on the screen said, "If you learn to be
brave, honest, and unselfish, then you will become a real
boy." Miss Scarlet stared raptly. I knew that if she had been
capable of weeping—one of the many things she dreamed
of—she would have cried. I stared down at my knees. I
could never have chosen such a world for myself.

A little longer and the story ended. We sat in silence,
Jane and Miss Scarlet and I. After a minute or two Jane
leaned forward and clicked something so that the screen
went black and the machine's hum was stilled. Miss Scarlet
slid from her lap to the floor and walked a few steps away
from us.

"Well," said Jane as she stood and stretched. "I figured
I'd find you here. I see that Scarlet has shown you her
favorite story."

I nodded, continuing to stare at the empty screen.

"She loves that one. When she was only a few years old—
after the operation . . ."

She lowered her voice. "One of the Keepers set up a
cinematograph in her room. That was the first one she ever
saw, that one you just watched." She pointed at the machine, then glanced over at Miss Scarlet standing by herself at the edge of the room, her back to us.

"She thinks it's true," Jane whispered. Her dark eyes
glazed with pity as they met mine. "You could never tell
her otherwise—not that I'd want to, it would break her
heart. And really, look at her! She's famous, the entire City
knows her and loves her, you would think that would be
enough.

"But *she* never thought it was enough. She's like the
Paphians. Dreams that someday the Magdalene will come
to save them all: overthrow the Ascendants, teach the Curators a lesson in humility, turn a chimpanzee into a
woman." She shrugged, sighing. "Turn me into a fox, if I
had *my* wish! Then I wouldn't have to worry about all this
nonsense tonight. Ha!"

She laughed, shaking the hair from where it flopped into
her eyes. "They found the lynx," she called to Miss Scarlet.

The chimpanzee turned, face rumpling into a smile. "But not before it killed Anatole Equestris's favorite bird-of-paradise."

"Oh dear," said Miss Scarlet. "Poor Anatole! I meant to ask him for another of those feathered flywhisks he made for me last year."

She rejoined us, tsk-tsking over the state of Jane's breeches and a fresh bloody cut upon the girl's arm. "I don't know how you can stand it, Jane. Those—"

She hesitated, searching for the right word. "Those animals, those *barbarians!* You with your carnivores and now you've got Wendy looking at snakes. . . ."

She shook her head. "But what time is it? Wendy and I should be thinking about meeting the others and setting up for *The Tempest.*"

Miss Scarlet gasped when Jane told her the hour. "And I meant to visit Koko and Effie!"

"Oh, there's still time for that," insisted Jane. "They're right on the way to the amphitheatre."

Miss Scarlet looked discomfited, but after a moment sighed. "I suppose I should: it's been almost a year. It's just so hard. . . ."

I followed them, looking back regretfully at the terrarium where the peepers clung to the glass until we had passed out of the Herp Lab, when I heard their ringing song once more.

Outside it had grown cooler. Dark clouds sailed across a blue sky rapidly turning gray. But there was a buoyancy to the air as we crossed the wide avenue where the Zoologists strolled, wearing clean tunics of green and russet and yellow, laughing and calling to Jane and Miss Scarlet, and even acknowledging me with bright smiles.

"They know you are one of Toby's troupe, Wendy," Jane proudly announced as we passed a group of laughing women carrying hooded gerfalcons, like small gloomily cowled monks perched upon their wrists. The women giggled. One who was hawkless pressed three fingers to her lips and winked, then rubbed her fingers across her palm to show her interest in me. I looked away.

"Aidan, I mean," Jane corrected herself, glancing to see if I had taken offense.

"That's all right," I said. "As long as no one else hears you."

"Oh, they won't," said Jane. "No one ever listens to me. Here, Scarlet—a new shortcut to the Primate House since you've been back. Follow me."

The Zoologists had laid an orderly path of smooth stones, with goldenrod growing alongside it and the day's ration of autumn leaves already raked up and burning nearby. Miss Scarlet coughed at the whiff of smoke and hung back from Jane and me. At the end of the path stood the Primate House. Not a large building, but constructed of glass and steel and other metals so that it seemed more massive than it really was. Over the centuries most of the glass had broken, to be replaced by boards and makeshift walls of iron bars salvaged from other cages. A sort of dry moat separated us from the overgrown habitats, empty except for sparrows and squirrels who dug industriously for acorns beneath the leafless oaks.

"They're inside for the winter," Jane explained. Miss Scarlet kept her head down, still walking a little behind us. Jane raised her eyebrows. "Scarlet, we don't have to go if you don't want to."

"No, no," the chimpanzee replied. She gazed at a small area barren of grass, the dun-colored earth hacked up and spattered with dried feces and rotting carrots. "I'll feel worse if I don't."

We entered by a heavy metal door, guarded by an older man who yawned and nodded as the gate clanged after us. "Hello, Jane," he said. "Scarlet Pan, how are you?"

She nodded, face drawn. Although this building was as neat and well-swept as the Reptile House, and better lit, she lifted her skirts with a grimace, as though afraid to let them touch the floor. I wrinkled my nose at the smell. A heavy musky air, cool but not very fresh. It was noisy, too, as we ducked down the corridor that led into the great covered courtyard where the primates were housed.

"Ah, Magdalene," Miss Scarlet said beneath her breath. Jane bit her lip. "They're really very well cared for," she told me. "What can we do? We are their Keepers, they all would have died years and years ago if not for us."

On every side immense bars rose from floor to ceiling. Behind them, on sloping concrete floors stained by centuries of damp and mold and urine, squatted figures much like Miss Scarlet. Only these creatures were huge, bigger than a man, with sorrowful heavy-browed faces that scarcely took note of us as we stopped to look at them. One cradled a little animal, a miniature of the great monsters rocking or sitting on the floor about her. The baby peered at us with inquisitive black eyes, but its dam gave us only a passing glance as she bowed her head to the infant. Her huge arms curled about the baby, her fingers moving in front of its wizened face in a repetitive series of gestures. When she dipped her head I saw that a number of black wires protruded from a shaved portion of her skull. Beside me Miss Scarlet shivered. My hair stood on end when I heard the creature in the cage mutter hoarsely, *"Men, men, men. Go."*

Jane Alopex looked away. "Come on, Scarlet, there's no need for this. . . ."

"But there is," Miss Scarlet retorted. "If I am ever to become truly human I must learn from these poor souls—"

"Why torture yourself?" said Jane angrily. She stopped in front of a cage where a single animal, massive and barrel-chested, with long matted auburn hair and hands the size of a bunch of plantains, crouched in front of a flattened sheet of polished metal. It regarded its distorted reflection impassively, fingers working the same strange patterns in the air, brow furrowed as though it sought to remember something.

"They are not torturing themselves," Miss Scarlet said at my elbow. Her pupils dilated and her hackles stiffened. "You have imprisoned them—"

"They would die without us!" Jane repeated. I left them and crossed to another cage, my heart pounding. In this one a number of small monkeys leaped and fought and howled. Several of them stopped and raced to the edge of the cage to stare up at me, paws writhing between the bars to pat at my knees as they squealed and chirped. But after a moment their cries grew petulant, their tiny black fingers clawing angrily when I did not acknowledge them. I pulled myself away.

In the next cage a family of the tall red-haired apes reclined against a log. The largest groomed one of the younger ones, parting its long fur so that I could see the scars where it too had been venesected. I hurried away to lean against a crooked metal railing, trying to breathe through my mouth so as not to smell the stench of fear and numbing boredom that seeped through that place.

"—then why do you never try to speak to them, Jane, why these endless games in the name of research—"

Jane stalked over to me, throwing her hands into the air as Miss Scarlet followed her, arguing. I pressed my thumbs to my eyes and breathed deeply. The sound of Miss Scarlet's shrill voice seemed to alarm the other animals in the Primate House. The small monkeys began to screech, the sullen mother ape to grunt, *"Go, go, go,"* in a guttural voice that grew gradually louder and louder.

"Scarlet, you know I hate it worse than you do—"

I opened my eyes. Beside Jane, Miss Scarlet swung her arms up and down furiously, heedless of her stiff garment tearing as she bobbed on her heels. "Why did you ever teach them, can't you see they are trying to remember—"

I let out my breath and asked, "What are they trying to remember?"

Miss Scarlet's long teeth gnashed as she cried, "Speech! They are descended from geneslaves, *they* taught them once to speak with their hands—"

"Hundreds of years ago!" exploded Jane. "They don't know what they're doing anymore, it's—"

"Then teach them!" cried Miss Scarlet. The monkeys exploded into screams and hoots of fright. Miss Scarlet crouched, rose up on her hind legs as though she were going to spring at Jane. Jane moved closer to me, her hand fumbling at her waist for her pistol. Then Miss Scarlet whirled and ran across the room to the cage nearest the outer door. In front of it she stopped, stock still, shoulders drooping and long arms dragging so that her knuckles grazed the floor. Jane turned to me, her eyes filled with tears.

"She gets like this every time she visits them," she said, her fingers dropping from the pistol. She motioned me to follow her to where Miss Scarlet stood in front of the last cage.

Two pathetic figures squatted inside it. They stared dully at a stream of urine threading to a rusted grate in the concrete floor. Grizzle-headed, naked, with red and listless eyes, they were still indisputably of Miss Scarlet's blood and kind. She hunched before them, her arms enfolded over her head, eyes shut, making a soft *hoo-hoo* sound as she swayed back and forth. Jane and I stopped behind her. I drew my hands to my throat—hairless, no scars there— and my eyes burned. But I could not cry: not when tears were denied my dear guide, who squatted before a cage and moaned with an animal's mute and ageless grief. I stood beside Jane Alopex, the girl staring at her feet with her hands clenched at her sides. In the cage sat the two chimpanzees, one of them scratching at the dirty floor, the other raising its head to regard Miss Scarlet. Dirt caked the lines about its eyes, and a fly lit upon its cheek before it dipped its head again to gaze at the concrete. Miss Scarlet buried her face in her paws.

"Come, Scarlet," Jane said after a few more minutes. "Your friends will be here soon."

"Yes. Yes, of course," Miss Scarlet said in a low voice. She stood, turning from the cage to take my hand. "Forgive me, Jane. Wendy."

The monkeys hooted as we crossed the courtyard, and one of the great apes bared its teeth at us. At the door of the Primate House the Keeper informed us that Toby and the other Players had arrived by pantechnicon and were already setting up in the amphitheater.

"Best hurry," he said, patting Miss Scarlet's head as she passed. "Come again, Scarlet. We miss you around here."

Miss Scarlet composed herself, smiling wanly. By the time we reached the path to the amphitheater she was calmly discussing the evening's performance; but she avoided looking into any of the cages.

* * *

Afternoon had faded into a clouded but promising evening. I felt that the day's heightened strangeness, its revelations and fears, all seemed to be leading up to this performance and this place: an ancient amphitheater dug into the earth, where already the first palanquins of costumed revelers gathered in small groups, and where I could spy Toby and the rest of the troupe struggling to unload a striped pantechnicon.

The amphitheater had been built into the hillside facing the Engulfed Cathedral, that sinister finger pointed accusingly at the sunset. Torchieres burned between rows of stone benches set into the damp grass, and a few children ran shrieking between their pockets of yellow light. A crowd of Zoologists had gathered to watch Toby and Justice and Fabian contend with the sets for *The Tempest*. A pair of striped horses were hitched to the gaily painted pantechnicon, the wagon piled with baskets of costumes and props. The horses whickered and kicked viciously at Fabian as he swung a papier-mâché column from the wagon onto the hillside.

"How thoughtful of you to drop by," he called as we slipped through the crowd. He tossed me a hamper, then turned to where Justice panted up the hillside.

"Perfect timing, Aidan. All the hard work's done," said Justice, wiping his brow as he climbed the last few steps to join us. "Toby was looking for you."

His hair had fallen from its thick braid, and he wore the heavy dark-blue smock we donned when building or striking sets, worn and stained: very much a Player and not a Child of the Magdalene. But I grinned to see him anyway. Glancing around for Gitana or Mehitabel, I spotted them with Toby at the bottom of the slope, stringing lantern globes across the grassy sward that would be our stage. I hefted the basket Fabian had thrown to me and started down the hillside with it. Justice grabbed another hamper and hurried after me, sliding on the slick grass.

"I wish Toby had let you come with us," I said. Behind us

I heard Jane's hoarse laughter and the excited voices of
other Zoologists greeting Miss Scarlet. "Miss Scarlet
showed me a cinematograph—"

Justice shrugged. "There was work to be done. And I
had to go over my lines—"

"With Mehitabel?" I sniffed. Justice looked back at me,
grinning.

"Yes, as a matter of fact. She's really quite talented."

I set the hamper on the ground, pretending to tighten its
fastenings. "I would have helped you, if you wanted."

From the stage area echoed giggles and Toby's booming
voice lamenting, *"Not* that one! Sweet Mother, the girl has
no sense at all!"

Toby raised his head and waved at me impatiently. "It's
about damn time, Aidan! The stupid girl's brought the
wrong costume for Caliban."

Justice laughed, steadying me as I swung the hamper
back onto my shoulder. "Maybe one of Rufus Lynx's people can help us find something," he said as Toby stormed
after the giggling Mehitabel. We ran the last few steps
down the hillside and dropped the hampers onto the grass.
"There's still a little time."

Gitana adjusted her spectacles and glared at him. "You
distracted her, Justice. Toby is *very* upset."

From behind a papier-mâché column came a shriek,
followed by the soft report of a slap. The column toppled to
reveal Toby and Mehitabel, the girl's face streaked with
tears, Toby rubbing his cheek ruefully.

"I suppose Aidan can improvise a costume," said Toby,
striding over to join Justice and me. Gitana glared at him,
then stalked off to take Mehitabel by the hand and lead her
up the hill. Toby watched them go, relieved.

The girls sauntered out of sight. On the hilltop Miss
Scarlet and Jane perched on the edge of the pantechnicon,
talking animatedly with a half-dozen Zoologists. Most of
the Curators had wandered into the twilight, flanked by
Paphians in feathered masks and beaks of gilt paper in
honor of the evening's theme, A Masque of Owls. Stars
pricked through the deepening sky. In the distance I could
hear faint music.

"There's a dinner first," said Toby. "Let it be noted that as usual we have been asked to sup with our hosts *after* the play." He stooped to retrieve a scarf blown from its hamper. "These damn Curators must think we perform better on an empty stomach. Ah, well. Come on, Caliban, let's figure out how you'll be dressed tonight. Did Miss Scarlet get her nap?"

To the strains of music piping down from the masque we readied the little stage. I stayed close to Justice, offering to help him with his lines. He refused, but seemed glad enough of my company. When the attention of the others had turned to preparing a smokepot for one of my entrances he drew me behind a tree.

"Did you mean what you said before, Wendy?" he asked. "When you said you wished I'd come with you?"

"Yes." I took his face in my hands and tilted it to the glowing torchlight. I stared at him a moment and then kissed him without biting (though I wanted to) and without trying to read his desires. They were apparent enough.

"None of that," Fabian snapped as he crossed upstage with an armful of props. "Haven't you got your costume yet, Caliban?" He prodded me with the blunted edge of a sword. I pushed Justice away and stumbled behind the gingko as though searching for something; but not before I saw Fabian wink at Justice, and Justice himself turn to stare after me in delight.

Gitana and Mehitabel returned soon, having left the feasting early. Mehitabel looked flushed and happy, owing no doubt to the contents of a silver decanter she pulled from beneath her skirts. In a tiny space made by stringing several sheets between gingko trees Miss Scarlet rested on a stack of heavy pillows, finally getting her nap. Her soft snores mingled with the creaks of crickets and the occasional whoop that echoed down from the Regent's birthday dinner.

An hour or so later the Zoologists and their Paphian guests began to straggle down into the amphitheater. Impossible to recognize the Paphians behind their elaborate headdresses and glittering dominos, although they made mocking bows to us, gloved fingers raised to masked faces.

One seemed particularly glad to see Mehitabel peeking
coyly from behind a tree ablaze with white candles. The
older Zoologist children pranced down the slope, carrying
torches and globes of *ignis flora* for their elders, many of
whom had by now succumbed to either lust or drink. They
leaned heavily upon the arms of their Paphian escorts, or
called boisterously to one another, mimicking the bleats
and yelps of their animal charges and inspiring the Zoo's
unseen inhabitants to respond vigorously from their pris-
ons in the surrounding trees. I spotted the young girl who
had been chosen to present the ceremonial lynx to the
Regent. Wearing a dove-gray robe and arching headdress
of emerald plumage she chattered happily at Rufus Lynx'
side. It seemed the actual lynx would not be appearing
tonight. The festivities would continue with our play.

Behind the curtains that designated "backstage" the
Players gathered their props. Miss Scarlet rose from her
nap. I assisted her into a gown, groomed her to assuage her
stage fright, and shook out Miranda's blond beribboned
wig.

"But where is your Caliban costume, Wendy?" she
asked. "You can't double in *that*—"

She pointed at the white shift spangled with silver
spiderwebs that I wore as Ariel.

I reached beneath an overturned basket and withdrew a
torn crimson tunic, the one Fabian had been wearing
when we had our cheerful backstage scuffle. I slipped it
over Ariel's costume and rubbed my face with dirt.
mussed my hair and stuck a few dead leaves behind my
ears for good measure.

"There," I announced, leering at Miss Scarlet and shambling to her side. "Caliban: the Gaping One himself."

Miss Scarlet shook her head. She tapped her foot, bent to
flick a twig from the sole of her high-buttoned boot, and
looked up at me with clouded eyes.

She said, "Wendy, you can't go on like that. There's a
houseful of Paphians out there: you'll cause a riot. This is
not a good idea."

"Too late: it's the only one I've got." From the slopes of
the amphitheater rang a chorus of bleary voices singing

"The Saint-Alaban's Song." If we didn't start soon the audience would be too unruly to play to. I shut my eyes, summoned the image of the Boy until His surge of imprisoned rage flooded me, helping me focus my impression of Caliban. That metallic tang in the back of my throat; a twinge of fire behind my eyes. Breathing deeply, I pushed back the shadowy figure groping through the darkness for me. I turned to bow to Miss Scarlet. Before she could warn me again I pulled aside the curtain and left her, scooping up my little pouch of cosmetics and taking my place behind the largest tree abutting the stage area.

In the middle of the grass stood Fabian. He cleared his throat and announced, "In honor of the Birthday of the Regent of Zoologists, Rufus Lynx, there will now be presented *The Tempest,* as adapted for this stage by Toby Rhymer and performed by this troupe."

Catcalls from the inebriated Zoologists. On the bench fronting the stage Rufus Lynx beamed, flanked by several Illyrians holding feathered masks in their laps. At the end of the row sat Jane Alopex. She spied me and waved. I waggled a finger at her (very unprofessional) and stepped back into the shadows.

My first entrance as Ariel provoked cheers from the Paphians. But this was nothing compared to their excitement when I reappeared a moment later as Caliban, red tunic askew over Ariel's gossamer. Leaves fell from my hair as I lumbered toward Toby, magnificent in his sorcerer's robes and turban. I cursed Prospero boldly and turned to snarl at Miranda cowering behind her father.

"Greetings, cousin!" a woman yelled from the hillside. From the corner of my eye I saw a Paphian stagger to her feet, a coronet of macaw feathers dipping rakishly over her brow. She bowed and made the Paphian's beck before the man beside her pulled her back down. But other Paphians took up her cry, saluting me as Aidan and Raphael and Baal-Phegor, the demon they called the Naked Lord. The Zoologists craned their heads and tried vainly to silence their guests.

Toby gave me a dangerous look, gazing fixedly at my costume as he finished the scene. I made a hasty exit to the wrong side to avoid confronting him. Fabian whistled softly as he slipped past me onstage, shaking his head. In the shadows behind one of the torchieres Justice waited, and pulled me to him in the darkness.

"Did you hear them?" I whispered gleefully. " 'Lord Death, Lord Baal!'—"

From the other side of the stage came Toby's voice reminding me of my cue. I motioned for Justice to wait, and began to sing offstage in Ariel's voice:

> " '. . . Nothing of him that doth fade,
>   But doth suffer a sea-change
>   Into something rich and strange . . .' "

As I sang I tore off the red tunic, spat into my hands, and tried to rub the dirt from my cheeks. I was so elated I was shaking, and reached for Justice's shoulder to steady myself.

"Shh!" He glanced over his shoulder, then pointed to the side of the hill where trees were crowded near the last row of benches. "Wendy, there are lazars here—"

I stared at him in disbelief. I smoothed Ariel's gossamer webs and tugged a leaf from my brow. "Where?"

"On the hillside there, among the trees."

A bellow as Toby repeated a line. Justice grimaced and ran onstage for a brief scene. He returned minutes later to whisper, "Look to the left when you next go on: hiding in the bushes by that big oak. I counted five, and something else with them too—aardmen, I think."

Beneath the flaking powder and rouge his face was ashen, and his voice shook as he said, "It's like the Butterfly Ball, Wendy—they'll take us—"

"No," I whispered, glaring at the dim silhouettes as though I might destroy them with my eyes. "No, they won't. I won't let them."

"Wendy! How can you—"

But here was another cue. I squeezed his hand and darted on, gave Ariel's speech and flitted offstage. I had several minutes before I would be on again as Caliban.

Behind the stage was a small stand of birch trees. I grabbed my tunic and crept among them unnoticed. I hugged close to one of the bigger trees and scanned the hillside for lazars.

And found them. My heart tumbled to see how near they were. They ringed the top of the amphitheater, hidden for the most part behind tall grass and brush. But they must be growing bolder. Several no longer crouched but stood to watch the play unfold—with great interest, it seemed, since in the wan torchlight I saw them covering their mouths to stifle their laughter. A quick count gave me ten. Not all children, either. I saw four tall figures standing close together, long hair matted and their faces filthy. But even from that distance I could make out the dusky skin and round eyes that marked them of the House High Brazil. They watched hungrily, like the weary dead envying the living their share of a feast.

A few steps away from them another tall form stood aloof: wiry and with long tangled hair, a silhouette that was somehow familiar to me. I stared for a long minute, trying to place her: no doubt an admirer from an earlier masque. I finally turned my attention to the other, stranger creatures pacing restlessly among the Paphians. At first I thought that more of the Zoo animals had escaped. Large powerful beasts, stooped like the apes I had seen in the Primate House, with spines curved as though they were unaccustomed to standing upright. I glanced at the stage to make sure I had not missed my cue, then turned back to them, fascinated. They slunk back and forth among the lazars, short wiry tails whipping through the high grass. Every few minutes they would pause to press close to the tallest Paphians. Pointed ears raised as they listened to the voices rising from the amphitheater. But large intelligent eyes glinted beneath their heavy brows, and their powerful forelegs ended in huge gnarled hands. I sniffed, caught their rank smell: canine servility and wolfish bloodlust just barely held in check by the presence of the human lazars.

Aardmen, and the enslaved Paphians who served the Madman in the Engulfed Cathedral. For the first time I realized how brave (or reckless) the Zoologists must really be, to live with them so near.

I turned back to survey my fellow Players and our audience. Zoologists and Paphians alike stared enthralled as Toby cast his spells and Miss Scarlet Pan defied him. For the moment the watchers on the hill were equally entranced. Lazars and aardmen tamed by an ancient play upon a stage: *that* would make a story Toby Rhymer himself would be proud to tell, only who would be left to hear it? A score of maddened chattering monkeys and countless caged beasts. I could make an escape now if I tried, might even alert Justice or some of the offstage Players to run to safety and leave the rest, actors and audience alike, to the mercy of King Mob.

But I could not leave them. I tried to imagine fleeing, tried to picture myself safe, taken in by one of the Paphian Houses or by the Curators, or even back at HEL. But each time I brought up an image of myself safe within the Horne Room or a seraglio at the House Miramar, a gory shade would thrust it aside. Miss Scarlet with her head shaved and electrodes protruding from her skull, starving behind iron bars. Toby Rhymer torn by the ravening jaws of the aardmen. Jane Alopex fighting bravely until she fell pierced by a lazar's arrow. And worst of all the thought of Justice lying dead, his golden hair matted with blood and his blue eyes cold and empty.

Sudden anger tore through me, frustrated rage that I should be thus enslaved. My head swam as I stared at the stage where Toby gesticulated wildly and tossed handfuls of glitter. Prospero's bitter words slashed through the air:

> " 'Poor worm! Thou art infected;
> This visitation shows it!' "

I nodded grimly. I could not leave them to die. Something bound me there to all of them, Justice and Miss Scarlet and sour Gitana, Jane Alopex and those nameless others, swaggering Zoologists and mincing Paphians and even the mute apes mindlessly signaling to one another in their barren cages. Voices whined in my ears: no longer

the Voices of the dead, but the remembered words of
those who watched or strutted nearby. Miss Scarlet reciting poetry, Justice weeping that he loved me, Jane
Alopex's hoarse laughter. I ground my teeth, trying to will
myself to turn and flee. But it was no use now. For good or
ill I had thrown my lot with this mess of Players and
Whores and Curators. I would die with them if I had to.

From the stage rang Fabian's sweet tenor, reminding me
that in a few moments I should make my next entrance. I
pulled on my tunic, trying to think of some way to keep the
renegade Paphians and aardmen from attacking. My bold
words to Justice earlier had been mere bravado. But I felt
an edge of exhilarated terror and expectation now, the
Boy's hypostate seething inside me: a leviathan beneath
calm waters. I recalled again Miss Scarlet's doggerel:

> *They that have power to hurt and will do none,*
> *That do not do the thing they most do show . . .*

And I felt terror and strength and desire all at once,
knowing that I was going to do the one thing I should not
do.

"Greetings, young Lord Death," I whisper, and laugh.

I step to the edge of the stage, tense my body and focus
on the image of a tree, new leaves and a softer air than stirs
this late autumn night. My hands clench as I summon Him;
very faintly the Small Voices wail, warning me—

"No, Wendy! He is too strong, so cold, he is so cold!—"

I push them back, draw up in the image of the doomed
twins among boughs of apple blossom, fragments of leaf
and flower sparkling in the air and their high voices intoning:

> *Here we stand*
> *Eye to hand and heart to head,*
> *Deep in the dark with the dead.*

The rush comes on, my heart hammers as though I have
received a crystal pulse of adrenaline. As I step onstage I
hear tiny frogs singing, whispered nonsense words; the
creak of a branch breaking beneath a dangling form as a
pendulum swings back from another time. My mouth fills
with bitter liquid, a taste like hot copper. Through the air
cascades the scent of apple blossom.

And He is there, green eyes shining with malicious joy as
He sights me: a shimmering figure like something made of
motes of light. The torches shine right through Him. I
exhale and blink, try to clear my vision so that I can see the
stage with its Players backlit by guttering lanterns. Waves
of light ripple in the air before my face. Fabian lifts his
head to greet me:

"Lo, now, lo!
Here comes a spirit of his, and to torment me . . ."

He stutters over his last line because suddenly he sees
that there is something in the air between us: a spectral
form, with hair like clear water and eyes that outshine the
dying torches, a beautiful boy's face and body turning from
me to extend a white hand to the terrified actor. From the
audience come gasps and muffled cries. Toby's curses turn
to loud amazement, and I hear Miss Scarlet cry my name.

I laugh, take a step toward the radiant phantasm commanding center stage. In the audience the Zoologists hush
their Paphian guests. They are delighted, certain they are
seeing some miracle of stagecraft engineered for their Regent's birthday.

For a moment everything comes to a halt: the actors
have forgotten their lines, the audience waits impatiently.
On the hillside the grass rustles as the lazars creep toward
the stage, and I hear the deep cough of the aardmen
breathing. The Boy too waits, hand cupped coyly beneath
His chin, emerald eyes winking.

And just when it seems that something terrible must
happen—an aardman will leap from the underbrush to rip
out Rufus Lynx's throat; the Boy will take Fabian's hand
and lead him to suicidal despair; Mehitabel will shriek and

ruin Miss Scarlet's next entrance—just when I think I will
collapse into a seizure and force the whole spectacle to
some awful conclusion—

Justice strides onstage, so white with terror that his pale
hair seems dark as blood in the firelight. With shaking
voice he cries, " *'What's the matter? Have we divels
here?'* "

A relieved sigh from the audience. The hidden figures in
the trees grow still. My voice rings out as I shamble toward
the glittering spectre, " *This spirit torments me!'* "

Scattered applause from the Zoologists. Paphians call on
the Magdalene with slurred whispers. I try to make eye
contact with Fabian. It is hopeless. He stands frozen, hands
raised to fend off the ethereal creature suspended in the
air before him, gazing with cold yet proprietary calm upon
the amazed audience.

Then, despite his own terror, Justice recites Fabian's
lines as well as his own, stumbling through his speech. I
crouch and strike at the air, as though there are demons
there, and reply:

> " *'His spirits hear me;*
> *For every trifle they are set upon me; sometime am I*
> *All wound with adders, who with cloven tongues*
> *Do hiss me into madness. Art thou afeard?'* "

With unsteady voice Justice calls back, " *'No, monster,
not I.'* "

The Boy turns to regard me, His eyes glowing with merciless delight as I continue:

> " *'Be not afeared, the isle is full of noises;*
> *Sometime voices*
> *That if I then had wak'd after long sleep*
> *Will make me sleep again; and when I wak'd*
> *I cried to dream again.'* "

And as Justice replies, and Caliban groans and shouts,
and finally Fabian breaks in with a line (not the right one),
the Boy stares past them to me, then slowly disappears.

The audience erupted into applause. For a quarter-hour all was in an uproar. Toby and Miss Scarlet took the stage to try to bring some order. I bowed and lurched offstage, then raced to where I could scan the surrounding hillside. The lazars and aardmen had fled, presumably to bear news of this marvel to their master in the Cathedral.

All but one of them. She stood brazenly in sight of the audience below, her tousled blond hair aflame by torchlight, her face raked by scars but no less recognizable to me now. Laughing softly she raised one hand and waved, calling out in a low voice:

"Hallo, Wendy! They killed Andrew, you know, and Merle and Gligor and Dr. Leslie and Dr. Silverthorn and everyone but me, everyone but Anna!"

Anna glanced over her shoulder, then called down, "I'm glad they're dead, Wendy. Dr. Leslie lied to me, Andrew lied to me, they all lied to me, and now they're dead, and soon I will be too."

The wind brought her sweet cold laughter, and I shivered. She slapped at her face, as though an insect had stung her, then stared dazed into the empty air before recalling me and looking back down.

"Listen to me, Wendy!" she said. "You should be careful. They weren't nice Doctors after all. That man, the Aviator —he's looking for you. He's crazier than Dr. Leslie was at the end. He knows you're with those actors—

"Be careful, Wendy. Stay away from the Masque at Winterlong—"

She grimaced and brought her hands to her temples, as though she might scream with pain; but before I could call out to her she turned and stumbled into the darkness.

I returned to the amphitheater, stunned. Toby had calmed the crowd sufficiently for us to complete the play. I remember little of the performance. Several minor scenes were skipped, due to Mehitabel's refusal to be onstage with me; but as Jane had told us that morning, no one noticed. And while thunderous cheers greeted me when I

took my final bow, the faint sour odor of disappointment
tainted the scene. There had been no further sign of the
Gaping One. The Zoologists crawled over the stage searching for wires or other evidence of technological sorcery,
but found nothing. I felt let down as well. My final speech
went poorly, and my head throbbed. Worst of all was the
memory of Anna's sudden appearance, but I said nothing
of this to anyone. Only Justice's delight at having salvaged
Fabian's scene made the next few hours bearable.

I left the private party that followed as early as I could.
While only Toby's troupe and a half-dozen Zoologists and
Paphians were present I was beset by questions, from Players and our hosts alike. Toby in particular was anxious to
preserve the illusion that the spectral appearance onstage
in Act Two had been carefully planned by himself. I revealed nothing, to Toby or anyone else. Piqued by my surly
mood, Justice finally turned his attentions to Mehitabel. I
reverted to sullen silence, then finally left. The party's
raucous laughter chased me out into the night, and I
walked angry and alone about the Zoo grounds.

The night had grown cold. The rest of the masquers had
retreated to the Lion House for the masque proper,
whence streamed music and brilliant candlelight and
more loud laughter. I avoided that part of the Zoo and
headed down a narrow road. Overhead shone a three-
quarter moon, dappling the barren earth with gray and
white. I kicked dispiritedly among dead leaves and feathers fallen from avian costumes. I wondered why, if I was
suddenly capable of feeling things, all I could feel was
unhappy.

My rambling brought me at last to the huge gates of the
Zoo's entrance, now chained shut. In front of them reared
the Regent's Oak, a massive tree centuries old, gnarled
and ominous in the moonlight. Through the iron barriers I
saw the Engulfed Cathedral atop Saint-Alaban's Hill: a
grim black shape glowing with subtle colors, as though
another, older moon cast its light upon it. I turned from
this disturbing vision to lean against the Regent's Oak. I
rested my cheek against its rough skin and sighed.

I would leave now. It would be easy to scale the gates; I

would make my way to the Cathedral and find certain death there. Miss Scarlet would be heartbroken, Toby furious at losing his prize actor. Perhaps Justice would blame himself for wasting this last evening with Mehitabel. . . .

From behind me came a soft sound, a snort as of suppressed laughter. I whirled, half-expecting to see Justice there. But it was not he.

Beneath the cold moon stood the Boy: leaf-crowned, naked, His skin shimmering white. He seemed completely unaware of His surroundings, as though like a hummingbird He moved through a finer air than held these things, moon and trees and iron gates, and perceived them as some kind of mist. But He saw me, and acknowledged me with a bow. Mockingly I thought: but when He raised His head His emerald eyes regarded me with respect.

"Greetings, Lady," He said. Laughter in that voice despite His serious demeanor. Laughter and what might have been pity, if He had seemed capable of it. He did not.

"I am called Aidan Arent." I moved away from the oak and smoothed my hair, then looked down the hill to where the bright strains of the Masque of Owls echoed.

"They cannot hear us, Wendy." The Boy shook his head, smiling. "And I know who you really are."

"Why are you here?" I drew closer to the tree.

"Because you called me," He said. "I always come when called."

"How do you know my name?"

He laughed. "I have always known you and I have always known your name, Lady. I knew Aidan Harrow too, though he would not recognize me now."

"Why wouldn't he recognize you?" I asked. I took a wary step away from Him.

"Because to him I am horror and corruption, and while he calls me by one name it is not my only name."

"And what name is that?" Suddenly I felt elated, almost bodiless. This was like a marvelous dream, like tapping some harnessed soul at HEL and discovering a secret strand of desire as yet untasted. I grinned, and He smiled at me. "Tell me, Boy."

He parried, "What do *you* think it is, Lady?"

WINTERLONG

I frowned a little at being called *Lady* again. Perhaps He was mocking me, after all. "The Paphians call you the Gaping One."

He narrowed his eyes, nodding slightly: as though He were an Ascendant rector who had received only partial answer to a complicated question. "The Paphians do not make a practice of calling things by their real names," He said. "They say, the Gaping One, the Naked Lord, the Lord of Dogs. Others have named me things similar to these: Baal-Zebub, the Lord of Flies; and Baal-Phegor, which means the Gaping Lord. But I am also called simply Baal, which is Lord; and Osiris, and Orpheus, and Hermes Chthonius; and in the East they named me Joshua, and Judas; and in Boeotia, Dionysus Dendrites, which means the God in the Tree."

He finished and looked at me expectantly.

"What did Morgan Yates call you?" I began slowly.

"Poetic Ecstasy."

"And that woman in the sleeplabs?"

"Sexual Desire."

I thought for a minute. I asked, "What did Melisande call you?"

"Peter Pan."

"And Dr. Harrow?"

"Unreason."

"And her brother Aidan?"

"Despair."

I fell silent. In the chill air the masque's clamor racketed more loudly. Even from here I sensed the revelers' desires, tugging insistently at me as they begged for release. How easy it would be to join them, pass among those bright figures and take from each whatever sensation I desired. I could let this other dream pass; but that was dangerous. Because if others had seen Him now, the Boy in the Tree, the Gaping One, then surely His power had grown beyond imagining; and how easy it would be for the Aviator to use Him against the City. I shuddered and bit the ball of my thumb, hard. That was how I used to wake myself from a patient's bad dreams at HEL.

I did not wake; the Boy did not disappear; but I was able to think clearly again.

I said, "So those are not your names?"

He grinned, flashing small even white teeth. "They are all my names."

I hesitated. "*I* think you are Death."

The Boy stared at me with those fathomless summer eyes. "I am."

"Then Aidan was right, to name you Despair." I held out my hand as if to take a prize.

"No," He said. "He was *not* right; because he did not want to learn the rest of it. Lazy thing."

Suddenly He laughed, tossing His head so that the crown of leaves sprang through the air and unfurled to reveal a froth of blossoms, white and gold and periwinkle blue. I caught and held them before me: leaves such as I had never seen, leaves like verdant stars and silvery blades and cupped hands, and all entwined with flowers that smelled of every spring that had ever been hoped for in the shrunken heart of winter.

"*You* must teach them the rest of my name, Lady!" He laughed again and bounced back on His feet as though he could scarcely contain Himself from leaping into the air. "You must tell them stories, you must tuck them in at night, *you must be their Mother!*"

I glared at His foolishness, and placed the crown of flowers upon my head. "And what will you be, Boy?" I said. "Their Father?"

"Of course! And your brother, and lover, and victim all in one! Just like before. All of it, all the same! All singing, all dancing, all dying!"

"You sound mad, like that Aviator they talk about, the one Anna called the Consolation of the Dead."

He frowned. "He is a fool, a neophyte. He does not understand what must be done. You will see for yourself when you meet him."

He turned away, for the first time noticed the moon and made a mocking bow to it, as He had to me earlier. Then he glanced back. "I go now, Wendy, sister mine. We will meet again; but not for a little while, and likely as not you won't recognize me, and you may not remember my names. Although perhaps by then you will recall your own." He shrugged, tossed His fair curls as though He had grown weary of this game.

"When will we meet?" Suddenly I was frightened of His leaving me, but as I reached to hold Him He skipped away, shaking His head.

"Why, at Winterlong of course," He cried, and laughing sprang into the air as though He would seize the moon. I shielded my eyes from its yellow glare; but when blinking I tried to find Him again He was gone.

A small sound by the Regent's Oak. I turned expectantly. But this time it *was* Justice, looking shy and uncertain as he stepped from behind the tree.

"I heard you talking," he said, looking surprised to see me alone. "I'm sorry, I'll leave you—"

My disappointment at losing the Boy eased. "No," I said. I took a step toward him. "I hoped you'd come."

Justice smiled, glanced up at the moon and then at me. He touched the crown of flowers upon my brow. "Really, Wendy?"

"Really," I replied, and took his hand. Together we walked down to the Masque of Owls.

Part Eight

The Gaping One Awakes

1. The central fire and the rain from heaven

They stood at the foot of the altar beside a stone basin: three young boys, all Paphians. Two had the tawny skin and black eyes that marked them of the House High Brazil, slender and long-legged. They still wore fine ropes of gold looped through their ears, and each had his dark hair braided down his back. The other was a Saint-Alaban, blond and blue-eyed and the youngest of the three. When he saw me he spat and crossed his arms before his bare chest, hands splayed in the protective gesture against the Gaping One. They were naked, save for wreaths of leafless vines about their necks. That morning before dawn they had been forced to gather the vines themselves. Aardmen led them to the river and watched panting on its banks while the boys pulled the plants from the earth. Their hands still bled where the vines had fought, and the Saint-Alaban's breast was scored with livid wounds like lashmarks. Now they waited while the Consolation of the Dead questioned them as to the whereabouts of the empath named Wendy Wanders.

I stared coldly at the Saint-Alaban, then shifted on my marble bench. Beside me Oleander shuffled, hissed under his breath as he nearly dropped the knife he held. He shot me a panicked glance. I shook my head and he averted his eyes.

Marble fountains stood at either side of the altar. They no longer held water, but twigs and powdered bricks of

opium taken from captive Botanists. Black smoke poured
from them, nearly obscuring the flames that licked at the
base of the fountains where small fires were tended by
other children, naked and filthy from rolling about on the
floor of the nave. Aardmen lolled among them as well,
scratching or biting at their flanks. A soft thrumming filled
the air, compounded of the fires burning and the drip of
rain seeping from holes in the ceiling high above, the
lazars' restless fidgeting and the Aviator's soothing voice
droning on and on.

"Have you seen her? A girl who looks like him, the very
incarnation of the Gaping Lord, the good Dr. Silverthorn
swore to me they were as alike as two drops of rain—"

The Paphians protested no, no, they had never seen her,
never. Only the Saint-Alaban continued to stare back at
me while the Aviator continued his tedious questioning.

Finally the Saint-Alaban called out, "I saw her. She is
disguised as a boy, and names herself Aidan Arent. I
thought she was *him*—"

He pointed at me, then continued, "She was with one of
my bedcousins, Justice Saint-Alaban, a paillard who went
among the Ascendants to betray us, may our Mother curse
him!"

The Aviator nodded. "Where was she, my darling boy?"

The Saint-Alaban gave me a look of such hatred that I
stared down at my hands, the stony lip of my sagittal
gleaming pale violet.

"With a group of traveling Players performing at the
House Illyria," he said. "She appears in blasphemous garb.
My people believe she impersonates the murderer
Raphael Miramar. They will be at the Masque of
Winterlong—" His voice shook with such fury that he
could not go on.

The Aviator nodded again. "But I know all this already,"
he said impatiently. "I want to find her *now. Where is she
now?*"

One of the boys from Persia cried out, "Can't you see we
don't know? Let us go, we'll help you, please—"

But already the Aviator had turned away, reaching for

the book he had dropped when he'd begun his interrogation.

". . . I am the bray of the brute in the night, whoever is deceived by me . . ."

Margalis Tast'annin, the Mad Aviator, lay upon a pallet at the back of the North Cloister facing me. At his feet sat the jackal Anku, still and white as a carven cenotaph. Even at that small distance I could not see them clearly through the roiling smoke and steam. Tast'annin's voice alone possessed a physical immediacy and potency. It cut through the opium's narcotic vapor, the thick stench of dread and hopelessness, so that even though I knew the man who lay there—knew every scar upon his body, knew the tenor of his groans as nightmares chased him, knew the place like a secret spring that bled slowly but ceaselessly, and the smell of his bloodstained raiment—even knowing all this I could sit here and imagine another man speaking in the gloom. A tall strong man with face unscarred and close-cropped wheaten hair, wearing metallic clothes that creaked, and smelling of scorched metal and ozone and (very faintly) of charred flesh.

"Lord Baal."

With a start I realized he had been calling me for some moments. I raised my head, my hair spilling down my shoulders and tangling about the hempen cord I wore around my neck.

"Yes?" I looked past the Paphian boys to where the Aviator had raised himself to stare at me with those translucent eyes.

". . . accept these offerings in your name . . ."

I dipped my head so as not to see them, or the firelight glinting off Oleander's knife. But I heard their fast and shallow breathing, and smelled the ammoniac reek of their terror.

The Aviator finished. A moment in which I could hear only the murmur of rain and the Paphians' choking breath. Then from opposite me came a soft command.

"Now, Oleander."

Oleander inhaled loudly. I closed my eyes, but not before I saw the two boys from Persia clutch each other, weeping. I lowered my head, hunching my shoulders as though this time I might somehow drown out what happened next.

I heard Oleander fumbling with the knife and cursing. An aardman growled: one of the Paphians must have tried to break away. I tried to hear only my own breathing, my heart thumping counterpoint to the boys' despair.

Suddenly Oleander cried out. A tearing sound and a scream; then the knife clattering to the floor, Oleander weeping as he retrieved it. I clenched my hands and squeezed my eyes more tightly, tried repeating loudly the words to the "Duties of Pleasure" and "Saint-Alaban's Song."

It was no use. Their screams and groans went on and on and on, for hours it seemed. Warmth spattered my bare legs and feet. Oleander sobbed and shouted, striking them again and again while I rocked back and forth on the marble bench, eyes shut tight.

Gradually their shrieks grew fainter, the bubbling sound of their breathing soft and labored. Something slippery brushed my leg, slid to the floor nearby. I heard Oleander panting, and the aardmen whimpering. I opened my eyes for an instant, saw blood pooled about my foot, blood sprayed in ribbons across the stone basin and the shapeless lumps strewn about the altar floor. The tip of a finger rolled beneath my boot, and a tuft of golden hair.

It took one of them a very long time to die. He made a choking sound, like someone swallowing syrup, then finally grew still. It was quiet, except for the sound of the other children crying and Oleander talking very slowly and calmly to himself, sentences I could not hear except for the words *save them* whispered repeatedly. I opened my eyes, saw my legs and thighs spattered with blood, smelled it like some warm tide spilling upon the altar. An aardman lapped noisily at the floor. On my wrist the sagittal burned a fierce and brilliant violet. I raised my hand slowly, the rays streaming from it to send ripples of light across the dim room. The lazars cried out, and Oleander tossed the knife across the room, then fell to his knees, retching. The Consolation of the Dead recited words I did not hear as I stared up to where the sagittal streaked the cloister's shadowy vault with amethyst radiance, and the cold rain dripped upon my bloodstained hands.

2. All traces of organic remains become annihilated

That night Oleander cried out in his sleep, thrashing so that his arm struck my cheek and woke me.

"Shh—it's a dream, Oleander, it's just a dream."

I reached across the pallet to embrace him. From the corridor behind the iron gates of the Children's Chapel echoed snores where an aardman lay guarding us.

"No! Oh god, no—"

I covered his mouth. "Be quiet! You'll wake Fury—"

He fell silent then, clutching at me as though he would crawl inside my skin. But for many hours we lay awake, staring into the darkness that engulfed us, the darkness that was everywhere like a poison in the air; knowing that the horror that awaited us upon waking was worse than any nightmare, and that it would never end.

3. The most remarkable of the beasts of prey

"He wants you, Raphael. He is ringing the changes."

In the darkness I could make out Oleander, frail and sallow as one of the few candles left guttering on the altar behind him. He cursed as he bumped against a chair, rubbing his arms to warm himself and finally standing atop the heap of pillows I had arranged next to my pallet. I blinked, sat up, and pulled my bedcovering—a woolen cloak taken from a dead Saint-Alaban—about my shoulders.

"So soon?" I coughed, shivering despite the cloak. From the number of candles that had burned out within the Children's Chapel I guessed I had been asleep for two or three hours. I never slept through the night—or day—anymore. Margalis Tast'annin murdered sleep as efficiently as he did those captives he tirelessly questioned in his search for the empath Wendy Wanders.

My sister, I thought. *That is why these others died, enslaved Curators and Paphians alike;* although mostly it was my own people who fell captive to their own faithless bedcousins.

"Hurry, Raphael," urged Oleander through chattering teeth. He fell onto the pallet beside me. He wore only loose white trousers, tied about his thin waist with a length of rope. I hugged him close, wrapping my cloak about him and feeling the spars of his ribs as he trembled with fear and cold. "I hate it, I hate watching them die—"

"Shh . . ." I stroked his lank hair, his scarred shoulders with their raw fretwork where the Madman had lashed him days before. "Don't cry, cousin, please don't cry."

He sniffled and buried his face in my shoulder. I moved my hand to guard him from my sagittal, though it slumbered now. Only my fear of the Aviator woke it—the Aviator knew this and delighted in it—and sometimes the sight of the dead lying pale as though sleeping in the nave.

A deep tolling note, far above us in the Gloria Belltower. A softer chime, an echo of the first; then silence. Oleander plucked at my arm. "Please, Raphael! Before he sends for others—"

I nodded, and groped on the floor until I found my boots. They were too big for me. Despite wrapping my feet in rags first, my ankles were scraped raw from wearing them and bled anew each day without healing. I blinked back tears of pain as I pulled them over my poor feet, waited for the throbbing to subside before standing to find my robe: a shapeless gray sack, long-sleeved and reaching below my knees, and with a motheaten hood. It was worn through at the elbows and unraveling at the cuffs, hideously ugly but the warmest thing I could find among the heaps of clothing torn from the dead and cast into piles about the nave. Each day the Aviator sent squalling groups of children to pick through these filthy remains, bringing to him and myself whatever seemed worth saving. Broken necklaces and armlets, dirty ribbons and brocade trim from Paphians' robes; occasionally some shattered sliver of machinery, timepiece or spyglass or monitor, buried beneath mounds of Curators' uniforms. The rest was burned, adding the stench of charred cloth to the reek that hung within the nave like a dense and poisonous fog. The hollow sound of children coughing was as ceaseless now as the winter wind howling in the broken west towers. This gray robe was the first and last prize I had found among the lazars' rags, before the Aviator forbade me to show myself among them except at his command. Now I was consigned to this chamber, half prison and half sacrarium to the Gaping One.

With a sigh I motioned Oleander that I was ready. We walked through the Crypt Church, I hobbling and Oleander skipping beside me. He was barefoot and tried to keep his chilblained feet from touching the icy floor, hopping and swearing as though he walked on hot sand. We started up the passage leading to the Belltower. A solitary candle pressed into an alcove threw its wan light down the steps. As we walked there came another loud peal, cut short so that we both stopped to listen for the next sound. Oleander stared at me, looking very much like Dr. Silverthorn in the cloudy light, with his hollow eyes and sunken cheeks and nearly all his hair gone. I looked away from him, staring at the arched ceiling high above us as though I might see through it to the bay floor. From the heights of the Gloria Tower came a tiny sound, what might have been a bat squeaking, or a child's wail. Then a soft thud. Oleander giggled nervously.

"Stop it!" I ordered, slapping him. He covered his mouth and ran a few steps ahead of me, his laughter turning to hiccuping gasps. I licked my finger, turned, and snuffed out the passage's single candle. I scraped it from the stone and ate it, choking on the oily taste. Then I hurried to Oleander's side.

At first glance the vast expanse of the Cathedral seemed empty, its bays and transepts filled only with clumps of debris and the fires burning untended among the huge columns and arches. The crackling flames and wind almost drowned out the other, softer sounds, choked coughing and, from some unimaginable space overhead, voices. Then the gray light filtering down through the great windows picked out the numbing details.

A white shape moaned and tossed its arm across what had seemed to be a rotting gourd or toadstool but was in fact a face. Dark forms laid like logs beside a dying bonfire were not logs at all but those who had died since dawn (not long past, to judge by the weak light), waiting their turn to be cast upon the smoking pyres. Many were the lazars Tast'annin had set to work outside: searching for the lost arsenal of the Ascendants, hacking at the frozen ground with whatever implements they could find—staves and

stones, the remains of autovehicles—until they were felled
by disease or exhaustion. Beside one of the immense columns holding up the Gloria Tower a pair of gargoyles had
toppled. But these raised their grotesque heads as we approached, unfurling long pink tongues as they yawned and
groaned a greeting.

"He waits, master," one said to me. His tongue wrapped
around the words so that I could scarcely understand him.
He stared at Oleander through slanted eyes and then
flopped back onto his haunches, scratching at his jaw with
one of his gnarled hands. "Little master, he shouts."

Oleander glared at me. "I told you we should hurry!"

The other aardman remained standing, attention fixed
upon the column looming above us. I followed his gaze
upward, to the tangled skein of ropes and boards and scaffolding that hung beneath the Cathedral bells. I could
scarcely see them there in the ruined tower: figures no
larger than the Angels and Saints who peered down at us
with unwinking stone eyes. But the figures upon the scaffolding moved. I began to pick out individual voices from
the faint garble that drifted down. Some cried or screamed
or even laughed shrilly. Others begged, and I heard several voices singing tunelessly the words to "Saint-Alaban's
Song."

And there was another voice, calm and soothing. Resonant, speaking slowly and with great clarity, with a pronounced drawl and accent unfamiliar to the City of Trees.
The Consolation of the Dead was ringing the changes.

A shriek. The aardmen's ears flattened against their
skulls. They flinched, looking askance at me before pointing their long muzzles skyward again.

"He shouts." The first aardman wriggled closer to me,
pressing his great head against my thigh and growling.
"He shouts, master."

"I know, Fury," I said, scratching the rough fur between
his ears. "It's all right."

Fury continued to growl, nostrils flaring as he stared into
the darkness above us. Oleander fidgeted by the door half-
opened in the column, the sole entry to the Gloria Tower.
"Raphael," he said again.

"Be quiet," I said. "I want to listen—"

If I squinted I could make them out in that dizzying space. Black figures that seemed to flail crazily as they walked across the few boards and rope bridges strung beneath the twenty-four bells, all that remained of the flooring that had rotted away in the past centuries. They clung desperately to a haphazard network of ropes, invisible from the nave.

At the entrance to the Gloria Tower stood a mass of shadows. I sifted through the crowd, trying to pick out among the writhing silhouettes Fancy's small form, her glorious golden hair.

But I did not see her. Except for Dr. Silverthorn's insistence that she was here, I had no reason to believe she was still alive. Still I looked for her everywhere. I forced myself to search among the faces of the dead in piles by the bonfires, and among those who scuttled with averted eyes past the iron gates of the Children's Chapel where I sat through endless twilit days and nights. I never found her.

Fury whined restlessly. I caressed his forehead, felt the short hairs bristling as his voice deepened to a more threatening note. I looked to see what alarmed him.

At the edge of the scaffolding were three figures, black and foreboding. Tast'annin's favorite lackeys, the aardmen he had named Blanche and Trey. Between them the Aviator himself lay upon a makeshift litter. At his feet crouched a smaller form, shining as a venomous lily: the traitorous jackal who had led my captors to me at the Butterfly Ball and then fled to join the Madman. They watched as two tiny figures struggled across the scaffolding. One child swayed, seemed to plunge from the narrow planks. But she caught an unseen rope, plummeted until it grew taut, so that it seemed she jerked and twisted in the empty air. She hung from the bell's black mouth, turned back to scream something through her sobs.

"I can't watch this," said Oleander. His footsteps pattered up the spiral stairs to the tower. At my side Fury whimpered, eyes furrowed as he stared at the tiny figure hanging limply from the rope.

"Master, master," he whined, tail thumping the floor. "Why?"

"I don't know why," I replied, and crouched beside him.

Sweat ran down my arms despite the cold, and I shivered. By now the other child had also shimmied up a rope. The two dangled from the ancient blackened bells. As we watched they kicked at the air and began to swing, back and forth, until the clappers struck metal and a harsh knell echoed through the Cathedral, first one clanking peal and then another. The figure seated amid the ruins of the Gloria Tower began to recite, pausing to wait for the clapper to swing back and strike once more.

"Master?" Fury turned to regard me with puzzled eyes. Throughout the nave small figures began to stir from the rubbish heaps, raising themselves to watch the macabre drama overhead.

"It means nothing," I said. "Nonsense he has made up, an invocation to the Lord of Dogs."

"Bad, master," he said. I nodded in agreement, then glanced up at the belltower. The Aviator droned on, the bells continued to peal. My heart had hardened in the past weeks, but still I pitied those children. "I must go, Fury," I said, and entered the column. The aardmen raised their freakish heads: bestial jaws and teeth and fur, but with human eyes that watched me take my leave, and human tongues bidding me farewell.

Inside the column all was silent, the air close and smelling of burning wax. I walked slowly, circling higher and higher, the icy metal stairs biting through the soles of my boots. On the uneven surface of the walls words and names had been scrawled in places, written in oily smoke or with the burnt end of a stick: *"Baldassare Persia died here"; "death to baal death to miramar"; "I loved Crescent Illyria tell Her."* In one spot had been scratched a crude stick figure with circles for eyes and open mouth, hanging from a tree. I did not pause to examine it closer.

At last the stairs ended. Most of the wall had fallen away, leaving a jagged gap through which I saw the miserable cluster of bodies I'd glimpsed from below. They were a children except for two: a girl unknown to me, tall and angular, with long straight blond hair and wearing a short blue tunic, like a Curator's gown but of different cut. The other was a young Paphian woman captured a few days earlier near the Rocreek. A Persian malefeant with eyelashes dyed carnelian and poppies tattooed upon her cheeks, she had been trysting with a Naturalist. Now the Naturalist sprawled outside the Cathedral, where he had tripped over one of the deadly parasitic trees. His face was still twisted into an expression of dazed alarm, his eyes staring at the blackened earth. I had seen him there, and stepped carefully around him. The dull buzzing that emanated from his body revealed that his corpse had been completely invaded by the animalcules.

His luckless consort stared wild-eyed over the void, clutching the shoulder of the louse-ridden child at her side. I thought with mean satisfaction how a week earlier she would have fled shrieking from that poor boy. Now he afforded her the last shred of human comfort she would know. I tugged the hood of my woolen cloak about my head, pulling it to shadow my face.

Above us soared the broken cusp of the Gloria Tower. The roofstones had long since fallen away, leaving it open to rain and snow and viral strike. Clouds raced across a pewter sky, so close it seemed the edges of the tower might snag them. The wind howled, tearing at my cloak and the children's rags. One or two of the lazars glanced at me as I slipped between them, then returned their attention to the two children who still hung from the bell ropes. I saw Tast'annin and his lackeys at the front of the small crowd, Oleander a few steps from the aardmen and eyeing them with distaste.

The Aviator had grown silent. He stared at the bells, the broken boards leading to the skeletal remains of the tower door. Without warning he turned, cast his glance upon the children huddled behind him, and pointed at the Paphian woman. She shrieked and grabbed another child at her side, as though she would put him between herself and the Aviator. A few steps away the blond girl watched with

amusement, her hands twitching at the hem of her tunic.
Tast'annin nodded, continuing to regard the malefeant
with an almost gentle expression as he leaned forward to
stroke Anku's back.

"Gelasia Persia," he murmured at last. "See, I remembered your name! Gelasia, come here please." He gave
Anku's fur a last fond tug and extended his hand to her.

Gelasia Persia shook her head. Her hair—still neatly
braided—whipped the air like the Aviator's quirt. She
shoved one of the children forward. The boy gave a small
squeak, scrabbling at the empty air; then tumbled from
the edge of the platform. The Consolation of the Dead
watched, perhaps with slight disappointment. Beside him
the aardmen growled and Anku whined. The blond girl
covered her mouth, snickering. The children murmured
and rustled and whispered, and a few of them peered
down after the unfortunate boy.

Gelasia Persia stared stupidly at the nave floor far below.
Then she turned and pushed her way through the crowd of
children.

Her eyes lit upon me in my gray Curator's cape. "Help
me, sieur!" she cried, grabbing my arm. "My lover was
Friedrich Durrell, a Naturalist, please help me—"

The Aviator drawled a command to Blanche and Trey.
The lazars pressed close together as the aardmen loped
across the rickety flooring. The malefeant stared back at
them, her fingernails digging through my worn cloak.

An arm's length from us the aardmen stopped. They
raised themselves upon their hind legs. One stroked his
jaw, puzzled, while the other looked at me with dispassion-
ate golden eyes.

"Girl, master," he snarled, indicating Gelasia Persia with
a flick of his head. I shrugged and tried to push her away.
Staring terrified at the aardmen she clung to me, panting.
My hood dropped. The aardmen crouched and warily approached us. Gelasia turned to me with wide mad eyes,
her gaze settling upon the sagittal dull-gray about my
wrist.

"Miramar," she gasped. She snatched her hands back.
"Dear Mother, it's true—"

I pulled the hood around my face. The aardmen grabbed
Gelasia Persia and began to drag her to the edge of the
platform. The lazars scrambled away. Some gazed at me
with sudden recognition; one boy crossed his hands before
his breast. But the blond girl beside him looked at me
boldly, then to my amazement burst out laughing. Before I
could get a closer look at her she turned and, glancing back
to make sure the Aviator did not notice, disappeared down
the spiral stairs.

Gelasia Persia only stared with utter loathing, mouth
working silently, too overcome with hatred even to curse
me.

At the edge of the scaffolding the aardmen halted. The
children clinging to the ropes dangled exhausted, hundreds of feet above the floor of the nave. The boy's head
was hidden by the bell's mouth. The girl had slipped so far
that only a few measures of rope remained for her to grasp.
She clung with eyes tightly shut, her bleeding hands sliding bit by bit down the hempen cord.

With pursed lips Tast'annin surveyed the bells, pale eyes
darting from one to another. Finally he pointed at one, an
immense black shape with glints of gold showing through
its patina of smoke and filth. It hung at least ten lengths
above the maze of rope and board, and a good twenty from
where the aardmen held their prisoner.

"That one," he said.

Gelasia Persia stared in disbelief. "I can't reach that!"
she cried. The tattooed poppies burned against her white
skin.

The Aviator shook his head and repeated, "That one."
He leaned forward on the litter, his scarred mouth more
hideous now as he smiled at her.

I looked down to see that lazars had already dragged off
the other child's body. A small group remained standing,
staring up expectantly at the bells.

Gelasia Persia shook her head. "I will die."

"You have nothing to fear from death, dearest child,"
said the Aviator. "Such a beautiful girl, the Gaping One
will be glad of such an offering." His smile twisted into a

horrible rictus, his eye bulging as though he enjoyed a lewd joke at her expense. He pointed at me. "See: there is his envoy, the one who has been consecrated to Baal-Phegor the Lord of Dogs."

"He is no lord!" spat Gelasia Persia. "I know Raphael Miramar—he is a traitor, a monster and murderer!" Her eyes flashed beneath their scarlet lashes. "He murdered his Patron and another Naturalist and my bedcousin Whitlock High Brazil, may our Mother's hands embrace him—"

The Aviator stared at her, still smiling. "But if your Mother will embrace you what have you to fear, beloved cousin?"

"Please—I don't want to die," she pleaded. "I am of the House Persia, I could serve you well—"

The Aviator shook his head. "But haven't you seen all my servants?" He spread his hands, indicating the restless lazars, Anku watchful at his feet, the aardmen Blanche and Trey and last of all myself standing aloof. "No, Gelasia: you go to serve a mightier Lord. I am but *His* servant; you may be His handmaiden."

A shriek pierced the air. I turned to see the little girl slide from the bell rope, her face crimson with weeping. Several of the lazars cried out. Then the other boy yelled, let go of his rope and plunged after her.

Gelasia Persia screamed and looked away, tried to bury her face in her shoulder. The Aviator grew stern. His voice rang out as he pointed to the ropes strung from the edge of the scaffolding.

"Ring the changes, Gelasia. I will console you in your need."

The aardmen pushed her shrieking toward the platform's edge. I turned away; but then heard the Consolation of the Dead command, "Watch her, young Lord Baal. Tell her she has nothing to fear. Tell her she goes to meet the Gaping One."

As I lifted my head she flailed and kicked desperately at her captors. The aardmen drew back, snarling. Blanche let go of her arm. Before Gelasia could grab one of the ropes she tripped, and screaming, plunged over the edge. I had a glimpse of her face, eyes livid and mouth contorted as she scrabbled helplessly for the ropes. As she fell her voice wailed above the wind:

"She will destroy you, Miramar!"

4. We shrink back affrighted at the vastness of the conception

"She referred to your sister, of course," the Aviator repeated softly.

It was much later, perhaps days later. I thought it must be·evening. When I answered the Aviator's summons a window like a gash in the Crypt Church had shown me a sliver of cobalt sky peppered with stars. I had returned to the Children's Chapel and slept for a few hours after my sojourn in the Gloria Tower; awakened and slept again, and again, until once more Oleander appeared in the chamber to bring me here to the very heart of the Aviator's stronghold: the Resurrection Chapel of the Cathedral Church of the Archangels Michael and Gabriel.

"She spoke of the Magdalene," I said for the third or fourth time, and coughed.

He reclined upon a dais, originally part of an altar, surrounded by massive blocks of granite fallen from the ceiling and scattered like so many broken tombstones. At his side was Dr. Silverthorn's black bag. The floor was littered with broken capsules, torn adhesive pads, half-empty tubes of morpha and octine and frilite. And everywhere were piles of trinkets brought him by the lazars—dolls and gowns and dead flowers, stones and bundles of twigs, a prosthetic arm and a scholiast's head. Scattered among these were braziers that burned damp green wood and old cloth.

At the base of each tripod were carefully placed three objects, particolored as though overgrown with moss or lichen. Stones, I thought the first time I had come here. But they were not stones. The lank stuff hanging like yellowed chaff was not dried moss but hair; the glints of silver were bits of glass and metal pressed into empty eyesockets. The sight no longer sickened me. They were dead now, whoever they had been, and at play in that green country I had glimpsed in Dr. Silverthorn's dying eyes.

In the midst of all this Margalis Tast'annin reposed like an effigy from one of the Museum's dioramas: his skin waxy and moist from the fevers that plagued him, a pallid yellow; eyes black pits from smoking uncured opium. In the firelight the scars upon his face appeared darker, and seemed to follow some pattern unknown to me; as though they had been scored there purposefully. Sometimes they seemed to move, writhing black characters etched upon his skin.

Set into the wall behind him was a window of colored glass with several panes broken or missing. The ones that remained formed a picture, the image of a woman draped in blue and carrying a lighted torch. In the chill winter sunlight her figure shone pale blue and white. Now it was dull, flat black and gray, the woman almost indistinguishable from the random patterns of glass and empty air. I stared at it with dread, this likeness of the Magdalene in such an awful place; and wondered who could have placed it there, aeons ago when the Cathedral was raised upon Saint-Alaban's Hill.

At Tast'annin's feet panted the white jackal, ruby eyes alert as ever. I had realized some days before that I had never seen Anku asleep. Now I believed that he did not sleep, that he was truly an immortal creature, one of the Egyptians' ancient demons somehow awakened by the Aviator; or, Magdalene forbid, awakened by me. The Aviator's shadow fell across his shrewd foxy face as he leaned over to poke at a brazier with a long white bone, clumsily carved and bound roundabout with strips of skin. Tast'an-

nin wore the remnants of his Aviator's uniform: heavy
breeches and a jacket of red metallic cloth, emblazoned
with the yellow triangle of the last Ascension. The jacket
was hung with teeth and small bones, broken blades of
knives and strings of glass beads all sewn neatly across the
leather. Oleander had done this; Oleander who sat patiently at Tast'annin's side, piercing a pair of leather trousers with a needle made of a finger bone, and stitching
bright ribbons culled from the braids of dead Paphians, up
and down the trouser legs in waves of gold and green and
blue.

"This Magdalene, then—"

The Aviator paused, the carven bone poised in the air.
He smiled at me with complicity: he would take another
tack. "Your sister might be the living image of the Magdalene, as you represent the Gaping One."

The bone clattered to the floor. His finger stabbed the
air in front of my face, then flicked a strand of wheat-
colored hair from his lip. He continued, "There would be a
certain symmetry; like in that masque the blond children
showed me. 'Baal and Anat': I quite liked that one."

His voice wandered off. He stretched his hand to pinch
Oleander's shoulder, kneading the loose skin as though he
were testing a bolt of fine silk.

"She might be," I said. "Only she was raised among the
Ascendants, who do not believe. And that masque is nonsense, a ghost story taught the Saint-Alabans by the Historians. *I* do not believe in the Magdalene or the Gaping
One."

Which was no longer strictly true, since I had seen with
my own eyes a spectral Boy walking in the Narrow Forest,
whom Dr. Silverthorn might have called an Angel, but
who I believed to be the Hanged Boy. And his jackal familiar sat not an arm's length from me. But I could not understand why an Ascendant would be interested in these
things. It was almost beyond comprehension to think that
he might *believe* in them.

Tast'annin looked at me with those vulpine eyes. They
glowed dull orange, as though banked embers burned
somewhere behind his shattered face.

"I was not a religious man," he said, his voice fallen to a whisper. From behind him billowed a sigh, the flop of a heavy leg upon the stone floor. The aardman Trey had turned over in his sleep. "I saw too many things, things you would not believe, my lovely child. . . ."

He motioned for me to draw nearer. I dragged myself across the floor, sweating as I came within the murky radius of firelight. I started to pull off my woolen cloak, decided not to. That would leave me only in a thin shift, and *that* would make it easier for the Aviator to grope at me with his large bony hands. Like many eunuchs his physical loss had honed his hatred to a fine dangerous point; he struck me whenever the temper took hold of him.

Not now, though. He merely tousled my unbound hair, then traced the edges of the hempen rope I wore about my neck at his command.

"No, darling boy: I ceased to believe after I saw entire cities erupt in liquid flame, and heard the sound a million people make when they die all at once. A sort of scream, so loud that my ears bled; and for many days afterward I heard a dull whining, as though flies whirred and banged inside my skull.

"I heard it so many times I went deaf in one ear—"

A draft of icy air shot up from one of the grates in the stone floor. The Aviator tapped his ear with a long ivory fingernail, then waved to disperse the smoke roiling around him.

"But the Governors repaired that. When I underwent rehabilitation, when I retired from active duty; when they decided to send me here to this accursed City."

He drifted into silence, running his front teeth over his lip again and again as though to strip the skin from it. I stared down at my hands folded in my lap. The sagittal glowed very faintly in here, the palest lilac; as though it drew strength from the stench of evil that hung about the Chapel. When the Aviator had been silent for several minutes Oleander lifted his head. His sunken eyes shone. As I took in his hollow cheeks, the unnatural brightness of his eyes, I realized that he really was starving. His cotton trousers had grown too loose to hang about his emaciated hips. He had discarded them for a pair of particolored breeches, a High Brazilian child's harlequin costume: gaudy gold and green, torn and bloodied at the knees (she too had been ringing the changes when she died), but fitting Oleander's demeanor, his somewhat melancholy gaiety.

"But you flew in the air!" he said. "You lived in the NASNA station!"

The idea delighted him beyond all measure. I had grown weary weeks before of the Aviator's exploits. Oleander, it seemed, never would.

Tast'annin let his lip slide slowly between his teeth until it curled back into its accustomed nerveless grin.

"Yes, I flew in the air," he said. He turned to look at Oleander, so slowly it seemed he was some huge automaton formed of metal and bone.

"I was one of the last. I was a NASNA Aviator, a remarkable soldier of the firmament; one of those who would save the world and bring about a final glorious Ascension, though not the one your people dream of, Oleander, nor yours, my dear Raphael. . . ."

He laughed mirthlessly. One hand groped through a pile of bright rubbish arranged by one of the smoking braziers. It withdrew a book, an archaic volume tied with string so that its pages would not come loose. I craned my neck to read the title faded across its mottled cover: *An Inquiry into Some Ethical Points of Celestial Navigation*. He glanced at it, frowned, and tossed it onto the heap of glowing embers. He raked his hand through the rubbish once again, until he drew forth another volume. Its cover was gone and many pages seemed missing, but it appeared to meet his satisfaction. He flipped through the matted pages, peeling them apart with great care, until he found the one he wanted. He began to read. The echo of his words hung in the heavy air, hollow and faintly threatening.

It was a terrible story, and it seemed to go on for hours. I moved closer to Oleander. He listened without looking up, and his stitches grew looser and more uneven, until when he jerked on the thread it broke, and the bone needle flew into the fire. Then he gave up all pretense of working. He

of ideals

huddled beside me, his hands slipping beneath my cloak to clasp mine as the Aviator's voice broke over us in inescapable waves, and the snores of the aardman droned on behind us, and in the shadows Anku stared unblinking as though he waited and watched for something to take shape and rise from the darkness of the Resurrection Chapel.

> " *'The conquest of the earth is not a pretty thing when you look into it too much. What redeems it is the idea only. An idea at the back of it; not a sentimental pretense but an idea—something you can set up, and bow down before, and offer a sacrifice to . . .'* "

As Tast'annin read this his tone grew dreamy, almost gentle. He lifted his head from the page.

"That is what we lost," he said. "The primacy of an idea, an idea worth dying for, something greater than ourselves and deserving of sacrifice . . .

"But you did not forget, Raphael, and your people did not forget, did they? And these others—"

He pointed at Trey snoring lustily. "The geneslaves have always looked for someone to bow down to: it is in their mongrel nature as dogs, and as failed men too I suppose, to find someone worth naming *master*.

"I think that is why I was not a religious man: I never found anyone or anything I could bow down to. Pasty weak men and women kneeling before insipid gods, gods with all the blood washed from their wounds, gods who died without a fight—else they'd still be getting their share of glory and blood and sacrifice, eh, Raphael?"

I had lost the sense of what he was saying. The words of his dreadful story still had me in a sort of trance, so that when the Aviator's cold fingers grabbed the rope around my neck I cried out, and Oleander nearly jumped into my lap.

I thought Tast'annin would kill me then, for no reason but that I had shown fear of him. But after a moment he dropped the cord and leaned back.

"The boy has no idea what I am speaking of," he whispered. In the dying firelight he looked even more like some ancient effigy, some terrible thing wakened from a long and restive sleep. But it was not the obvious symbols of his derangement that frightened me, the bones and braids and broken knives, or even the rope he made me wear. No, it was the more subtle emblems of the outer world that filled me with a growing unease: that triangle of shining cloth adorning his breast, a type of luminous cloth I had never seen; the little icons emblazoned on his Aviator's jacket, stars and moons and shapes like arrows or the prows of boats. The ring upon one gnarled finger, a circle of heavy gold set with a large blue stone and surrounded by letters spelling out NASNA. I could not imagine that his people would have weak gods. I could not imagine that they would have gods at all, and I told him so.

"You do understand, then, Miramar; a little at least. Yes, they had gods; but not such as you have in this City, a corpse and a whore!"

He laughed, a harsh hooting noise. At his feet Anku turned to regard him before laying his muzzle back upon his paws. As if the jackal reminded him of more serious business the Aviator fell quiet.

"The Gaping One," he said softly. "Now there is a god whose time has come: a god of death and destruction and despair. Because what have we now to live for or hope for, and what is there left to repair?"

He leaned forward until I felt his breath upon my cheeks and smelled the taint of opium. Oleander crawled away from us and crouched beside a brazier. I swallowed, drew back before replying, "But I do not believe in the Gaping One—my people do not believe, it is an ancient superstition that only the House Saint-Alaban gives any credence to."

Tast'annin smiled. His upper lip drew up like an animal's, catching on one of his front teeth. "But your people *do* believe, Raphael," he said. "I have used my time wisely in the City of Trees. I have used the tools put in my hands, the geneslaves and the children of the plague and now the

Children of the Magdalene, and from them I have learned many things.

"About six weeks ago there was an atmospheric disturbance. We lost one of our stations to the Balkhash Commonwealth. Your people believed the blast signaled a new Ascension; many felt it heralded the Final Ascension."

"I saw it," I blurted. "It was—" I started to speak of my meeting with the Hanged Boy, but stopped. "It was very unusual."

The Aviator fixed me with a strange look. "It was indeed. I was fortunate enough to be watching the skies from the Gloria Tower. As I was fortunate enough to have an intelligent little girl who had joined my little family here, a child named Pearl, whose people had discarded her as they might have tossed away a bad fruit, once they saw she could not run fast enough to escape the fougas."

His face contorted. He threw his hands open, as though to dismiss everything in the Chapel, toys and aardman and Oleander cowering in the shadows.

"Pagh! *You* are the real animals, you Paphians and Curators who let your children die and kill these poor misshapen creatures that would have served you bravely, if only you had not been so corrupted by fear! But they have found a better master now, a truthful man if not a kindly one; because it is better in these days to embrace death than to flee him, and offer what solace we can to ourselves since no one will escape him."

He reached for Dr. Silverthorn's bag, his hand rummaging around until he withdrew a capsule. Without glancing at it he popped it into his mouth. He continued, "Pearl saw you by the river, in your torn clothes and with a vine about your neck, and with this circus animal protecting you."

He roughed Anku's fur affectionately. " 'I have seen the Lord of Dogs, master,' she told me when she came back that evening. 'The one the Paphians talk of, I saw him walking in the river.'

"I had her describe this strange figure to me, because as you know I was searching for an escaped empath. Until that evening I retained some foolish hope that if I found her and returned her to my superiors they would reward me, forgive me for my failure to assume command of the City.

"But when I saw the explosion of the NASNA station that night I knew that I no longer had any superiors."

He paused, staring confused at the book in his hands, as though he had no idea how it had gotten there. After a moment he folded it shut and looked up at me, the black holes of his eyes so filled with despair that I glanced away.

He said, "In a way it really *was* the Final Ascension; for me at least. I have died many times, in aerial strikes and skirmishes, and been reborn, rehabilitated by the Governors more often than you could imagine, my lovely boy. And even when the Curators betrayed me, and the aardmen took me and tortured me and dismasted me: even from that I was saved, and when Lawrence Silverthorn arrived with his Physician's bag I began to grow stronger still.

"But when I saw the explosion that evening I knew this would be my last life. Everything and everyone I lived for died then. *That* was my world and my home, not this—"

He waved his hand, indicating the braziers and blocks of fallen granite surrounding us upon the altar; but with a chilling certainty I knew that he did not really mean *this* at all: not the Resurrection Chapel or the Cathedral or even the City of Trees itself. He dismissed an entire world with that small gesture, the vast world outside that I had never known and would never know, but which included myself and my people and my City nonetheless.

And as I stared up at him with growing unease he smiled; a very small, knowing smile.

I knew then that he meant to destroy us as that other small world, his world, had been destroyed. He only knew how to do one thing, you see, he only understood one thing. That was why the image of the Hanged Boy appealed to him; that was why he searched obsessively for a girl who could deal death with her mind.

But that day I still retained some hope of salvation, of the supremacy of a gentle goddess I had never really believed in. I had not yet grasped that the Aviator's truth might be the only truth worth knowing; and so that smile filled me with more horror than the sight of him sacrificing the children in the cloister or Gloria Tower ever had.

"There is an arsenal here," he said. "On the hillside beneath the Cathedral. A stockpile of weaponry NASNA put there two hundred years ago. One of my duties as Governor was to set up a janissary outpost here."

He chewed his lip. "Of course there is no reason whatsoever to guard it now: there's no one left to guard. There's no reason for anything, really."

"But we are here," I protested. "And the Curators—"

"But they're all dead, darling boy. All of them. No one could possibly have survived."

Oleander stared at the Aviator, puzzled. "They aren't dead. I know they're not de—"

The Aviator struck him, so hard that Oleander's lip split and blood sprayed my cheek as the boy sprawled backward. Tast'annin never even looked at him. He continued to stare at me, his smile frozen, and reached for my robe to wipe the blood from his hand.

"They are all dead," he repeated. "If anyone survived the rebel strike they will have killed them by now. There is no one left to answer to, dearest child; no one except me."

I sat rigidly, waiting for him to strike me or continue with this disordered talk. But he said nothing, only stared at me with that ghastly fixed grin. I stared back, afraid to look away lest he kill me, until my eyes swam and all I saw was his idiot grimace floating in the gloom like a disembodied skull.

Gradually his consciousness seemed to waver. His pupils shrank until they all but disappeared in his watery eyes. He continued to gaze vacantly into the darkness. I glanced at Oleander, sniffling quietly as he nursed his bleeding lip. When after some time it was obvious that the Aviator would say no more, indeed that he had entered some kind of trance, I quickly and quietly fled the Chapel, abandoning poor Oleander to stand watch over the Madman.

5. A lapse of misrepresented time

I had no clear idea as to where I was going, only that I wanted to get as far from Tast'annin as I could. I dared not leave the Cathedral. No one would have stopped me, no one would have dared; but the landscape of this part of the City itself was threat enough to keep me here.

It was winter now. Snow had drifted through the holes in the Cathedral roof to form shallow gray banks. In places the children had sculpted figures from it, men and women and animals—aardmen?—blackened with soot and melted into grotesque shapes. As I wandered I could look out windows and see the City dusted with white, the distant river sheathed in gray ice beneath a new moon's feeble gleaming. Only the ashen slope in front of the Cathedral was untouched by snow. Whatever poisons had leached into the earth there melted it so that the ground remained black as rotten ice, dotted with the corpses of those fallen prey to the parasitic trees. Not even the ravens crying in the frigid air would light upon the Cathedral grounds. I would not venture there.

So I wandered through the twisting halls and bays of the ancient Church, and thought how strange it was that every path in the City seemed to lead here: how the corridors in the House Miramar and the other Paphian Houses had brought me to the labyrinthine passages of the Museum of Natural History, and from there I had lost myself in the Narrow Forest, and the House High Brazil, until finally the tortuous path had led me to Saint-Alaban's Hill. Like the whorls and swirls upon my sagittal, dizzying complexity in such a small thing; and how much more complicated were the windings and turnings of the City of Trees—a place that was only one of the world's besieged sectors, if I was to believe Dr. Silverthorn.

It was night when the Aviator had summoned me to him. It was night still. I was beginning to think that perhaps the Madman was right. Maybe the very nature of the world itself had changed to accommodate the coming of the Gaping One, and there would never be another bright dawn. Certainly I could scarcely recall the last time I had seen the sun: when we fled the Butterfly Ball, perhaps.

I leaned upon a parapet overlooking the nave. Nothing moved down there save the smoke from a half-dozen feeble bonfires left untended through the night. Despite the raiding parties that returned daily with captives, mostly Paphian children, it seemed to me that the number of those who dwelled within the Cathedral grew fewer and fewer each day. Those who did not succumb to disease were slaughtered by the Aviator. A fetid smell hung in the frigid air, the smell of blood and decay, of bodies lying unburned and unburied outside the Cathedral walls. I shivered, sighted a figure nosing among the still forms below. An aardman, starving as we all were, searching for food.

I turned away. I wished I had not left Oleander behind; wished I had been able to do something to save the Persian malefeant, the Illyrian boys, or even the Saint-Alaban. But the Aviator's strength lay in this, his power to command. It was as Dr. Silverthorn had said. One must serve somebody, and only Margalis Tast'annin remained to command. I was not a fighter. My only power had been to inspire worship through my beauty. I took my place here passively as I had upon the Hill Magdalena Ardent, receiving whatever the Aviator offered me: a rain of blood instead of petals, curses and imprecations instead of lustful glances, a hempen cord rubbing raw against my neck instead of flowers upon my brow. I tugged uneasily at the rope. He had knotted it so tightly that I would have to cut it off; but Tast'annin guarded his weapons carefully, and Oleander had refused when I asked him to remove it.

I heard a small sound down the corridor. Perhaps an aardman had crept upstairs, thinking me an unsuspecting lazar and hoping to surprise me. I moved so that the moonlight shining through a window revealed who I was.

But the figure stepping from the shadows was not an aardman.

"Hallo, Wendy."

My hair stood on end at the husky voice and the name it spoke. Backing against the parapet, I pulled my hood about my face. She stood in a small bay flanked by twin Angels of pocked stone, a wiry girl peering at me amused.

"Don't worry," she said airily. "He's forgotten all about me. After Dr. Silverthorn died, I guess. Nobody cares, nobody remembers about Anna. Nobody misses Andrew but me."

She stepped into the corridor. It was the girl I had seen in the Gloria Tower a few days before, the blond girl who had winked at me. Now I could see that her smile was the only fair thing that remained of her face. She was gruesomely scarred.

"Who are you?" I said, trying to sound bold.

"Who am *I*?" she retorted mockingly. "Who are *you*?"

"I am Raphael Miramar." When she made no move to come any nearer I let my hood droop back and peered at her. "But you think I am Wendy Wanders."

She shrugged. "Maybe. Dr. Silverthorn told me about you. *He* turned out to be a nice Doctor after all, didn't he? He tried to save Gligor—"

Suddenly she doubled over, racked by a fit of coughing. When she raised her face again tears streaked it, and when she brushed them away blood smeared her cheeks. The rain of roses had left suppurating wounds across her face and arms and legs, any place that had not been protected by her short tunic. "You were smart to leave when you did," she said hoarsely. "They killed all the rest of us."

"What is your name?" I asked. I tried to imagine what she had looked like before the rain of roses, this Ascendant girl, but it was impossible to tell. Her skin had cracked and blackened like scorched bark; flesh hung in tiny curls from her arms. Only her eyes still shone with sharp intelligence within her ravaged face.

"Anna," she said. A flash of white as she smiled again. "I had a brother too, you know. An independent personality. Andrew. They fed him to the NET. I'm alone now, Wendy."

I nodded. She seemed harmless, and I was lonely. "Yes. I'm alone too, Anna."

She coughed again, covering her mouth with her hand, then gazed surprised at the film of blood upon her fingers. When she looked up her eyes were unfocused, her words slurred.

"I was looking for you, Wendy. To warn you: he means to capture you. They will kill you just like Andrew and Gligor, just like me. . . ."

She took a step, weaving as though drunk. Then she stopped. With a smile she stuck her hand into a pocket. I drew my breath sharply: I had misjudged, she had a weapon hidden there. I glanced around to see how I might escape, but when I looked back she held her hands out to me one at a time, chanting in a hoarse childish voice:

"Now: this is for me, and this is for you."

There was no weapon. One raw palm held a slender cobalt capsule, its casing dull as though she had carried it for a long time. In the other was some bit of gaudery, cloth or feathers mashed flat and pickled with dirt. As I stared uncomprehending she pushed her hand closer to me, the one holding the filthy cloth.

"Take it," she urged.

Gingerly I picked it up, held it at arm's length. A narrow headband made of feathers, matted together with grime and all but colorless.

"Andrew and I made it for you after you left," she said softly. "After they killed him I finished it. That was why I followed Dr. Silverthorn and Gligor. I was afraid they'd forget to give it to you."

I stared at it numbly, this pathetic bit of frippery.

"Don't you like it?" she asked with a twinge of anxiety.

I nodded. "You came all the way here just to give this to her?"

She shrugged. "They would have killed me anyway," she said. "Silverthorn was mad at first, but then he didn't have much time to stay mad, did he? And I remembered how much you liked the other one."

She smiled then, a smile of ineffable sweetness. "It's funny, after Andrew died I felt so horrible, but it was different than before, when we tapped them. I wanted to ask you about that, and about that Boy you showed me—"

A spasm shook her. She waved her empty hand across her face, then looked down at the capsule in her other hand as though she had forgotten it. "But I guess I won't have time now."

Before I could stop her she tossed the capsule into her mouth, making a wry face. She waited a moment, then shook her head apologetically.

"I was the one who betrayed you to the Aviator, Wendy. I was still mad at you. One of the blond children told me about the masque at Winterlong. I was the one who told the Madman. I'm sorry now. I felt bad afterward, that's why I wanted to warn you, to give you a chance to escape."

She hiccuped, then grimaced. "Dr. Silverthorn told me it would taste awful, and he was right: it does. Augh. Well, I was afraid I'd never see you again, Wendy. I'm glad I was able to give you your bandeau—"

Turning, she took a few steps, then stumbled and fell, suddenly hidden in the shadows of the bay.

"Wait, Anna!" I cried. I shoved the headband into a pocket and rushed after her. I knelt at her side, turning her body so that she faced me. Moonlight fell from a window in the granite wall above us, a thread of fine white light across her face.

But it was not the face I had seen an instant before. As I held her the broken skin rippled and then grew smooth and pale, her eyes blinked open and stared up at me with an expression of faint derision.

"Franca!" I cried.

She pulled herself up and shook her head, the hair whipping across her face no longer tawny but silver-fair. The eyes staring at me from behind that gossamer cloud were green as unripe apples.

I staggered back. Without thinking I crossed my hands in front of me, but He only laughed.

"Raphael Miramar!" He scolded. He reached for the rope about my neck and tweaked it teasingly, pulling me near Him. "You saw how little protection that afforded the Saint-Alaban in the cloister."

I dropped my hands. "But you were not in the cloister," I stammered.

"Oh, but I was," He replied. He looked at the bit of rope, let go of it and settled back upon His heels. He seemed heedless of the freezing stone floor, for all that He was naked as an egg. "I am with you always, Raphael. With all of them: Franca and Anna and Dr. Silverthorn, Margalis and Oleander and yes, your little friend Fancy—"

"Fancy? She is alive, you know where she is?"

I tried to grab Him, torn between rage and hope, between wanting to rend Him or embrace Him if what He said was true. But as my hand closed about His a burning pain shot through it. I snatched it back.

"Not yet, Raphael," the Boy murmured, a note of menace in his voice. "You should wait until you are invited. Soon enough, darling boy, soon enough."

His tone had deepened to the Aviator's soft drawl. I looked up, then stumbled to my feet. Because the Aviator stood there, staring down at me with pale mad eyes.

"Did you kill her?" he asked. He stooped, took Anna's corpse by the hair and yanked it so that her head lolled backward, gazing at him blindly. I stared in disbelief, then glanced around the tiny bay. Her scars were unhealed, and she was certainly dead. And the alcove was empty, the Boy gone. The chink in the wall showed a fingerlength of pale gray, bright enough that I knew it must be morning.

He let go of the girl. Her body fell back to the floor with a thud. He stood, continuing to stare at me with that knowing smile, his eye bulging.

"Your little friend," he said. "Fancy."

I felt as though he had driven a knife through my stomach. "Yes," I said at last.

The Consolation of the Dead extended his hand, took the end of the cord about my neck and tugged it.

"Come," he said, as though promising wonderful things. "She is in the cloister, waiting to see you again."

Without a word I rose and followed him.

It was not until we reached the cloister that I saw a tendril of living vine had clasped itself like a green finger around the hempen rope that bound me to him.

6. The most formidable of the many tyrants

She was hanging from a metal spike protruding from one of the columns in the center of the room. Her throat had been slashed, ripped from chin to breast, the blade wrenching through flesh and sinew all the way to her backbone so that her vertebrae were exposed, a necklace of twisted coral. The stone basin that had been dragged beneath her was half-filled with blood. Her face was a color I had never seen before: the color of a winter sky scraped of sun, so utterly bloodless that the whites of her eyes seemed blue in comparison. Her mouth twisted as though she had tried to scream, an expression of such unrelieved torment that I could only imagine she had been alive when the knife tore through her.

I walked up to the basin, reached to touch one of her bare feet. The blood had thickened where it dripped from her toes in a blackening stalactite. A spider clung there, uneven threads marking the beginning of a web strung from one foot to the other. I stretched my finger to caress her foot, the skin white and glistening, striped with crimson like an overripe fig. When I dug my nail into her heel the flesh split as though it were a sheet of parchment. As I withdrew my finger the spider scurried away. I turned and fell to the floor.

Many minutes passed before I opened my eyes. Darkness seethed around me, waves of black and scarlet. I was sick again, and again; felt a burning in my bowels so that I

Lope

empty/void vs.

hoped
fecundity

squatted and defecated upon the stones, then stumbled until I found another column and embracing it slumped to the floor. I lay with my face pressed against the cool stone, weightless, feeling nothing but darkness and cold, as though my skin had been flayed from me and my bones had become part of the stone blocks of the Cathedral. An immense and mindless relief flooded me, an emptiness more soothing than any lover's touch, a wakeful void that held more promise than an aeon of undisturbed sleep. I felt the very stones of the Cathedral melt away; I saw the sky above me, brilliant, limitless, glazed with a multitude of stars. Then the stars began to wink out, one by one, until whole patches of the vast firmament stretched dead and black across my vision, and the horizon itself disappeared. I hung suspended in that void, watching as the last points of light flickered and went out, until finally there was nothing there, nothing at all.

It was then that the Voice began to speak.

—*You have seen Me*, it said.

—I see nothing, I replied. I tried to move my hand before my eyes. Nothing: no hand, and no eyes to see it. I am dead, I thought; and the thought was comfort.

—*But that is Me*, it said: *Nothing. You see now that is all there is: only this and nothing more.*

I waited but it was silent. Finally I had a thought.

—There is something, I said. There is an Enemy.

It replied, *You know that there is.*

I said, What is its name?

I saw something then. A hand, or something like a hand; a flame like a smaller tongue of blue ice rising from its palm.

—*Her name is Anat*, it replied.

—*Her name*, it went on, *is Tiamet, and Astarte, and Isis, and Maria, and Ariadne, and Aphrodite.*

—*Her Name*, it said, the blue flame leaping, *is Wendy.*

—*Her Name*, it said after a long moment, *is Hope.*

The Voice fell silent then. The flame licked at the empti-

ness and was gone. The echo of that last word hung in the
air for hours, a hissing venomous breath that meant to
extinguish me, the sound the stars made as one by one they
died.

Then gradually I began to feel something, gradually I
began to feel cold, as though drop by drop every atom of
my body had been replaced by slivers of ice. My head
ached; my cheek felt bruised. When I opened my eyes I
saw not black but gray, the surface of the Cathedral floor,
granite slabs fitted together so that the cracks between
them were no wider than hairs. I raised myself, coughing
at the stench of my own body, my own filth and that which
surrounded me.

"He is awake," whispered the Consolation of the Dead.
He lay at the other end of the cloister on a pallet strewn
with rags. At his feet lay the white jackal and the aardmen
Blanche and Trey, and half-hidden behind him squatted
Oleander.

I stood. I felt weak, but no longer ill. I felt as though I had
crept from a husk that lay behind me, a shapeless thing
with gray eyes and tawny hair and a beating heart now
stilled. I looked back but only my gray robe lay there.
When I glanced down at myself I saw that I was naked,
wearing only a length of green vine that hung from my
neck to my thighs, a living vine the rich deep green of
summer.

The child's body still hung in the center of the room. I
walked to it and placed my hand upon it, then wrenched it
from the metal spike so that it fell, the head with its tangled golden hair spilling into the blood-filled basin at my
feet and the torso sprawled beside it. I glanced down, then
kicked it so that the rest of the body tumbled into the
basin.

I lifted my head to stare at the Consolation of the Dead
as he watched me. I raised my hand to point, first at the
aardmen and then Oleander.

"Bring me all of the girl children who are still alive in
this place," I said. I turned and walked to the marble
bench upon the dais and sat there upon it.

The Consolation of the Dead regarded me for a long moment, then slowly began to smile.

"It is as you wish, Lord Baal," he replied.

I waited upon the marble bench until they returned. I watched unblinking all that followed, all that I commanded. I felt no need for sleep, or for any sustenance besides that offered me from the stone basin where the Consolation of the Dead presided. I felt nothing, nothing at all.

Part Nine

Winterlong

Jane Alopex joined us at the theater the morning of the eve of Winterlong. We were eating a more formal and elaborate breakfast than we usually did: dried fruits and bread, the last of Toby's gingko brandy and my own sweet-mint tea hoarded all these weeks, pickled carp and a smoked ham from the Zoologists that Toby had been saving for a special occasion. No one said what we feared this occasion was: the last time we would all be alive together.

"Maybe we shouldn't go," Mehitabel said for the tenth time. "Aidan told us, that lazar warned him not to attend the Masque Winterlong."

"But we have to," said Miss Scarlet, sipping from her demitasse. "The Show Must Go On."

Even she sounded doubtful. For all that it was still early morning—the sky was sunless, the trees pleached with snow and ice—we had the air of campaigners working through the night, or of party-goers reluctant to end a bibacious evening. The room smelled of brandy and woodsmoke. A half-dozen empty bottles and the shards of candicaine pipettes added to the scene of exhausted if desperate gaiety. Only Jane seemed unconcerned. She sat beside Miss Scarlet, cleaning her fingernails with a bread knife.

"God forbid the Paphians should miss a party," she said dryly. "If it were up to me, I'd be home in bed. But there were aardmen skulking around the Zoo last night. The animals went half-crazy and I was up all night trying to calm them. When I saw the weather this morning I thought I'd better come here, in case you needed an escort to the House Saint-Alaban."

She looked out at the snow, heavy wet flakes that hissed against the windowpanes. I had seen snow only a few times in my life, and wondered what this storm portended.

"Well, thank you for coming, Jane," said Toby, and poured her the last of his gingko brandy.

That night we talked for hours, Jane and Miss Scarlet and Justice and myself, all of us crowded into the little room I shared with my Paphian consort. I suspected the other Players were up too, Gitana and Mehitabel gossiping in their chamber, Toby and Fabian keeping unease at bay by practicing their fencing in the gymnasium. Justice and I sprawled on one bed, enjoying the luxury of being with trusted friends. A fire smoked in the little stove that heated the room. Jane's boots sent up plumes of steam and a muddy smell where she had leaned them to dry against the grate.

"Will there really be a Final Ascension, d'you think?" she wondered aloud. Through the narrow windows with their panes of diamond glass we could see the snow still slanting down. Now and then a gust would shake the window, and Jane and Miss Scarlet would pull their hassocks closer to the stove.

"My people think so," Justice replied softly. He stroked my neck, staring at me with eyes wide but unafraid. "All the signs are there: the brilliance in the sky the night of the Butterfly Ball, the massacre at High Brazil; aardmen and lazars hunting together in the Narrow Forest; a boy who impersonates the Gaping One, and the Madman in the Engulfed Cathedral. And now it is Winterlong. We have only to wait, and see if the Magdalene awakens as they say She will, to confront the Gaping One."

"A man," Jane snorted. "Remember the Aviator's only a man, and not even much of a man anymore, eh Scarlet?"

She nudged Miss Scarlet's hassock. The chimpanzee shook her head, continuing to stare at the embers glowing in the grate.

"It is the end of something," she murmured. "The end of the way things are now, at least."

Jane tucked her feet under the hassock and glanced over at me. "The beginning of something else, too, I guess." She sniffed, eyeing Justice as he toyed with my hair. "So much for the chaste young Sieur Aidan."

She made a face and turned to Miss Scarlet. "Aw, don't get all worked up over it, Scarlet, it's just another costume party." She tugged at the hair flopping into her eyes, then reached to pat the chimpanzee. Miss Scarlet sighed, adjusted the collar of her gown, and pursed her lips.

"I consulted the pantomancer Zuriel Persia when we gave *The Spectre's Harlequinade* last week," she said.

"That fraud!" snorted Justice. He reached for another candicaine pipette.

I propped my chin on my hand. "So that's why you weren't at the supper afterward," I said. "I wondered."

Justice cracked a pipette beneath my nose. I shut my eyes, tried to think what it reminded me of, this cold rush of pleasure. But all I came up with was the memory of the supper at the House Persia, where Justice and I had lingered with the suzein over candicaine and morpha tubes. Lately all I could think of was Justice, his hands and mouth and the taste of his skin, his hair soft as feathers. When I tried to remember what had haunted me since leaving HEL, the eyes I drew up were not green but blue, the loveliest sapphire blue: a boy's shining eyes and not a demon's.

"*You* needn't have stayed there quite so long, Wendy," said Miss Scarlet. "You two certainly made a sight, carrying on like that."

She pulled up her skirts, stretched her furry legs until her toes curled in front of the glowing stove. "Although I don't imagine it matters much anymore."

She sighed, hunching forward to gaze into the coals. Justice leaned to kiss my shoulder. I closed my eyes and murmured happily, looked up to see Jane Alopex staring at me in disgust. Justice drew three fingers to his lips and made the Paphian's beck, winking.

Jane looked away. "So what did Zuriel Persia, that fraud, *say* exactly? Tell me, Scarlet. I didn't come all this way in a snowstorm to watch the Gaping One roll her eyes at Justice."

"*He said,*" Miss Scarlet began, drawing herself up to

command us with her sober brown eyes, "that the Masque at Winterlong would not be the one traditionally performed."

"Well," said Justice, "we haven't heard that they've changed it, have we?"

I shook my head. I started to reply but Jane silenced me with a glare. "Go on, Scarlet," she ordered.

"I met him in the Chamber of August Divination. He took an impression of my face in heated wax. 'For the Ages,' he said. 'So that we may remember the greatest glory of our Stage.' He was really quite charming, although he had an odd sort of voice."

Jane frowned. *"That* doesn't sound so charming, Scarlet. Taking a death mask before you're dead."

Miss Scarlet shrugged. Outside, the snow tapped against the windows. I moved closer to Justice.

"Well, nothing he said was very encouraging," she admitted. "After the mask he burned some joss sticks, then smoked quite a lot of honeyed tobacco and a pipeful of opium. Then he killed a squirrel—poor thing, it was half-dead already, it looked starved. None of the animals look very healthy this winter, do they? Then he drained its blood into a bowl and he, he—"

She hesitated. At Jane's impatient cough she looked at her, aggravated, and said, "Well, he *drank* it. Really, it seems as though barbarism is quite the fashion these days. But what could I say, when I had consulted him?

"So I waited, while he smacked his lips over the blood and muttered about there not being enough of it; until finally he performed a kind of divination with books. *Stichomancy,* he called it. I was surprised to see that he had books at all. Surprised he could read, actually.

" 'The Curators taught me,' he said. That nasty voice, for all that he was quite handsome. 'These books came from the Museum of Natural History, they gave them to me when I exorcised the Hall of Archosaurs after Nopcsa's murder.' I glanced at some of them—you know how I love to read—but they were mostly very old textbooks, natural-history books I suppose. He chose one at random, then flipped through it and selected phrases—quite aimlessly, *I* thought.

"This is what he gave me."

She took a rolled-up bit of parchment from her reticule, unfolded it, and began to read.

" '. . . the traces of the existence of a body . . . as to the succession of life upon the earth . . . the course of nature will be a continuous and uninterrupted one . . . an interminable vista is opened out for the future . . . the central fire and the rain from heaven . . . all traces of organic remains become annihilated . . . the ancient peace once more came to reign upon the earth.' "

She finished, stared down at the parchment, and then rolled it up and replaced it, closing her reticule with a snap that made me jump. Then she folded her paws upon her lap.

"That is what he told me," she said. "That, and to beware of the Masque Winterlong. 'The Masque of the Gaping One,' he called it. He said *he* would not be in attendance."

"He sounds quite intelligent for a pantomancer and a fraud," said Jane Alopex. "I think you're mad to go there tomorrow, Scarlet. And you too, Wendy, after you've been warned that the lazars plan an attack."

I shrugged. "Anna was—she was never very reliable, actually." I spread my hands in front of the stove. "And really, what else are we to do? The whole City can't hide forever, and you said yourself we have no weapons to fight back with."

Jane said nothing, only turned to stare out the window until Miss Scarlet crept into her lap and engaged her in more cheerful conversation.

So we passed our last night in the theater. The four of us talked until a few hours before dawn, recalling the glories of past performances, giddy sleepless nights of rehearsals and the triumphant applause that followed. We fed the little woodstove with sticks of applewood until first Justice and then Jane nodded off, leaving Miss Scarlet and I watching the embers turn gray and cold.

"There was something else, Wendy."

I started, bumping my chin against Justice's shoulder. I
had almost fallen asleep.

"What, Miss Scarlet?" I mumbled, sitting up.

"What he told me. The pantomancer; there was more
that I didn't tell them."

She tilted her head to where Justice slept beside me and
Jane snored stretched out upon the floor, her traveling
cloak rumpled beneath her. Miss Scarlet smiled wistfully.
She had removed the lace mobcap she wore to cover her
nearly hairless skull, the coarse ridge of fur that bristled
across her head. Her paws kneaded restively at her throat.

"I—I asked him what he saw for me, if he saw anything."
She glanced to make sure the others were really asleep. "I
wanted to know whether—well, you know. If it *was* to
happen, if there really is a Magdalene—whether She
might make me truly human. He put down the book and
closed his eyes, and sat for a long time, so long I thought he
had fallen asleep. I decided he'd forgotten me, and started
to go, to find the rest of you, when he suddenly threw back
his head.

" 'Nothing!' he exclaimed. He looked quite alarmed. 'I
see nothing in this City of a talking chimpanzee, nor of
your companion Aidan Arent, nor his Paphian leman.
Nothing, nothing at all; but of this I will say no more.' "

She was silent then. The snow rattled against the windows. Jane's snores mingled with Justice's gentler breathing. After a few minutes Miss Scarlet crept from her
hassock to Jane's side, and curled in the crook of her arm to
sleep.

A pantechnicon from the House Saint-Alaban arrived
the next afternoon. The Players embarked, Jane Alopex
riding beside us on Sallymae, her pistol hanging from her
waist. Darkness crept across the City, the Narrow Forest's
shadowy fingers groping across the Museums and up Library Hill, to fall just short of the white lawn where sheep
no longer grazed. The solitary young shepherd still stood
guard there, silent and watchful, his round face more

pinched than it had been in the autumn. He watched us pass without a word. Only when the pantechnicon clattered around the curve and began the long slide down Deeping Avenue he raised his hand and called out:

"The Magdalene guard you through Winterlong."

I stood in the back of the wagon and waved, clutching my cape against the bitter wind, and stared until I saw him no more.

The Saint-Alaban elders driving the pantechnicon were well fortified with apricot negus and a steaming tin of hot whiskey that they shared with Toby and the others. Faces hardened or bodies too frail to barter with the City, still they were good-natured, not resentful as were so many Paphian elders. I sat a little apart from them all. Even Justice's company seemed too much for me this afternoon. I smiled wanly as they raised their tumblers to salute me.

"Hang the boy and raise the girl, Arent!"

"We'll break the old whore Winter's back, eh Aidan?"

Then they burst into one of the lewder choruses of "Saint Alaban's Song," stopping often to repeat the words for the benefit of Jane Alopex.

As we turned from the Deeping Avenue toward the Hill Magdalena Ardent, Curators poured from the Museums. Black-clad, brown-clad, they carried tall poles each topped with an animal's skull, whipped by ribbons of green and blue and red. In front of the Museum of Natural History a small group gathered around the slender figure of the new Regent, Clara Brown, and struggled to hoist the immense beribboned skull of an archosaur upon their shoulders. The other Curators stopped to help them, then swept them along in the growing crowd that trailed us. They greeted us boisterously, tromping through the snow and raising their skull-topped icons, tugging the ribbons so that the skulls' jaws clattered as they fell in behind us in a long parade.

At last we mounted the Hill Magdalena Ardent and came to the House Saint-Alaban.

"Sweet Mother, look at them all!" Fabian stumbled against me as the wagon jounced up the icy drive. "The whole City must be here—"

"There's less of the whole City than there used to be,"
one of the Saint-Alaban elders intoned, then hiccuped
"The other Houses decided to throw their luck with us
tonight. They'll all be there. . . ."

He swayed, grabbed a passing pole so that its skeletal
embellishment clacked mournfully. Justice crossed to the
back of the wagon to join me.

"Did you hear that, Wendy? The whole City here! That's
never happened, especially at Saint-Alaban! It really *is* like
the old stories—"

I nodded, took his hand and squeezed it. I felt as though
every nerve in my body was firing at once. Bright images
flared in my mind as the Curators and Paphians shouted—

> ### *"hang the boy and raise the girl*
> ### *'til Winterlong is broken!"*

—figures resplendent as though painted on glass. Aidan
Harrow; Emma Harrow in the Horne Room, flinging a
broken hibiscus blossom into my lap; the Paphian child
Fancy standing on tiptoe to embrace Raphael Miramar, his
face flushed as he gathers her to his breast, as he turns to
me and it is my own face there, my arms enfolding the
child. Sorrow pierces me and I feel my knees buckle. Dark
ness whirls behind my eyes. Justice catches me before I
can fall.

"Wendy—"

I lift my head and see him, his blue eyes worried. Behind
him stands Toby Rhymer staring at me, his hand tight
about a mug of steaming wine. He says nothing but contin
ues to stare. I know then that he heard Justice name me
that he has suspected for some time and now he knows
Slowly a smile creeps across his face as he raises the glass
his eyes glittering.

"Through Winterlong, Wendy Wanders," he murmurs
and drains the mug. He turns to gaze at the House before
us, Paphians like brilliant pennons waving from the step
and balconies and snowdrifted terraces of Saint-Alaban.

* * *

Adonia Saint-Alaban, the suzein of the House, greeted us as we clambered from the pantechnicon.

"Through Winterlong, cousins," she called as she descended the main stairway to the drive. She wore a long tunic of scarlet cloth worked with green thread. Even in mourning, the Paphians would be fashionable. She was older than most of the other suzeins, older than any Paphian I had ever seen. Small and plump, she was still beautiful, with the same slanted blue eyes that marked Justice and Lalagé and others of the House Saint-Alaban. On each high cheekbone a crescent moon was tattooed in red and violet ink. She chanted her words in a voice raspy from years of smoking kef and opium.

"Justice, my dear cousin, *everyone* is waiting to see you!" She made him the Paphians' beck, then kissed him. Behind her, Paphians radiant in gold and crimson and blue swarmed down the steps to join the crowd outside. Some of them began lugging props and baskets of costumes from the pantechnicon. Others brought steaming bowls of wine and whiskey to the Curators, and then helped them carry their macabre standards inside. Still others greeted the Players, bowing to Toby and kissing Miss Scarlet's gloved paws. Before I could rejoin Justice several of his bedcousins lifted him onto their shoulders. Laughing resignedly, he waved to me as they bore him up the steps. After greeting Toby and Miss Scarlet, Adonia Saint-Alaban took me by the arm and led me indoors.

"Dear Sieur Aidan, our House is honored to have you here, tonight of all nights." She leaned against my shoulder, her tongue flicking unsettlingly close to my ear. I smiled uneasily, tossing back the folds of my heavy cape.

"What a lovely costume!" she exclaimed, admiring my boots and crimson tunic. Her eyes lingered on the ornament I wore around my neck, a gift from Justice: a necklace of gold worked to resemble vines and trumpet-shaped flowers like lilies, traded from the Historians.

I nodded my thanks. "Your bedcousin Justice helped me

with it," I said. We paused at a set of massive wooden doors,
flung open to reveal the Great Hall. I blinked at the sudden
blaze of candles and gaslights, huge cylinders of glass and
metal suspended from the ceiling by chains and so dazzling that I had to look away for a moment.

"At Winterlong we set the night on fire to keep the
Gaping One at bay," said Adonia, smiling. Her eyes darted
across the sweep of marble, as though to make sure there
was no corner left unlit.

I wished for a shred of darkness: my eyes ached at so
much radiance. Hundreds of revelers moved across a floor
of polished marble, blazing nearly as brilliantly as the
chandeliers overhead. The masquers seemed to course
through a forest of flame. Evergreens were everywhere,
trees that would have dwarfed the theater but here made
copses of green and silver, their boughs so heavy beneath
dripping candles that I marveled they did not break. Beside each one stood a Saint-Alaban child, clad in shifts of
diaphanous yellow so that their slender forms were silhouetted in the candlelight. The children held salvers of water, and laughed and sprayed one another until their
costumes hung wet and limp. I wondered aloud at this
unreliable method of firefighting.

"Oh, there's never any problem," Adonia assured me.
"The candles are set far beneath the leaves, and besides
the trees were all cut this morning. Green wood shouldn't
burn."

A young boy from Illyria sidled beside her. A wreath of
pine cones crowned his black curls. "The masquers from
Illyria want to know where their seats are during dinner,"
he said.

Adonia's hand fluttered before her face. "Oh! I forgot
and put them with that spado from Persia—well, come
quick, Hilary, you can help—"

Her fingers brushed my mouth and she kissed me fleetingly, so that I had a quick taste of the raw fear beneath her
coy posings. Then she was gone, the spangled hem of her
tunic lost among the masked harlequins and columbines
and mock-Raphaels milling about the room.

I looked around at the trees like waterfalls of fire, the

white smoke curled beneath the domed ceiling high above me. I inhaled the heady scent of evergreens, fir resin, and the hundreds of red roses the Botanists had brought from their greenhouses and piled beside the tinkling fountains where the children refilled their salvers.

She is afraid, I thought. *She is thinking of the lazars and the Madman in the Cathedral.*

I glanced at those around me: Persian dominatrices with tattooed eyelids; three swaggering boys from Miramar; an Illyrian gynander swathed cap-a-pie in ropes of emerald feathers woven to look like verdant leaves. Did they know the lazars had planned an attack this evening? If so, why were they here?

Why was *I* here?

I grabbed a passing girl, a Saint-Alaban with chalk-white face and eyes painted to resemble holly leaves. She went with me laughing, but her smile died when she saw who held her.

"Greetings, cousin," she said gravely. "You honor me, Sieur Aidan."

"What is your name?" I pulled her into a small alcove where a fountain bubbled gaily, hidden behind sheaves of dark-green holly and magnolia leaves. She trembled in my arms. "I will not harm you—"

"I know." Her pupils had dilated with fear, but she did not resist as I drew her face to mine. "Tansy. Tansy Saint-Alaban. I was paired with your consort Justice last year at the Glorious Fourth."

"Tansy," I repeated. I would tap her, learn what it was that made her come tonight and perhaps face her death. "Kiss me, Tansy."

She turned her face from me. I could see tears in her cornflower eyes.

"Why are you afraid, Tansy?" I asked, taking her chin and forcing her to look at me. "I am Aidan Arent, a Player. You've seen me?"

"Yes," she answered, her voice scarcely audible above the fountain. "At the Chrysanthemum Carnival at Illyria."

"Then why are you afraid of me? Why are you here if you are so afraid?"

She gave me a look of such sadness that I let her go. "This is my House," she pronounced with dignity. "In 'The Duties of Pleasure' it says that great sorrow will come to it, but also that a Saint-Alaban will be the one to wake the Magdalene from Her long sleep. We believe that the Final Ascension is coming, now. We believe it will begin at Winterlong. So we are afraid, all of us upon the Hill; but we will not run away. Too many of us are already dead, and what good will it do to flee and join our cousins who have gone to serve the Lord of Dogs?"

I turned to the fountain. The water tasted of oranges, and I splashed some upon my cheeks. "That doesn't answer my question," I finally said, drying my face on my sleeve. "You are afraid of *me*. Why?"

She smoothed her costume, a chemise of blood-red silk that barely covered the tops of her thighs. "Because they say you are the same one who rules in the Engulfed Cathedral, the one who commands our cousins to slaughter us as offerings to him. The Gaping One. The Hanged Boy."

"But I'm not," I said. "How could I be? He rules the Cathedral, and I am a Player. I have never been near the Cathedral—"

She stared at me with huge eyes blank as a small child's. "I do not know how this can be true. But I saw the great star the night of the Butterfly Ball. And for three nights running I have dreamed of monstrous things, wolves with the faces of men racing through a flaming forest, and myself lying dead in the snow. I do not know what any of these things mean, and I am afraid. But I will stay here tonight with my people to await the waking of the Magdalene."

Before I could stop her she turned away. "I will leave you now, Aidan Arent."

Anger throbbed in my temples. I started to snatch her back, to force myself upon her and draw from her that dream, as though it might help me understand this madness. But as my hand fell upon her arm she turned and smiled, then leaned forward to kiss my mouth.

"May the Magdalene guard you through Winterlong, Aidan," she said, and left.

I lingered for a few more minutes by the fountain,

splashing idly at the falling water. *So that is why they are here,* I thought. My anger melted away. This was like the old religions Dr. Harrow had taught us about, the ones that had been suppressed by the First Ascension. To see the waking of the Magdalene. Not even lazars would frighten them from it, and Justice was too embarrassed to tell me.

As I walked out of the alcove I laughed, so loudly that an Illyrian malefeant admiring an evergreen's young steward dropped her whip in surprise. As she retrieved it she bowed, then flashed me a quick smile. "May She guard you through Winterlong, young Aidan."

"May She guard all of us, cousin," I replied.

Our performance of *The Spectre's Harlequinade* was not the evening's highlight. The little play went well, my appearances as the Spectre—costumed after Raphael Miramar, and wearing a crimson death's mask until my final revelation as the ghost of the dying heroine's beloved—provoking not gasps but enthusiastically polite applause. But the Paphians in the treelit ballroom awaited other entertainments.

We took our bows. Adonia beckoned us to where she reclined with visiting Regents and the suzeins of the other Paphian Houses. Gower Miramar sat there, clad in a simple tunic of dark green, his only ornament a wreath of holly. He greeted me but did not smile, nor make the Paphian's beck. I turned to help Miss Scarlet onto the cushion between myself and Justice. Jane Alopex stood nearby, biting her nails as she gazed across the room.

The Great Hall had grown eerily silent. Paphians stood grouped around the blazing fir trees, their bright costumes incongruous with the air of trepidation that had replaced the afternoon's urgent revelry. Beside them stood the Curators, holding their skull-crowned staves. They glanced often at their Regents, but they too were silent. I heard only my own breathing, the hiss of candles, and the purl of water in the fountains. Burning wax nearly overpowered the scents of balsam and roses and musk. Only the youngest children waited with expectant faces, grinning and smirking at one another beneath the radiant trees. Miss Scarlet slipped her hand into mine, her glove not disguising how cold it was, nor how her long fingers trembled. Behind her simple black domino her eyes glanced nervously about the room.

Silence. Then from somewhere high above us came a single deep note, the tolling of a great bell. The tocsin that warned of attack by lazars or fouga strike; the tocsin that also each year marked the beginning of the Masque Winterlong. It echoed into the whisper of flame.

The bell sounded again. A rustle throughout the hall. Heads craned upward. I glanced at the main entrance, where sentries in blue and crimson shifted uneasily, armed with pistols and swivel guns borrowed from the Curators.

A final gong. It scarcely died away when there came a boom, the hammering of a knocker upon the entrance to the Great Hall. The sentries looked to Adonia Saint-Alaban. I saw her take the hand of the Regent at her side, her face dead white except for the scars of the crescent moons upon her cheeks. She nodded. The sentries pulled open the doors.

Flurries of snow rolled through the hall, a bitter wind sent a thousand candles guttering.

"Who will let the Winter in?" cried a voice from the shadows.

No reply; only the wind rushing through the room.

"Who will let the Winter in?" the voice repeated.

Adonia stood, the blast ruffling the fillet of leaves in her hair. "Not I!"

"Who will let the Winter in, who will let the Winter in?" other voices chanted. I glimpsed figures stirring in the darkness outside. Then suddenly the entry was filled with them, throwing back capes heavy with snow to display their costumes, shifts trimmed with gold and silver, tuxedos of very old black satin, robes trimmed with lumens blinking red and green and blue. Their eyes shone behind elaborate masks, masks of flowers and leaves, masks of holly and balsam and magnolia. Vines—dead grape vines, living nightcoils, frail ivy—curled about their brows. They pushed aside the guards, tossing handfuls of rose petals to drift with the snowflakes to the marble floor.

"Send her on," cried Adonia Saint-Alaban, her voice rising shrilly. A Regent grabbed her as she stumbled and pulled her down beside him. I waited for the others to join in, as they had when I tapped Fancy and spied last year's masque, the joyous children and roisterous masquers in the House Miramar. There was silence.

"But there is nowhere left to go."

A masquer stepped forward from the group inside the door. A man dressed as a woman, his blond braid laced with greenery. Beside him was a boy in mask of emerald holly holding a child-sized bow and arrow. "All the City of Trees is here tonight, and Winter is tired of wandering—"

All about me I heard whispers, voices truly fearful now at this breach with tradition.

"Send her on!"

Beside me Miss Scarlet cried out, pulling the domino from her face to show flashing eyes, her mouth bared in a snarl. "Send her on, her power is broken, we light the end of Winterlong!"

The man-woman bowed, turned to gesture behind him. From the darkness a figure strode into the hall, tall and draped in crimson and black. Atop its head was a horse's skull hung with red ribbons. At its side crouched a pair of wolvish creatures with the eyes of men, and between them a small form, gleaming white with glowing ruby eyes. It lifted its head and wailed. The figure with the horse's skull lifted one arm and pointed at Adonia Saint-Alaban.

"There is no end to it. The Lord of Misrule will not be overthrown this time—"

I heard Justice and Miss Scarlet gasp at that voice, heard the sound ripple across the hall as I felt them all turn to me, Players and Paphians and Curators, strangers and friends; then from me to the figure in the doorway now pulling the horse's skull from his head. For the first time I saw him in waking life: his russet hair bound with vines, his gaunt face powdered ghastly white so that his eyes burned above his cheeks.

Raphael Miramar. The Gaping One.

I knocked Miss Scarlet from her perch as I stumbled forward. "No!" I shouted.

He searched the room until his eyes found me. For a moment he stared as his mouth worked silently about a name; my name. Then:

"To me, Scarlet! Wendy, run!"

I heard Jane shout, the click of her pistol turning uselessly; then a booming report. One of the chandeliers shattered, showering us with glass and liquid flame and the smell of gas. A scream. I stepped backward, tripped, and shielded my eyes from the blistering fumes.

Figures raced across the hall. I saw Raphael shouting at the aardmen and lazars. Then he raised his hand. It held something, a globe of dull-colored metal. As Paphians fled past him he threw the globe into the center of the Great Hall. There was a whistling shriek, a soft thump; a deafening explosion. A wall of flame erupted, subsided, and then leaped again as it claimed a stand of evergreens.

"The arsenal!" Miss Scarlet cried. "They found the arsenal beneath the Cathedral—"

Behind her Toby yelled, waving the Players to follow him. Jane grabbed Miss Scarlet. Justice lunged for me, but I was looking for Raphael amid the screaming revelers.

"Let me go!" I shouted, pushing at Justice as he tried to drag me away. "They're looking for me, it's me they want—"

"Stay with me, Wendy!"

I cried out as I tripped over a flaming bough, twisted away from a great evergreen roaring as it tottered and then collapsed.

"Wendy!"

I glimpsed Justice's face, his arm thrown up to protect Miss Scarlet from the embers and flaming branches that pelted them as the tree crashed down. I shouted his name, tried to break through that wall of flame; but it was no use. Smoke rolled over me. Flames seared my cloak. Something slashed against my cheek; I drew my hand away streaming with blood. I covered my mouth, pushed my way through the mass of bodies that crowded me, everyone trying to reach the doors in the torrent of smoke and flame howling through the room.

An explosion from overhead. More screams as glass and metal cascaded down from a window shattered by the inferno. I fell back against a crush of bodies. A struggling woman suddenly collapsed, her breast pierced by a spear of broken glass. Someone else stumbled to his feet. I was thrown down once more. I rolled blindly across the floor to keep from being trampled, until I slammed against the wall. For a minute I lay there dazed, pulling the tattered ends of my tunic to my face and coughing into it as I tried to catch my breath.

After a few moments I raised my head and saw the doorway, midnight blue behind a scintillant tapestry of orange and black and scarlet. It was only a hand's-throw from where I lay. Looking back I saw nothing but a blazing horror, black figures racing screaming through the holocaust, trees bursting into flame, the hanging gaslights exploding and showering the hall with liquid fire. If Justice or Miss Scarlet or the others were back there they were dead. I turned and crawled along the wall toward the doorway, pushing away bodies, some of them already dead, others sobbing or gasping for breath.

At last I reached a spot far enough from the conflagration that I could stagger to my feet and lean against the wall, breathing freely for a moment. I rested, wheezing and wiping my eyes, and kept my gaze from the atrocity behind me.

"Master," I heard suddenly: a voice like a groan of thunder. I looked up at the doors leading outside.

In the opening loomed three deformed creatures made more repulsive by the leaping play of shadow and flame. The tallest raised its great head, snapping its jaws as it weaved from side to side as though looking for someone.

"Master." Its deep voice echoed above the Paphians' screams and the crackling fire. The other two followed it a few paces into the ballroom, snarling and swiping at the masquers trying to flee.

One stiffened, pawed its face as though to disperse the

smoke. It raised its head as though scenting something, then turned.

"Master?" it said again, taking a step toward me. It sniffed, then snarled a command to the others. I started to run, stumbled, and was knocked to the floor by one of the aardmen.

"Master!" it howled. It straddled me with its long legs, its breath worse even than the stench of burning. The others slunk beside it, lowering their heads to gaze at me and sniff doubtfully. One nosed my cheek where it bled, then raised its head and howled. Surely no one could hear it above the din of screams and roaring flame; but someone did.

"Trey—let me see—"

An emaciated lazar in harlequin's breeches, his bare chest and face black with soot and red-streaked. In one hand he clutched a knife, in the other the torn hem of some feckless reveler's costume. The aardman who guarded me stepped back. The boy stared down, coughing and shaking his head.

"Raphael," he murmured. Then he turned and looked around, excited, and yelled, "Raphael!"

"He is gone, little master," said one of the aardmen. "This one, this one?" It pawed at me anxiously.

The boy stared down at me, dropped to one knee, and pointed his knife at my chest. "You are the girl called Wendy Wanders? The actor disguised as Aidan Arent?"

Behind me I heard screams, the boom and crash of a gas chandelier exploding, or perhaps another of the Aviator's explosive weapons. In the ruin that had been the Great Hall of Saint-Alaban trees still burned. I thought numbly of the yellow-clad children, of Justice and Miss Scarlet fleeing through the carnage.

"Yes," I said at last.

The boy dropped his knife in excitement, hastily shoved it into a sheath at his side. "You are," he said. "I can tell, you look just like him—"

"Tell me—" I took his hand, ignoring the aardmen's growls. "My friends, the Players—a blond Saint-Alaban and a talking chimpanzee, a Zoologist girl—have you captured them? Are they alive?"

He gazed down at me, childish eyes in a shrunken face.
"I don't know. Or—yes, maybe, there were guards at the
front gate said they had an animal there—"

It was all I had to hope on. I nodded and let go his hand.
"What will you do with me?" I whispered.

The boy stood, shouted at a group of lazars struggling
with several captives.

"You! Come here, leave them and help me—"

The lazars obeyed, their prisoners staggering for the
gate and what freedom might await them outside.

"Tie her and bring her to the Cathedral," the boy commanded. "I'll go with you to make sure she doesn't escape." He flourished his knife again, but glanced
apprehensively back into the Great Hall.

I did not fight when they bound me, nor when they laid
me on a palanquin stolen from those left outside Saint-
Alaban. As they bore me away I lifted my head to gaze
back at the burning ruins, sparks and smoke leaping
through the snowy darkness, the end of the oldest of the
Houses of the Hill Magdalena Ardent.

There were other prisoners in the long file that made its
way to Saint-Alaban's Hill and the Engulfed Cathedral. I
glimpsed them through gaps in the curtained palanquin
that let in the snow and wind along with a shred of view.
Paphians sobbing and sometimes falling to their knees,
begging their captors for release; Curators walking silently, some still bearing their skeletal standards. The boy
who had overseen my capture—Oleander, he introduced
himself to me almost shyly—would occasionally stick his
head through the palanquin's drapery. He would start to
speak. But fear or shyness would overcome him, and he
would prod me (but gently) or brandish his knife before
rejoining the horde of lazars and aardmen. When I could
peer through the curtains I searched as best I could for
Justice, Jane Alopex, or Miss Scarlet; listened for their
voices among those weeping or cursing or laughing shrilly

in the mob. But I heard and saw nothing; only once imagined Miss Scarlet's voice wafting to me:

> *Whoever the searchlights catch, whatever the loud-speakers blare,*
> *We are not to despair . . .*

But surely this must have been my own imagining.

Now even breathing exhausted me. I coughed ceaselessly, my lungs still heavy with corrosive smoke and the painfully frigid air. But at last I must have dozed, despite the jarring of the palanquin, the aardmen's howls and groans, and the Paphians' piteous cries.

What woke me was silence. The palanquin had stopped, though its subtle motion told me that my captors still bore it upon their hairy shoulders. I sat up, pulled back a curtained panel to peer outside.

We stood on a barren heath near the top of a tall hill. In the darkness about me Paphians and lazars stood without speaking, without moving. Only an occasional cough floated back to me on the wind. The snow had stopped. Across the starless sky swept heavy clouds, so close it appeared they might settle upon the towers and spars of the great edifice looming above us.

From the Zoological Gardens, the Cathedral had appeared to me as a single column, a dark and broken spar much like the Obelisk. But it was not. A thousand spires and turrets and broken towers stretched across the leaden sky. Light rippled across immense windows of colored glass, their patterns shattered or twisted into horrible forms by the passing centuries. Within the soaring vaults of stone grinned fantastic figures, creatures lovelier than any Paphian or more horrible than the geneslaves who bore me to their master: the eidolons of a dead god, a god resurrected by a deranged Aviator and a kidnapped whore.

I shivered. What sort of men had built such a monstrous edifice, how many had labored to bring those stones to life and lift them to unimaginable heights above the black and hungry earth? Did they know that centuries hence it would still stand, that sacrifices would once again be offered within its dismal nave? Even the aardmen cowered at the sight of it, and Oleander stood between them, hugging his thin arms to his chest and shaking his head as though begging to go free.

From within the tallest spire of the Cathedral came a sound. A clang as of a single bell; magnified until the frozen air splintered with its clamor. One of the great windows shone brilliantly, lit by some inner fire. For an instant a dazzling figure glowed from within the labyrinthine patterns of scalloped glass. Young man or boy, one hand raised to grasp a flaming heart, the other clasping the neck of a small white animal. The bells pealed thunderously as it stared out into the night, the Ascendants' abandoned god trapped within the embrasure.

There was a bellow, a deafening explosion. The glowing window burst apart, white flame and smoke tearing through iron mullions and melting glass. I clapped my hands to my ears. Captives and captors alike cried out, sheltering their heads from raining debris.

More shouting; then the flames subsided to a steady flicker. The palanquin lurched forward to the Cathedral's South Gate.

He was gone from me now, the Boy in the tree; but I knew where He had fled.

We crossed the charred earth leading to the gate. Petrified trees littered the ground, and among them the bodies of the dead, their eyes still staring upward, hands clasping at the ground. The air was loud with a humming like that of many wasps. My guardians bore me carefully among these corpses, and thence into the Cathedral.

Inside wandered the numbed guests of the Masque Winterlong, their costumes torn and dragging in the half-frozen muck that covered the floor. Many still held masks before their faces; faces that had been burned or scarred in the conflict with the lazars. A few smoky fires burned from makeshift altars of fallen stone or overturned braziers. Fig-

ures milled about them, haggard children or their shriveled elders clad in rags. They scarcely acknowledged the
newcomers, only glanced as they passed among them. Occasionally a soft cry or shout of recognition would flare up,
to fade into sobbing or anguished shrieks. I thought I
glimpsed Fabian, a tiny figure across the Cathedral's vast
interior; but before I could cry out the aardmen laid my
palanquin to rest. The boy Oleander yanked back the
frayed curtains.

"Come with me," he said. He grabbed my arm, but I
struck him and sent him reeling.

"Don't touch me," I spat.

I stumbled from the litter. The aardmen shied away.
One regarded me with calm yellow eyes, and something
like pity. I rubbed my cheek where the blood had stiffened
and cracked. My hand brushed my throat; I still wore the
necklace of golden vines. "Where are you taking me?" I
croaked.

Oleander sucked at his teeth. "The Aviator would see
you," he said, fingering his blade. I glared at it disdainfully.
"The Consolation of the Dead; and Lord Baal, the Gaping
Lord."

"He is here? Raphael Miramar?" My disdain withered. I
thought of my friends. "What of those I asked about: Justice Saint-Alaban and Miss Scarlet Pan and Jane Alopex?
And the others, the Players from the masque—"

Oleander looked across the nave to where a group of
new captives huddled about a fire. "I told you, I don't
know. But: we were told to take prisoners, not to kill them.
No more than we had to."

No more than we had to . . .

How I longed to rend him, taste his blood and trace
within it whatever path might lead me to my friends, my
beloved leman! I groped at his hand. He pushed me away,
fearful, and commanded the aardmen, "Follow me! To the
Crypt Church—"

They led me down passages so dark that only the
aardmen could tell where to step safely, the only sound our
breathing and their loud snuffling as they sought the way.
Candles glimmered here and there, throwing into sudden

relief the hollow contours of a skull, a sleeping effigy's calm face. Oleander turned to blow out each one as we passed. When I looked behind us I saw only darkness.

At last the passage ended. We stepped into an open space. It was still dim, but enough pale light glimmered from crevices and narrow windows and even torches that I could see. The ceiling rose above us in a series of vaults, leading north and south and east in an endless progression of archways. Rows of tiny candles lined one wall. As we passed, their smell assaulted me, burning fat or flesh.

Some subterranean furnace must have warmed that place. It was cold, but not so frigid as the nave above us. I recalled someone speaking of engines in the earth, was momentarily grateful if they still ran here. But my guards were not eased by it. I smelled the aardmen's fear, and Oleander's blunt terror as he walked beside me.

"What will he do with me?"

The boy jumped at the sound of my voice. I heard his knife slide from its sheath, then slip back again. "I don't know," he replied after a moment. He paused at the intersection of two passages, chose the one lit by rows of tapers set upon the floor, two by two. "We're almost there now."

The passage twisted. A doorway opened before us, iron grates pulled back to show a long room dim with smoke curling from crackling braziers. A raised dais was at one end; before it a sort of tub or basin of stone, stained black along the lip. Many people stood against the walls, children and Paphians and lazars and Curators, gaunt and unmoving. A column reared from the center of the room, pale marble wrapped about with vivid green vines, their leaves shining even in that murky light. Someone sat upon the dais, and something white crouched at his feet.

We hurried through the iron gates into a small alcove, from this into an adjoining alcove that hid us from those watching in the chamber, though we could see them by peering through the narrow doorway. Here Oleander turned and bade the aardmen hold me fast. Then he ripped a panel from my tunic and gagged me with it. He stared at me for a moment, then tugged at the necklace I wore until its clasp gave way and took it.

"Hold her here."

He slipped out. A minute later I saw him weaving through the lazars until he reached the dais. The figure there stepped forward, a small white shape coiling about his legs like a cat. His face was darkened with ash and he had bound back his hair. When he raised his hand to greet Oleander something glimmered there, the faintest lilac.

They spoke softly. I saw Raphael glance back at the alcove and smile. Then Oleander handed him something, a flash of gold in the firelight. Raphael dipped his head and Oleander fastened my necklace about his neck. Then the younger boy stepped back to disappear through a door at one side of the altar.

Raphael stood a little longer, fingering the necklace's intricate turnings of leaf and flower. He stared back at where I stood hidden by the shadows. The aardman Trey whimpered at that look, and tightened his grip upon me. Then behind Raphael something else took shape in the darkness of the doorway. It remained there where I could not see it clearly. Silence, except for the crackling of the braziers, the hissing of tapers set about the floor, the soft stir of lazars shifting their feet where they watched.

Abruptly Raphael looked away, to another alcove opposite mine.

"Bring him here," he said. "I want to see him."

From the alcove two aardmen emerged, half-dragging a third figure. When they reached the center of the room the murky firelight touched his hair with a faint cast of gold. The aardmen pushed him forward roughly, so that he fell to his knees in front of the dais. I tried to cry out, the gag cutting my mouth as I fought against Trey and Fury.

"No, lady," Fury growled softly.

At the foot of the altar Justice crouched, coughing. When he raised his head I saw a gash across his forehead still bleeding slightly. He blinked at the smoke, ran a hand across his eyes, and shook his head, dazed. Then he stumbled to his feet, swaying as though drunk, and looked up.

On the dais stood my brother, clad in torn red tunic, his matted hair pulled back. At his throat shone the necklace Justice had given me. Behind him in the doorway stood the

Aviator. Two aardmen supported him, their slanted eyes
livid in the firelight.

"Wendy," Justice said. He shook his head again, wincing,
and looked back at Raphael.

"Yes, Justice," Raphael called softly. He held out his
hands and beckoned Justice toward him. About his wrist
glowed a band of violet light.

Justice took a step toward the altar, stopped. At
Raphael's feet the white animal, dog or small wolvish creature, stared with blazing eyes at my lover. A murmur
passed through the chamber; several of the children
turned away or covered their eyes. Still no one spoke or
tried to warn him. I tried to scream, choking on the cloth
in my mouth.

"Do not watch," croaked Fury. He tried as gently as he
could to twist my head from the sight. I kicked at him until
he loosened his grip and I could turn to watch.

Very slowly Justice mounted the steps, slowly as someone in a nightmare. I shut my eyes and tried desperately to
draw something up, tried to turn his steps as I had those of
countless dreamers at HEL. But when I opened them
again he had mounted the last step and stood unsteadily
before Raphael, his hands open before him.

"Wendy! I was so afraid—"

He took one last step, reaching for Raphael's hand. As he
did so my brother embraced him, pulled him to his breast,
and bowed his head so that their hair fell in tangled waves,
mingled gold and russet. Raphael caressed him, murmuring. There was an uncanny lavender glow against Justice's
neck.

My brother stepped away. For a moment Justice stood
before him, confused. He touched his throat, as though to
ease a bruise there. My twin gazed at him, toying with the
gold chain around his neck.

"You are mine now," he said.

Justice raised his eyes to Raphael and choked out a single
word, his knees buckling.

"Miramar—"

He sank to the floor and was still.

Raphael turned to the shadows behind him, raised a

shaking fist encircled by a band gone dark and gray. Without looking back he strode across the altar to the sanctuary. The white jackal sniffed at Justice's body, then turned and darted after Raphael. The Aviator let him pass. He stared out across the nave to where I stood, Fury and Trey pressed close against me. He made a cutting gesture with his hand.

"Ungag her and bring her to the armory," he called. He turned and followed Raphael.

Fury struggled with my gag. As it fell to the floor I commanded him, "Free me!"

The aardmen stared at me uneasily, tails switching.

"Free me!"

Trey crouched, growling, then dropped his hold and loped across the room to the sanctuary. Fury stared after him. "Please," I whispered.

He let go of me. I stood shivering, rubbing my arms. Before me flames darted across the floor, licking at pools of melted tallow and dried grass and ruined cloth. I walked slowly from the alcove to where Justice lay upon the steps. In the shadows the silent lazars watched.

"Justice."

I knelt beside him, brushing back his long hair to see a tiny mark upon his neck, like an insect's bite. A drop of blood no larger than a bee's eye pearled there. I touched it, brought it to my lips not caring if it were poison. Then I bent to kiss him, pulling oh so gently at his jaw still warm in my fingers. My tongue slipped between his teeth, his mouth unyielding now for the first time, the only time, as I kissed him, my Justice, kissed him and found nothing, nothing at all: only my own tears falling upon his lips and throat and he was not there, he was gone, gone past all redeeming. Justice Saint-Alaban whom I had loved was dead. The Gaping One had claimed him.

I drew back, stunned. Dark bruises had begun to erupt on his skin, the beautiful pale skin that had not been a vanity to him. And at the thought of that, of his beauty ravished in death, horror and grief overwhelmed me so that I knotted his hair about my fingers and began to sob. Fury crept to the altar to slink warily between the flames.

The lazars slipped from the shadows and approached me, murmuring.

I wept then, who had never wept before; while behind me in the crypt I could hear the hiss of the bonfire where they would lay him—my friend and companion, who had led me from HEL and lived only long enough to teach me the beginning of love.

And now I would never know what it was to be human; now all there had been of love in me would burn upon a madman's pyre. My brain seethed as though it might explode, as inside me I heard the weeping of all the ones I had taken, all those who had gone to feed the Gaping One: Emma and Aidan, Morgan Yates, Melisande, all the others for whom it had been too much, this life, this waking horror that was the world; their voices rising to a shriek, until I shook and my hands dropped from him.

And I screamed, striking at a lazar who had reached to touch Justice's hair. She fell back, her head striking a marble pillar. She slipped to the floor, a seam of blood like a crack upon her pale face.

"Don't touch him! Don't try to hold me!" I shouted. *"None* of you can hold me!" Another child slipped and fell in his haste to run from me. I lunged to grab him, held him above me, and hurled him across the chapel. He screamed, and the voices of the other lazars echoed his end.

"The Gaping One, the Gaping One!" they cried. "He wakes, he wakes—"

I stood, panting as they cringed in the shadows of the Chapel, weeping and coughing from the bitter smoke. Then someone else limped from the altar, the reflection of firelight scorching his tattered crimson jacket until he seemed another flame approaching me.

"No!" he shouted, kicking a knot of crouching children so they scattered like a nest of voles before a stoat. *"That* is not the Gaping One!"

He staggered toward me: the Consolation of the Dead, the mad Aviator, Margalis Tast'annin. The torn jacket flapped like some withered basilisk clinging to his shoulders. From its tattered sleeves hung myriad tiny bones that clattered as he moved.

I stood frozen, staring; and finally I knew why they feared him: because now I too was afraid.

"Go back," I hissed. "I will destroy you—" I bared my teeth and swiped at the air in front of his face.

"You are not the Gaping One," he said. He jabbed at me, knocking me to the floor, then grabbed my shoulders. I could smell the plague on him, the fetor of rotting flesh. I fought him with all my strength, twisting, snapping at the air until my teeth felt his skin split beneath them. He swore, kicked me as his blood ran into my mouth and I choked, trying to find the strand there that would unleash the horror upon Tast'annin and disable him. I tried to escape, but succeeded in getting my head free so that I could shut my eyes and try to call it forth, the One who lived inside me, the Boy who lived on blood. . . .

There was nothing there.

Not a thought, not a darkness, not even the black wraith of a nightmare to feed it. Instead I gagged, my mouth filling with hot blood. As when I had tried to tap Justice when he died: He was gone, truly gone. I was helpless before the power of those who worshiped the Gaping One.

I was bound again, my legs left free so that I could walk. Trey and Fury watched me as the lazars dragged Justice's body away, the children looking at me fearfully as the Aviator shouted at them to hurry. Then I was alone with him in the Crypt Church, with only the aardmen guarding me.

"Wendy Wanders. Subject 117."

He licked his cracked lips and reached for a taper burning upon the altar. Dried blood caked one side of his face so that it appeared he wore a grisly half-mask. He raised the candle, held it close enough to my cheek that it burned me and I turned away. "Emma's prize subject. You led us quite a chase, Wendy; and for what? It doesn't even work anymore, does it? You couldn't save your friend, you couldn't fight me. What good are you now, Wendy?"

I spat at him. He laughed, drew the candle to my temple

until I heard the hiss of hair burning and smelled where he scorched me. Beside me Fury growled. "The scars are gone, you can't even tell anymore, can you? I would have given anything to see how you did it; but I don't suppose we'll ever know now, will we?"

He stepped back, kicking at something: a heap of bones, the twisted remains of a white robe. A skull clattered across the floor and came to rest beneath a smoking brazier. He stared after it for a long moment, then turned to me.

"I asked them to show it to me once. Aidan Harrow told me. He told me everything. I was his confidant, his only real *friend* at the Academy—

" 'Show me,' I begged him; 'let me see what it is.' I wasn't afraid of it, you see, as he was and Emma was. I knew even then that this was something that shouldn't be kept a secret.

"But he was a coward, Aidan, and we all know what happened to him." He laughed, flicked melting wax so that it spattered my arm. "Emma was no coward but she was a fool, to think she could hide this—"

"She didn't know what she was doing!" I tried to pull away from the aardmen, but they only held me tighter. "The implants were part of her research—"

"She knew exactly what she was doing." His voice was very soft. He took my chin in his hands and turned it so that I faced the brazier and blinked in its fiery light. "Not so pretty as you were, Wendy Wanders." He traced a jagged cut upon my cheek, and I winced as he prodded where I had been burned at Saint-Alaban. "She knew there had been a boy, your twin brother; I read it in your file. She hoped to awaken this—*thing*—she wanted to see it again. . . ."

I closed my eyes, trying to recall Him, the face peering from spring leaves and the color of His eyes. But it was Justice's face I saw, pale beneath the film of blood, his eyes dead and gray. They were both gone: gone as though it really had been a dream. Justice dead. The other had forsaken me as He had Aidan and then Emma; and they had killed themselves to find Him again. That beautiful face, those eyes . . .

When I looked up the eyes boring into mine were pale blue and threaded with blood.

"Why?" I asked. I struggled to shake myself free of the aardmen. Tast'annin glanced at them, nodded. They stepped back to crouch in the shadows. "Why would you care after all this time, about—about Emma, and me, about all of this?"

His gaze drifted upward, seeking something in the smoke-blackened figures that watched us from the vaulted ceiling. "I told you, I was Aidan's friend," he said at last. "I wasn't—happy—about his relationship with his sister. And I was curious.

"To see a god like that, or a demon; even just a hallucination! Something that strong, something to die for—surely you can understand that, Wendy?"

He was silent for a long time, staring at me and then past me, seeing something in the darkness of the Crypt Church, something perhaps in the bones he had scattered across the floor.

Finally he said, "There is a play the courtesans have, a play about twins."

I nodded, my flesh prickling. "The masque of Baal and Anat."

He beckoned at Fury. The aardman slunk back beside me, Trey following. "That's right. *Baal and Anat.* I have seen it many times, I had the children perform it for me. But then I thought, how much better if there were *real* twins, that would give it more impact, more—"

He waved at the air, his hand stabbing at my chest. "More *depth,*" he finished.

"I—I don't know the play," I stammered. "It's a sacred text of the Paphians, of the House Saint-Alaban. Waking the Magdalene—"

"It's very simple, really. A sort of sacrificial drama. They fight. One dies, the other doesn't. I've arranged a place for the performance—"

Abruptly he turned away, gesturing at the aardmen. "Bring her to the armory."

He sounded weary, and limped as he crossed the altar. Before he reached the door leading upstairs he looked back at me.

"Even I must serve something," he said, and began to climb the stairs.

I was half-carried out of the Cathedral. The wind had fallen, the air was still and cold and silent except for muted voices in the distance. A few stars showed through the clouds drifting across the sky. Trey and Fury dragged me hurriedly across the frozen ground, their flanks rippling as they shivered in the darkness. About me I heard the sounds of running feet, coughing, and urgent whispers.

In a few minutes Trey and Fury skidded to a stop, snarling and snapping. I fell between them, tried to brace myself against the ground. There was nothing there. Inches in front of me the earth fell away abruptly. At my side the aardmen hunched, panting.

We were on a ledge ten or fifteen feet above a gaping hole large enough to swallow the Crypt Church. Brilliant white light streamed from it. Many figures moved there, black against the glaring lanterns.

They had excavated a great pit in the earth. Frozen mounds of dirt and gravel surrounded it, heaps of stone and sand lay scattered about its floor. It was the ruins of an ancient arsenal. Banks of monitors and metal pilings, immense shining globes and myriad metal chairs had been lined around the perimeter in a feeble attempt at order. Spikes and rotting timbers protruded from the earthen walls, hung with lanterns or chains or frayed costumes.

In the center of the pit loomed some kind of launching mechanism, its hollow nose pointed skyward, jointed steel legs splayed across the uneven ground like those of a mantid. From within it protruded a long silvery missile. Nearby a small generator had been propped, its tiny operating lights blinking red and green through a film of dirt. Wires strung from it led to floodlamps pitched from crazily tilted poles and scaffolding made from warped wood and metal rods. The whole place was blindingly lit, so that it was impossible to ignore those who had died during the excavation, the stench of bodies heaped along the walls and beneath the launcher.

"Come," said Fury. He nosed at the earth until he found something, the lip of a rickety metal ladder. He mounted it with difficulty, hind legs scrabbling at the narrow struts as he clambered down, until finally he slipped and fell the last few feet. Shivering, I followed, my hands sticking to the freezing metal, and stepped carefully to the bottom. Trey crouched at the rim of the pit, his eyes glowing as he stared down at us. After a moment a smaller shape joined him, foxy muzzle and ruby eyes watching shrewdly.

"This way, lady," Fury ordered. I turned to follow him. Lazars squatted exhausted against the walls. Others dragged more captives down from above, and hurried to avoid us as we passed. I shielded my eyes against the glaring lights, stumbling against broken chairs, the gutted shell of some kind of robotic server. Beneath the missile launcher the ground had been swept clear except for a few metal screws, a tooth, and shards of glass. "Here," said Fury.

As he turned away another voice cried my name, hoarse but unmistakable.

I whirled, tripping so that I grabbed one of the launcher's legs to keep from falling. In the shadows behind a narrow scaffold stood Jane Alopex, her arms held tightly by a slender lazar still wearing a columbine's purple shift. A bruise welled beneath one eye, but she held her head high and stared at me with relief.

"Jane!" The word came out in a whisper. Then I nearly wept, because from behind her a smaller figure emerged dragged by a lazar scarcely bigger than herself. Her gown filthy, mobcap gone, limping slightly because she wore only one boot. "Miss Scarlet—"

Another person was pushed forward. Fabian, staring dazed at the ground. Even at this distance I could see him shaking, his torn clothes fluttering from thin wrists. Of Toby and the others I saw nothing.

"Well! We seem to have all the principals assembled. Not as large a cast as usual, but sure to be an interesting one."

At the base of a ladder weaved Tast'annin, clutching at Oleander and Trey for support. Behind him stood Raphael Miramar, calm as though just awakened from untroubled sleep.

I drew myself up and called out, "Let my friends go free, Tast'annin! You have no fight with them, you had none with Justice—" I stammered the name, halted.

Tast'annin shook his head. He looked weary beyond belief, his eyes sunk within his ravaged face, his face almost bloodless as it turned from me to Raphael. As his gaze lingered upon my brother loathing writhed across his features, loathing and a dull sort of recognition. He raised one hand to Raphael, with the other grasped at Trey as though to pull him closer. For a moment I thought he would speak, command the aardmen to bear my brother back into the fastnesses of the Engulfed Cathedral, and slay him there as a final offering to the Naked Lord.

Then the light died in his pale eyes. He turned back to me, his voice a raven's croak.

"No. It must be done—"

He pointed at the far wall where Fabian cowered beside Jane Alopex. "You—whore there, you *actor*—introduce them."

Tast'annin's hand flailed at the air. Fabian gasped, then was shoved forward into the ring of light.

"What—I don't—"

"The masque of Baal and Anat," prodded Tast'annin. He leaned heavily upon Oleander. The boy grimaced, moved the belt and sheath around his waist, and stepped forward bearing his master. Raphael followed them, then walked until he stood a few paces from me.

"The masque—" Fabian began in a wavering voice. The Aviator stared at him coldly, his lip catching on one upper tooth. "The masque of Baal and Anat, performed by—by—"

Tast'annin grinned and clenched his fist. A cry as Fabian was struck and sank to the ground, and another lazar stood pale and trembling where he had.

"You may begin," whispered Tast'annin. "Wendy—Raphael—"

My brother stared back at the Aviator as though for the first time. His hair had fallen unbound to his shoulders; his face was white as ash, his mouth red against its pallor. Blood caked at the corners as though he had been bitten. My necklace still hung about his throat. Then he turned to gaze at me, his unearthly calm finally shaken.

There was not a sound, not a breath, in that place. I felt as though even the freezing air had fallen away; I felt nothing, nothing at all.

"Wendy?" he asked, so softly that I almost could not hear him. He reached one hand to touch me, his fingers sliding from my wrist to my arm. Maybe I did not really hear him, maybe it was only that I knew what he would say, perhaps the name had been fluttering in my mind waiting only for him to say it. Not Aidan Arent but Wendy Wanders. Not a solitary wanderer but Raphael's sister; not a research subject but a real girl. He stared where his fingers stroked my arm, marveling, shut his eyes for a moment as he traced the crook of my elbow.

"You're just like me." He pulled me closer, until our faces almost touched. I could smell the blood on him, the breath of poison that had claimed Justice. I wanted to draw away from him but could not. To see him like this, to touch him for the first time; to realize that it was true, that all these years there had been this other part of me, this changeling boy living in the City of Trees, and never knowing it, never knowing me; never knowing him. He stroked my face, took my hand, lifted it so that I could see our fingers entwined and the same thin wrists, the same broken nails and slender fingers, then pulling back my other sleeve to show me my arm, his arm, the veins like new young vines and their patterns both the same. He dropped my hand and gazed into my eyes once more.

"You are so beautiful," he whispered. And staring at him I nodded, and murmured his name; because it was so. I glimpsed the beauty that had held the City in sway, the sweetness in his features beneath their film of blood; the high cheekbones and gray eyes that, had they not been so striated by fatigue and madness, would have been lovelier than any eyes I had ever seen, lovely eyes, eyes I dared not meet in dreams, the eyes of the Boy in the tree . . .

And suddenly I saw it, saw Him; suddenly I knew that *this* was what Miss Scarlet had glimpsed at our first meeting, and knew at last what it was those others had seen through me:

A demon, a god. Revenant and revered one, the eternal victim and He who holds the knife. A boy of unearthly beauty, different from the One who had haunted me but also the same, as Raphael was like me and yet not me; as though Raphael's corporeal body had been transformed and this other one shone through him as though he were a beaker of clear water. As I gazed into those eyes I knew that He had found His final place, He had found His way into the world. I had been an imperfect vessel; Raphael Miramar had become His ideal host.

"Wendy. My sister—"

He drew my face to his and kissed me. For one instant I felt in him a spark of something that was neither hatred nor desire but perhaps relief, and peace. Then he groaned, turned so that his cheek crushed against mine. His eyes clenched shut as though to keep from seeing some horror beside him. His hands clutched my side, his tongue slipped between my lips as he pulled me tight against him.

"No—" I cried, trying to pull away.

But in this, at least, he was different: he was stronger than I was. I fought and bit, tried to scratch at him, went mad thinking, *This is the one who killed him, this is the one who murdered Justice;* but it was no use. Neither hatred nor will nor force could shake him from me. My struggle only aroused him more until finally I kicked him, knocking him aside for a moment as I fell. I staggered to my feet. He threw himself against me and knocked me down, then grabbing my shoulders forced me back and smashed my head against the earth, so hard that it felt as though he had taken a knife to my temple. I nearly passed out from the pain; perhaps I did. . . .

* * *

Because now there is a thrumming in the air, a sound
like wind in the leaves or something else, a sound I have
never heard, not in waking; only perhaps in dreams. The
sound of waves returning to some distant shore, the sound
of voices chanting. Gradually their words become clear:

> We came upon Baal
>   Stricken on the ground:
> Mot had slain him. We cried,
>   "Puissant Baal is dead,
>   The Prince, Lord of Earth, is perished."

> Our lamentation wakes Anat.
> She descends from the throne,
> Pours dust of mourning on her head.
>   In her face she cuts a gash with a stone,
> She gashes her cheeks and her chin,
>   She plows her breast like a garden,
> Harrows her back like a plain.
>   She lifts up her voice and cries:
> "Baal's dead!—what becomes of our people?
>   What becomes of the earth?
>   After Baal I'll descend into earth."

> Anat goes and wanders
>   Every mount to the heart of the earth,
>   Every hill to the earth's very bowels.
> She comes to the Wasteland
>   To the horror of Mot's field.
> She comes upon Baal
>   Stricken on the ground.
> Then weeps she her fill of weeping;
>   Deep she drinks tears, like wine.

> Loudly she calls
>   Unto the Mother above.

"Lift Puissant Baal, I pray,
  Onto me."

The Mother wakes.
She picks up Puissant Baal,
Sets him upon his sister's shoulder.

Anat lifts up her voice and cries:
"Now will I sit and rest,
And my soul be at ease in my breast.
For alive is Puissant Baal,
My brother, king of the earth."

When I open my eyes once more I see him above me, his hands tight about my shoulders as he thrusts against me, grunting, his face contorted into a mask of such despair and terror that I try to turn my head so as not to see it, not to see him, my own face there above me in the throes of such torment as I can no longer imagine, a horror even worse than mine at being ravaged by him.

But He is too strong; I cannot look away . . .

And suddenly they are there with me, all of them: Morgan Yates with her face pressed against a bloodstained window, Emma Harrow staring as her brother's body twists slowly from a leather belt, Jane Alopex recoiling as He turns to her and extends His hand, Fabian a gray wraith twisting in the night. Just as suddenly they are gone. I am alone. It is me there, for one moment my own face hangs above me in the darkness, not Raphael but Wendy. Then he tosses back his head and cries out: a scream that echoes from the walls and is taken up by those who watch, until the air is filled with it: a shriek of such horror and misery and loathing that it deafens me, and I shut my eyes so as not to see the anguished face that would make such a sound.

It is over. He rolls from me and lies prostrate upon the blackened earth. I turn onto my side to stare at him, reach to touch him: my consort, my enemy, my brother. He does not move; he lies there as though dead.

A shadow falls across his face. Dimly I become aware of

other sounds; cries and the sound of fighting, metal against metal, granite crushing bone. There is a smell of burning, of flesh. Above me stands the Aviator. Blood slicks his arm and hand, and he holds a piece of metal like a bloodied scythe.

"Kill him!" a voice shrilled. I twisted to see Oleander hanging from a spike beside the ladder, his face contorted as his arms flailed. Blood frothed from his mouth as he strove to free himself. *The missiles—he will destroy us all —kill him!"*

His hand flopped against his side. With his last bit of strength he pulled a knife from the folds of his trousers and tossed it. It skittered across the floor and halted beside my brother's body.

With a roar Tast'annin leaped from where he swayed above me. Stumbling against the ladder he raised his arm, the light blazing crimson from his scythe as it struck at the boy's neck. For one instant Oleander's mouth mirrored Tast'annin's own, a frozen mask of loathing and horror; then with a rush of blood his head toppled from his shoulders.

"Kill him?" shouted Tast'annin. But no one seemed to hear him but me. Everywhere lazars ran blindly, scrabbling at ropes and ladders, kicking as they fought to climb the walls of the pit. "Kill him? No one can kill him! It is the Final Ascension: he will rise again!" His voice rose to a scream, bubbling from his twisted mouth so that I could not be certain what words I heard and what I only imagined in my delirium. "He is not dead, he doth but sleep—"

Then there was a flash of light. The generator exploded with a hollow sound, showering me with sparks. Tast'annin disappeared in the shadows. There was only torchlight and a few sullen candles glowing fitfully above the melee.

I turned dully to stare at the stricken form on the ground in front of me: so like myself I might have aligned my body beside his, the two of us forming twin curves of a human arabesque, gray eyes deadened, tawny hair a wasted wave upon this bleak shingle, our broken limbs entwined cold and unmoving. Raphael Miramar. Neither god nor Gaping One: only my brother given to the dark.

"Kill him," another Voice whispered. I lifted my head; but Tast'annin had forgotten me. I heard him growling as he lunged and struck at something in the dark.

—Kill him, Wendy.

The yellow points of the lazars' torches guttered and went out. With them it seemed the very voices of the lazars died. A terrible silence encloaked me, although I could still see the wraithlike figures of the damned children soundlessly spinning about the abyss, contorted like insects trapped in a lamp. Even the pounding of my heart stilled. For a moment I thought, *We are all dead.*

Then, from the charred ground in front of me a brilliant white flame leaped up like a fountain, a flame with neither heat nor color besides that painful argent. The stench of rotting flesh arose with it. I blinked and shielded my eyes and mouth.

—Oh, Wendy, the flame sighed. The brilliant light danced and faded to a harsher yellow, then began to shape itself into a more substantial form. Slowly it rose and fell, as though trying to draw strength from the freezing air.

—Poor Wendy! Alone now, you are truly alone—

—But I can still hear you, Small Voice, I said in surprise. If I am alone you must be gone—

—No. I am still here, for the moment. Kill him, Wendy. He is an abomination; you cannot both live. Kill Raphael.

With difficulty I turned from the flame; it seemed to will me to stare at it, be consumed by it. But I looked back down at the boy lying there. So frail now, and white. His eyes were closed but I knew that even if he opened them there would be no light there, no reflected glory to madden me, no maenad's Dionysus there now but only a broken shell.

—Kill him, hissed the flame. *There is a knife, take it and kill him!*

I nodded and reached for the knife Oleander had thrown: a golden knife with a curved blade, so keen the light refracted from its edge in dazzling waves of blue and white. I held it a long time. It seemed to have no weight at all in my hand.

—*Kill him,* the flame repeated. *Kill him, Wendy.* Each time it leaped higher beside me.

—Be quiet, I commanded it. I was trying to remember something, something the Boy had told me at the Zoo:

We will meet again . . . but you may not remember my names. Although perhaps by then you will recall your own . . .

—*Your name?* the flame screamed. *Your name? You know it now! Kali is your name, and Athena; and Morgan and Mayuel; Clytemnestra and Artemis and Hecate!*

"No," I said suddenly. I recalled that strange sound, a noise like waves, like many women chanting. "I am Anat, the consort of my brother Baal. But I am also Wendy Wanders, the lover of Justice Saint-Alaban.

"I am the Magdalene."

I stared down at him, the bright one broken, my own face stricken and bloodless before me, Raphael Miramar, Aidan Harrow, the Hanged Boy: my beautiful brother in the dark.

And there came to me then a great sound, the sound of singing. And I saw all of them, Emma and Aidan, Gligor and Merle and Anna, Dr. Silverthorn and Toby Rhymer, a white dog with eyes like burning ice and a girl who longed to fly with finches, all of them like lights dancing in the air. With them shrilled the voices of the lazars like wounds bleeding song, all of them crying out to me. Loudest of all was the piercing cry of a boy with fair tangled hair and green eyes, his hands streaming through the darkness like the purest moonlight and his eyes two burning stars. And the song they sang had only one note and one sound and one word, and the word they sang was Death; the song they sang was Supplication to slay him there where he lay with his white throat awaiting the knife, his eyes shut against the blade. And the song they sang went on and on and on, their voices grew higher and louder until the sky whirled with them and the stars began to wink out one by one. And within me I felt my heart wither, and the knife Oleander had tossed me grew heavy and cold in my fist as I raised it above my brother.

As abruptly as it had begun the singing ceased. I heard

only a dull hissing from the flame still flickering before me.
I stared at the golden blade in my hand, then carefully
looked around. Where the flame leaped a fissure had
opened, a black pit that descended endlessly into the
earth. Unsteadily I got to my feet. I walked to the edge of
the pit and stared down into it. Then I dropped the knife.

For a moment it seemed to hang in the air, blindingly
golden, a scythe or perhaps a crescent moon. Then it fell,
its light extinguished. With a shriek that deepened to a
thundering roar the flame leaped as though it would con-
sume us all, leaped until the sky vanished as though behind
a curtain of light. The flame dwindled, and finally disappeared. I blinked, trying to adjust to the darkness, and
walked to my stricken brother.

Something moved behind me. I whirled around, and
there stood Miss Scarlet, rubbing her arms where the ropes
had fallen from them. Only with her bonds it seemed that
the dark hair had fallen from her arms and face so that they
gleamed like smooth brown glass, and she stepped delicately from a shriveled thing like a filthy robe of fur and
walked toward me. And though I knew her face it was
changed. Instead of the shrunken features of a wizened
monkey I saw now that she was a woman, and suddenly it
seemed to me that she had *always* been a woman. It had
been myself that was the blind animal, and my own eyes
had never seen before the colors that the world showed to
me now, the colors that Miss Scarlet Pan saw as well and
laughed to see.

From the ground beneath my brother a faint light glittered, and grew brighter, until the black stones cracked
and split like a great fruit. And to my amazement it was not
my brother who lay there after all. It was Justice. But
Justice as I had never seen him, laughing with joy as he
leaped from the frozen earth and reached for me and glad,
so glad! to see me. He gathered me to him and then it was
myself who was laughing and crying to see him again, not
dead but alive, alive! and his hands warm about me and his
mouth soft and laughing as he pulled me to him.

As he drew me to him he also reached for Miss Scarlet.
He pulled her to him as well, until the three of us stood

Dante

embraced. It seemed the world had stopped turning except for our mingled tears and laughter and their hands in mine, hands strong and small and strong and large. And suddenly I felt inside me the vibration of my heart thrumming and my breath coming loud and hard in sobs that were not sorrow but a joy I had never known. I don't know how long we stood there; a long time, I think, because when I opened my eyes once more I blinked at the light: not lantern light but dawn. I drew away from Justice and Miss Scarlet.

At my feet lay Raphael. He was bathed in golden brilliance. I heard a wailing as of some creature falling from the air and looked up. I saw the stars, one by one, coming into sight once more, and the sky folding itself back like the dark underside of a leaf turning to the rain.

I drew my breath and turned to my friends there beside me, Justice and Scarlet Pan. Justice looked at me and smiled. He took my face in his hands and kissed it, and said, "Now you know, Wendy. Now you are truly awake and you can see, it's not all horror and confusion; even death."

I kissed his mouth. "Now I know."

He stooped to lift Miss Scarlet and kissed her as well; and then holding her he turned to me and said goodbye.

"But it's only started," I cried.

He nodded. His eyes were not sad, but still they held something in them of pity.

"I know," he said; "but I have to go on, you see. Because I've done what I had to do. And besides, I've already left."

He set Miss Scarlet gently back upon the ground and pointed to where my brother lay, his face so pale and his eyes twitching beneath their lids in troubled sleep.

"There is your brother to be made whole," he said. His arms swept out to encompass the dark pit about us, barren glassy Saint-Alaban's Hill and the sky pale and still, the lazars still struggling to flee. "A City to be made whole, a world perhaps . . ."

He took me once more and kissed me, and I wept. But this time there was no bitterness, nothing of vengeance or horror but only sadness to see him go.

"You still have your good Angel there," he said, smiling

as he pointed to Miss Scarlet. "Even though you have grown a conscience of your own."

He touched me on the forehead and quoted, laughing softly: " 'If you learn to be brave, honest, and unselfish, then you will become a real girl.' "

He bowed to us both, drawing three fingers to his mouth in the Paphian's beck, then dropped one and then the other until only his index finger remained upon his lips.

"Remember, Wendy: It is all one," he whispered. "Death and growth and desire and fear. It is all one." He was gone.

I stood, dazed, and stared at the sky. Above me reared the launcher. As I watched it shuddered, then recoiled as with a tremendous shriek the missile shot from it, speared the clouds and burst into flames of white and red. The launcher shuddered again, then was still. After a moment debris rained down like hail, but I was heedless of it striking me.

The explosion in the heavens faded to black smoke, streamers of gray and white. In the distance the horizon glowed pale pink. The Cathedral's dark spires pointed heavenward where the last stars gleamed faintly: all but one that flared brightly and then faded to a prick of white like the others upon that black map. Beside me stood Miss Scarlet: not a woman but the same small wizened figure as before, staring at her gnarled hands in disbelief.

"Wendy?" She turned to me pleading. Her eyes fell upon Raphael, the small forms scattered about the pit, and she was quiet. After a moment she said, "It doesn't matter, really, does it? We're alive, at least—"

"Yes," I said. I reached to take her small hand. "But it did happen; something did happen."

For a moment we stared at each other, and I wept to remember Justice Saint-Alaban.

Then a shout rang through the air. We turned, and saw against the wall something slumped beside a small body covered with a rainbow cloak. The Aviator lay there, dead, his ruined face staring at the dawn. Above him stood Jane Alopex, disbelief turning to joy as she waved her pistol, then with a whoop threw it so that it bounced over the rim of the pit. I smiled despite my sorrow, and looked down.

He lay there still, the broken boy; but his face was not so tormented as it had been. It seemed even that he might dream of gentle things, for his eyes no longer twitched beneath their lids, and the soft full curve of his mouth now turned slightly upward. I stood a moment, then looked to the east where the sky now was yellow. I waited until the first brilliant blade of sunlight sliced across the Cathedral's tallest tower. I stooped and brushed the tangled hair from my brother's brow, and kissed him upon the forehead.

"Wake, Raphael," I whispered. His eyes twitched and opened to stare at me, a gray flash of alarm that faded as quickly as the stars.

"Wh—" he started, but I touched his mouth with my finger.

"We are waking now," I said, and stood.

Behind me Jane started to say something, fell silent. I felt Miss Scarlet's hand slip into mine.

"Where are we going?" she asked. "Or doesn't it matter now?"

I shrugged. "I don't know. Well, yes; I suppose it probably does."

I brushed the hair from my eyes. I took Miss Scarlet into my arms and with Jane behind me climbed the ladder until we stood above the pit, gazing down from Saint-Alaban's Hill.

The sun had risen above the horizon, and I could see the entire City of Trees laid out before me, trees and ruined buildings and four fair Houses upon a hill. Far far beyond these I made out the faint sparkling cusp of the river.

"Well," I said, tightening my grip upon Miss Scarlet's hand. I looked at her and then at Jane. "I guess we'd better go."

They nodded. Together we walked down Saint-Alaban's Hill.

E quindi uscimmo a riveder le stelle.
—And thence we came forth, to see again the stars.

Author's Afterword

My concern in *Winterlong* is the relationship between consciousness and reality, and in particular the
way in which an artistic medium may be used to explore
the interstices between the objective, waking world
and those other, more richly textured and deeply shadowed realms that most of us visit only fleetingly.
Winterlong explores these regions through the peculiar
sensibility of Wendy Wanders. In *Aestival Tide,* an independent companion novel, I take a different route: we
move outward from the disfigured City to the broader
stage of a transmogrified oceanscape, conducted (or
kidnapped) by a narrative consciousness that is even
more out-of-the-ordinary than Wendy's.

Wendy, Miss Scarlet, Jane Alopex all appear in *Aestival Tide.* But the primary narrative is that of Jenny-the-
fox, neophyte in an arcane cult whose members live in
the ruins of an ancient weather-tracking station in the
coastal town of Occis. Jenny is caught up in the ongoing
intrigue between the Ascendant hegemony and the
Balkhash Commonwealth. She is also increasingly ob-
sessed with what she believes is her crucial role in
bringing about the necessary destruction of Occis itself.
Aestival Tide, the annual celebration of the summer
solstice, brings hundreds of carnival-goers to the former
ocean resort—among them Wendy and Scarlet and
Jane. There's a kidnapping, a geneslave insurrection
involving the reluctant Miss Scarlet, messianic obses-
sions and the looming threat of a killer hurricane that
has been predicted for over three hundred years. As in
Winterlong, I'm using subtexts drawn from Near Eastern mythologies, along with the more familiar elements
of the Demeter/Persephone myth, the story of the

Magdalene, and even the Biblical tale of Lot's wife. And I hope that the different narrative structure, alternating between third-person and yet another first-person narrator (a la Lawrence Durrell's *Alexandria Quartet*) will give even more depth and texture to my continuing exploration of the coming of the Magdalene.

ABOUT THE AUTHOR

Elizabeth Hand has published short fiction in Bantam Spectra's *Full Spectrum 2* anthology and *Twilight Zone Magazine*, as well as book reviews and criticism in *Washington Post Book World* and *Science Fiction Eye*, of which she is an associate editor. She worked for six years as an archivist for the National Air and Space Museum. She lives on the coast of Maine and is deep at work with her second novel, *Aestival Tide*.